There is no one who can write better about love than Jacqueline Susann. This novel is a testament to that. It is her most human book, her most deeply felt, and for that her most satisfying in every way.

ONCE IS NOT ENOUGH

The novel's theme—daring, poignant, sensitively rendered—is a daughter's obsessive love for her father. It is January Wayne, named by an adoring father after the month in 1950 when she was born, who is in love with her father, Mike Wayne. He is a renowned movie and theatre producer, lover of many women, and, above all, a gambler.

"Our girl has done it again. There is no place for this sensational novel to go but straight up the bestseller lists. This is Jacqueline Susann's best written novel to date."

—PUBLISHERS WEEKLY

Also by Jacqueline Susann

THE LOVE MACHINE
VALLEY OF THE DOLLS
EVERY NIGHT, JOSEPHINE!

and published by CORGI BOOKS

JACQUELINE SUSANN

ONCE IS NOT ENOUGH

CORGI BOOKS
A DIVISION OF TRANSWORLD PUBLISHERS LTD

ONCE IS NOT ENOUGH

A CORGI BOOK 0 552 09615 6

Originally published in Great Britain
by W. H. Allen & Co. Ltd.

PRINTING HISTORY
W. H, Allen edition published 1973
Corgi edition published 1974

Corgi Books are published by
Transworld Publishers Ltd.,
Cavendish House, 57–59 Uxbridge Road,
Ealing, London W.5.
Made and printed in the United States of America
by Arcata Graphics,
Buffalo, New York

To Robert Susann, my father,
*who would understand**

and to Irving,
who does understand

ONCE IS NOT ENOUGH

PROLOGUE

Him

HE BURST upon the theatrical scene in 1945. He was Mike Wayne—a born winner. He had been known as the best crap shooter in the Air Force, and the thirteen thousand dollars in cash, strapped around his waist, proved the legend to be fact.

When he was in his late teens he had already figured the stock market and show business to be the two biggest crap games in the world. He was twenty-seven when he got out of the Air Force and crazy about girls, so he picked show business. He parlayed his thirteen thousand into sixty with five hot days at Aqueduct.

By investing it in a Broadway show he became co-producer. The show was a hit and he married Vicki Hill, the most beautiful girl in the chorus.

Vicki wanted to be a star, and he gave her the chance. In 1948 he produced his first big lavish musical on his own and starred his wife. It was a hit, in spite of her. The critics praised his theatrical know-how in surrounding her with talented performers, a foolproof book, and a hit score. But they all agreed that Vicki was less than adequate.

When the show ended its run, he "retired" her. ("Baby, you gotta know how to walk away from the table when the dice are cold. I gave you your shot. Now you give me a son.")

On New Year's Day, 1950, she presented him with a

baby girl. He promptly named her January, and when the nurse put the baby in his arms, he silently swore he would give her the world.

When she was two, he greeted her before he greeted his wife.

When she was four, he went to California and produced his first movie.

When she was five, he produced two hit pictures in one year, and was nominated for an Oscar.

When she was six he won the Oscar and his name was linked with several beautiful stars. (That was when his wife began to drink and took a lover of her own.)

When she was seven, he named his private plane after her and his wife killed herself trying to abort their unborn son.

And then there were just the two of them.

He tried to explain things the day he drove her to the boarding school in Connecticut. "Now that Mommy's gone, this fancy joint will teach you to become a lovely lady."

"Why can't you teach me, Daddy?"

"Because I travel a lot. And besides, ladies are supposed to teach little girls."

"Why did Mommy die, Daddy?"

"I don't know, honey . . . Maybe because she wanted to be somebody."

"Is that bad?"

"Only when you aren't, and it eats away at your insides."

"Are you somebody, Daddy?"

"Me? I'm a super-somebody." He laughed.

"Then I'll be a somebody," she told him.

"Okay. But before you can be anybody, you have to be a lady."

So she had accepted Miss Haddon's school. And whenever he was in New York, they would spend the weekends together.

His fame grew, and like all good gamblers, he knew when to push his luck and when to quit. He had been known to change the odds at the track with one bet. Once he lost his plane on the roll of the dice, but he walked away with a grin because he knew there would be another time.

And if you asked him when his luck ran out, he could tell you the exact day.

Rome. June 20, 1967.

The day they told him about his daughter. . . .

IF YOU ASKED her when her luck ran out, she wouldn't have been able to tell you because she only thought of herself as *his* daughter. And being *his* daughter was just about the most marvelous thing in the world.

From the start she had accepted Miss Haddon's school as merely something to "get through." The girls were all friendly and fell into two categories. The older girls worshipped Elvis and the younger girls were "Linda followers." Linda was Linda Riggs, a student. She was sixteen. She could sing and dance and her hyper-enthusiasm was noisy but infectious. (Years later when January came across some early school photographs, she was amazed at Linda's resemblance to Ringo Starr.) But at the time, when Linda was the undisputed star at Miss Haddon's, no one seemed to notice the skimpy shaggy hair, the broad nose, and the heavy silver braces on her teeth. It was an accepted fact that when Linda graduated she was going to become a top musical comedy star on Broadway.

In Linda's senior year, she starred in the school's watered-down version of *Annie Get Your Gun*. When rehearsals began, Linda singled out the eight-year-old January to be her "special little friend." This meant January would be given the privilege of running errands for her and of cueing her on her lines and lyrics of the songs. January had never been a "Linda follower," but she was

4

pleased with the arrangement because most of Linda's conversation centered on Mike Wayne. Linda was a great admirer of his work. *Had January invited him to the school play? Was he coming? He* had *to come! After all, hadn't Linda seen to it that January had gotten into the chorus?*

He did come, and after the performance January watched the star of *Annie Get Your Gun* dissolve into a stammering blushing high school girl when Mike Wayne shook her hand.

"Wasn't she great?" January asked as they walked off together.

"She stank. You stood out more in the chorus than she did in all of her numbers."

"But she's so talented."

"She's a fat ugly broad."

"Really?"

"Really."

But when Linda was graduated, Miss Haddon's suddenly seemed empty. A beautiful girl named Angela starred in the school play the following season, but everyone agreed she was "no Linda."

Two years later, Linda jumped back into the news when one of the girls ran screaming down the hall with a copy of *Gloss* magazine. On the masthead, in small print, was the name Linda Riggs: junior editor. Everyone at Miss Haddon's was wildly impressed, but January was secretly disappointed. What had happened to Broadway?

When she told her father about it, he didn't seem surprised. "It's amazing that she even made it as a gofer on a fashion magazine."

"But she was so talented," January insisted.

"Talented for Miss Haddon's. But this is nineteen sixty, and there are girls who look like Liz Taylor and Marilyn Monroe pounding the pavements, hoping for a break in anything. I don't say beauty is everything . . . but it helps."

"Will I be beautiful?"

He grinned as he fingered her heavy brown hair. "You're gonna be more than beautiful. You've got your

mother's brown eyes. Velvet eyes. The first thing that
attracted me to her."

She didn't tell him that she'd rather have his eyes.
They were so unbelievably blue against his perpetual tan
and his black hair. She had never been able to take his
extraordinary good looks for granted. Neither could her
classmates, who saw their fathers as beleaguered men
who sometimes needed a shave, worried about losing
their hair or jobs, and constantly argued with a mother
or a kid brother.

But the weekends January spent with her father in
New York, she only saw a handsome man who lived to
please her.

It was because of these weekends that January discouraged all attempts at any "buddy-buddy" relation-
ships with the girls at school. Having a "buddy-buddy"
meant holiday dinners at their homes and occasional
weekend "sleepovers"—on a reciprocal basis. And January had no intention of sharing any of her weekends
with her father. Of course, there were times when he
was in Europe or on the Coast, but the weekends they
spent together more than compensated for the lonely
ones. Those Saturday mornings when the limousine
would arrive and whisk her to New York . . . to the
large corner suite at the Plaza which he kept on a year-
round basis. Invariably he'd be having breakfast when
she arrived. A secretary might be taking notes; a production assistant going over weekly grosses; a publicity
man checking advertising copy; phones would be going,
sometimes three at once. But when she entered the room
it was as if an alarm went off. All activity stopped and
he'd sweep her into his arms. The smell of his aftershave
lotion was like pine . . . and the feel of his arms around
her gave her a sense of all-encompassing security.

She would have some lunch while he quickly disposed
of the business at hand. It never failed to fascinate her.
The wheeling-dealing, his staccato decisions on the long-
distance phone. She'd nibble at her food and watch him,
trying to etch into her mind the way he hunched the
phone between his shoulder and his ear as he made notes

. . . and that warm feeling that shot through her when he looked at her in the midst of it all and winked. A wink that said, "No matter what I'm doing, I still stop and think of you."

And after lunch there were no more phones or interruptions. The rest of the day belonged to her. Sometimes he'd take her to Saks and buy her everything in sight. Other times they'd go ice-skating at Rockefeller Plaza (he'd sit inside and have a drink while the instructor took her around). If he was putting on a new show, they'd stop by and watch rehearsals. They saw every show on Broadway; sometimes they went to a matinee *and* an evening performance. And they'd always wind up at Sardi's and sit at the front table under his caricature.

But she hated Sundays. No matter how much fun they had at their Sunday brunch, there was always the shadow of that big black limousine that was waiting to take her back to Miss Haddon's. And she knew she had to go, just as she knew he had to return to his phones and his productions.

But his favorite "productions" were her birthdays. When she was five he had hired a small circus and invited her entire nursery school class. Her mother had been alive then, a vague lady with huge brown eyes who sat on the sidelines and watched everything without too much interest. When she was six there had been a sleigh ride to the Tavern On The Green in Central Park, with a Santa Claus and a bag of toys waiting. Another time there had been a magician, and a puppet show.

But on her eighth birthday there had been just the two of them. It was her first birthday since her mother's death. It fell on a weekday and the car had picked her up at Miss Haddon's and brought her to the Plaza. She had stood solemnly as he opened the bottle of champagne and poured her a quarter of a glass. "This is the best there is, babe." He raised his glass. "Here's to my lady . . . the only lady I'll ever love." That was how he introduced her to Dom Perignon and caviar.

And then he had taken her to the window and pointed

toward the Goodyear Blimp that was passing by. But instead of "Goodyear," the huge red letters blazed "Happy Birthday, January!" And from that time on, Dom Perignon and caviar became a ritual for all important occasions.

On her thirteenth birthday, he took her to Madison Square Garden. The marquee was dark when they arrived, so she assumed they were late. He took her hand and led her inside. Oddly enough there were no ushers to help them. No attendants . . . no people . . . no lights. He led her down a ramp, into the cavernous darkness of the empty Garden. It was eerie as they walked hand in hand . . . down . . . down . . . deep into the belly of the Garden. Then he stopped; and when he spoke his voice was quiet. "Make a wish, baby, a big one, because right now you are standing on the exact spot where some of the biggest champions stood. Joe Louis, Sugar Ray, Marciano." He raised her hand in the fighter's victory pose and, mimicking the nasal tones of a referee, chanted, "And now Ladees and Gennelmen . . . introducing the greatest champion of them all . . . Miss January Wayne . . . who has now entered her teens!" Then he said, "That means you're in the heavyweight division now, babe."

She threw her arms around him and he leaned down to kiss her cheek, but in the darkness their lips met and held . . . and then the scoreboards all exploded with lights, sparkling, HAPPY BIRTHDAY, JANUARY. A table was set with caviar and champagne; a waiter was standing at attention to serve them, and an orchestra played and sang "Happy Birthday."

After the song, the musicians began a medley of her favorite show tunes. They sipped the champagne, and then Mike held out his arms and asked her to dance. At first she was nervous, but after the first few awkward steps she snuggled against him, and suddenly it felt as if she had been dancing with him all of her life. As they moved to the music, he whispered, "You're on your way to becoming a lady. One day a boy will come along who'll mean more than anything else in the world . . .

and he'll hold you in his arms like this and you'll know what it means to be in love." She hadn't answered because she knew she was already in the arms of the only man she could ever love.

He was producing a picture in Rome when she was graduated from Miss Haddon's. She didn't mind his missing the graduation. She would have liked to skip it herself, but she had auditioned and been chosen to deliver the valedictory speech, and now there was no way out. But she was joining him in Rome for the summer.

And she had won the argument against college.

"Daddy, I've been away at school all my life."

"But college is important, baby."

"Why?"

"Well, to learn things, to meet the right kind of friends, to prepare you for—hell, I don't know. I just know it's the right thing. Why do other girls go to college?"

"Because they don't have you for a father."

"Well, what do you want to do?"

"Be an actress maybe."

"Well, if you're gonna be an actress, you have to study for that too!"

And so it had been arranged. Once he finished the picture in Rome, he was scheduled to do one in London. And he had managed to get her enrolled at the Royal Academy of Dramatic Art for the fall term. She wasn't dedicated to the idea of the Royal Academy. She wasn't even sure she really wanted to be an actress. . . .

But she was going to Rome! There were just the graduation exercises to get through. Under her cap and gown was a blue linen dress. Her plane ticket and passport were in her bag. And her luggage was already in the trunk of the limousine waiting outside the school. All she had to do was deliver the speech, get that diploma, and run!

And then it was all over and she was making her way up the aisle; accepting congratulations from parents of classmates; pushing through a wall of tearful farewells;

promising to write. Goodbye! Goodbye! Tearing off the gown. Tossing the cap to Miss Hicks of the drama department. Goodbye! Goodbye! Into the limousine and on the way to Kennedy Airport.

704 . . . first class half empty . . . too excited to concentrate on food or the movie. Hours and hours of magazines, daydreams and Cokes . . . then finally the descent . . . seven o'clock in the morning, Rome time. And there he was . . . standing with some important-looking officials . . . right on the airfield . . . with a private car. Out of the plane . . . into his arms . . . the arms of the most fabulous man in the world . . . and he belonged to her!

The long black car drove them to customs . . . her passport was stamped . . . they entered the busy terminal where two attractive young Italian boys in skinny dark suits stood waiting to attend to her luggage.

"They don't speak English, but they're great kids," Mike said as he handed them some crinkly paper money. "They'll get your baggage and take it to the hotel." Then he led her outside to a long low-slung red Jaguar. The top was down and Mike smiled at her obvious delight. "I thought it would be more fun if we drove ourselves. Get in, Cleopatra. You are about to make your entrance into Rome."

And that was how she saw Rome on that sparkling June morning. The wind was soft and the early morning sun warmed her face. A few shop people slowly raised their blinds. Young boys in aprons began washing down the streets of sidewalk cafés. An occasional timid horn squeaked off in the distance, a horn that would join a pack that would blend into a screaming crescendo when traffic reached its peak.

Mike pulled the car to a stop in front of a little restaurant. The proprietor ran out and embraced him and insisted on personally making them eggs and sausage, with the hot rolls his wife had just baked.

The city was bursting with noise when they finally reached the block of the Via Veneto that housed the Excelsior Hotel. January stared at the small expanse—

the sidewalk cafés lining both sides of the street, tourists reading *The New York Times* and Paris edition of the *Tribune* as they tried to drink the heavy espresso.

"*This* is the Via Veneto?" January asked.

Mike grinned. "Yep, this is it. Sorry I couldn't arrange to have Sophia Loren passing by. The truth is, if you sat here for a year you might never see Sophia Loren on the Via Veneto. But in one hour, you will see every American who's in town."

She was overwhelmed with the enormous suite at the Excelsior. The ornate marble fireplaces, the dining room, the two large bedrooms—it was almost palatial.

"I left the room facing the American Embassy for you," Mike said. "I figured the street noises might not be as loud there." Then he pointed to her bags which had been delivered. "Unpack, take a bath and go to sleep. I'll send a car to pick you up around four. You can come to the studio and we'll drive home together."

"Can't I go to the studio with you now?" she asked.

He smiled. "Listen, I don't want you to be tired for your first night in Rome. Incidentally, we don't dine here until nine or ten."

He started for the door and stopped. He stared at her for several seconds and shook his head. "Know something? You really are goddamned beautiful!"

They were still shooting when she arrived at the studio. She stood in the back and watched in the darkness. She recognized Mitch Nelson, the American actor whom the press releases billed as the new Gary Cooper. Through a granite jaw and seemingly immovable lips, he was playing a love scene with Melba Delitto. January had seen Melba only in foreign films. She was very beautiful, but her accent was heavy, and several times she fluffed her lines. Each time, Mike would smile, walk over to her, reassure her, and then start the scene again. After the fifteenth take, Mike yelled, "Print it," and the lights came up. When he saw January he broke into that special smile that belonged only to her, and he crossed the sound stage. He linked her arm through his. "How long you been standing there?"

"For about twelve takes. I didn't know you were also a director."

"Well, it's Melba's first English-speaking part, and the first few days were pistols. She would fluff . . . the director would scream at her in Italian . . . she'd scream back . . . he'd scream louder . . . she'd walk off the set in tears. That meant an hour for new makeup plus another half hour for her to accept the director's apologies. So I learned that if I just walk over and soothe the lady and tell her how well she's doing, we save a lot of time and money and finally get a decent take."

A young man came toward them eagerly. "Mr. Mike, I was through work two hours ago but I wait, because I so much wanted to meet your daughter."

"January, this is Franco Mellini," Mike said.

The young man was in his early twenties. His accent was heavy, but he was tall and undeniably handsome. "Okay, Franco, you've been presented. Now scram." Mike's voice was gruff, but he smiled as the boy bowed and backed away. "That kid has only a small part, but he may walk off with the whole ballgame," he said. "I found him in Milan when I was scouting locations. He was doubling as a singer and a bartender in a dive. He's a natural. It's wild to see the way he's charmed every broad on the set. Even Melba." Mike shook his head. "When an Italian has charm, forget it." They walked arm in arm. The studio was empty and she felt as if all of her unspoken prayers had been answered. This was the moment she had longed for, the moment she had dreamed about. Walking beside him . . . being a part of his life . . . his work . . . sharing his problems.

Suddenly he said, "By the way, I've lined up a bit for you in the picture. Just a few lines—hey." He tried to pull away from her embrace. "You're strangling me!"

Later, as they inched through the unbelievable traffic, he told her about his troubles with the picture. Melba's anxiety with her English . . . her antipathy toward Mitch Nelson . . . the language barrier he had with some of the crew. But most of all he groaned about the traffic. And she sat and listened and kept telling herself it wasn't a dream . . . she was really here . . . this wasn't just a Saturday . . . there would be no limousine to take her away from him tomorrow . . . she'd be with him like this every day . . . and she didn't care if the traffic took forever . . . she was with him in Rome . . . just the two of them!

When they finally reached the hotel another slim attractive young man was waiting in the lobby with several large boxes. January wondered how all the men stayed so thin. Didn't Italians eat their own food?

"This is Bruno," Mike said, as the grinning young man followed them to their suite. "I figured you might not have enough clothes, so I sent him out a few days ago. He shops for a lot of the V.I.P.'s. Take whatever you want, any or all of it. I'm going to shower, make some calls to the States—that is, if I can break through the language barrier with the operators here. Sometimes we never get past *Pronto*." He kissed her cheek. "See you at nine."

He was waiting for her when she walked into the living room at nine o'clock. He let out a low whistle. "Babe, you're built like a brick—" He stopped suddenly and smiled. "Well . . . let's say you're better than any top fashion model."

"Meaning I really haven't got enough on top." She laughed. "That's why I adore this Pucci. It clings and makes me look—"

"Fantastic," he said.

"I took this and a skirt, some shirts and a pants suit."

"That's all?" Then he shrugged. "Maybe you'll have more fun finding all those hidden little shops the dames all talk about. I'll have Melba tell you where to look."

"Daddy, I'm not here for a fashion collection. I want to watch you make the film."

"Are you kidding? Jesus, babe . . . you're seventeen. You're in Rome! You don't want to stick around on a hot movie set."

"That's exactly what I want to do. I also want that bit part you promised me."

He laughed. "Maybe you will be an actress at that. At

least you're beginning to sound like one. Come on. Let's get going. I'm starving."

They went to a restaurant in the old ghetto section of Rome. January adored the old buildings . . . the quiet streets. They went to a place called Angelino's. Dinner was served by candlelight in a Renaissance piazza. There were even strolling musicians. The entire evening took on a feeling of beautiful unreality. She sat back and watched Mike pour her some wine. She realized that another of her favorite fantasies was actually unfolding . . . she was alone with Mike in a storybook setting . . . he was pouring the wine . . . women were looking at him with admiration but he belonged to her. No phones could take him away, no long black limousines could take her away. She watched him light his cigarette. The waiter was just pouring their espresso when Franco and Melba came into the restaurant. Mike waved them over to the table and ordered another bottle of wine. Melba began talking about one of her scenes in the picture. When her English failed, which was often, she got her point across with gestures. Franco laughed and turned to January. "I speak the English language very poor. You will help me?"

"Well, I—"

"Your father, he all the time talk about you. He count the hours until you come."

"He did?"

"Of course. Just like I count the hours until I meet you tonight." He reached out and touched her hand. She pulled it away and turned toward her father, but he was whispering something into Melba's ear. The actress giggled and rubbed her cheek against his.

January looked away, but Franco smiled. "Maybe love needs no language, right?"

"I think your English is excellent," she said stiffly. She tried not to stare at Melba's hand, which was resting on her father's thigh.

"Oh, I learned from G.I. uncles." Franco laughed. "My mother was widowed from war. She was very young . . . *multa bella*. . . she speak no English then,

but she learn and teach me. And G.I. uncles good to my
mama. But she's fat now and I send her money because
now no G.I.'s to help out. Just Franco."

January was relieved when Mike signaled for the
check. He left a pile of bills on the table and they all
stood up. Then he turned to January with a smile. "Well,
I guess I've hogged you enough, babe. Besides, a beautiful young girl should spend her first night in Rome with
a handsome young Italian. At least that's what it says in
all the movie scripts I've ever done." He winked at
Franco. Then he put his arm around Melba as they
walked out of the restaurant.

For a moment they all stood together on the narrow
cobbled street. Then Mike said, "Okay, Franco. I'm
gonna let you show my daughter some of the night life
in this town. But take it easy. After all, we're all gonna
be here two months." Then he took Melba's arm and
headed for his car. January watched them drive off. It
all happened so fast she couldn't believe it. Her father
was gone and she was standing on a strange street in
Rome with a handsome young Italian, courtesy of Mike
Wayne.

Franco took her arm and led her down the street to
a tiny car. They squeezed into it, and with skillful ma-
neuvering he managed to dart in and out of the crowded
traffic. She was silent during the drive. Her first inclina-
tion had been to ask him to take her back to the hotel.
But then what? Sit there and wait . . . and wonder what
they were doing? *No!* Let *him* sit and wait and wonder
what *she* was doing. He had walked out on her . . . left
her with this boy. Okay. She'd show him how it felt.

"Small car only thing to use in Roma," he said. They
went through winding streets and stopped at an outdoor
ice cream parlor. "We go downstairs," Franco said.
They climbed out of the car, and he led her down a dark
narrow staircase. "You'll like . . . best discotheque in
Roma."

The entire building looked as if it were ready for the
demolition ball, but they entered a cavernous expanse
that was packed with couples gyrating to blasting

music and psychedelic lighting. Franco seemed to know
everyone in the place, including the waiter, who led them
to a choice table in an alcove. He ordered some wine
and then pulled her onto the floor against her will. She
was embarrassed because she didn't know the new
dances. She looked around. All the girls seemed to be
undulating, oblivious of their partners. The entire floor
looked like a mass of worms . . . wriggling . . . squirm-
ing . . . twisting. She had never tried it. Her last term at
Miss Haddon's had been dateless by choice, because
Mike had been in New York and she had spent every
weekend with him.

But Franco laughed away her doubts. The beat of the
music was strong, and under his guidance she began to
move slowly . . . tentatively. Franco nodded encour-
agement and swayed to the tempo. His smile radiated
confidence and approval. She found herself falling into
a modified imitation of the other girls on the floor.
Franco nodded . . . his arms waved in the air . . . his
hips slithered . . . she followed his pace . . . the beat
of the music grew louder . . . soon she was dancing
with complete abandon. They fell into each other's arms
from exhaustion when the music stopped. He led her
back to the table and she drank an entire glass of wine
in one long swallow. Franco ordered a bottle and refilled her glass. Several of his friends came to the table,
and soon a large group of young people had gathered.
Very few spoke English, but they all danced with her,
smiled easily, and even the girls seemed warm and
friendly. She would actually have enjoyed herself except
for the nagging thought of Melba and her father. She
had seen the way Mike had looked at Melba . . . the
way their eyes had held. She drank another glass of
wine. Melba meant nothing to her father. She was just
the star of the picture. He wanted to keep her happy.
Hadn't he explained that was why he went over and
whispered to her between each take? But what had he
whispered? She took another long swallow of wine and
nodded in agreement when another handsome young
man asked her to dance. The music was blasting. She

was moving with the exact precision of the other dancers. (Were Melba and her father sitting somewhere listening to good music—music for lovers—sitting alone
in some quiet place with violins?) She suddenly stopped
dancing and walked off the floor. The boy hurried after
her, jabbering in Italian, waving his arms questioningly.

"Tell him I'm tired, that's all," January told Franco.
She sat down and listened to the exchange of Italian.
The boy stopped frowning, smiled, shrugged, and asked
another girl to dance. At one o'clock the group began
to disband. She wondered if Mike was home. Was he
worried that she was out this late? Maybe he wasn't
home yet. She finished her glass of wine and reached for
the bottle. It was empty, and Franco immediately ordered another bottle, but the waiter shook his head. A
heated argument began. Finally Franco stood up and
tossed some money on the table. "They are closing.
Come, we go somewhere else."

She followed him up the steps. "Where does everyone
go now?" she asked. "I mean, people who want to stay
up late? Is there a place . . . well, like in New York
we have P.J.'s . . ."

"Oh, you mean meeting place? No, only Americans
meet late here. Italians don't stay up or go to late clubs.
They have home-type social life."

"But—" She stopped as they reached the street. That
would mean Mike was coming home just about now.

"I tell you what," Franco said. "We go to my place. I
have the same wine." He turned to another couple who
were standing with them on the street. "You come too,
Vincente and Maria."

Vincente shook his head with a wink and walked off
with his arm around the girl. Franco led January to his
car. Suddenly she said, "I think I'd better go home, too.
I've enjoyed it very much, Franco . . . honestly. It's
been really neat."

"No. We have nightcap. Your papa think I am very
bad escort if I bring you home so early."

She laughed. "Is that what you are? An escort?
Courtesy of my father?"

His face went dark. He stepped on the gas of the small car and it careened through the streets, swerving, taking corners at an unnerving speed.

"Franco, we'll get killed. Please. Have I insulted you?"

"Yes. You call me a gigolo."

"No . . . really . . . I was just kidding. . . ."

He pulled to a stop on a small side street. "Look, one thing we get straight. Your papa important man. But I am good actor. I am superb in film. I see rushes. I know. Zeffirelli wants me to read for part in his new film. I will get it. You see. Most of my part is finished in your papa's picture so I am not playing the politic. I take you out tonight because you are beautiful. Because I want to see you. Your papa talk much about you, but I did not believe. But when I see you this afternoon . . . ah . . . then I believe."

"Okay, Franco." She laughed. "But one thing . . . there's no such thing as gigolos anymore. And you've got to learn not to be so touchy."

"What you call a man who is bought?" he asked.

She shrugged. "No *man* is ever bought . . . or kept. The ones that are . . . I suppose you'd call them escorts, or fags, or muscle-beach types . . . male whores."

"I am not male whore."

"No one said you were."

He started the car but he drove slowly. "In Naples where I was born, we learn we have to fight for what we want. Women, money—even to stay alive. But we cannot be bought by women. We are maschio." Then he smiled. "Okay . . . I forgive you . . . if you come back for some wine."

"But—"

"Or maybe I feel you are only with me to please your papa unless we have one glass of wine."

"All right. One glass of wine."

He drove through winding streets . . . over cobblestones . . . past massive dark buildings with courtyards. Finally he pulled up in front of an imposing old house. "Way back this was private palazzo of rich old lady. Mussolini once stayed here with his mistress. Now it is run down and made into apartments."

She followed him through a dark courtyard with cracked marble benches and a broken unworkable marble fountain. He fitted his key into a massive oak door. "Come in. This is my place. Not neat . . . but nice . . . yes?"

The living room was a wild contrast of modern disorder against old-world antiquity. High ceilings . . . worn marble floors . . . sofa strewn with newspapers . . . littered tin ashtrays . . . tiny kitchen stacked with dirty dishes . . . bedroom door ajar, with unmade bed. Here he lived in typical bachelor chaos.

He seemed unabashed by the appearance of the apartment. He flicked on the hi-fi and suddenly music seemed to be coming from everywhere. What he lacked in furniture he made up for in speakers. She studied the moldings and fine marble while he worked on the cork of the bottle of wine.

"This is same like we had," he said as he came to her with the glasses. Then he led her to the couch, swept the newspapers to the floor and motioned for her to sit. The stuffing and some springs were leaking through the bottom, but there was pride in his voice when he said, "All my furniture donated by friends."

"This is a marvelous couch," she said. "If you had it redone and—"

He shrugged. "When I become big star I furnish place good. Maybe."

"Maybe?"

"Well, if I'm big star enough, they send for me to come to America. That is where the real money is, no?"

"Melba Delitto is a big star and she stays here."

He laughed. "Melba is already very rich. Besides, she is thirty-one . . . too old to go."

"But she made all that money here."

"No. From lovers. She has had many lovers . . . many diamonds. She make good money in films but more from lovers. See, is different for a woman. Your papa already give her big pin with diamonds."

She stood up. "I think I'd better get home."

"You just arrive. You didn't drink the wine. I opened whole bottle."

"Franco, it's getting late, and—"

He pulled her back on the couch. "First drink your wine." He handed her the glass. She sipped it slowly. His hand dropped from the back of the sofa onto her shoulders. She pretended not to notice, but it felt heavy, as if it had a life of its own. The fingers began to play with the back of her neck.

She made an effort and swallowed some of the wine. Then she stood up. "Franco, I think I'd like to go."

He stood up but held out his arms. "Come. We dance. Old-fashioned style."

"I really don't want . . ."

But his arms went around her and he held her close as he led her into a slow dance. She felt the hardness of his body . . . the bulge in his pants . . . he was pressing against her . . . moving his body to the rhythm of the music. Her thin Pucci dress felt like paper. Suddenly he kissed her. His tongue pressed her lips apart. She tried to pull away, but he held her head with one hand and with the other he began caressing her breasts. She kept trying to get away from him, but he laughed at her efforts. Then, with one quick move, he lifted her up and carried her into the bedroom and tossed her lightly on the unmade bed. Before she could move, he had her dress up and was pulling at her pants. She screamed when she felt his hands on her bare buttocks.

He stared at her. "What is it? What is wrong?"

She jumped off the bed, pulling down her dress. She was too angry for tears. "How dare you! How *dare* you!" She ran into the living room, grabbed her purse and ran toward the door. He leaped in front of her and blocked her way. "January—is something wrong?"

"Is something wrong!" she said hoarsely. "You ask me here for a drink and then try to rape me."

"Rape?" He stared at her. "I try to make love to you."

"To you, it's obviously the same thing."

"What same thing? Rape is crime. Making love is two

people whose bodies long for one another. You agreed to come here, no?"

"For a drink . . . and to . . . Well, I thought your feelings were hurt."

"Maybe I have big temper," he said. "But you are acting like spoiled American girl."

"Well, I am an American girl."

"Ah yes. But you are maschio's daughter. That is the big difference. See, they say American girls . . . have rules. First date . . . maybe goodnight kiss. Second date, maybe a little feel. Third date more touching and feeling. But never no lovemaking until after fourth or fifth date. And American men follow these rules. But Mike Wayne makes his own rules. I thought his daughter would be like him."

"You mean . . . just like that . . . you thought I'd go to bed with you!"

He laughed. "Well . . . just like that . . . you went for drinks with me. You danced with me. It's all very natural and very good. Making love follows." He leaned over and stroked her breasts. "See. Nipples are hard. Right through your dress. Your lovely little breasts want Franco . . . even if you don't. Why not let me just make love to them?"

She pushed his hands away. "Franco, take me home."

He leaned over and kissed her, pinning her against the door. She fought violently . . . kicking . . . pulling at his hair, but he only laughed as if it were part of a game. With one hand he took her arms and pinned them behind her. With the other hand he tried to pull down the zipper in the back of her dress. In the midst of her panic she remembered to be grateful that it was only a six-inch zipper. He tugged and tugged. Then, quickly, he reached down and pulled the dress up around her head. It trapped her arms against her head and muffled her screams. She wasn't wearing a bra and suddenly she felt his lips against her breasts and in spite of her fury she felt a strange sensation in her groin. He slid one hand under her pants and groped between her legs. "See, my little January. You are moist with love . . . waiting for me."

With one frantic burst of strength she broke away and blindly groped at her dress. As she pulled it down she gasped between sobs, "Please . . . please let me go."

"Why are you crying?" His amazement was real. He tried to put his arms around her again and she screamed.

"January, what is wrong? I will be a good lover. Please. Take off your clothes and come to bed with me," He was fidgeting with the buckle of his belt. He stepped out of his pants. His grin was boyish, as if he were cajoling a stubborn child. "Come. Look how very much I want you. Please look." He was standing before her in brief shorts.

She tried not to stare . . . but she was hypnotized. He smiled modestly. "Franco is like a stallion. You will be pleased. Come . . ." He held out his arms. "We make love. Your body is calling out to me. Why you try to deny this happiness to us both?"

He took her hands and shoved them under his shorts. "Feel how much I want you. Can't you see it has to be?"

"No . . ." It was a plea mixed with a moan. "Oh, God, no. Not like this . . ."

He looked bewildered. Then he looked toward the bedroom. "You mean because of bed? Look. I never made love on those sheets. I just slept on them."

"Please! Please let me go!" Tears were blurring her vision. She hugged herself protectively and tried not to look at him. Suddenly he stared at her closely and reached out and touched her cheek as if he could not believe her tears. A curious expression came on his face. "January . . . you have made love before?" he asked quietly.

She shook her head.

For a moment he was silent. Then he came to her, smoothed her dress, and brushed the tears off her face. "I am sorry," he whispered. "I had no idea. You are what . . . twenty-one . . . twenty-two?"

"Seventeen and a half."

"Mama mia!" He slapped his forehead. "You look so . . . so filled with knowing . . . so . . . like the Ameri-

cans say . . . so cool. Mike Wayne's daughter a virgin."
Again he slapped his forehead.

"Please take me home."

"Right away." He got into his pants, grabbed his
shirt and jacket, and opened the door. He took her
arm and led her through the garden to his car. They
drove in silence through the deserted streets. He didn't
speak until they reached the Via Veneto. Then he said,
"There is someone you care about in the States."

"No."

He turned to her. "Then let me . . . oh, not tonight
. . . not tomorrow . . . not until you want me. I won't
touch you until you ask me. I promise." When she didn't
answer, he said, "You do not trust me?"

"No."

He laughed. "Listen, little beautiful American virgin.
In Roma there are much beautiful Italian girls. Actresses, models, married women. All want Franco.
They even make my bed, cook for me, bring me wine.
Know why? Because Franco is good lover. So when
Franco asks to see you and says nothing will happen,
you must believe. Hah! I do not have to fight to have
love. It is all around. But I want to apologize. We start
fresh. Like this never happened."

She was silent. She didn't want to say anything to
make him angry; they were close to the hotel. She just
wanted to get out of that car and get away from him.

"It is very sad that you do not want me," he said
quietly. "Especially because you are a virgin. You see,
my little January, the first time a girl gives herself to a
man it is not always enjoyable . . . to her or to the man.
Unless the man is expert and gentle. I would be very
tender. I would take you so carefully. Make you very
happy. I will even get you the pills."

He was so serious that her fear began to dissolve. And
the wild part was he actually felt he had done nothing
wrong.

"I upset things tonight," he went on. "I fight you because I think maybe it is part of your game. One American lady I met—she made me chase her around her

suite at the Hassler and then she lock bedroom door.
I start to leave and she holler, 'No, Franco, you must
break down door and tear off my clothes.' " Again he
slapped his forehead, but he was grinning. "Ever try
breaking down door in Italian hotel? Like iron. She
finally open it and I chase her again and then I tear off
her clothes. Whooey . . . buttons . . . lace . . . stocking pants ripped . . . everything torn . . . and it was
crazy . . . we make love all night. She married to very
big American star so I don't tell you her name. But he
like to do it that way too. But see . . . I am gentleman
. . . I never tell who I sleep with. Not right. Yes?"

She found herself smiling. Then she caught herself
and stared ahead. It was insane. This man had just torn
at her clothes, tried to rape her, and now he was asking
for approval of his past exploits. Obviously he sensed
her mood, because he smiled and patted her hand almost condescendingly. "You will ask me to make love
to you. I know. Even now I can see your nipples harden
through your dress. You have much sexual desire."

She folded her arms across her chest. She should
have worn a bra. She hadn't realized the dress was so
thin.

"You're not too big on top," he said pleasantly. "I
like that."

"Franco . . . Stop it!"

Once again the familiar slap against his brow.
"Whooey . . . how can Mike Wayne's daughter be so
. . . such prude?"

"I'm not a prude." She felt safe at last. He was pulling
into the driveway of the Excelsior.

"I have no call tomorrow," he said as he sprang out
of the car and opened the door. He helped her out. "We
see each other . . . no?"

"No."

"Why? You are not angry?"

"Not angry? Franco, you treated me like . . .
like . . ."

"Like a beautiful woman," he said with a smile.
"Please. Tell you what . . . You have good night's

sleep. I call tomorrow and we spend day together." He held his arms open. "No touch, I swear. We take ride on my motorcycle. I show you Roma."

"No."

"I call tomorrow. *Ciao*."

She turned and walked into the deserted lobby. It was almost three o'clock. Mike would be frantic . . . probably waiting and tapping his foot. Well, she wouldn't tell him the truth. She'd just say she didn't want to be stuck with Franco again. She'd tell him he made a slight pass. She thought about it as she rode up the creaky elevator with the sleepy attendant.

She put the oversized key into the door. He was up. She could see the streak of light under the door. She walked in. "Mike . . ." Then she looked around. The door to his bedroom was shut. There was a pile of paper money and a note propped up against the lamp on her desk.

"Waited until two, Princess. Hope you had fun. Sleep late. Remember the shops all close between one and four. So just see some sights in the early part of the afternoon. Visit the Spanish Steps. A guy named Axel Munthe once used the little house down there to take in stray animals. Also a guy named Keats lived there too. You can visit his apartment. After four go to the Via Sistina. Melba says there are some great shops there. If you run out of money you can always send things to the hotel C.O.D. Sleep well, Angel.

Love, Daddy."

She stared at the note . . . then at his closed door. He was asleep! He wasn't even concerned about her! But then, he probably never dreamed Franco would dare to come on so strong.

She went to her bedroom. Some of her anger evaporated. If he had waited up until two . . . that meant he had gotten home around one . . . maybe earlier. So he probably really just had a nightcap with Melba. Nothing more. The big love affair was all in Franco's mind. Melba was old . . . well, old for a movie star

. . . in her thirties . . . she needed sleep. She couldn't take a chance of staying up late with Mike. She was too career-minded. She walked into the bathroom and ran the bath. But what about the diamond pin? Well, what about it? Mike always gave the stars of his productions lavish gifts. Of course . . . It was all in Franco's mind. The entire evening was like a dream. She took off her clothes and stared at her breasts. But the evening *had* happened. Franco had touched her breasts . . . sucked at them. His fingers had been between her legs. She got into the tub and scrubbed herself violently.

Later as she lay in bed in the strange room, she felt wide awake. She stared at the dim outline of her bedroom door. Outside was the living room . . . and then there was his door. He was sleeping in there. Oh God, if she could only slip in there and climb into his arms the way she used to do when she was little and had a bad dream. Why couldn't she slip into his arms and tell him all the terrible things that had happened tonight? Let him hold her close and tell her it would be all right. He was still her father. Why was it wrong now? And yet . . . she felt she couldn't do it. Was it because she *wanted* to feel Mike's body against her own? Yes. But in the nicest of ways. She wanted the soothing strength of his arms. She wanted to kiss his cheek, especially the side where the dimple almost formed. She wanted to hear him say, "It's all right, baby."

There was nothing wrong in it. She got out of bed quietly and opened the door. She crossed the large living room and turned the handle of his door gently. It opened easily. At first, she saw only the darkness. But gradually she saw the dim outline of the bed across the room. She tiptoed over, feeling her way along the wall. She reached the bed and pulled aside the sheet and slid in. Her side of the bed was cool and crisp with clean sheets. She inched over and reached for him. But her hand touched another cool crisp pillow. The bed was empty!

She sat up and switched on the lamp on the night table. The bed was turned down . . . the linens were clean. He wasn't there! She got out of bed and walked back into the living room. She stared at the note and the money.

Everything Franco said was true . . . he was with Melba. But why didn't he tell her . . . why did he have to lie to her . . . leave the note about waiting up for her. She went back to the desk and reread the note. But he hadn't said he had waited *up* for her. He had said, "Waited until two." Sure . . . he and Melba had waited until two . . . and then gone off together. Right now they were probably making love.

She went back to her bedroom. He had every right to be with Melba. Why was she so upset? He always had girls. But she was the only one he really loved. Their love was beyond sex . . . people had sex without love. Animals had sex . . . and they weren't in love. They mated, that was all. Like the time when she was five and she had a poodle. It had been mated and it wouldn't even look at the male after it was over. And then when it had puppies . . . it had loved them . . . *until* they were three months old. She had been so amazed when her mother told her they had to give away the male because to the girl poodle he was no longer a son . . . just another male. And that was all Melba was to her father . . . just someone to have sex with.

She got into bed and tried to sleep. She held the pillow in her arms as she often had at school when she was lonely. But suddenly she pushed it away. The pillow had always been a symbol of Mike, of comfort. But now Mike had Melba in his arms. . . . She had to stop thinking this way! After all, what did she think he had been doing all these years since her mother died? But she had never been *there*. Okay, now she was *there*. And she must get him used to the idea that she was an adult, that she could be a great companion, a help to him. He had been alone so much. He was used to latching on to anyone.

When she did fall asleep her dreams were strange and disjointed. She dreamed she was at the funhouse in Coney Island where her father had taken her when she was small. Only there was jarring blasting discotheque music now. She looked at herself in the mirror and laughed . . . first she was long and skinny . . . then short and squat . . . over her shoulder she saw Melba . . . only Melba's face wasn't distorted . . . it was beautiful . . . and she was laughing . . . her face grew larger and larger until it covered the mirror. Melba kept laughing . . . then she heard Franco laughing . . . his face was on the mirror with Melba's and they were both pointing at her grotesque foreshortened image and laughing. Why was the funhouse mirror making her look so funny when it let Melba and Franco look beautiful? She looked around for Mike. He was at the shooting gallery. Melba walked over and stood close to him, her hand on his leg. "Daddy—" January cried out. "Come and take me away from the mirror." But he laughed and said, "Let Franco help you. Besides, I'm shooting all the clay ducks and pipes. I'm doing it all for you, baby. I'm winning all the prizes to lay at your feet." And he kept shooting and each time he shot he hit the bull's-eye and the bell rang and rang.

She opened her eyes. Coney Island and the funhouse were gone. A blotch of sunlight had found its way onto the rug through the drapes. As she came fully awake she was aware of the shrill cacophony of Rome's famed traffic. Horns of all ranges screamed their demands. Soprano horns . . . tinny horns . . . bass horns . . . And through it all there was still the sound of a bell ringing. It was coming from the phone in the living room. She stumbled in. The marble clock on the mantel chimed softly—eleven o'clock. She picked up the phone.

"Franco here," the cheerful voice called out.

She hung up.

Then she called room service and ordered coffee. The door to her father's bedroom was ajar. The light on the night table was still on, just the way she had left it. She turned it off, and on sudden impulse ruffled up the bed. She didn't want the hotel maid to know he hadn't come home. But that was ridiculous. Probably there were a lot of nights when his bed was unused. Or maybe it had been used . . . by Melba.

The phone rang again. She hoped it was Mike. She must sound as if nothing had happened. Cheerful. Or sleepy. Yes, sleepy, as if she had really had a marvelous evening. She picked up the phone.

"Franco here. We were snipped off."

"Oh . . ." She didn't even try to hide her disappointment.

"Dumb operator. She snip us off."

"No, I hung up."

"Why you do that?"

"Because I haven't even had my coffee yet and—" She paused. "Well, golly . . . why shouldn't I hang up on you?"

"Because it is a beautiful day. I pick you up. We go to lunch in a cozy little place—"

"Listen, Franco . . ." She began to sputter. "What you did last night was . . . well, it was terrible, and I don't ever want to see you again."

"But last night I didn't know you were a child. Today I treat you like a child. Okay?"

"No."

"But you get mad if I treat you like a beautiful woman. Look, I have been shining up my Honda for two hours. It is so beautiful . . . Tell you what. No cozy little place for lunch. We go to Doney's. Like tourist. We sit right out in the open. I buy you your coffee, then we take ride. *Ciao*." He hung up before she could answer.

Her coffee from room service never arrived, and when Franco called from the lobby she decided she might as well go with him to Doney's. After all, she had to have coffee. She scooped up the money Mike had left. Then on an impulse she put it back . . . along with the note. She called the hotel maid and told her to make up her room immediately. Let him come back and wonder whether *she* had slept home last night!

It was impossible to remain angry at Franco. He ordered her coffee and croissants. He was warm and volatile. And it seemed half of Rome stopped at the table to talk to him. His boundless enthusiasm gradually melted her reserve, and she found herself laughing and enjoying her breakfast. This sunny, easygoing boy almost made her forget the Franco of last night. She realized he was trying to apologize, trying to please her, and it would be fun to see Rome with him. She was wearing dungarees, and she realized that subconsciously she had intended to go on the motorcycle with him.

The Honda was bright red. He gave her a pair of over-sized goggles and told her to sit behind him. "This time you must hug me." He laughed.

He drove through the traffic carefully and pointed out churches and important buildings. "Next week we see the Vatican," he told her. "And I also take you into some churches. Michelangelo's work in marble you must see."

After a short time they left the city and headed for the Appian Way. He did not speed. He let her get the feel of the seat, of the wind blowing through her hair and cooling her face. He pointed out important villas . . . bits of ruins . . . the house of a movie star. Then he cut off and went down a winding country road. They stopped at a small family-run restaurant. Everyone including a barking dog greeted Franco eagerly. They called him by his first name . . . beamed radiantly at January and brought out bread, cheese, and red wine.

"The Appian Way is the road to Naples," he said. "We must go there someday. And Capri." He kissed his fingers to the sky. "Tomorrow I have filming, but I take you to Capri on Sunday. See Grotto Azura and . . . oh, we have so many places to see."

Later as they walked back to the Honda he put his arm around her shoulders in a brotherly fashion. As they were about to get on the bike she turned to him suddenly. "Franco, I want you to know that this has been a fabulous day. Really neat. Thank you so much."

"Tonight I take you to a great place for dinner. Ever eat clams Posillipo?"

"No . . . but I can't have dinner with you."

"Why? I took promise I won't touch you."

"It isn't that. I . . . want to be with my father."

"You what?"

"My father . . . I haven't seen him since last night."

"Okay, you see him when you go home now. Then at nine o'clock you have dinner with me."

"I want to have dinner with my father."

"Perhaps your papa has other plans." He climbed on the motorcycle.

"No. I'm sure he expects to have dinner with me."

"Before you come . . . every night he take Melba to dinner."

"But I'm here now."

"And you expect to eat dinner every night with your papa?" He was no longer smiling.

"Perhaps."

He started to rev the motor. "Get on. I see everything now."

"What do you see?"

"No girl wants to eat with her papa. You must have other date."

"Franco, for heaven's sake. I don't have another date."

He grabbed her wrist. "Then you have dinner with me tonight like I say."

"No."

He released her hand. "Get on," he snapped. "I take you home. Hah! And I believed the virgin story. Now I know. You just don't dig Franco."

They started down the country road. He drove quickly, bouncing over potholes and rocks. Several times she was almost hurled off. She clung to him as they turned onto the Appian Way. A sightseeing bus filled with Japanese tourists passed. He careened past, almost skinning its wheels. The driver screamed some profanities . . . Franco shook his fist at the driver and went faster. She shouted for him to be careful. But her voice was lost in the noise of the motor and the wind. She was frightened now. There was violence in his driving. She pleaded with him to slow down until she was hoarse. Finally she could do nothing but cling to him and pray. As they rounded a curve she saw a car trying to pass another. He saw it too and tried to swerve the motorcycle off the road. It seemed to rear on its hind legs like a horse . . . she felt herself going through the air . . . and in that split second before she lost consciousness, she felt only a sense of amazement that there was no pain when her body was flung against the stone wall.

When she opened her eyes she saw her father. Two of him . . . three of him . . . She closed her eyes because everything blurred. She tried to reach out for him, but her arm felt like lead. She opened her eyes again. Through the haze she saw the dim outline of her leg raised in traction. Then she remembered the crash. The wild drive . . . the white stone wall . . . and now she was in a hospital with a broken leg. It would ruin the summer, but she felt lucky to be alive. But these days they fixed it so you could walk with your leg in a cast, didn't they? She tried to move, but her entire body felt like cement. She forced her eyes open again, but the lights made them tear. Why was her body so taut? Why couldn't she feel anything in her right arm? Oh God, maybe it was more than just a broken leg.

Mike was standing across the room talking to several doctors. A nurse was bustling about. They were whispering. She wanted him to know she was awake.

She called out, "Daddy . . ."

She tried again. It seemed as if she were shouting. But he didn't move. No one moved. She was screaming but no words were coming out. She was screaming but her mouth wasn't moving. She was screaming inside! She tried to move her left arm . . . she wriggled the fingers, and then everything blurred into a soft gray sleep.

When she opened her eyes again, there was just a small light in the far corner of the room. A nurse was reading a magazine. It was night now. The door opened. Her father and the nurse began to whisper.

He dismissed the nurse and pulled a chair to the side of her bed. He stroked her hand. "Don't worry, baby. Everything will be all right."

She tried to move her mouth. She strained every muscle, but no words would come. He went on talking. "They tell me that even when you open your eyes you don't see me. But they don't know everything. You're gonna make it . . . for me!"

"Make it!" What was he talking about? She had to tell him she'd be fine. A broken leg would heal. She felt awful. Here she was causing him all this trouble. She had probably made him lose a whole day's shooting just because Franco had lost his temper this afternoon. But it was ridiculous for him to be so worried. But why couldn't she talk? She wriggled the fingers on her left hand . . . that worked. She tried raising it. That worked too. He was staring off into space. She reached out and touched his shoulder. He almost leaped off the chair.

"January! NURSE! Oh, babe . . . you moved! You moved your arm! NURSE!"

She tried to tell him she was fine, but suddenly she felt herself falling through space . . . and the thick gray sleep was trying to take over. She didn't want to sleep! She fought against it. The room was suddenly crowded. She saw two white-coated men closing in on her. One white coat raised her right arm and let it drop. Another stuck a needle into it. She saw it rather than felt it. That was odd . . . she felt nothing. Another doctor stuck a needle into her left ankle. Wow! She felt that! And then the gray sleep took over.

When she opened her eyes she saw a big jar of fluid hanging over her ankle. The doctors were all gone but her father was bending over her.

"Nod if you understand me, baby."

She tried. Oh, God. Did they have her head strapped down? It was like a rock.

"Blink your eyes, January. Blink if you understand."

She blinked her eyes.

"Oh, baby—" He buried his head in her shoulder. "I promise you everything is going to be fine." Then she felt the dampness on her neck. Tears. His tears. She had never seen Mike Wayne shed a tear in his life. No one had. And he was crying over her. And suddenly for that one second she was happier than she had ever been. She wasn't worried about her leg or her arm. He loved her . . . he cared for her this much . . . she would get well . . . she would heal so fast . . . they'd have their summer together . . . on crutches . . . with a cast . . . it didn't matter.

She reached out to touch his head . . . to stroke him . . . but her gauge of distance was suddenly crazy and she touched her own head. It felt like stone. Mike stood up. His face was composed. He saw her left arm flailing toward her head.

Her head! What was wrong with her head? Maybe her face was hurt, too. The panic shot through her; a sudden wrench of nausea twisted her stomach. But she forced herself to touch her face.

He understood her frantic gesture immediately. "Your face is fine, baby. They had to shave your head, but your hair will grow back."

THEY HAD SHAVED HER HEAD!

He read the panic in her eyes, and took her hand and held it tight. "Look, I'm gonna give it to you straight because you're gonna have to do a lot of fighting. We both will. So I'll give you the bottom line. You have a fractured skull along with a brain concussion. They had to operate to release some blood. They were afraid of clotting or something. It's all right now. The operation was a complete success. Your back is broken. Two vertebrae, but they'll mend. You also have what they call multiple breaks in your leg. You've got casts all over you . . . that's why you can't move. You can't move your right arm because of the brain concussion. But they say that will all come back." He tried to smile. "Outside of that, baby, you're in great shape." Then he leaned over and kissed her. "You don't know how great it is to see you look at me. It's the first time you've really looked at me in ten days . . ."

TEN DAYS! Ten days since she had fallen off the motorcycle!

Was Franco hurt? How long would she have to be here? Once again she tried to talk, but no words came out. He held her hand and said, "That's part of the concussion, baby. The side of your head that was hit affects the speech area. Don't panic. It will all come back. I swear to you. . . ."

She wanted to tell him she wouldn't panic. As long as he was there, everything was okay. She wanted to tell him to go back to the studio . . . he had a picture to do . . . she wanted to let him know these things . . . that as long as they were a team . . . as long as she knew she'd see him the end of each day and that he loved her and was thinking about her—nothing would stand in her way. She scratched furiously with her left hand. She wanted a pencil. She had to tell him these things. Tears of frustration streamed down her face. She wanted a pencil. But he didn't understand.

"Nurse!" he called out. "Come here quick . . . maybe she's in pain!"

(Daddy, I'm not in pain . . . I just want a pencil.)

The nurse was all starched efficiency. January felt the needle go into her arm . . . the numbness began to seep through her and in the distance she heard her father's voice . . . "Just relax, babe . . . everything's gonna be all right. . . ."

ONE

WHEN MIKE WAYNE WALKED into the V.I.P. Lounge at Kennedy Airport, the hostess was positive he was a movie star. He had that look of someone you've seen many times but know you've never met.

"Is Flight Seven, Swissair, still scheduled for a five o'clock arrival?" he asked as he signed the guest book.

"I'll check," she said, flooding him with one of her warmest smiles. He smiled back, but experience told her it was the smile of a man who already had a girl. A girl arriving on Flight Seven. Probably one of those Swiss-German beauties that were crowding the market lately. It was getting so a domestic stewardess didn't have a chance.

"Half an hour late. Due at five-thirty." Her smile was apologetic.

He nodded and walked to one of the leather chairs by the window. She studied his scrawl on the book. Michael Wayne. She had heard the name, and she *knew* his face, but she couldn't place him. Maybe he was on one of those television series . . . like that dreamy fellow on *Mannix* whom she watched whenever she was dateless on Saturday nights. He was older than the men she usually dated, maybe in his forties. But for Mr. Michael Wayne with the Paul Newman blue eyes she could easily forget the generation gap. In a final bid for attention, she came over with some magazines, but he shook his head and continued to stare at the planes being serviced on the ground. She sighed as she returned to her desk. *No way!* This one really had something on his mind.

Mike Wayne had plenty on his mind. She was coming back! After three years and three months of hospitals and therapy . . . she was coming back.

When she crashed on that motorcycle, his own crash dive had begun. It started with the flop of Melba's picture. He took the blame for that himself. When your kid is busted into pieces, you can't worry about a spaghetti western. And January's prognosis had been dismal. In the beginning none of the surgeons held any hope that she would ever walk again.

The paralysis was due to the concussion and called for immediate physical therapy. For weeks he studied X rays he didn't understand . . . electroencephalograms . . . spinal pictures.

He flew in two surgeons from London and a top neurologist from Germany. They agreed with the specialists in Rome—the delay in physical therapy lessened the chances of recovery from paralysis, yet nothing could be done until the broken bones healed.

He spent most of his time at the hospital, going to the studio to make sure that most of Franco's scenes were cut from the picture. He didn't buy Franco's story —that January had insisted he drive faster—and when he put it to January she had refused to deny or confirm it. But he threw Franco off the set and let the director cut and edit the picture. He wanted to get out of Rome . . . and take January with him.

But three months later she was still in a partial cast and unable to talk. The picture opened in Rome to murderous reviews and tepid business.

In New York it was yanked out of a first-run house after one week and went straight to Forty-second Street on the bottom half of a double bill. In Europe the press labeled Mike Wayne the only man who ever made Melba Delitto look sexless.

He tried to be philosophical. Everyone had to have one flop. And this was long overdue. He had been on a

winning streak since 1947. He told it to himself. He
told it to the press. Yet as he sat beside his daughter's
bed, the thought nagged like an exposed nerve. *Was* it
just one flop—or had his luck run out?

He had two more pictures to release through Century,
and he could amortize the loss of this picture against the
profits of the others. And he didn't see how the next
picture could miss. It was a spy story from a best-
selling novel. He started principal photography in London, in October. Each weekend he flew back to Rome;
forcing himself to walk into that hospital room with a
smile to match the one she always had for him. He tried
not to be disheartened at her lack of progress. She
would make it. She had to! On her eighteenth birthday
she surprised him by taking a few laborious steps with
the aid of the therapist and crutches. Her right arm had
improved, but she still dragged her right leg. Her speech
was coming back. There were times she halted or stut-
tered on a word. But he knew that was just a matter of
time. But damn it! If she could talk and use her right
arm, what was holding up the progress of the leg? Certainly not the concussion anymore. But her smile was so
bright and victorious. Her hair had grown back short and
shaggy—she looked like a frail little boy. His throat felt
dry. He felt it tighten as he forced a smile. Eighteen years
old, and so many months lost.

After her birthday he had to go to the States to film
the chase scenes in New York and San Francisco. Then
there was the editing and final scoring in Los Angeles.
He had high hopes for the picture; it had the smell of
a winner. And somehow he tied up his hopes for the
success of the picture with January's recovery. Like a
mind bet. If the picture made it big—her recovery
would be rapid.

It opened with a big charity premiere in New York.
The klieg-light bit; the celebrities; Barry Gray interviewing the V.I.P.'s. The audience applauded and laughed in
the right places. When the lights came up, the heads of
Century walked up the aisle with him . . . back-slapping
. . . smiling. Then on to the party at the Americana,
where they heard that the first reviews on TV had been

bad. But everyone said it didn't matter. *The New York Times* was all that counted. At midnight they learned the *Times* had murdered it (that was when the heads of the studio left the party). The head of Century publicity, an optimistic man named Sid Goff, shrugged it off. "Ah, who reads the *Times*? For movies, it's the *Daily News* that counts." Twenty minutes later they learned the *News* had only given it two stars, but Sid Goff was still optimistic. "I hear the guy at the *Post* loved it. Besides, word of mouth will make the picture."

But neither the *Post* nor word of mouth was good. Business was weak, but Sid Goff was still cheerful. "Wait till it plays across the country. The people will love it. That's where it counts."

It received a lukewarm reception at the Chinese in Los Angeles. It limped along in Detroit. In Chicago it bombed completely. And Philadelphia and other key cities refused it at first-run houses.

He couldn't believe it. He had been so sure of the picture. Two flops in a row. And now he faced the old show business superstition. Everything bad comes in threes. Deaths . . . plane crashes . . . earthquakes—and flop pictures. Obviously the heads of Century pictures felt the same way, because when he called, everyone was always busy in meetings or had "just stepped out of the office." And the final clincher was when word came from the New York office that they would allot him only two million dollars (including advertising) for his third picture.

He couldn't bring it in on that kind of a budget unless he settled for actors whose names went under the title and a new director or an old one with a long backlog of flops. But he had no choice. He had to do the picture; it was part of his contract. He had a three-picture deal. Well, if that's the way the cards were stacked he'd get the third flop out of the way, pack it in, go back to New York, and do a smash Broadway show. The more he thought about it, the more his confidence grew. His return to Broadway would be an event. Money would be no problem. Hell, he'd back it himself. He was worth several million. What was a few hundred

thousand bucks? The only thing—he had to come up
with a hot script.

These were his emotions that summer of '68 as he
started his third picture. He was in high spirits when he
flew to Rome to see January, but when he saw her hobble
toward him, still dragging her leg, it hit him for the first
time that she just might not walk again. Her bright
smile and eager excitement only added to his feeling of
despair. She wanted to know all about the new picture.
Why had he picked unknowns? Who was the leading
man? When could she read the final shooting script? He
forced himself to invent stories and gossip with an enthusiasm that came hard. He held his panic until he
was alone with the doctors. Then his rage and fear exploded. What was all this crap about her making steady
progress? All the good reports he had received during
the past few months? She hadn't improved one iota.

They admitted she was not responding as quickly as
they had hoped. But he must realize . . . They had not
been able to start the physical therapy as soon as they
should. Then they told him the facts. She would im-
prove. But she would always limp and possibly have
to use a cane.

That night he went on a wild drunk with Melba
Delitto. And when they wound up at her apartment, he
paced and raged about the doctors, the hospital, the
hopelessness of it all.

Melba tried to calm him. "Mike, I adore you. I not
even hold my one big flop against you. But now you
have done another bad picture. You must not let your
daughter's misfortune destroy your life. This next one
must be good."

"What do you want me to do? Just go to work and
forget about her?"

"No, not forget. But you have your own life to live.
Stop fighting for the impossible."

His anger made him suddenly sober. His whole life
had been a fight to attain the impossible. Son of a
mother who deserted him when he was three. Father, an
Irish prizefighter who died from a lucky punch from a
third-rate kid. A life of growing up on his own in South

Philadelphia. Enlisting in the Air Force at seventeen because anything seemed better than the world he knew. And then the war . . . being in the midst of it . . . seeing guys you lived with and slept with catch a bullet at your side . . . wondering why *they* got it and not you. *They* had families who were waiting for them to come home. Families and sweethearts who wrote long letters and sent food packages. And gradually the idea hits you that maybe they got *your* bullet because there was something back there, waiting to be done . . . by *you*. And it's your job to go back and do it. He felt he had been given luck—luck to accomplish the impossible. And he had to make good so that the guy who got his bullet would understand. He wasn't religious, but he believed in paying his dues. That had always been his philosophy, and it still was.

"My kid will walk," he said quietly.

Melba shrugged. "Then try Lourdes. Or if you really want to spend money, take her to the Clinique of Miracles."

"What's that?"

"In Switzerland, in a remote section of the Alps. It is very expensive, but they have accomplished great things. I know a racing driver who crashed at the Monte. They said he'd be paralyzed for life. He went to the Clinique of Miracles—they made him walk."

The next day Mike flew to Zurich, then drove to a rambling château hidden in the mountains and met with Dr. Peterson, a fragile-looking man who seemed incapable of creating even the smallest miracle.

It was just another wild chase. Another blind alley. But he was there. So he toured the Clinique with Dr. Peterson. He saw old people who had suffered strokes wave cheerfully at the doctor as they struggled with crutches and braces. He followed the doctor into a room where small children were singing. At first glance, it appeared to be an ordinary songfest, until he realized that every child was performing against odds. Some had cleft palates . . . some wore earphones . . . some had facial paralysis. But they all smiled and forced some sounds through their lips. In another wing there were

Thalidomide children working with their artificial limbs, smiling as they made some slight progress with a new and cumbersome prosthesis. Mike felt his mood changing. At first he didn't quite understand. But then it hit him. Everywhere he went, there was an absence of despair. Everywhere he looked was an attempt at accomplishment. The fight to attain the impossible.

"You see," Dr. Peterson explained, "every waking moment is spent in therapy. In striving to get well. We have one little boy who lost both his arms in an accident with a tractor on a farm. With his prosthesis he has learned to play the guitar. We have songfests every night. Sometimes we put on plays and ballets—all part of the therapy. But there is no television or radio."

"But why cut out the outside world?" Mike asked. "Aren't they segregated from life as it is by their illnesses?"

Dr. Peterson smiled. "The Clinique is a world of its own. A world where each patient helps the other. News from the outside world concerns wars, strikes, pollution, riots. . . . If it is not a world that healthy people enjoy, why should our patients want to fight insurmountable obstacles just to return to it? Also, a child born without legs who has worked six months to take two steps can be disheartened if he sees the violence or apathy of people born more fortunate. The Clinique of Miracles is a world of hope and the will to recover."

Mike looked thoughtful. "But there is no one here my daughter could relate to. Everyone is very old . . . or very very young."

"Who is she relating to in her hospital room in Rome?"

"No one. But she's not surrounded by sickness and mutilation."

Dr. Peterson looked thoughtful. "Sometimes seeing others less fortunate helps one to recover. A boy comes here with one arm and sees a boy without any arms. Suddenly, having one is not the end of everything. And the boy missing two arms takes great pride helping the boy without legs. And that is how it happens here."

"One question, Dr. Peterson . . . do you really think you can help my daughter?"

"First I must study her records and the reports from the attending physicians. We accept no one whom we cannot help. And even then we cannot always promise a complete cure."

Three weeks later Mike chartered a plane and flew January to the Clinique of Miracles. He had not spared her. He told her what she would find, the condition of some of the patients. But at least—here—she had a shot at getting well. He did not tell her that Dr. Peterson had some reservations about her complete recovery.

The nearest village was five miles from the Clinique. He checked into the inn and remained a week to see how she would take it. If she felt any revulsion she did not show it. Her smile was always bright, and she praised everyone at the Clinique.

He returned to the Coast and went through the motions of making the final picture. It was a dog and nothing could save it. But he had already started the publicity going on his "return to Broadway." Agents, actors and directors began calling. Each night he holed up in his bungalow at the Beverly Hills Hotel and read scripts. Scripts from established playwrights, new authors, amateurs. He read everything, including galleys of new novels. His attaché case was stacked with them when he flew to Switzerland. January had been at the Clinique two months. Her speech was perfect. Her right arm was as strong as it had ever been. But her leg still presented a problem. She was walking better, but with a decided limp.

The picture was finished in December. He gave it to the director to edit and score and walked away from it. He had a long meeting with his business manager. He sold his plane and some stocks. But he refused to relinquish the suite at the Plaza.

On the day before Christmas he flew to Switzerland five hundred dollars in overweight, with three suitcases loaded with toys for the children. He brought January a record player and albums of all the show tunes of the past ten years.

They celebrated her nineteenth birthday in the little dining room at the inn. She chattered about the albums

—how much she liked them, how she wished she hadn't missed the shows of the past year. Then her face grew serious and she reached out and took his hand. "Tell you what. Next time you come, I'm going to be able to dance with you. That's a promise."

"Take it easy." He laughed. "I haven't danced in a long time."

"Well, brush up," she said. "Because I'll be waiting." Then she smiled. "I don't mean discotheque stuff. But maybe a quiet little waltz. At least it's something to shoot for."

He nodded and managed a smile. Just that day he had a long talk with Dr. Peterson, who also was concerned over the lack of improvement of her leg. Dr. Peterson suggested they send for one of the top orthopedic surgeons in London for consultation.

A few days later Mike met with Dr. Peterson and Sir Arthur Rylander, the English surgeon. After Sir Arthur studied the X rays, it was his opinion that the bone had healed improperly. The only chance for a cure was to rebreak it and reset it.

When Mike put it to January, she didn't hesitate. "Let's break it. I've always thought wearing a cast in the Alps was rather chic. Didn't you do a picture like that, where the heroine sat in après-ski clothes and looked beautiful?"

"I've done three of them." Mike laughed. "And all my heroines always recovered. Remember that."

The operation was performed in a hospital in Zurich. Two weeks later she was back at the Clinique of Miracles. Those who were able signed her cast, and her unbelievable spunk sent Mike Wayne back to the States with fresh determination. Anyone with her guts deserved to have a kingdom waiting on her return. Nothing could stop him now.

He went to the Coast, cleared out his office at Century pictures, and went to the races at Santa Anita. He bet a long shot. It came in and he won five thousand dollars. He wasn't really surprised, because he knew his luck had changed. And that night he read a script from a new author, and knew he had found his play. He decided to back it himself. He went to New York, put extra phones in his suite at the Plaza, took a lavish office in the Getty building, and called a press conference. Michael Wayne was back on Broadway!

For the next few months he was an explosion of frenetic energy. There were discussions with set designers, directors, actors, interviews at Sardi's, appearances on the talk shows, quick dinners at Danny's Hide-a-Way to unwind with the comedians, dropping by and sitting up half the night with Long John Nebel on his radio show. His return generated the excitement of a superstar. He was well liked by the press . . . his enthusiasm and "rough cut" charm were infectious to everyone around him. When rehearsals began he sent daily reports to January. He sent her the script; the newspaper stories; wrote to her about rehearsals; and kept her informed on every development of "their" prospect. The only thing he neglected to tell her about was the ingenue who had moved in with him after the first week of rehearsal.

The play opened in October in Philadelphia and got mixed notices. Revisions were made and the ingenue lost two of her best scenes and stopped talking to him. It went on to Boston, where it received excellent notices. Three weeks later it opened in New York to a rousing ovation and murderous reviews. The consensus was "Old hat" . . . "Cumbersome" . . . "Badly cast." The playwright went on talk shows and said Mike had changed his original conception, taken away all the mystical quality. The ingenue went on talk shows and said the playwright was a genius and Mike had ruined his work (she had already moved out of the Plaza and in with the playwright).

He refused to close it. The cast took cuts and went on minimum salary. He poured another two hundred thousand dollars into signs on buses and subways, full-page ads in *The New York Times,* radio and television spots, full-page ads in the trades, in weekly *Variety.* He reprinted the Boston notice in full-page ads in out-of-town newspapers. He papered the house and gave it the razzle-dazzle he had always given his hits. He flew to Switzerland and told January it was a smash—it would run forever and he would have at least three companies on tour.

Two months later, after a long session with his accountant, he was forced to close. The market was down, but he sold more stock and arrived in Switzerland for her twentieth birthday, walking like a winner, and carrying the usual amount of overweight in gifts.

And when January walked into the reception room without crutches and without a trace of a limp, he felt like the winner of all time. Her steps were slow and measured, but she was walking. He clamped his jaw and swallowed hard. She was so damned beautiful with those great brown eyes and her hair hanging to her shoulders.

And then she was in his arms, both of them talking and laughing at once. Later, over dinner at the inn, she said, "Why did you tell me the show was such a hit?"

"It was . . . with me. Just had too much class for the public."

"But you put your own money into it . . ."

"So?"

"Well, you've had three flop pictures . . ."

"Who says?"

"*Variety* says."

"Where in the hell did you get *Variety*?"

"You left it here last time. Dr. Peterson gave it to me, thinking you might want it back. I devoured it. But why did you tell me it was a hit?"

"It was . . . in Boston. Look, forget the play. Let's talk about important things. The Doc says you'll be ready to leave in six months."

"Daddy—" She leaned across the table and looked into his eyes. "Remember when I entered my teens, you said that was a special night. Well, tonight I've left my teens. I'm twenty. I'm a big girl now. I know the clinic costs over three thousand a month. Erik, the little boy who taught me to play guitar, had to leave because it was too expensive . . . so I've been thinking . . ."

"The only thing you've got to think about is getting well."

"What about money?"

"Hell, I made money from the flop pictures. I was on a percentage of the gross, baby—got it right off the top."

"Honest?"

"Honest."

He had gone back on the plane determined to knock down windmills. His talk with Dr. Peterson had been unsettling. ("Mr. Wayne, you must think of January's future with much care. She is so very beautiful but also so very innocent. She talks of being an actress, which is natural because it is your business. But you must realize how protected she has been in the world of our Clinique. She must be eased back into your world, not thrown into it.")

He thought about it on the plane. Somehow he'd manage to have one hell of a world waiting for her. When they ran into some rough weather, he was hit with the crazy idea that a plane crash might solve everything, until he realized he had already cashed in his insurance.

A hit picture was the only solution. Maybe with the three bad ones behind him, the curse was off. He returned to Los Angeles and once again holed up at the Beverly Hills Hotel reading scenarios and treatments. Oddly enough he found one almost immediately. It was from a writer who had not had a hit in the past ten years. But in the fifties, he had one blockbuster after another. He had Oscars for doorstops. And this one would get him another. It had everything. Big love interest, action, a violent chase scene. He met with the author and paid him a thousand dollars for a month's option.

Then he went to the heads of the big studios.

To his amazement, he couldn't raise any money or any interest in the script. The answer was the same everywhere. The industry was in a slump. A scenario from a screenwriter meant nothing. Now if he had a best-selling novel . . . perhaps. But scenarios were flooding the studios. And everyone seemed in a state of quiet panic. Changes were happening everywhere. Studio heads had come and gone. At some studios he didn't even know the new people in charge. The top independent film-makers also refused to back him. They felt he was a bad risk and the author was old hat. At the end of the month he was forced to relinquish the property. Three days later, two kids in their twenties who had come up with a sleeper the year before grabbed it and got immediate backing from a major studio.

He returned to New York in a frantic search for some action. He invested a hundred thousand in a show a top producer had in rehearsal. The trouble began when the leading man quit the second week of rehearsal. The out-of-town tryout was a nightmare—eight weeks of hysteria, fights, cast replacements, and finally his decision to close the show without bringing it in.

After that he spent two months pouring money into an idea for a television series. He worked with the writers; he paid for the pilot himself, spent over three hundred thousand dollars. The networks looked at it, but "passed." His only chance to recoup some of the money would be as a one-shot slot filler in the summer.

A few weeks later he went to a private screening of the picture he had lost. The production room was filled with young men with beards, tank shirts, and hair hanging from their armpits. The girls wore tank tops and no bras and their hair was either Afro or long and stringy. He felt sick as he watched the picture. They had ruined a great script. Put the ending at the beginning, flooded it with flashbacks and out-of-focus camera work, made the love scene a psychedelic dream sequence with hand-held cameras— the *cinéma-vérité* crap. Sure, they had to play it that way with the beasts who were passing as actors and actresses today. There were no more faces around like Garbo's or Crawford's, or actors like Gable and Cary. . . . Today was the world of the Uglies. That's what everything seemed to be, and he didn't understand it.

A week later he went to a sneak preview on Eighty-sixth Street. The same crowd was there, along with college kids and young married advertising executives. The audience cheered.

Three weeks later it opened, and broke box-office records all over the country. That really rocked him. Because it meant he really didn't know what was good or bad. Not in today's market. Three years ago he could call the shots. Studios had believed in him . . . and more important, he had believed in himself.

It was time to walk away from the table. Mike Wayne was tapped out. How had the chemistry changed in such a short time? He looked the same, thought the same. Maybe that was it. He hadn't gone along with all the changes, the nudity, plays and movies without plots, the new trend of Unisex. Well, he was fifty-two. He had lived through some great times. He had known what it was like to walk down Broadway without worrying about getting mugged. He had known New York when it had nightclubs and lines of beautiful girls, not just porno movies and massage parlors. But most of all he was sad—because this was the world she was coming back to.

He sat in the V.I.P. Lounge and stared at the gray sky. She was flying home through that leaden muck. He had always promised her a bright shining world. Well, goddammit, he was keeping that promise.

The smiling hostess was back. She announced that Flight Seven was arriving. He had arranged for January to receive courtesy of the port. An official would be waiting to whisk her through customs. Hell, what could a kid who had spent three years in hospitals have to declare? He walked out of the lounge and never noticed that the hostess had leaped up to say goodbye. Ordinarily he would have turned on the charm because she was a pretty girl. But for the first time in his life, Mike Wayne was scared.

He spotted her the moment she walked into the airport. Hell, you couldn't miss her. Tall, tan, long hair swinging—she would have caught his eye even if she wasn't his daughter. She seemed oblivious of the men who turned to look at her. A little man was walking double time to keep up with her long strides as her eyes scanned the airport. Then she saw Mike and suddenly he was enveloped in bear hugs, kisses, and she was laughing and crying together.

"Oh, Daddy, you look super! Do you realize I haven't seen you since June? Oh, wow! It's so wonderful to be home again . . . to be with you."

"You look great, babe."

"You too! And . . . oh . . . this is Mr. Higgens." She turned and introduced the little man. "He's been so nice to me. I never even had to open my bag and . . ."

Mike shook hands with the customs official, who was carrying her overnight case. "I'm very grateful, Mr. Higgens." He took the bag. "Now if you'll tell me where the rest of my daughter's luggage is, I'll arrange to have it brought to the car."

"That's all there is, Mr. Wayne. And it was a pleasure. And such a pleasure to meet you, Miss Wayne." He shook hands with both of them and disappeared into the crowd.

Mike held up the overnight bag. "This is it?"

"Yup! I'm wearing my best outfit . . . do you like it?" She stood off and spun around. "I got it in Zurich. They said everyone was wearing pants suits and this suede outfit cost me three hundred dollars."

"It's beautiful. But—" He stared down at the small bag he was carrying. "No other clothes?"

She laughed. "Oh, that's loaded with clothes. Like three pairs of jeans, a couple of faded shirts, some sweaters, sneakers, and oh . . . a gorgeous shortie nightgown I got in Zurich. I ran out of money or I would have bought the robe to go with it. But other than that little omission, I'm practically set for any emergency."

"We'll take care of the clothes tomorrow."

She tucked her arm through his as they walked to the exit. "I saw so many different skirt lengths on the plane. Mike, what *are* people wearing?"

"Mike?" He stared at her. "Where did *Daddy* go?"

"Oh, you're too gorgeous to be called Daddy. You are gorgeous, you know. I like the sideburns . . . and the gray in them."

"They're white; and I'm a dignified elderly gentleman."

"That'll be the day. Hey, look, that girl is wearing

an Indian outfit. Think she's part of some act or something—with the headband and the braids and all?"

"Come on, you know how kooky everyone is dressing today," he said.

"How would I know? Most of my friends wore bathrobes."

He stopped suddenly and looked at her. "Holy Christ, that's right. No TV . . . no nothing?"

"No nothing."

He led her outside to the car. "Well, everyone dresses like they're going to a costume party today. That is, kids your age." But she wasn't listening. She was staring at the car. Then she let out a low whistle. "Wow . . . I'm impressed."

"You've been in limos before."

"I spent my life in them. But this is not just a limo —this is really super." She tossed him a smile of approval. "A silver Rolls-Royce—the *only* way a girl should travel." She got in and nodded. "Pret-ty nice . . . chauffeur's uniform matches upholstery . . . a telephone . . . a bar . . . all the necessities of life *if* you're Mike Wayne." Then she threw her arms around him. "Oh, Daddy . . . I'm so glad for you." She leaned back as the car inched its way out of the airport. She sighed. "It's so great to be back. If you only knew how many times I've dreamed of this moment. Even when I felt it could never happen, I kept dreaming the dream—of *walking* into your arms, of us together in New York. And it's all happening just as I dreamed it. Nothing's changed."

"You're wrong, baby. A lot has changed. Especially New York."

She pointed to the traffic as their car slipped into the speed lane. "This hasn't changed. And I love it all—the traffic, the noise, the crowds, even the smog. It's just so wonderful after all that sanitary snow in Switzerland. I can't wait until we go to the theater. I want to walk through Shubert Alley . . . see the trucks pull out of the Times Building . . . I want to get my nice clean lungs all polluted."

"That'll happen. But first we have a lot of catching up to do."

She nestled against him. "We sure do. I want to sit at our table at Sardi's . . . I can't wait to see *Hair* . . . I want to walk down Fifth Avenue . . . see the clothes. But tonight, I just want to stay in and do the caviar and champagne scene. I know it's no birthday. But you've got to admit it's one hell of an occasion. And most of all I want to know all about your big hit picture."

"My hit picture? Who told you that?"

"No one. But I know how you operate. When I got all those postcards from Spain this summer with mysterious hints of a big new project . . . well, I knew it had to be a picture and you were afraid of jinxing it by telling me. But now . . . when I see all this—" she waved her hand. "Well, come on—tell me about it."

He looked at her. And this time he didn't smile. "You tell *me* something. Are you still the most resilient girl in the world? Because you're gonna find a lot of changes and—"

"We're together," she said. "And as long as that never changes, nothing else matters. Now tell me—is it a movie or a play? And can I work with you? In any capacity—a walk-on, a script girl, a gofer . . ."

"January, did it ever occur to you that there are better things in life than the theater and tagging along after me?"

"Name one."

"Well, like you finding the right guy . . . getting married . . . making me a proud grandpa . . ."

She laughed. "Not for a long time. Listen—beside you sits a lady who has spent three years just learning to walk and talk again." She reached out and touched his face tenderly. "Oh, Mike . . ." Her sigh was happy. "I want to do all the things we've always dreamed of doing together."

"Sometimes we change our dreams," he said. "Or perhaps I should say . . . exchange them."

"Fine. What have you in mind?"

"Well, as you know, I was in Spain," he said slowly. "But it wasn't for a movie."

"A TV series," she said. "That's what it is! Right?"

He looked out of the window. His words were measured. "I've made some pretty good moves in my life and this is about the best I've ever made. I've got some big surprises for you. Tonight you're going to—"

She cut in. "Oh, Mike, please, no surprises tonight. Just us and the champagne. If you knew how many months I've dreamed of being with you in our suite at the Plaza, looking out at the park, seeing my old wishing hill and toasting to—"

"Will you settle for the Pierre?"

"What happened to the Plaza?"

"Mayor Lindsay donated it to the pigeons."

She smiled, but he saw the disappointment in her eyes. "The view is almost the same," he said quickly. "But I'm afraid you'll have to forget about your wishing hill. Drunks and junkies have claimed it now. Along with a few large dogs who use it as a lavatory. Everyone has large dogs now. Not for pets—for protection." He knew he was talking too much. He stopped and stared at the approaching skyline, the uneven beauty of the buildings shrouded in smog. Lights beginning to glow in tiny square windows . . . evening in New York.

And then the skyline was gone and they merged into New York's traffic. As they made their way down Sixtieth Street, Mike called out to the driver. "Stop at that cigar store on the corner opposite Bloomingdale's." They pulled up and before the chauffeur could get out, Mike jumped out of the car. "I'm out of cigarettes." He turned to the chauffeur. "You can't double-park here. Drive Miss Wayne around the block. I'll be out by then."

He was standing on the corner when the car rounded the block. He lit a cigarette when he got into the car. Suddenly he extended the pack as an afterthought. "Do you?"

"No, I don't. But did you?"

"Did I what?"

"Make the call."

"What call?"

She laughed. "Oh, Mike . . . there's a whole carton of cigarettes right here in the bar area of the car."

His jaw tightened. "Okay . . . what call did I make?"

She slipped her arm through his. "To order the caviar and champagne. I could tell by your face that you forgot."

He sighed. "Maybe I forgot a lot of things."

She put her fingers across his lips. "Just tell me one thing. Did I guess right about your call?"

"Yep, you guessed right."

Her voice was soft. "Mike, you haven't forgotten anything."

When she opened her eyes, she thought she was still at the Clinique. But the darkness in the room was unfamiliar; the dark shapes of the furniture were different. And then consciousness took over and she realized she was in her new bedroom at the Pierre. She switched on the lamp on the night table. Midnight. That meant she had been asleep only two hours. She stretched and looked around the bedroom. It really was beautiful. It didn't look like a hotel bedroom at all. The entire suite was luxurious and huge. Bigger than anything Mike had ever had. He had explained the hotel had co-op apartments and some people sublet their suites. Well, the people who owned this one sure had taste. The living room had been so beautiful when she arrived. Candlelight, caviar, and champagne all iced, the velvet darkness of the park so many stories below. Then they had toasted one another, eaten the caviar . . . And, after just one glass of champagne she had suddenly gotten drowsy. He had noticed it immediately. "Look, babe, it's only nine o'clock here, but by Swiss time it's two or three in the morning. You go right to bed. I'll take a little walk . . . get the papers . . . watch some TV and turn in early too."

"But we haven't talked about you . . . what you're doing . . . or anything."

"Tomorrow." His voice had been firm. "We meet in the living room at nine and have breakfast together and do a *lot* of talking."

"But Mike—"

"Tomorrow." Again that strange quality in his voice.

Almost like a cut-off. An odd new hardness. The way it had been with the photographer in the lobby who had snapped a picture of them. He had seemed like a nice young man. He had followed them to the elevator and said, "Tell me, Mr. Wayne, how does your daughter feel being the—"

But he had never finished the question. Mike Wayne pushed January into the elevator and snapped, "Beat it. This is no time for any on-the-spot interview."

She thought about the incident now. The whole thing had been so unlike her father. To him publicity had always been a way of life. She had been on the cover of a national magazine with him when she was nine. And she had felt so sorry for the young man in the lobby.

When she had asked her father about it, he shrugged. "Maybe Rome did it to me. I don't go for these guys who take pictures on spec—pictures that can turn up anywhere, in any cheap magazine. I'm all for giving an authorized interview or posing for a photographer for pictures to *accompany* a story. But I don't like guys popping out from dark corners at me."

"But he was waiting in the lobby. He looked very nice."

"Forget it." (Again that cold determined cut-off tone.) Then he had opened the champagne. When she toasted and said, "To us," he shook his head. "No . . . to *you*. It's your time now, and I'm here to see that you get it."

She lay in the dark bedroom. She had the whole night ahead of her. She should try to go back to sleep. But she was wide awake and thirsty. She was always thirsty after caviar. She slipped out of bed and went to the bathroom. The tap water was lukewarm. She decided to forget it and got back into bed. She switched on the dial of the radio beside her bed to an album station. She was just drifting off to sleep when the commercial break came, and an enthusiastic announcer began his pitch on a new diet cola. The way he began to sell that damn soda— suddenly she *had* to have a glass of cold water!

She got out of bed. There was a big kitchen in the

suite. She could get some ice . . . She started for the door and stopped. She had no robe! And she was wearing the short see-through nightgown. She opened the bedroom door cautiously and called out, "Daddy?"

The living room was empty. She tiptoed out. She looked into the darkness of the dining room . . . the large den . . . and down some long corridor off the kitchen. Mike had said there were servants' quarters. But the apartment was empty. She went to his bedroom door and knocked. Then she opened it. Empty. For a fleeting second she thought of Rome . . . and Melba. But he wouldn't do that, not on her first night home. He had probably gone for a walk and run into some friends. She went into the kitchen. The refrigerator was stacked with Cokes, 7-Up, ginger ale, along with every kind of sugar-free diet soda. She took a Coke and poured it into a glass. Then she ambled into the living room. She stood staring out at the park. The tiny sparkling lights gave it a Christmas-tree effect. It was impossible to believe there was anything to fear in that soft darkness.

Then she heard the click. Her father was fitting the key into the lock. Her first impulse was to run and greet him. Then she looked down at her nightgown. It was ridiculous to have bought something so short and sheer. But after three years of flannel pajamas at the Clinique, the sheer gown had been a symbol. Part of being well . . . and leaving. Well, she'd better tell him to keep his eyes closed and lend her one of his robes.

The door opened and she heard the woman's voice. Oh, good Lord . . . he had company. She looked frantically across the long living room. If she tried to make it back to her bedroom, she'd have to pass the foyer and run right into them. The nearest door led to his bedroom. She dashed inside just as they came into the living room. His bedroom was dark. Oh, God . . . where was the light? She groped along the wall searching for the switch.

"Mike, this is absolutely ridiculous for me to have to sneak in here." The woman's voice was petulant. "After all, she's not a child."

"Dee"—his voice was firm but cajoling. "You've got

to understand. For three years she looked forward to the way she wanted to spend her first night back."

The woman sighed. "But how do you think I felt when you called and told me to get out of the apartment after I had gone to such pains, getting the best caviar, the right champagne. It was going to be my 'getting to know January night.' Instead I'm dismissed like some chorus girl. Thank God I was able to catch David. We sat in that bar at the Sherry for hours. I'm sure I dragged him out of the arms of some beautiful young thing—"

"Come here," Mike said softly.

There was silence, and January knew he was kissing the woman. She didn't know what to do. It was wrong to stand in the darkness and listen. If only she had a robe.

Her father spoke softly. "January and I are having breakfast tomorrow. I want to have a long talk with her before you two meet. But believe me, I was right . . . handling it the way I did tonight."

"But Mike—"

"No buts. Come on, we've wasted too much time already."

The woman laughed. "Oh, Mike, you've ruined my hair. Oh, would you be a love and pick up my purse . . . I left it on the table near the hall."

January stood very still. They were coming into the bedroom! The door opened and there was a sudden burst of light as the woman flicked on the wall switch. For a split second they both stared at one another. For some reason January felt she looked strangely familiar. She was tall and slim with frosted hair and incredibly beautiful skin. The woman recovered first and called out, "Mike . . . come on in. We seem to have company."

January didn't move. She didn't like the funny smile of composure on the woman's face, as if she had the situation well in hand and had her next move planned.

Mike's first reaction was surprise. Then an expression came to his eyes that she had never seen before. Annoyance. And when he spoke his voice was cold. "January, what the hell are you doing snooping around in here?"

"I . . . I was having a Coke—" She pointed toward the living room where she had left her drink.

"But what are you doing in here . . . in the dark . . . *without* the drink?" the woman asked.

January looked toward her father, waiting for him to end this horrible scene. But he stood beside the woman, waiting for the answer.

Her throat was dry. "I heard the door . . . and voices . . ." She forced the words out. "I had no robe, so I dashed in here."

For the first time they both stared at the filmy nightgown. Her father walked into the bathroom quickly and returned with one of his dressing gowns. He tossed it to her without glancing up. She struggled into it and started for the door. The woman's soft voice called out, "Stay a moment, January. Mike, you can't let your daughter go without introducing us."

January stood with her back to them waiting for her release.

"January—" her father's voice suddenly seemed weary. "This is Dee."

January forced a slight nod in the woman's direction.

"Oh, come now, Mike," the woman slipped her arm through his. "That's not really a proper introduction."

Mike looked at his daughter and said quietly, "January . . . Dee is my wife. We got married last week."

She heard herself congratulating them. Her legs felt like weights, but somehow she managed to walk out of that room . . . through the living room and into the safety of her own bedroom. Only then did her knees begin to shake . . . and she rushed to the bathroom and was violently ill.

TWO

SHE SAT by the window for the rest of the night. No wonder the woman looked familiar. Dee wasn't just Dee. She was Deirdre Milford Granger, often reported as the sixth richest woman in the world! No one really knew whether she was the sixth or sixtieth. It was obviously a tag some reporter had dreamed up, and it stuck. The girls at Miss Haddon's used to kid about the title whenever her picture appeared in the newspapers or magazines. And in those days, Deirdre's marriages kept her in print constantly. First there had been an opera singer. Then an author, followed by a top designer. That marriage had made *Vogue* in January's time. He had been killed four years ago in an automobile accident in Monte Carlo. There had been newsreel pictures of Deirdre in heavy widow's weeds at the funeral, tearfully claiming the dead man to be the only man she had ever loved, swearing she'd never marry again. Unfortunately, she had changed her mind.

Or had Mike changed her mind! Of course! She had been his big new project. All those postcards from Spain. Dee had a house in Marbella—she had seen that in *Vogue*. Dee also had a Palm Beach estate where she kept forty in help—she had seen that in *Ladies' Home Journal*. And there was a yacht in Cannes—that had come into the news when Karla had been Dee's guest at sea. Karla had retired from the screen in 1960 and was more

59

of a recluse than Garbo or Howard Hughes. So much so that her appearance as a guest on someone's yacht made *Time* magazine. All of the girls at Miss Haddon's had been fans of the Polish actress. In 1963 January's biggest claim to fame came when her father offered the great Karla a million dollars to come out of retirement. She never accepted or declined, but it had gotten Mike a great deal of publicity. Later her father had told her that it had been one of his big dreams just to meet the great Karla.

Well, he'd probably meet her now. Maybe he had already.

So the big new project was Deirdre Granger! In a porcelain-muted way, Dee was beautiful. But she seemed bloodless and fragile. Could Mike really love her? She seemed so cold, so unable to give affection. But maybe that was the fascination. Mike always loved a challenge.

She sat at the window until the first hint of light filtered through the darkness. She watched the black sky turn gray. She knew the sunlight was beginning to creep over the tall apartment buildings on upper Fifth Avenue. Everything was so silent—that intermediate time between night and morning.

She put on a pair of jeans, a sweater, and sneakers and slipped out of the apartment. The elevator man's greeting was a cross between a yawn and a nod. The desk clerk looked up with weary disinterest. A man in coveralls was mopping the floor of the lobby. He stopped to let her pass.

New York was still shadowy. Empty, desolate—a vacant city. In the gray morning light the streets seemed curiously clean. She walked to the Plaza and stood for a moment looking up toward the corner suite. Then she cut across the street and walked into the park. A bedraggled woman, wearing a man's overcoat, was poking into a trashcan. Her legs, swollen to twice their size, were swathed in dirty rags. Drunks were sleeping on benches, empty liquor bottles smashed on the ground at their sides. Others slept in fetal positions on the grass. She walked quickly—to the Zoo, back toward the Carousel. The sun worked its way through the smog and

fought to clear the sky. Two young men dressed in sweat-
shirts jogged by. Pigeons began to cluster on the grass,
searching for breakfast. A squirrel came right up to her,
cupping its paws, its bright little eyes demanding a nut.
She shrugged and held out her empty hands and it scam-
pered off. Three black girls on bicycles waved, holding
up their fingers in the Peace sign. She continued to walk.
The sleeping drunks began to stir. A woman came into
the park carrying an elderly dachshund. She placed it
on the ground gently and said, "Come on, Baby . . .
make ca-ca." Neither the woman nor the dog looked at
January. The dog performed—the woman praised it,
picked it up, and left the park.

The drunks were pulling themselves to a standing position now. Those who staggered were helped by others.
Suddenly the park became alive with dogs: a professional walker with six dogs of assorted breeds, a man
with a schnauzer, a woman with rollers in her hair and
a fat cocker on a leash. The park that looked like velvet
in the darkness last night was now harsh and dirty. The
sunlight seemed to spotlight the beer cans, the broken
bottles and sandwich papers. A wind stirred the trees,
and the sighs of the leaves dropping to their death
seemed despairing and gentle against the belching snorts
of the huge buses. There were sounds of horns, riveting,
blasting—the monolithic monster was awake.

Babies were coming into the park now. Babies in
strollers, pushed by young mothers who looked pale and
weary. Sometimes an elderly dog tagged jealously along,
attached to the stroller, thinking of fonder days when
he was the main concern of the family. There were other
carriages where an infant slept while a two-year-old
perched perilously on a jump seat as the mother trudged
them toward the playground.

And then the Fifth Avenue brigade entered. A stream
of large English prams, with pure silk initialed blanket
covers concealing the tiny babies inside. Nurses in stiff
uniforms wheeled these sparkling carriages to nearby
benches, where they gathered and talked while their tiny
charges slept.

January glanced at them enviously. Those tiny bits of life . . . yet each one felt at home in this park. They belonged in this city. Each one had an identity, a name, a home.

She walked with no real direction and found herself heading toward the wishing hill. It was such a small hill. But it had seemed like a mountain when she was little. When she was five she had climbed to the top of it triumphantly, and her father had raised her arm in victory and said, "Now this is your own hill. Close your eyes and make any wish . . . and it will come true." She had silently wished for a doll. Then he took her to Rumpelmayer's for hot chocolate, and as they were leaving he bought her the biggest doll in the place. From that moment on it became the wishing hill.

But now the hill seemed so bare and ugly. She kicked through dead leaves as she walked to the top. She sat down, drew her knees up to her chin, hugged them, and closed her eyes. Oddly enough it seemed as if the sounds of life around her were suddenly intensified—the noise of the traffic below, the barking of dogs in the distance. . . . Then she heard leaves crackle, and she knew someone was approaching. All the stories of violence she had heard rushed to her. Perhaps it was someone with a knife. She didn't move. Maybe if she just kept her eyes shut it would all be over. Quickly and painlessly.

"January . . ."

Her father was standing beside her. He held out his hand and she struggled to her feet.

"This is the third time I've come back to this hill in the past half hour," he said. "I figured you'd come here." He took her arm and led her out of the park. They crossed the street and he stopped in front of the Essex House. "They make pretty good coffee here. C'mon, let's have some breakfast."

They sat in the impersonal dining room without speaking; the untouched eggs before them. Suddenly he said, "Okay. Yell, get mad . . . but say something."

She started to speak, but the maître d' appeared and asked if anything was wrong with the eggs.

"No. We weren't hungry," Mike said. "Take them away and just leave the pot of coffee." He waited until the waiter left, then turned to her. "Why the park? My God, why? You could have been killed."

"I couldn't sleep," she said.

"Who could! Even Dee had to take an extra sleeping pill. But no one goes walking around New York at dawn. I sat up all night just waiting till morning. I smoked two packs of cigarettes waiting—"

"You shouldn't," she said tonelessly. "Cigarettes are bad for you."

"Look, let's not worry about my health right now. Christ, when I found your room empty . . . I went crazy. Dee woke up just as I was calling the police. She calmed me down and said you were probably walking to think things out. That's when I got the idea of the wishing hill."

She didn't answer, and he reached out and grabbed her hand.

"January, let's talk it out." When she didn't answer, he looked at her and said quietly, "Please, don't make me beg."

"I wasn't snooping or intentionally eavesdropping last night," she said.

"I know. I was just caught off guard. I was angry at myself, not you. I—" He hesitated and lit another cigarette. "I wanted to write to you about Dee—"

"Oh, Mike, why didn't you?"

"Because until the very end, I didn't think I'd actually marry her. And when our seeing one another began to break in all the newspapers, I was worried it might leak to you. Thank God for Dr. Peterson and his rules about keeping the world locked out. Because this was something I felt I had to tell you in person. I had intended to tell you on the ride back from the airport. But when you said you had waited so long, that you wanted to be with me alone, well, Christ, I felt you rated having your first night the way you planned it. So I made the phone call and told Dee she had to get out. I figured I'd tell you at breakfast today."

"When did you fall in love with her?"

"Who's talking about love?" He looked directly at her. "Look, for the record, the only broad I ever loved in my whole life—or ever will love—is you!"

"Then why? *Why?*"

"Because I was tapped out. Through!"

"What are you talking about?"

"Through. Finished. After three years of straight flops, I couldn't raise a dime for even an Off Broadway show. On the Coast they treated me like I had some communicable disease. And then the Clinique gave me the great news. They were releasing you in September. Jesus, here was the moment we had both lived for . . . and I was wiped out. Know where I was when I got the great news? Shacked up with Tina St. Claire on the Coast."

"You used her in a picture once."

"Yeah, I used her when she was seventeen. No talent, but beautiful. She still has no talent, but she's on a television series that's in the top ten and will keep going for a long time. She's got a big house filled with servants and hangers-on. That was me—prize hanger-on number one. Why not? She had a nice house, a well-stocked bar, and all I had to do was accommodate Tina." He paused. "This is a lousy way for a father to talk to a daughter, but there's no time for a dress rehearsal. I've got to give you the script . . . cold." He stabbed out his cigarette. "Okay, so there I was at the pool at Tina's, sopping up the sun like a beach boy. A Chinese houseman to bring me drinks, a sauna to relax in. I've got everything any man can want except cash. It's July. And I get the news that you can leave by September. And like I said, I'm just sitting there getting a tan and wondering what to do. And wham! That night, I get the idea from Tina. We're at an opening. The old klieg light bit doesn't mean a thing anymore, but they make the effort once in a while, and like a jackass I'm walking down that red carpet with her—as *her* escort—and as she snuggles in the seat next to me, she starts telling me how she wouldn't know what to do if I ever left. She kept rambling on about how hard men were to find, that she hadn't had sex for a month until I arrived. Then suddenly she says,

'We look so great together and I have enough money for both of us. How about getting married? Then at least I'll be sure of having someone to take me to next year's Emmy Awards.' "

He looked past his daughter. "I realized at that moment that I was at the bottom of the barrel. She was only in her late twenties and she wanted to keep me. I began to feel like the movie *Sunset Boulevard* in reverse. The next day I took my usual spot at the pool and tried to find the answers. I decided if I was gonna be kept it wasn't going to be for meals and a swimming pool from a Tina St. Claire. If this was the last port of call, at least I'd go down first class. So I began to think. Barbara Hutton was married. Doris Duke I didn't know about. The Baroness de Fallon was a beast . . . And then I thought of Deirdre Milford Granger. We had met once when I was riding high and she had been good-looking in a faded way." He stopped. "Nice story, huh? But at least I'm giving it to you straight. Not the 'I-met-this-broad-and-fell-madly-in-love-and-I'm-giving-up-my-career-just to-make-her-happy' jazz. Oh, no . . . I made her a project. I learned she was in Marbella. I sold everything I owned. My car . . . the Patek Philippe watches . . . the last of the IBM stock. All together it gave me forty-three thousand bucks. It was a big roll of the dice and I was putting it all on the line. I went to Marbella to court the lady . . ." He frowned at the memory.

"I didn't know that after our first date she had a Dun and Bradstreet on me. She sat back and played it cool while I handed out twenty-buck tips to captains . . . picked up eight-hundred-dollar tabs for groups of her friends in nightclubs. Three weeks of this and I couldn't even get close enough to kiss her goodnight, let alone even have dinner for two by candlelight. No, we traveled in packs. During the day I mixed drinks for everyone and watched her play backgammon. Then just as I was beginning to get flop sweat, I arrived at her villa at cocktail time, expecting to find the usual crowd, but she was alone. She handed me a drink and said,

'Mike, I think you'd better get around to asking me to marry you because you only have twenty-six hundred dollars to your name.' "

He smiled at January's expression. "Yep, she knew my bank balance almost to the penny. Then she said, 'But first I want you to know that I will never back any of your projects—pictures *or* plays. Now, do you still want to marry me?' "

He lit another cigarette. "Oh, it gets even better," he said with a grim attempt to smile. "Once the lady let me know how much she despised show business and everything it stood for, I naturally came up with all the stock lines, like 'Look, Dee, maybe that was what I had in mind when it started, but now I've really fallen for you and I wish I had three hits running on Broadway now because then I could ask you to marry me.' " He paused. "Does it make you sick? Because it does me . . . just in repeating it."

"Go on," January said. "Did she believe you?"

"Well, at least she didn't stick to the script and simper and go coy. Oh, she's nothing if not original. She smiled and said, 'Well, Mr. Mike Wayne, if you had those three hits, you probably never would have even gotten a date with me.' " He paused thoughtfully. "I don't know what it is. She has some hang-up about show business. Maybe way back she was rejected by an actor or maybe it's just snobbism, but I had to promise not to go back in show business if she'd marry me. So there I sat, with her calling the shots. Before I accepted I told her about you. But of course she already knew all about that too. I explained that your future was the most important thing. And when she agreed, that was it!"

"Where was the wedding?" she asked.

"We got married the end of August, quietly and secretly in London. But the news got out and then the parties in our honor began. Suddenly *Sunset Boulevard* turned into a Fellini movie. Contessas, semi-royalty, top international models, a few real princesses thrown in. It's a world where the women are all thin, gorgeous, and titless, the men have no asses, and English is everyone's second language. She runs with that crowd in New

York, too. No one plays golf; tennis is the *in* game and gin rummy is for peasants. Backgammon is their game." He sighed. "Okay, that's the whole ballgame. Any questions?"

"Just one. Do we both stand in line every Friday and get our allowances?"

Their eyes met and he said, "Where did you learn to hit so hard?"

She fought back tears but held her gaze. "Well, it's true, isn't it? Dee supports you—as you said—in style."

"Real style, honey." His voice was hard. "But she does it with class. She's made me a director of one of her companies. Sure, it's just a title. What in hell do I know about real estate or oil tankers? But I sign things once a week; and everyone in my office acts like I'm needed." He smiled. "Every man needs an office to go to. You'd be surprised how it breaks up the day. I go there and close the door so my secretary will think I'm busy. Then I read the trades. Wednesday is the big day— *Variety* comes out, so that takes up the whole morning. Then I stop down at the brokerage office in the same building, have a shoe-shine, and on to the Friars Club for lunch and a game of gin. And I get a salary too— one thousand a week. I used to spend more than that on tips—but it's a great life. I've got the New York apartment, the houses, a chauffeur . . . I've got everything any man would want."

"Stop it," she moaned. "Oh God, stop it! I'm sorry for what I said. I know you did it for me." She felt her throat close with tears but she forced herself to go on. "Couldn't we have gotten a small apartment somewhere? Maybe I could have gotten a job."

"Doing what?"

"Acting maybe, or even working for a producer . . . reading scripts."

He shook his head. "The whole business has changed. Some of the top playwrights refuse to write for the theater now. Why should they? Work their asses off for two years and have a guy on the *Times* close it in one night. Sure there's Neil Simon who rarely misses; but even stars stand in line to get into one of his plays. Then

there's Off Broadway . . . and even Off Off Broadway.
But that's another civilization. I know nothing about it.
And it's not what I want for you."

"What do you want for me?" she asked quietly.

"To hand you the world."

"And by marrying Deirdre Granger do you think
you've given me that?"

"At least I'm handing you a bright new world. A
world where people talk about something else besides
theater or box-office grosses. Look, for you, show business can be like a great dessert. Something you enjoy
maybe a few evenings a week. But it shouldn't be your
whole life. Besides, you saw it as Mike Wayne's daughter. When you went backstage you only saw the star's
dressing room. Never the drafty ones on the third floor
in Baltimore or Philadelphia. You saw success, baby.
The bright side of the moon. It's only normal for you
to think that it's your world. What other world have I
ever given you?"

"But why should I want another world? You loved
show business. I know you did."

"Nah, I loved the horses just as much. I loved the
gamble of doing a show or a picture. I loved the money,
the fame, the broads. Look, you don't think I took you
to the theater every Saturday because I loved it, do you?
Hell, I took you there because I didn't know what else
to do with you. Now don't get angry," he said as he saw
the color come to her face. "But what does a man do
with a little girl every weekend? I had no real social life.
Only broads who I shacked up with. Some of them were
divorcées with kids your age who called me Uncle
Daddy. That would have made a big hit with you, right?
Jesus, it's a wonder you turned out as perfect as you
did. Because I sure as hell gave you nothing. But that's
all changed now. At least I can give you a chance at
another kind of life. All I ask is that you try it this
way."

"And what is this way?"

"See how other people live. Meet Dee's friends. Give
it a shot. If you don't, then I've struck out all around."

She managed a smile. "Of course I'll try."

"And try to give Dee a chance, too. She's a great broad. I don't know what she ever wanted with me."

"The same thing Tina St. Claire wanted," January said. "And Melba Delitto . . . and probably every girl you meet."

He shook his head. "Sex isn't all that important to Dee." He looked thoughtful. "I get the feeling that she wants something more than that with me. Companionship maybe . . . a togetherness . . . to be part of a team. I don't know too much about that kind of life. But please give Dee a chance. If you could see all the trouble she went to arranging tonight's dinner party. And she's invited her cousin, David Milford, as your escort."

"Is David Milford also one of the six richest people in the world?"

"No. Dee's father had all the big money. And—"

"And he died when Dee was ten," January chanted. "And six months later Dee's beautiful young mother committed suicide because of his death. Oh, Daddy, at Miss Haddon's we all read about Dee's life story every time she got married. The magazines called her 'The Lonely Little Princess' always seeking happiness." She stopped. "That sounds bitchy, and I didn't mean it that way. It's just that I may have been out of touch with the world during the past three years, but at Miss Haddon's Deirdre Milford Granger was like an institution. Some of the girls had mothers who knew someone who knew her. I grew up knowing everything about her—except that one day my father would marry her."

He was silent and waved to the waiter for the check. She tried to smile. "Mike, I'm sorry." She made her voice soft and traced his fingers with her fingertips. "Come on, tell me about David. Have you met him?"

"Several times," he said slowly. "He's good-looking. In his late twenties. Dee never had any children. Her mother and David's father were brother and sister. The Milfords have no real money. Oh, they live well. In fact, they do very well." He paid the check. "He works at a brokerage house. He handles Dee's accounts. His father is a lawyer with his own firm and David is Dee's principal heir and—"

"Wow," January said softly. "You really made a package deal. A girl for you . . . a boy for me . . ."

His eyes flashed. "Boy, you sure as hell are my daughter. Always a direct hit. But first . . . I haven't got David lined up for you. I think David has his own idea of who *he* wants to marry. But I'd be a goddamned liar if I didn't admit that through Dee I hope you meet someone with class. David probably has a lot of friends. He'll introduce you around. In that way maybe you'll meet someone you really like, someone you'll eventually marry. I'd love to have a grandchild, maybe two . . . three. Sure, I'd like it. But I'll tell you what I wouldn't like—to have you wind up a female version of me."

"That's too bad," she said softly. "Because that's exactly what I am. And what's more, I planned it that way."

"Why?" His voice was almost a snarl. "What kind of a model am I? I've never given a woman a fair shake in my life. But I'm gonna play it straight with Dee. It's about time I started paying my dues. And between you and me, I owe plenty."

She was silent for a moment. When she spoke she looked off into space. "But my dues are paid in full. Maybe I could have brought us some luck. We could have tried it together." Then she smiled. "But that's in the past. I'm sure I'll like David Milford and I'll do my best to charm him so he'll introduce me to all his fancy friends. So the first thing I'd better do is buy something dreamy to wear tonight." She stopped suddenly.

"Don't worry. That's all arranged. No, not what you think." He dug into his pocket and took out a card. "Here, go to this bank and ask for a Miss Anna Cole. You'll have to sign some things. There's money in trust for you. You can open a checking account right away."

"Mike, I don't—"

"It's not Dee's money," he snapped. "When your mother died, she left a small insurance policy—fifteen thousand dollars. I stuck it in trust for you. Thank God I did . . . or I would have gone through that, too. With the interest and all, there should be close to twenty-two or twenty-three thousand bucks waiting for you. Now go buy out Bonwit's and Saks."

They walked down the street and stopped in front of the Pierre. Subconsciously they both looked up half expecting to see Dee at the window. Mike laughed. "She took another sleeping pill when I left. Besides, she rarely gets up before noon. Oh . . . here's a key to the suite. You're registered, so always check at the desk for your messages."

She laughed. "Mike, you're the only person I know in New York. So maybe you ought to leave me a message—"

"I don't have to. I think you got it." Then he turned and walked into the building.

THREE

SHE WAS EXHAUSTED when she returned to the Pierre. It was almost four o'clock and she was carrying only one large box. And it hadn't been easy to decide on that! She didn't know *what* to wear to a dinner party with Dee. At Bergdorf's, a saleslady told her *midi* skirts were *in* and *mini* skirts were *out*. But at noon, as girls poured out of office buildings on their lunch breaks, Fifth Avenue became flooded with minis and *micro minis*. On Lexington Avenue she saw Indian headbands, blue jeans, knickers, and long granny skirts. It was like a costume parade. She finally settled on the long patchwork skirt and red jersey blouse she saw on the mannequin in Bloomingdale's window. The saleslady assured her it would fit any occasion.

When she walked into the hotel she stopped at the desk on a whim and asked if there were any messages. To her amazement the clerk handed her two slips of paper. Balancing the box under her chin and one arm, she studied them as she rang for the elevator. One had come at three, the other at three-thirty. Both asked her to call the same Plaza number and ask for Extension 36. She looked at the name on the message form. It was for her, all right. Suddenly she smiled. Of course . . . the Plaza number was probably Mike's office.

When she came into the apartment, a maid was dusting some little jade elephants on the mantel. In the daylight the apartment looked even more beautiful. The sunlight mirrored itself on the silver frames that covered the top of the piano. There were so many pictures. She recognized a United States Senator, Nureyev, an Ambassador, and the remarkable face of Karla. She walked over and studied the childish scrawl in faded ink. "To Deirdre . . . Karla." January stared at the high cheekbones, the fantastic eyes. The maid came over. "There are three princes on the left. And a Rajah."

January nodded. "I was looking at Karla."

"Yes, she's very beautiful," the maid said. "Oh, by the way, I'm Sadie. And I'm glad to meet you, Miss January."

January smiled. The woman was in her mid-sixties and looked Scandinavian. Her light faded hair was pulled into a tiny skimpy knot and her face was clean and shiny. She looked spare, bony and strong. "Miss Deirdre told me to hang your things. I took the liberty of rearranging your drawer space. When do your trunks arrive?"

"They don't," January said. "There's just what you saw. And now this new outfit from Bloomingdale's."

"I'll press it out. Miss Deirdre is out now, but if you want anything, there is a button beside your bed. It connects with the kitchen and my bedroom out back. I'll hear it wherever I am. And I didn't know if you smoked, but I put cigarettes in all the boxes in your room. If you prefer a certain brand, let me know."

"Thank you, no. I think I'll take a bath and rest."

"Be sure and ring if you need anything. I also left all the latest fashion magazines in your room. Miss Deirdre thought you might like them. She said something about you had a lot of catching up to do." Then Sadie took the Bloomingdale box and left the room. In less than a second she had popped back. "And Ernest comes at six if you need him."

"Ernest?"

"Miss Deirdre's hairdresser . . . every night at six."

January suddenly remembered the phone messages she was holding. She went into her bedroom, flopped on the bed and gave the number to the operator. After three rings a switchboard operator answered. January dutifully asked for Extension 36.

There was a pause . . . a click . . . another voice. "Miss Riggs' office."

"Who?" January sat up.

"Who are you?" The voice was annoyed.

"I'm January Wayne. And who is Miss Riggs?"

"Oh, I'm Miss Riggs' secretary. One moment, Miss Wayne. We called you. I'll connect you." There was some more clicking. Then a voice drawled, "January, is that really you?" It was a sleek voice, aristocratic, smooth and cool.

January tried to place it. "Who is this?" she asked.

"Good God, January. It's me . . . Linda. Linda Riggs!"

"Linda . . . you mean from Miss Haddon's?"

"Of course. You think there's another?"

"Oh, wow! Well, it's been so long. How are you, Linda? How did you find me? And what've you been doing?"

Linda laughed. "I should ask you that. But first things first. Why was your father so snotty to Keith Winters?"

"Keith?"

"Keith Winters . . . the photographer . . ."

"Oh, you mean last night?" (Good Lord, was it *just* last night?)

"Yes, I sent him down to get a picture of you for our magazine."

"What magazine?"

There was a slight pause. Then in a voice tinged with annoyance, Linda said, "Well, I am editor-in-chief of *Gloss,* you know, and—"

"Editor-in-chief!"

"January, where on earth have you been? I was a smash on the Mike Douglas show last month. And I've been asked to do the Merv Griffin show the next time I'm on the Coast."

"Oh, well. I've been in Europe and—"

"But everyone knows what I've done for *Gloss* magazine. I'm one of the youngest and most famous editors-in-chief in the world. Of course, I'm not Helen Gurley Brown. But then *Gloss* is no *Cosmopolitan*. But give me time. I'm going to make this magazine the biggest thing going."

"That's marvelous, Linda. I remember after you left Miss Haddon's. I was about ten. And we all went crazy when we saw you were a . . . a . . . "

"Junior editor," Linda finished the sentence for her. "It might have looked impressive to everyone at Miss Haddon's, but it was just a fancy label for slave. My God, I ran all over town sixteen hours a day. Tracking down jewelry for fashion layouts . . . getting coffee for photographers and models . . . running errands for people in the art department . . . returning an earring left by a fashion director—all this for seventy-five dollars a week. But at eighteen it seemed like a lark. I'd get four hours' sleep and still manage to get to Le Club every night and dance. God, I'm weary just thinking about it now. Incidentally . . . how old are you?"

"I'll be twenty-one in January."

"That's right. I'm twenty-eight. Funny how it evens out now. The age thing. When I was sixteen and you were about eight, I didn't think you were even human. I mean, as I recall, you were one of the moppets who followed me around at Miss Haddon's, weren't you?"

"I suppose so." January saw no reason to tell her she had never been a "Linda follower."

"That's why I sent Keith Winters to the Pierre. Celebrity Service had it that you were arriving from Europe and I thought I'd run a picture of you and Daddy in *Gloss* along with a cute story about Daddy's young lady meeting Daddy's new lady. Your father was a real horror to Keith, but the picture turned out fine. Either you're very photogenic or you've turned into a real tearing beauty. Listen, why not pop in tomorrow . . . say about three-ish. I'll dream up some kind of story and we'll take some good pictures."

"I'd love to see you, Linda, but I don't know about a story."

"We'll talk about it tomorrow. You know where the

Mosler building is, don't you? Fifty-second, near Madison. We have the entire top three floors. Come to the executive penthouse. See you then. *Ciao.*"

January ran the bath and got into the tub and closed her eyes. She hadn't realized how tired she was. She thought about Linda—so ugly, so eager, so energetic . . . And now she was . . . well, she sounded important. January felt so tired. She knew she was falling asleep. It seemed just seconds later when she heard Sadie whisper, "Miss January, wake up."

She sat up. The water was tepid. Good Lord, it was six o'clock!

"Miss Deirdre says it's time for you to dress for dinner," Sadie explained. "I pressed your dress. It's hanging in the bedroom closet."

She was dressed when Dee knocked on her door and swept into the bedroom. For a moment they both stared at one another. Then, self-consciously, January held out her hand. "Congratulations. I'm afraid I forgot to say that last night."

Dee pressed her cheek against January's cheek. "I don't think either of us said too much last night. It wasn't exactly the best way to become acquainted."

"I—oh, good Lord . . ."

"What's wrong?" Dee asked.

"I forgot to buy a robe!"

Dee laughed. "Keep Mike's. It looked marvelous on you. Some women look fabulous in men's robes. I'm not one of them."

January decided Dee was more attractive than she had originally thought. Tonight she wore the frosted hair in a Gibson-girl style. And January knew the globs of diamonds on Dee's ears were real. She looked very feminine in black silk harem pants, and January suddenly wondered if the patchwork skirt was right.

Dee stood back and appraised her. "I like it . . . but I think we need a bit of jewelry." She buzzed Sadie who appeared instantly. "Get my box of gold jewelry, Sadie."

Sadie returned with a huge leather jewel case, and Dee began draping gold chains around January's neck.

She insisted January wear gold hoop earrings. ("Darling, with your tan it's perfect . . . gives you a gypsy effect.")

January felt weighted down with four chains, a jade figa, and a lion's tooth set in gold. (Dee explained she had shot the lion herself on a safari.)

"I like your makeup," Dee said as she came up close. "They're your own lashes. Fan*tas*tic! I love that no-lipstick look you young girls affect. And your hair . . . well, it's marvelous. Today you young things have it made, wearing it just long and straight. When I was your age, I was all clipped and permanented for the bloody Italian cut. That was the rage in the early fifties. I always told Gina I could kill her for starting that style. I have straight hair, and it seems to me I've spent half my life in rollers under driers. And now that long straight hair is in . . . well, one really can't wear it hanging down to her shoulders after thirty-five. At least I don't think one should . . . although God knows Karla hasn't changed her hair style since she was eighteen."

"What is she like?"

Dee shrugged. "Karla is one of my oldest and dearest friends . . . although God knows why I put up with her eccentricities."

"At Miss Haddon's," January said, "we all watched her movies on television. To me she is even greater than Garbo or Dietrich because she moves like a dancer. Imagine having the guts to retire at forty-two and stay retired."

Dee reached over and lit a cigarette. "She never cared about acting. She always said that as soon as she made enough money she would quit. And she's got the first dime she ever made!"

"Where is she now?" January asked.

"I believe she's back in town. She'll get around to calling soon. She keeps an apartment at the East River View. Marvelous building, but aside from a few good paintings that were gifts and some good rugs—also gifts—the apartment is barely furnished. Karla has a sickness about spending money. She was supposed to come to Marbella. Your father was so disappointed . . . I know he wanted to meet her. Good Lord, until

this summer she was always around. Last spring poor
David was stuck taking both of us around. Not that she
gads about, but she adores the ballet. Other than that,
Karla still sticks to her old movie routine—up at seven,
four hours of ballet exercises, long walks, bed at ten.
But she will go to dinner with a close friend and she
adores watching television. Actually, she's quite dreary
once you get to know her. And then there's her disap-
pearing act. She does that. Like last June—she just goes
off without so much as an 'I'll see you.' Personally"
—Dee lowered her voice—"I think she went off to have
her face done. She was just beginning to sag a bit . . .
and God forbid anything happened to hurt that Polish
bone structure that is now so immortal."

January laughed. "Now I'm really nervous about
meeting David."

"Good Lord, why?"

"Well, if David felt 'stuck' taking Karla around as a
favor to you, then taking me out must be the Big Daddy
of all favors."

Dee smiled. "You darling child. Look in the mirror.
Karla is over fifty and David is twenty-eight." She put
out her cigarette. "And now it's time I checked on your
father. If I know him he's watching the news and still
hasn't shaved. Why do men hate shaving twice a day?
Women put on makeup at least that many times. Oh, by
the way, I've told everyone, including David, that you've
been away at school in Switzerland at the Institut International. It's an excellent college."

"But why?"

"You do speak French, don't you?"

"Yes, but—"

"My dear, trust me. There's just no point in bringing
up the accident. Why have anyone think you might have
brain damage? And some people get sticky the moment
they hear one has been at a sanitarium. Now we want
you to meet the right people and have a wonderful life
. . . so we mustn't handicap ourself with a past illness."

"But a brain concussion and broken bones isn't an
illness—"

"My dear, anything with the brain throws people off.

I remember Kurt . . . I almost married him until he told me he had a steel plate in his head from a skiing accident." She shuddered. "I just couldn't bear the thought of touching a man's head with steel in it. There was something Frankensteinish about the whole thing. Besides, if one has a piece of steel against one's brain . . . well, it stands to reason the pressure *must* do something. Do it my way, dear. Now then . . . I've asked David to come twenty minutes before the others. You stay in your room until he arrives. I'll give you the signal when to come out. One must always make an entrance." She started for the door and turned. "You'll fall in love with David. Every woman does. Even Karla found him a little more than entertaining; and Karla's not capable of falling in love with anyone. So don't let his good looks throw you. Just play it cool and pour on the charm. I'm sure you have some. After all, your father has almost too much." She opened the door, and stopped just as January was about to sink on the edge of the bed. "No . . . no. Mustn't sit. You'll crease your skirt. One must be perfect for an entrance. Now I must dash. Ernest is waiting to put the final spray to my hair. You just stay here . . . until it's time to meet David."

FOUR

At six-thirty, David Milford rushed to his apartment to change his clothes. He jammed in the plug of his electric razor. Goddammit but he hated Dee! But anything Cousin Deirdre wanted—Cousin Deirdre got! The acceptance of her autonomy had come into full cognizance with his promotion to a vice-presidency at Herbert, Chasin and Arthur. In a down market, with most brokerage houses cutting back—*he* had been promoted. And his future with the firm was assured—just so long as he handled Dee's stocks. Damn Dee! And damn his father for not having his own fortune. No, he didn't mean that. After all, the old man worked hard, made close to a hundred and fifty thousand a year. But with his mother insisting on the ten-room Fifth Avenue co-op, three in help, and the house in Southampton . . . well, there certainly wasn't going to be anything left for him to inherit. But then no one was expected to amass a fortune; because Cousin Dee had enough for them all.

Her marriage to Mike Wayne had thrown them into shock. His mother went into one of her major traumas —three days of Librium and tears. Dee's past husbands had never been a threat. They had all been of the same cut. Charming, well-bred lightweights. But Mike Wayne was no lightweight. And his past record indicated that his romantic affiliations had always been with girls half Dee's age. But their major concern was the absence of the "will ritual." His father handled that end of her business. Dee had what the family jokingly referred to as the "loose-leaf will." Before every marriage, she and her "husband-to-be" would arrive at his father's office, and Dee would dictate a new will with a generous inheritance for her new groom. On the day of the wedding, a signed copy was presented to him. The following day, Dee would return to the office alone, draw up a new will, allotting a nominal sum to the new husband *if* he was still her husband at the time of her death.

She had been married to Mike almost a month. And Mike's name hadn't been entered in the loose-leaf will. As it now stood, he and his father and Cliff (his mother's younger brother, who was also in the law firm) would serve as executors of her estate. Each of them would wind up with several million on that end alone. The bulk of the estate would go to the Granger Foundation, and he would be designated to officiate as president at a salary of one hundred thousand a year.

Of course, Dee was still very much alive, and fifty was not old. But Dee's prospects for a golden age didn't seem very likely. For years the newspapers had given extensive coverage to her consistent bouts of illnesses. First there were the fainting attacks which medical tests diagnosed as an organic heart murmur and chronic high blood pressure (but Dee refused to give up the strong diet pills and reveled in her high-fashion gauntness). There were also several operations . . . female stuff. And the "influenza" that had almost killed her a few years ago (that had really been an overdose of sleeping pills over some mysterious love affair). Odd, he had never thought Dee capable of feeling any desperate emotion. But why not? He had never thought he could ever feel any real emotion either.

He pulled out the plug of the razor and slapped some aftershave lotion on his face. Might as well look at the cheerful side. So far as the will was concerned—maybe Mike wasn't playing the super-operator, maybe he was really in love with Dee. Maybe he didn't care about her money. Hell, there was enough for everyone as long as Wayne didn't get greedy. But why did he have to have a daughter to complicate things! No one knew she even existed until a week ago when Dee's call came. "David, darling. Mike has this divine daughter who is arriving any day. You've got to help me out and take her around. It would please me to know she was taken care of by someone *I* care about. I'd consider it *such* a favor."

Favor? It was a command!

And once again he swore softly. Goddammit but he hated Dee. But hell, he hated everything and everyone these days. Everything and everyone who kept him away from Karla.

Karla! For a moment he stood and stared at himself in the mirror. It didn't seem possible. He, David Milford, was Karla's lover! He wanted to shout it to the world, to stop people on the street and tell them. But he knew that absolute silence was the major law in his relationship with Karla.

Karla! At fourteen, he had masturbated with her picture propped up before him. His friends had their school lockers loaded with pinups of Doris Day, Marilyn, Ava, and other glamor girls of the fifties. But with him it had always been Karla. At seventeen, the first girl he had gone to bed with was a horse-faced debutante who had hair like Karla's. In the years that followed he often found a girl who had a quality that was reminiscent of Karla. But as he matured he accepted each girl on her own individual charm, and the image of Karla receded into some kind of mystic dream.

And then, eight years ago, he had come across a newspaper picture of Karla on Dee's yacht. He had immediately written Dee an impassioned letter pleading for an introduction. She had ignored it. But he never failed to renew the request every time he saw Dee. And then, last spring, when he had all but given up, Dee had casually said, "Oh, by the way, David, Karla is in town. Would you care to take us to the ballet?"

He had been like an idiot that first night. He hadn't done any work at the office all day. He had rushed home and changed suits three times before he decided which one would be proper. And then . . . Dee's casual introduction . . . Karla's firm handshake . . . he knew he had stood there just staring at that wonderful face . . . listening to the low voice he had heard so often on the screen. He had moved about in a catatonic state that night, unable to comprehend that he was actually sitting beside her, unable to concentrate on the ballet on the stage, unable to believe the casual way Dee behaved in the presence of this magnificent woman. But then, when you had Dee's kind of money maybe nothing really turned you on. To Dee, even Karla was just another "fun" person, a name to encase in a silver frame to join the exclusive gallery on the piano.

The day after the ballet he had sent Karla three dozen roses. His office number was on his card, but he also added his unlisted apartment number. She called just as he was leaving the office. The cool low voice thanked him but told him firmly never to do that again as she was allergic to flowers. She had already sent them off with her maid. When he began to stutter, she laughed and said, "But in return, I will give you a drink. Come to my apartment this afternoon at five."

He was shaking like a schoolboy when he rang her bell.

She opened the door herself and greeted him with outstretched hands. "My so very young admirer. Come in. Come in. And please do not be so nervous, because I want you to make love to me."

She had led him into the apartment as she spoke. His eyes never left her face. But he was aware of an empty spaciousness to the room. A few paintings, a TV set, a large couch, a wood-burning fireplace that looked as if it had never been used, a staircase that obviously led to a second floor—but most of all, he felt no reflection of Karla's personality in the apartment. It was almost as if she had "borrowed" it. For a moment they looked at one another. Then she held out her arms and the schoolboy vanished. And when their bodies came together, David suddenly knew the difference between sex and making love. On that late spring afternoon, his one wish was to please her . . . and when he did, oddly enough his own gratification seemed intensified.

It was later when they were lying together that she

gave him the rules. "Dee must never know. If you want
to go on seeing me, *no one* must know." He agreed. He
held her close and poured out devotion and promises.
And he heard himself say, "Any way you want it, Karla.
You see, I'm in love with you."

Her sigh was tremulous. "I am fifty-two. Too old for
love . . . and much too old for you."

"I'm twenty-eight. That's not exactly a boy."

She laughed. "Twenty-eight, and so very handsome."
She stroked his cheek. "A very young twenty-eight. But
. . . perhaps we can be happy for a time. That is, if you
behave."

"How do you want me to behave?"

"I have told you. Also, you must promise never to try
to reach me. I shall not give you my phone number and
you must never come here unless I invite you."

"Then how do I see you?"

"I will call you when I want you. And you must not
speak of love. You must not imagine yourself in love
with me or you will be very unhappy."

He smiled. "I'm afraid that happened when I was fourteen . . ." He stopped. Goddammit, that was wrong,
showing the disparity of their ages. But she had smiled.

"You love the Karla you saw in movies; you do not
know the real Karla."

He had held her close and knew a strange excitement
as he felt her small flat breasts against his body. He
liked breasts. But oddly enough it hadn't bothered him
that she had none. Her body was strong and firm. A
dancer's body. He had read stories about her early training in Poland for the ballet—how she had been forced
to escape to London during the war and went directly
into pictures as an actress. How she still worked out on
the bar four hours a day. She had changed studios many
times because of photographers who learned the address
and waited to catch her. He had also heard that she had
been a lesbian during her early days in Hollywood. All
these thoughts came to him as he held her in his arms.
But these stories were part of the legend . . . the woman
of mystery . . . the woman photographers still chased
everywhere. But at that moment she seemed to belong

to him completely . . . her ardor and passion were young . . . she clung to him when they made love. Yet when it was over, a curtain came down, and Karla, the legend, returned.

That had been last spring. They had spent a fantastic month together. A month in which he wandered around feeling everything was unreal except his meetings with Karla. A month when he awoke each day not really believing this miracle was happening to him. But there was always the frustration of not being able to call, of having a sandwich sent in at lunch for fear of missing her call, of walking through all work and conversation until the call finally came.

And then one day there was no call. He tried not to panic. Perhaps she didn't feel well. Maybe she had the curse. Hell, did women of fifty-two still get the curse?

The following day there were the familiar pictures in the newspaper. Karla ducking photographers at Kennedy Airport. She was off to Europe, destination unknown. He had tried to check her plane reservations, but it was obvious she had used another name. One enterprising reporter claimed a ticket agent thought she was going to South America. But it was all just speculation. She was gone. That was all he knew.

He had tried to sound casual when he phoned Dee that night. He had talked about stocks, the weather, about her plans for Marbella . . . And when he finally managed to bring up Karla's disappearance, Dee had laughed. "Oh, dear boy, she always does that. Karla refuses to have roots. That's why her apartment is hardly furnished. If it were too comfortable, she might feel she actually lives there."

"Has she always been like this?"

Dee sounded bored. "Always. I met Karla in California at the height of her fame. I was married to Emery then, and his book had just been bought by Karla's studio. Naturally, Emery was frantic to meet her—most people still are—but you can imagine what it was like then. Well, Emery knew a director who knew Karla, and one great day—for Emery, that is—Karla actually appeared at a Sunday brunch. That was about 1954. Karla was at the peak of her fame and beauty. I must say she did generate a certain magnetism when she entered that room. She was painfully shy . . ." Dee laughed and he realized she was warming to the subject. "But she gravitated to me that day because she has an animal cunning and she knew I was the only one in that room that wasn't impressed and it amused her. I was nice to her for Emery's sake. And she actually invited us to her place for a drink the following week." Dee sighed. "Talk about Falcon's Lair. This was it. Not in the chic part of Beverly Hills, but way up in some godforsaken hills, surrounded by a twelve-foot stone wall she had had built. The house was barely furnished. It looked as if she had just moved in. I swear there were still crates in the halls, and she had lived there five years. No one ever saw the rest of the house, but I understand that aside from the living room and bedroom, it was empty. She didn't do Emery's picture, and years later after I had divorced Emery and Karla had retired, we met and became friends. But one must take Karla as she is. The key to her personality is the three S's. Secretive, stingy, and stupid! Once you realize that—you understand Karla."

Dee had gone off to Marbella and he had tried to put Karla out of his mind. He had gone back to the models he had been dating. He got involved with Kim Voren, a gorgeous Dutch model who adored him but told him he was an unsatisfactory, selfish lover. That had rattled him. He had always been a good lover. But with Karla on his mind . . . perhaps something was missing in his lovemaking. On top of this came the explosive news of Dee's marriage, which threw the family into panic and jolted him back to reality. Dee was their security. Karla was gone, and he had to get back to the business of everyday living.

He gave his full attention to his work. He turned on the charm for Kim, and within a few days she exuberantly retracted her opinion of his lovemaking. And as he settled into his normal routine he almost appreciated the security of knowing what each day would bring. No wild highs . . . but also no agonizing lows. No sitting and waiting for the private phone in his office to ring.

And then, eight days ago, it rang again. Right in the middle of an active trading session. The low voice . . . the heavy accent. She was back! Ten minutes later he was ringing the bell of her apartment. When she greeted him he had not been able to conceal his amazement. It was as if she had stepped out of one of her old movies. She looked barely thirty. The magnificent face had no lines . . . the skin was taut across the cheekbones. She had laughed as she grasped his hands. "I am not going to tell you Karla had a long rest," she said. "I will tell you the truth. I was so tired of my face not matching the firmness of my body. So I had something done. A wonderful man in Brazil. . . ."

She had not called Dee and she told him to keep her arrival secret. "I am not up to Dee's questions about my face. Or her gossip with her friends."

And now it was as if she had never left. They saw each other every day. He would either go to her apartment at five, or they would meet and go to a ballet picture or a foreign movie. Then they would return to her apartment and make love. Afterward they would go to her kitchen and watch television as they ate the steaks they cooked together. Karla had no servants—she hated strangers to be around her. A maid came in every few days at nine, and left at noon.

She also adored television. She had a set in every room. She wasn't interested in the news . . . she hated the war . . . pictures of it made her shudder. David realized she had lived through World War II in an occupied country. She refused to talk about it and he never pressed it. He was not eager to remind her that in 1939, when Poland was occupied, he had not even been born.

He finished dressing and looked at his watch. Six forty-five. He walked into the living room and mixed himself a short martini. In less than an hour he had to be at Dee's to meet this stepdaughter she had inherited. Dee hadn't sprung this dinner engagement on him until yesterday. And when he told Karla about it last night, she had smiled and said she understood. "Do not be upset.

I shall invite an old friend over to eat your steak to-morrow."

She hadn't called today. Because she had no reason to call. She had told him to come by at the usual time tomorrow. If only he could call her now. This was the most frustrating part of their relationship. How could he play the man if he had to sit like a love-sick girl and wait for her to call the shots? He sat back and sipped his drink. He felt oddly unsettled. He wasn't quite sure what bothered him the most—the idea that he wasn't going to see her tonight, or the realization that she wasn't in the least upset. And now he was racked with a frantic kind of desperation, a sensation he had never known until he met Karla. If only he could call her and tell her he missed her, that perhaps it would be an early evening and they could still be together. He swallowed his drink. It was an impossible situation, not being able to call her; she had even taken the precaution of removing the number from the dial of her phones. It robbed the affair of some of its intimacy. What intimacy? He made love to her and she enjoyed it. *He* was the one who was emotionally involved. Actually she didn't give a damn. But it didn't matter. All he lived for was to be with her, and tonight *he* had been forced to break the date because of Dee. Dee didn't know what it meant to feel like this. Goddammit but he hated Dee!

His mood was still heavy when he pressed the buzzer to Dee's apartment. Mario, who doubled as chauffeur and butler when Dee was in New York, answered the door. Mike greeted him, and Mario set about to fix him a martini.

"Dee's having her hair combed," Mike said. "One of those guys with the tight pants comes up every night." Then the door opened and Dee swept into the room. She put her cheek to Mike, who dutifully kissed it, floated over to David and told him how perfectly marvelous he was looking, and he in turn kissed her cheek and told her how marvelous she looked. Then he sat on the edge of the couch; made the proper small talk with Mike and wondered where in hell the daughter was.

He had almost finished his martini when she came into the room. He heard himself accepting the introduction, asking the stock questions—How was her trip? Did she feel the jet lag everyone talked about? But he knew he was staring like an idiot. Holy God! She was a real knockout!

He heard himself promising to take her to Le Club, to Maxwell's Plum, Daly's Dandelion—to all the places she hadn't seen. Good God, he was saying he'd get tickets for *Hair*. He lit a cigarette and wondered how he would ever manage to extricate himself from all these offers he had suddenly made. He had been talking from nerves. Well, he was plenty unnerved. He hadn't expected anything like this. He sat back and tried to think rationally. Okay, January was an exceptionally beautiful young girl. But she wasn't Karla. Yet one day Karla would pick up and leave again. He must realize that. Karla was just something insane and wonderful that was happening in his life.

Suddenly he realized he was just staring. He had to say something.

"Do you play backgammon?" he asked.

"No, but I'd like to learn," January said.

"Fine. I'd be delighted to teach you." He finished his drink. (Oh, great! Now he was going to teach her backgammon!) He'd better shut up and go easy on the martinis. He decided to keep it impersonal and began talking about the backgammon tournaments in Vegas, London, and Los Angeles. Dee was their family champ. She always did well. He heard himself explaining how the tournaments went, about the betting . . . Suddenly he stopped. He had a feeling that she really didn't give a damn about backgammon and was just listening to please him. This couldn't be happening! He was Karla's lover. And this young girl was throwing him off base. It was her incredible cool. That easy half smile that was making him run off at the mouth like an idiot.

The doorbell rang and Mario admitted two couples who had arrived together. David found himself accepting another martini. He knew he shouldn't, but the girl had a disconcerting effect on him. He watched the easy nonchalance with which she accepted the introductions. And always that quick smile . . .

He also noticed that her constant focal point was her father. Her eyes followed him wherever he moved, and occasionally they would exchange a wink as if they shared some private joke.

Dee's guests were paying January extravagant compliments. She accepted them quietly, but he could tell she wasn't impressed. Then it hit him that maybe she wasn't overly impressed with him either. This was a new experience. Like when the Dutch girl told him he wasn't great in bed. Was he allowing Karla to swallow him alive? Drain him of all of his personality? For the rest of the evening he made a concerted effort to put Karla out of his mind and concentrated on January. Yet as the evening progressed, he had the uneasy feeling that he wasn't reaching her in any way.

Actually he was having an extremely disconcerting effect on her. After Dee's "selling job" she had been prepared to dislike him on sight. Instead she found this marvelous-looking young man who didn't seem at all taken with himself. He was very tall. Ordinarily she didn't like blond men, but David's hair was dark brown and sun-streaked. He was tanned and his eyes were brown.

She liked him. She really did. And that half smile that bothered him had been the nearest thing to a mask that she could manage. The muscles of her face actually ached, trying to hold that smile as she watched Mike in the role of "Dee's husband." Because from the attitude of everyone—Dee's friends, even the waiters and maitre d' at the restaurant—she was still Deirdre Milford Granger . . . and Mike was just her newest husband.

They had gone to dinner at Raffles, a discotheque restaurant next door to the Pierre. Dee directed the seating arrangements at the large round table. Mike was wedged in between two women: a Rosa Contalba, a middle-aged Spanish lady whose escort was a young Yugoslavian artist she was sponsoring, the other woman was plain and a bit on the large side. Her diamonds

were also large. And her husband was enormous. He sat
to the left of January and felt it was his duty to make
small talk. He went into an endless story about their
ranch in Montana. At first she tried to appear interested
but soon realized that an "Oh, really!" or "That's very
interesting!" was all he seemed to need. There was cross-
talk back and forth—summer vacations and winter plans.
Rosa was going on a photographic safari to Africa. The
stout woman was too tired after the season in East Hamp-
ton to even *think* of the winter yet. And everyone asked
Dee when she was opening the Winter Palace in Palm
Beach.

"In November. But I'll play it loose with houseguests.
They'll have to understand that we're going to pop off
for all the backgammon tournaments. Of course, we'll
always be in residence for the holidays. January will
probably come down for Thanksgiving and Christmas,
but I imagine she'll spend most of her time in New York
on a fun job."

Fun job? Before January could speak, the large man
said, "Now Dee, don't tell me this gorgeous creature is
going to work."

Dee smiled. "Stanford, you don't realize. Today the
young people want to do things—"

"Oh, no," Stanford groaned. "Don't tell me she's one
of those types who wants to change the world. Give
the land back to the Indians, or march demanding
equality for females and blacks."

"What about those religious nuts who paint their
faces and shave their heads?" the large woman added.
"I saw a group of them beating tom-toms and chanting.
Right on Fifth Avenue in front of Doubleday's."

"They're no worse than the weird types we see on
newsreels on the college campus," Rosa cut in. "And
they march, too. Arms around each other . . . boys and
girls . . . boys and boys . . . you can't tell the difference
unless one of them has a beard."

"Oh, that reminds me"—the stout woman leaned into
the table and everyone knew a choice bit of gossip was
coming. "Pressy Matthews is *not* really at a spa at all.

She's having a complete nervous breakdown at some sanitarium in Connecticut. It seems that this summer her daughter ran off with a Jewish boy. They bought a secondhand truck and loaded it with supplies and a big mongrel dog and traveled across the country, staying at communes. Pressy's psychiatrist told her to be permissive about it, that little Pressy would get the rebellion out of her system. But this fall little Pressy will not return to Finch. She's having a baby with this Jewish boy and they're not going to get married until *after* the baby is born because little Pressy wants the baby at the wedding. Well, you can imagine! Big Pressy just collapsed . . . they're trying to keep it a secret . . . including the sanitarium thing . . . so let's keep this among ourselves."

Then the stout man said, "Well, at least it's not all guitars and hard rock. Look at January."

Everyone murmured that January was indeed a beauty, but then as Dee pointed out, January had studied abroad. Rosa asked her what she had majored in, and Dee quickly said, "Languages. January speaks French fluently." Then Dee launched into a story about some darling little nursery school where the wee ones were taught languages immediately. January watched her father snap to attention with his gold Dunhill lighter every time one of the women on either side of him picked up a cigarette. He was even nodding and smiling at a story the Yugoslav artist was telling. He sure was paying his dues. She watched the way he leaned his handsome head in a listening pose as the large woman rambled on and on. Once he caught her staring and their eyes met. He winked and she managed a smile. Then he went back to his work. Suddenly she heard Dee saying, "And January will love it."

January will love what? (You couldn't leave this conversation for a second.)

Dee was smiling and explaining in detail about the nursery school. "The idea is—teach the tots early. Make them bilingual. That's why Mary Ann Stokes had made such a hit out of La Petite École. Mary Ann and I went to Smith together. The poor girl got polio in her junior year. Then her family lost everything . . . and with no money and a shriveled arm . . . Well, naturally poor Mary Ann's chances of a decent marriage were nil. So when she wanted to start this school some years ago, I agreed to back her. It's practically self-supporting now."

"Oh, Dee, darling," the stout woman boomed, "you are so modest. All these years . . . I never knew you started Mary Ann. It's a divine school. My grandniece goes there."

Dee nodded. "And of course the minute I told her that French was January's second language, she leaped. After all, that's part of the premise—beautiful socialites teaching the tots. They'll adore January."

"Me teach?" January knew her voice had actually cracked.

David was watching her carefully. "When does she start?" he asked.

Dee smiled. "Well, as I told Mary Ann, it will take at least two weeks to get January's wardrobe in shape. I'd say we'll shoot for the beginning of October. Mary Ann is coming by for tea tomorrow. We'll settle it then."

The music switched from rock into standards. January looked toward Mike. Their eyes met. He gave her a slight nod and stood up. But Dee rose at the same moment. "Oh, Mike . . . and I was afraid you wouldn't remember. They're playing our song."

Mike looked slightly startled, but he managed a smile. Dee turned to the table as she led him toward the floor. " 'Three Coins in a Fountain.' They were playing it in a little restaurant in Marbella when we first met."

Everyone watched them leave. Suddenly David stood up. He tapped January on the shoulder. "Hey, I'm your date." He led her out to the floor. The crowded floor made actual dancing impossible. They moved among the other couples. David held her close and whispered, "This will be over soon, and then we'll cut out."

"I don't think I can." She glanced toward her father who was whispering into Dee's ear.

"I think you'd better," he said evenly.

He led her back to the table when the set was over. There was espresso, after-dinner drinks, more talk and somehow the evening finally ground to an end and everyone was standing up telling Dee how marvelous it had all been.

"I'm taking January for a nightcap," David said. Then he quickly thanked Dee and Mike for the evening, and before January could voice any objections, they were in a cab, heading for Le Club.

The place was jammed, the music was loud. David knew almost everyone in the room. There were several couples who were friends of his, standing at the bar. David suggested they join them. "We're not staying long, so we really don't need a table."

She accepted introductions, danced with some of his friends. Dee's chains felt like an anchor, but it seemed every girl on the dance floor wore them. Some wore twice the amount of chains, but they didn't appear cumbersome. The girls' long hair swished as they moved, and the necklaces clinked in rhythm. She was in the midst of being shoved around the floor by an effeminate-looking boy who held her too close and insisted on making a date for the following night. She was trying to be politely evasive when David cut in. "I had to save you from Ned," he said. "He's a real closet queen but feels he has to score with all the beautiful girls to prove otherwise."

Miraculously the music changed and some Bacharach-David songs came on. They moved closer. He obviously felt her relax, because he whispered, "I like this kind of music too. I have most of these records at home."

She nodded and felt his hand stroke the back of her neck. "I'd like to sleep with you," he said.

They continued to dance. She couldn't believe the matter-of-fact tone he had used. No ardent pleading like Franco. No promises. Just a statement. Weren't you supposed to be insulted if a man said this on a first date? At Miss Haddon's, you were. But this wasn't Miss Haddon's. This was Le Club, and David was a sought-after, sophisticated man. Besides, the way he had said it—not like a question, but almost like a compliment. She decided that no answer was the best course.

When he led her back to the bar he joined in the conversation, and everything seemed casual and impersonal. They talked about the upcoming World Series. The girls discussed their summer vacations, how the "season" was really on, the cost of lengthening a sable coat—*Women's Wear* said the mini definitely was *not* coming back . . .

January smiled and tried to appear interested, but she was suddenly very tired. She was relieved when David finished his drink and suggested they leave. Once they were in the cab she kept up a steady barrage of conversation—How interesting Le Club was . . . How nice his friends seemed to be . . . Why did they play the music so loud? . . . She never stopped until she saw the canopy of the Pierre. David told the driver to hold the clock. And he walked her to the door.

"I had a wonderful time," she said.

"We'll have a lot of them," he said. Then, without any warning, he pulled her to him and gave her a long kiss. She felt his tongue prying her lips apart. She knew the doorman was tactfully looking the other way. And she was dismayed that she felt the same revulsion she had always felt when a man tried to kiss her.

When he broke the embrace, he smiled. "It's going to be great between us. I can feel it." Then he turned and walked back to the cab.

Mike and Dee were huddled over the backgammon board when she came in. "I beat her," he called out. "For the first time, I beat her!"

"He broke every rule," Dee drawled. "He just had incredible luck with the dice."

"I always break rules." Mike grinned.

Dee turned her full attention toward January. "Isn't David divine?"

Mike stood up. "While you two broads rehash the evening, I'm going to get a beer. Anyone want anything? A Coke, January?"

"No thanks." She began taking off Dee's jewelry.

The moment Mike left her room Dee said, "Wasn't I right about David? He is beautiful, isn't he? When are you seeing him again?"

January suddenly realized he hadn't actually made a date. She handed Dee the earrings and began taking off the chains. "I want to thank you for the jewelry . . ."

"Anytime. Now tell me about David. Where did you go?"

"To Le Club."

"Oh, that's a fun place. What did you two young things talk about?"

January laughed. "Dee, no one talks at Le Club. Unless you use sign language. We danced, and I met a lot of his friends."

"I'm so glad. David knows all the right young people and . . ."

"Dee, I've got to talk to you about the tots."

Mike walked into the room. "What tots?"

Dee wandered back to the backgammon board. "Oh, January and I have a project in mind. Now set up the board, Mike. I've got to beat you before we go to bed to prove you don't really know the game at all. Run off to sleep, January. We've got a lot of chitchatting to do tomorrow."

She blew a kiss at her father and slipped into the bedroom. For a moment she stared at the closed door. Mike Wayne . . . sitting up playing backgammon. She thought of David . . . Maybe he had just meant the "I want to sleep with you" as a compliment. And she had gotten all uptight over it. After all, it wasn't as if he had tried to grope her, or said it in a slimy way.

But it still wasn't right!

Or was it?

Things had changed since Miss Haddon's. Mike had changed, the whole world had changed. Maybe it was time for her to change.

And David was so nice. He was so good-looking. Maybe she had turned him off. Maybe he had felt her stiffen when he said that. But then, he *had* kissed her goodnight. Only she hadn't been exactly wildly responsive. But maybe he hadn't noticed that.

Or had he?

He hadn't asked her for another date. But then maybe he had just forgotten. After all, she hadn't realized it either until Dee brought it up.

The phone rang. She reached for it so eagerly she almost knocked down the lamp.

"Hi, babe." It was Mike's muffled voice.

"Oh, hi, Daddy."

"Dee's in the bathroom. I figured we've got a few things to talk over. How about meeting in the living room for coffee tomorrow morning at nine?"

"Okay."

"And don't sound so blue. I promise you—you're not gonna teach any tots."

"Oh." She managed a slight laugh.

"See. I'm always there to fix things. Right?"

"Right."

"Goodnight, babe."

"Goodnight, Daddy."

Mike was sitting on the sofa drinking coffee and reading the *Times* when she came into the living room the next morning. Without saying a word, he poured a cup and held it out to her. "Sadie sets this up before she goes to bed," he said. "Dee usually sleeps until noon, so there's not too much action for breakfast around here."

"Do you always get up this early?" she asked.

"Only since you came to town."

She sat down and sipped her coffee. "Mike, we have to talk."

He smiled. "What the hell do you think I'm doing here?"

She fastened her eyes on the coffee cup. "Mike . . . I—"

"You don't want to teach at La Petite École."

She looked at him. "You knew about that?"

"Not until you did. And I settled it with Dee last night. No Petite École. Next?"

"I can't live here."

His eyes narrowed. "Why not?"

She got up and walked to the window. "Oh, look, I can see my hill from here. There's a large French poodle on it and . . ."

He came to her side. "Why can't you live here?"

She tried to smile. "Maybe it's because I can't stand sharing you."

"Come on. You know damn well you're not sharing me. What we have together belongs to us."

"No." She shook her head. "It won't work. I can't stand to see—" She stopped. "Forget it."

"What can't you stand to see?" he asked quietly.

"I . . . I can't stand to see you play backgammon!"

For a moment neither of them spoke. He looked at her and forced a smile. "It's not a bad game . . . really." He took her hands. "Look, she redid that bedroom for you—new wallpaper, special hangers in the closets, all that jazz. I think she'd be hurt if you didn't at least give it a try. Besides, we're going to Palm Beach the beginning of November. In six weeks you'll have the whole place to yourself. Try it for a while anyway. Then, if you want to move—okay. But at least give it a shot. Please?"

She managed a smile. "Okay, Mike."

He walked over and poured himself another cup of coffee. "What did you think of David?"

"I thought he was . . . well . . . very groovy-looking." She caught his look of surprise. "You wanted me to like him, didn't you?"

"Sure. But I guess I'm like all fathers. I know one day you'll fall in love—I want you to fall in love—yet when I hear about it, I'll probably hate the whole idea." He laughed. "Don't pay any attention to me. I never was any good in the morning. Now, what's on your schedule? Want to meet me for lunch?"

"I'd love lunch . . . another day. I've got to get some clothes. David said the kind of places I'd like are on Third Avenue. So I'm heading there. And I have a three o'clock appointment with Linda Riggs."

"What's a Linda Riggs?"

"She's the girl from Miss Haddon's—the one we all thought would be a star. That is, everyone but you. She's editor-in-chief at *Gloss* magazine now."

"Okay. That takes care of your day. Now tonight Dee is having some people in for cocktails at seven, and then we're going to '21.' Do you want to join us? Or are you all set with David?"

She laughed. "Last night we went to Le Club. It was mobbed . . . the music was so loud . . . David knew everyone there. It was impossible to talk. And . . . well . . . we just forgot about making a date. That's crazy, isn't it?"

He lit a cigarette. "No, it happens." He paused. "Look, babe, don't go off the deep end for him. Take it real slow and easy."

"Mike, you wanted me to like David. Something is bothering you. What is it?"

"Well, I can see right now that you're in a pretty vulnerable spot. You come back . . . New York is strange . . . I've got a new wife . . . you're at loose ends . . . a sitting duck for the first halfway attractive guy who comes along. I like the idea that you like him, but there are a lot of beautiful broads in this town, and he's a very eligible guy."

"And?"

"Well, he might not have *forgotten* to make a date. He might just be booked up for the time being."

"Mike, you know something?"

He got up and walked to the window. "I know nothing. I saw him coming out of an art movie with Karla last week. I have to admit I was very impressed, because that's one lady I want to meet. I wouldn't have thought anything of it. But two days ago, I also saw him standing on Fifty-seventh Street outside of Carnegie Hall. Dee tells me Karla rents a studio there. And sure enough, down she comes, and they go off. He didn't see me. And I've said nothing to Dee."

"Are you trying to tell me he goes with Karla?"

"I'm also trying to tell you there's a gorgeous Dutch model named Kim Voren. She's on the cover of *Vogue* this month. Maybe I gave you the idea that we were

serving David to you on a silver platter. Dee would like
it that way. But David is his own man. And I don't
want you to be hurt. I would like to plunk the world in
your lap. Last night I did a lot of thinking, maybe because I saw you for the first time as a gorgeous girl out
on a date. A gorgeous vulnerable girl. And I don't want
you sitting around just waiting for this guy to call."

"I have no intention of doing that. I want to work."

He walked over and poured himself another cup of
coffee and lit a fresh cigarette. "What do you want to
do?"

She shrugged. "Until now I always assumed I'd be in
show business because of you. In some way, I guess I've
felt as if I've been in it all of my life. I think I can act.
But I've had no experience. And I know there aren't
many jobs open. But there's Off Broadway. Maybe I
could try for an assistant stage manager . . . or an understudy . . . a walk-on . . . anything. Dee was right
about one thing—I do want to do something."

He looked thoughtful. "Most of the producers and directors I know are on the Coast now. As for Off Broadway, that's a whole new breed. Tell you what—I'll call
the Johnson Harris agency. It's a hell of a good talent
agency. Sammy Tebet is vice-president in charge of motion pictures. He owes me a few favors. I'll get him to
introduce you to whoever runs the legit department
there." He looked at his watch. "I'll try them in about
an hour."

"That would be great. Maybe they can see me tomorrow." She stood up. "And now I'm off to buy out
New York—like you told me to do yesterday."

He smiled. "Only today . . . you really feel like doing
it."

She nodded. "Just shows you what a good night's
sleep will do."

FIVE

THIRD AVENUE WAS a whole new world. She had dropped off boxes at the Pierre loaded with pants, long skirts, shirts, dungarees—enough to fill most of those heavy brass hangers Dee had put in her closets. Now her wardrobe was as freaked-out as everyone else's in New York.

Gloss was a factory of mod clothes and frenetic activity. The receptionist announced her, then pointed the way down a long hall. People stood in clusters studying layouts. Young men carried art portfolios. Girls rushed about carrying sketches. Bright simulated daylight flooded most of the windowless offices. There was a "now" look about everyone, from the skinny girls with the long hair and tinted glasses to the young men with the well trimmed beards. She was glad she was wearing one of her new outfits.

She stopped at the end of the hall before a large lacquered white door with the name LINDA RIGGS in impressive block wooden letters. The secretary, sitting in the small cubicle outside, led January into a striking corner office with windows from floor to ceiling. A beautiful young woman was sitting at the desk, a phone cradled against her shoulder, making notes as she listened. The office was colorfully modern. White walls . . . orange rugs on stained black wooden floors . . .

paintings that looked like colored Rorschach tests . . .
white leather chairs . . . a black velvet couch . . . plex-
iglass tables . . . copies of *Gloss* everywhere. In spite of
the decor, there was a worked-in feeling about the office. January sat down and waited until the woman got
off the phone. It was incredible to envision Linda of the
shaggy hair and funny face in this sleek setup. The
woman on the phone smiled, and signaled that she was
trying to get off. January returned an understanding
smile and stared at the manuscripts that lay piled on
the windowsill. *Ladies' Home Journal, Cosmopolitan,
Vogue,* and other rival magazines lay on a table.

The woman got off the phone. "I'm sorry. That call
was endless." Then she looked at January and smiled.
"Well, you really are quite a beauty. But then why not
—with a father like Mike Wayne."

January smiled politely and wondered where Linda
was. This smooth attractive woman was staring at her
as if she were some kind of a specimen. January stood
up. "I'm supposed to see Miss Riggs at three and—"

The woman laughed. "January! Who do you think *I*
am!"

January looked bewildered. But Linda only laughed.
"I forgot. Good Lord! How long has it been?"

"About ten years." January finally managed to speak.

Linda nodded. "That's right! Well, you didn't think I
intended to stay stuck with that face all of my life, did
you? The braces came off, a few caps were added, and
of course the nose job—that was my graduation present
—and I've lost about twenty pounds of what we used
to call baby fat . . ."

"It's unbelievable," January said. "Linda, you're
beautiful. I mean . . . your personality was always so
great that people thought you were beautiful, but—"

"I was kinky-looking—before it was 'in' to look kinky.
Now that I've gone all through this, the uglies have come
in. I swear, sometimes I wish I had my old nose back.
Incidentally, Keith doesn't know about the nose job or
the teeth or anything." She pressed a buzzer and the
receptionist's voice came through the box on her desk.
"Norma, when Keith Winters arrives, send him right in."

Then she turned to January. "I wish you had worn something with more color. I love those pants, and the suede jacket is divine . . . but it's all so beigy and Keith is coming with reams of color film."

"Linda, I didn't come here to be photographed. I came to see you. I want to hear all about you and the magazine. I think it's just fabulous."

Linda came out from behind the desk and sat on the couch. She reached for a pack of cigarettes in a large glass bowl. "We've got just about every brand here . . . except grass . . . so help yourself."

"I don't smoke."

"I wish I didn't. How do you manage to stay so thin without it? I worry sometimes with all that cancer talk, but they say until women have the menopause, they have some secret ingredient that protects them. Speaking of menopause, tell me about Deirdre Milford Granger."

"She's Mrs. Michael Wayne now."

"Of course." Linda smiled. "I'd love to get a story on her and your father. We cater to the twenty-to-thirty crowd, but *everyone* loves to read about the really filthy rich. We've tried and tried, but she's always turned us down. That's why I'm keen to do a story on you. It will really grab our readers. I'm surprised Helen Gurley Brown or Lenore Hershey hasn't gotten to you. Although it's more of a *Cosmo* story than *Ladies' Home Journal*. I swear that Helen Gurley Brown will drive me back to my analyst."

"Why?"

"She's so damned successful. And it all started from writing about how a single girl landed a divine husband. And the wild part is, no one gets married anymore . . . except older people. Anyway, that's going to be my angle. Stories don't drop in your lap. You've got to find them . . . be first. That's why I'm in my office from eight in the morning until eight at night. It's not easy. But it's the only way. Because I intend to make *Gloss* bigger than *Cosmo*. Bigger than them all one day."

"Don't you believe in marriage?" January asked.

"Of course not. I live with Keith and we're divinely

happy. We live for today. Because nothing is permanent
. . . not even life."

"He's the photographer?"

Linda smiled. "Actually he's really an actor. He
moonlights as a photographer. I give him all the jobs I
can. He's damn good. Of course he's no Halsman or Sca-
vullo. He could be, if he dedicated himself to it, but he's
determined to become the Marlon Brando of the seventies. He's really marvelous. I saw him do *Streetcar* in an
Equity Library thing. But there are just no jobs. And
he hasn't really ever had a break on Broadway."

"I thought you'd be the big star," January said. "We
all did at Miss Haddon's."

Linda shook her head. "I tried. But even with the
nose job and all . . . nothing really happened. I mean
it was all so tacky—girls working as waitresses at night
so they could study and job hunt during the day. I tried
it for a while. I even got a job as a waitress in a
coffeehouse. And then one day I saw a girl applying
for a job who was also an actress, only she was in her
thirties. That's when I quit . . . and got the job on *Gloss*.
The magazine was on the verge of folding, and I had
a lot of ideas of things that could make it go. But no
one would listen to me. I stayed on as a gofer for about
two years. And then someone in the advertising department dropped it to me that John Hamer was going to
close *Gloss* down. He's chairman of the board of Jenrose
—they own *Gloss* and several other publications. Everyone was already looking for other jobs. So on a wild
chance I went to him and told him my ideas. I told him
it should stop competing with *Vogue* for high fashion
. . . to gear it to the younger woman . . . the working
girl . . . or housewife . . . to go after ads for new bras
. . . buy stories that didn't all have an 'up' ending. To
do articles on marriages that *couldn't* be saved by a
pastor or a marriage counselor . . . stories about the
'other woman' who suffered while the wife who didn't
give a damn had a ball. He took a chance and made me
editor of special subjects. After a year we had doubled
our circulation. At the end of that year I became editor-
in-chief. We were the first to do a photo layout on the

topless beach at the Riviera. I also did articles for and
against natural childbirth, for and against children . . .
We've done great and we're still climbing in circulation.
But if I want to beat out *Ladies' Home Journal* and
Cosmo, I have to keep coming up with firsts. And if I
can't get Deirdre Milford Granger *Wayne* . . . then I
want January Wayne. I want to run a picture layout
of you in our January issue, with the heading: 'January
is not a month. She's a girl who has everything.'"

"Linda, I don't want a story done on me."

For a moment Linda stared. "Then why did you come
to see me?"

"Because . . . well . . . I had hoped we could be
friends. I . . . don't really know anyone in New York."

"The lonely little princess? Come on, that's your stepmother's bag. Or at least it was until she married your
father. He must be a great stud. Know something? I've
always had a thing for him."

January stood up, but Linda grabbed her arm. "Oh,
for God's sake. Don't take it that way. Look . . . okay
. . . so you're lonely. Everyone's lonely. And the only
way not to be lonely is to go to bed with the man you
care about . . . and waking up the next morning and
finding yourself still in his arms. I've got that with Keith,
and that's one of the reasons I want this story. Because
I'll be able to give him some decent money on the assignment. You see, I feel that if he got some real recognition for his photography he'd take it more seriously.
Then I wouldn't have to worry that he might take off
for six months with a bus and truck company of some
show." The intensity of Linda's feelings changed her entire face, and suddenly January was looking at the
Linda of Miss Haddon's. The Linda who was raucous.
The Linda of *Annie Get Your Gun.*

They were both silent. Then January said, "Linda, if
you care this much for Keith, why don't you get married?"

"Because as I told you—we don't believe in it." She
was Linda Riggs of *Gloss* magazine again. "He's my mate
and we live together and it's fine and . . ."

They both looked up as the door swung open and

Keith Winters walked into the room. January recognized him immediately as the photographer in the Pierre lobby. His hair was long and shaggy, he wore a Dutch boy cap, an army surplus jacket, a T-shirt, sneakers, and dungarees.

"Sorry, Keith," Linda said. "I'm afraid there is no assignment. The lady says no."

He shrugged and took off the camera he had slung across his shoulder. He also had one around his neck. January began to feel slightly guilty.

Keith reached for a pack of cigarettes from the bowl. Then he turned to Linda. "Listen, you better not plan on me for dinner tonight."

"But this is the day Evie comes to clean. I told her to make a big meat loaf—the kind you adore."

He shook his head. "I have an appointment with Milos Doklov. I have to be downtown at five-thirty."

"Who is he?" Linda asked.

"Just one of the best Off Broadway directors there is. He was nominated twice for an Obie." He looked at January. "That's an Off Broadway Tony."

She smiled faintly. "Oh. I didn't know."

"Cheer up. Neither does Linda."

"Keith, I have nothing against Off Broadway."

"How could you? You've never been there."

"I'll come for the opening of this."

"Cool it," he said. "This is for Off Off Broadway. But it's good enough for Milos to have done it, so it's good enough for me."

"Why, that's wonderful," Linda said with a forced enthusiasm. "Tell me about it. What's the part like? When does it open?"

"It's opened and is a hit—by Off Off Broadway standards. The leading man is splitting to do another show. So I may replace him."

"Well . . . that's marvelous. I'll freeze the meat loaf and wait up for you. We'll have pâté and wine to celebrate."

"I don't like pâté." He looked at January. "Sorry you're goofing out on us. I could use the bread and my old lady needs a good story. She doesn't sleep nights unless the circulation climbs."

January felt an undercurrent of hostility between them. Linda's smile was forced and her hands fumbled as she tried to light a cigarette. Suddenly January felt Linda needed this story desperately—and not just for the magazine.

"Linda, maybe, if I phoned my father and asked him . . ."

"Asked him what?" Linda was staring at Keith.

"About the story . . . I mean, what you suggested doing on me . . ."

Linda brightened. "Oh, January, do. Call him now. Use that phone on my desk."

January realized she didn't know her father's office number. Maybe Sadie would know. She called the Pierre. Sadie knew the number and also told her two dozen roses had arrived. She waited while Sadie read the card. "It's from Mr. Milford. It's on his business card. It says, 'Thank you for a lovely evening. Will call you in a few days. D.' "

She thanked Sadie and dialed her father's office. His secretary told her to try him at the Friars Club. She thought about the flowers as she waited for them to page him at the Friars Club. "Will call you in a few days." Well, as Mike said, he hadn't been just sitting around waiting for her to arrive. He probably was dated up. And the flowers were to show her he was thinking of her.

When her father came on the phone, he sounded breathless. "What's up, babe?"

"Did I get you away from something important?"

"Yeah. A hot gin game and a double Schneid—"

"Oh, I'm sorry."

"Well, look, sweetheart, from where I'm standing I can see the guy I've got on the blitz trying to sneak a look through the pack. You want something special? Or is this a social call?"

"I'm at *Gloss* magazine and Linda wants to do a story on me."

"So?"

"Is it okay?"

"Sure . . ." He paused. "That is, if it's a story on *you*. I don't want Dee kicked around. Look, get it in writing that you have complete approval of the story before it goes into the magazine."

"Okay."

"Oh . . . and listen . . . you're all set with Sammy Tebet tomorrow at the Johnson Harris office. Ten A.M."

"Thanks, Mike!"

"See you later, babe."

She hung up and told them Mike's demands. Linda nodded. "Fair enough. I'll have a letter drawn up immediately. I'll put Sara Kurtz on the story. Keith, you can start right in with the pictures." She pushed an intercom buzzer. "Send Ruth in to take some notes." She pushed another buzzer. "Janie, hold all calls. Unless Wilhelmina calls back. I want that new German model she has for the February cover . . . Shotzie something. Good Lord, you know I'm bad on names. What? No. And tell Leon to leave the artwork for the new novel excerpt. I've got to see it before I leave tonight. Yes, that's about it." She looked up as an ugly birdlike girl timidly entered the room clutching a notebook. Linda gave her a brief nod and then hung up.

"Sit down, Ruth. This is January Wayne. Ruth is gorgeous at shorthand. I'll ask questions, because I know the way the story should go. Then in a few days we'll set up a date to put you and Sara together . . ."

Keith had finished loading his cameras. He took out his light meter, changed a lamp, then took a quick shot with a Polaroid to check composition. He stared at it, nodded, and started snapping with another camera.

Linda's smile was all business. "Okay, January. After Miss Haddon's, where did you go to school?"

"Switzerland."

"What was the name of the college?"

January saw Ruth making all funny curlicues on the pad. She hesitated. She couldn't remember the name Dee had given her. What Dee wanted to tell her friends was one thing. But she didn't want to lie about it in print. Besides, it might get Linda in trouble. And to add to her personal confusion, Keith was suddenly all over the place, taking shots of her at crazy angles. She turned to Linda. "Look, let's concentrate on *now*. I don't want any stuff on Miss Haddon's or Dee or Switzerland. I'm going to start job hunting tomorrow, and . . . well, let's go from there."

"Job hunting?" Linda laughed. "You?"

Keith came up close and snapped his camera. January jumped. "Ignore me," he pleaded. "You and Linda keep talking. I shoot better that way."

"If you want a job," Linda said, "come work for me."

"Here?" January was getting jittery. Keith's clicking was nerve-racking.

"Sure, I'd love a name like yours on the masthead. You could be a junior editor. Only you wouldn't be a slavey or a gofer. I'll pay you one hundred and twenty-five a week and let you do some pieces."

"But I can't write!"

"Neither could I," Linda answered. "But I learned. And now I don't have to. I have plenty of rewrite people. But all *you* have to do is get the interviews, go out on them, take notes or use a tape recorder. Then I'll assign someone to rewrite them."

"But why would you want me?"

"For your muscle, January. Look, last year Sammy Davis Junior was in town and there was no way I could get to him. Now if you had been working for us then, it would have been just one telephone call from your father to Sammy. Mike Wayne may have retired, but he still has entrée to people we could never reach. Right now we're going after the young beautiful-people readers. You could do a monthly column—what's doing with that set, where do they go. Also, your new stepmother knows the great Karla. Now—if we could get a story on her!"

"Karla's never given an interview in her life," Keith said.

"Of course not," Linda agreed. "But who's talking about an interview? If January happens to see her at one of Dee's dinner parties and just happens to overhear some pearls dropping from that beautiful Polish mouth . . ."

"January, I've got six shots of you frowning," Keith said. "Give me a different mood."

January got up and walked out of camera range. "This is wild . . . the way you two are going on. I come to see an old friend and wind up doing an interview. I say I want to work, and you ask me to be Mata Hari. As you would say, Linda, NO WAY!"

"What kind of work do you want to do?" Linda asked.

"Act."

"Oh, God," Linda groaned.

"Any experience?" Keith asked.

"Not really. But I spent my life watching and listening. And at the—in Switzerland—I used to read aloud a lot. Every day for two hours. Shakespeare . . . Marlowe . . . Shaw . . . Ibsen."

Keith clicked as she spoke. "Come along with me this afternoon. I'll introduce you to Milos Doklov—he always has some project going. He may know someone else who might be doing something you could audition for. Do you sing or dance?"

"No, I—"

"That's a great idea," Linda said. "And Keith, see if you can get some pictures of January with this Milos. Also get some background shots of her in the Village . . ." Then as Keith started packing his camera, Linda said, "I'll check with you in a day or so, January. I'll have the letter your father wanted drawn up and I'll set up an appointment for you and Sara Kurtz." She looked at Keith. "I'll keep the meat loaf hot until eight. Try to get back by then."

"I'll try. But don't count on it," he said. "Come on, actress," he took January's arm. "You're on your way."

When they got outside, Keith said, "Well, rich girl, you're about to travel out-of-work-actor style."

"How's that?"

"On the subway—Dutch Treat. Got thirty cents?"

"Yes, sure. Know what? I've never been on a subway."

He laughed as he led her down the steps. "Keep talking, baby. You're blowing my mind."

She sat beside Keith fighting off a queasy feeling as the train rattled its way downtown. She decided there was nothing wonderful or colorful about poverty. The man sitting near her had body odor. A woman across from her had a large shopping bag cradled between her legs and was working diligently at picking her nose. There was a dank feeling in the car and the walls were covered with names and graffiti. She sat very straight and tried not to show her revulsion as Keith chattered through the noise of the car. At one point he almost broke his neck trying to stand on a seat across the aisle to get her picture. The train lurched and he sprawled across the floor. His camera slid down to the other end of the train. January ran down the car to help. It struck her as odd that no one else bothered to help or even seemed to notice. She was relieved when they got off.

They walked two blocks to a dingy building. Then they climbed five steep flights. "Milos keeps his office up in a loft," Keith explained. They both stopped several times for breath before they reached a wet-looking steel door. Keith rang the bell and a strong voice boomed, "It's unlocked. Enter."

The voice was the only strong thing about Milos Doklov. He was a skinny, dirty-looking little man with long thin hair that only partially covered a shiny scalp. His fingernails were long and dirty and his smile revealed decayed teeth.

"Hi, man. Who's the chick?"

"January Wayne. January, this is Milos Doklov."

"So you've come home to Daddy," Milos said, ignoring January.

Keith took out his camera and snapped January, who was openly staring at the place. "I didn't get the job with Hal Prince, if that's what you mean," Keith answered as he tore open a new role of film with his teeth.

"Baby . . . baby . . ." Milos sprang to his feet like a cat. "That Broadway shit will kill your potential. After you make it here and find out what it all means, then you can go uptown for a season to make some bread. But always remember—this is the scene, this is where it's at."

"Cut the sales pitch, Milos . . . I'll take the job."

Milos smiled sadly. "You could have had the part originally . . . gotten all the reviews. Look what's happened to Baxter—he's going into *Ashes and Jazz*."

Keith clicked the camera again. "That's still Off Broadway."

"Yes, but he's up for an Obie."

"Look, I said I'll take the part."

"Split with the fashion lady?"

"No."

"Then why the change of heart? Seems to me that was the main reason you wouldn't take the part before."

Keith began to reload his second camera. He checked the light meter. "I was still hoping for the Hal Prince deal. Let's cut it. When do rehearsals start?"

"We'll have just two days. Maybe next Monday and Tuesday. You watch the performance every night— learn the part and the moves. No sweat."

"Okay, Milos." He took a final shot of January.

"Why the pictures?" Milos asked.

"Doing a setup on the lady."

"You a model?" Milos asked.

"Nope." Keith strapped his camera back in its case. "She's an actress. Know anyone who needs someone who looks like her?"

"Are you any good?" Milos asked her.

"I think so. That is, I feel I am," she said.

Milos rubbed his chin. "Look, one of the Muses is leaving the same time as Baxter. I was going to call Liza Kilandos. It's only ten lines and pays . . . ah . . . are you Equity?"

"Not yet."

"Fine. Go see the show tonight with Keith. It's the part Irma Davidson plays." He tossed the script to Keith. "Bone up on it, man. And January, you come back tomorrow at four and read for the part."

When they got out on the street she grabbed Keith. "Did he mean it? I mean, that I might have a job right away? Wouldn't that be fabulous?"

The weather had changed. There was a sudden rumble of thunder. Keith looked at the sky. "It's going to come down like bullets, but it won't last. Let's go in for some coffee." He led her to a little cellar. "We can have a sandwich here and kill time until we go to the theater. No point in spending money going back uptown. Do you have to call anyone to say you're not coming back?"

She called the Pierre. Her father wasn't home and Dee was resting. "Tell them I can't have dinner with them," she told Sadie. "I—I have a date." It wasn't exactly the truth. But it was better than a long explanation.

She walked back to the table. The rain was slicing across the pavement. They both sat in the small booth and stared out at the wet gray street. They ordered hamburgers and Keith took a few more shots of her in the restaurant.

"Linda says you're a good photographer," January said.

"I get by."

"She said you could be one of the best."

"Look, I'd rather be a half-ass actor than the best photographer in the world."

She was silent. Then he said, "The lady makes thirty thousand a year. I don't want any more mercy jobs!"

"But she says you're good."

"Yes, but not with the camera."

She knew she had blushed and she busied herself adding more relish to her hamburger. He began telling her about his career—the few decent roles he had in summer stock . . . his roles Off Broadway . . . the Industrials . . . the one TV commercial which kept him going for a year. "But that's run out . . . my unemployment insurance is out too . . . and I have no intention of trying to be better than Avedon and all the others."

"But you could learn," January said.

He looked at her. "Why?"

"Why?"

He nodded. "Yeah. Why? Why should I kill myself trying to learn something I don't enjoy doing? Sure there's rejection in the theater. But it's like getting a turn-down from a chick you got a hard-on for. At least you keep trying because you got a chance she might say Yes. The other way you're working just as hard to settle for a chick who doesn't turn you on. Dig?"

"But you'd be with Linda."

He stared into his coffee cup. "No rule says I can't be with her as an actor."

"But . . . I mean . . . as an actor you have to tour a lot and be away from her."

"Ever hear of a thing called self-respect? Before you can be with someone every night you want them to respect you. And for them to respect you, you got to respect yourself. I know too many actors who sold out . . . turned queer to get a job . . . or got kept by someone . . . And know something? They never really make it, because it kills something inside of them."

She was silent. Suddenly he said, "What about you? What's your scene?"

"What do you mean?"

"You love someone?"

"Yes. I mean, no."

"How can you mean yes . . . and then no?"

"Well, I love my father. I know that. But that's not being in love, right?"

"I should hope not."

"And then I've met someone. But when I think about love—" She shook her head. "I mean, I'm not quite sure how you're supposed to feel when you're in love. I like him, but—"

"You're not in love. That's the story of my life. I've never been *in* love."

"You haven't?"

He shook his head. "To me love will be when I stand on that stage and know the whole fucking audience is there just to see me. That's the real orgasm. What I feel for a chick—" He shrugged. "That's like eating a good meal. I love good food . . . I love life . . . I love tasting new things . . . new sensations." He stopped. "Look . . . don't look so shocked. Linda knows the score. She's been my old lady for a long time, yet she knows I might split at any time. But if I do, it won't be because I've fallen in love with some chick. It'll be for some other experience. For some other scene. Dig?"

"No."

"You're a real put-on, aren't you? I mean no one, like no one, can be this straight. Look, I'm a life freak. I want to wring it dry. Linda only pretends she is. But she isn't. She lives only for that magazine. Sure, she digs me. But I'm not the first man in her life. I think she'd feel worse losing a big story than losing a guy. Dig?"

"The rain's stopped," she said.

He stood up. "Your end is ninety cents. That means we're leaving a thirty-cent tip—fifteen apiece. Okay?"

"Okay."

The streets were wet and a few occasional drops fell from the trees. They walked the few blocks in silence. January dredged her mind trying to think of something to say that would put Keith into a more romantic frame of mind toward Linda. He seemed so turned off. . . . Maybe he was just talking, maybe he was nervous. After all, a lot of people said things they didn't really mean when they were nervous. He was attractive in an earthy kind of way and Linda was really in love with him. Maybe after he got in the show things would change. Mike always said he was more relaxed when things were going great.

Suddenly it began to rain. Keith grabbed her hand and they ran the rest of the way, ducking under awnings and trees. They were breathless when Keith stopped in front of a store.

"Well, here we are."

"But . . . Where's the theater?"

"Follow me." He led her through the store, which was empty except for a few wooden plank tables with lemonade and peanut butter crackers stacked in readiness for the intermission break. A girl stood beside a homemade ticket box. She waved when she saw Keith. He led January past her into a long narrow room. There were rows and rows of hard-looking folding chairs. Up front was a stage without a curtain. Keith led her to the third row. "These are house seats," he said with a grin.

"This is the theater?" she asked.

"It was an old store. But they've turned it into a playhouse. The dressing rooms are upstairs, and Milos keeps a pad on the third floor for starving actors. It's like a dorm . . . co-ed . . . and they live there rent-free if they're out of a job."

By eight o'clock the house was full, and to January's amazement, extra chairs were being jammed into every available spot.

"It's a real hit, isn't it?" she asked.

"It's caught on pretty big . . . mostly word of mouth. I see a lot of uptown people. Maybe some of the producers will come down at that."

The lights dimmed and the entire cast came on. They bowed, introduced themselves and exited. Three girls remained. "The one on the left—that's the one you're replacing," Keith whispered. "They stay on stage all the time. They're the Greek chorus."

The three girls were dressed in gray coveralls. They chanted a few lines and then the young man they were talking about came on. He looked like Keith. He had a long diatribe which January barely understood. The Greek chorus cut in occasionally with an "Amen, brother." Then a girl came on. There was a violent argument. They sat down and went through the elaborate motions of smoking pot. The stage filled with artificial smoke.

"This is a hash-dream sequence," Keith said. "They're using a smoke screen now. This is the scene that's bringing them down from uptown."

When the smoke cleared, the two leads were nude. The Greek chorus was also nude. Then actual lovemaking began on the stage between the boy and girl. At first it was slow . . . almost like a dance . . . the Greek chorus hummed to background music that came from an offstage speaker. As the music grew louder, the chorus grew louder . . . everyone moved faster . . . the dance turned into a frenzy as the leading man broke into a song and began stroking the breasts of the Greek chorus and the leading lady, while the leading lady in turn stroked everyone. Then the Greek chorus began stroking each other until everyone was intertwined in a song called "Move, Touch, Feel . . . That's Love."

Then the stage went dark and the house lights came up and it was intermission.

January suddenly scrambled to her feet. "I'm leaving."

"But there's another act. Your big scene is in it." He laughed. "You have ten lines alone."

"With or without clothes?" she asked.

"Say . . . are you uptight about frontal nudity?" He grabbed her arm as she pushed her way up the aisle. "I mean, nudity is a natural thing. To hide the body is an idea planted in our mind from birth. I guess it started when Eve ate the apple. But a baby has genitals . . . yet everyone loves a bare-assed baby. Our body is part of the expression of love. Do we cover our faces because our eyes send out signals of love or because our mouth talks of love? Our tongues caress someone's lips . . . yet is a tongue obscene?"

"We see with our eyes and talk with our tongue," she said.

"Yeah . . . and we pee with our pricks and our cunts but we also make love with them."

She broke away from him and ran outside. People were crowded in front waiting to pay a dollar for a cup of lemonade. There were limousines parked outside. Keith reached the street and grabbed her by the arm.

"Okay, so maybe I'm not crazy about doing a sex number right on the stage either. Why do you think I didn't take the job when the play first opened? I knew Linda would blow her top. But it's the way things are today. If I'm not uptight about nudity, then I shouldn't be uptight about the sex act. It's a normal function."

"So is throwing up, but no one wants to pay to watch it!"

"Look, January, the play has caught on. It's a big chance for me. Besides, everyone is doing it. Big-name movie stars are doing nude scenes. It's just a matter of time before they'll go all the way. And it's not Keith the man they'll be looking at on that stage. It'll be Keith the actor. And that's all I care about. I'd rather live in Milos'

dormitory and do hard-core porno *acting* than sit around
in a Park Avenue penthouse holding a camera."

They had walked halfway down the block. A light
misty rain was falling. The trees that lined the street
partially shielded them. Keith tried to smile. "Come on.
The second act is starting. Let's go back."

She continued to walk in the opposite direction. For
a moment he hesitated. Then he shouted, "Go on. Run
home. Go back to the Pierre where your father is being
kept by a dame. At least *I'm* trying! If guys like your
father hadn't thrown in the towel, maybe we wouldn't
have to do this kind of shit. But it's guys like him who
played it safe and refused to experiment. Well, fuck
them! And fuck you! And fuck Linda too!" He turned
and ran back to the theater. For a moment she stood very
still. There had been tears in his anger. She wanted to
tell him that she understood . . . that she wasn't angry.
But he was gone. People were returning to the theater.
The second act was beginning. And suddenly she was
alone on a deserted street. There wasn't a sign of a cab.
She walked back to the theater and looked at the license
plates of the limousines. Several had X's, indicating they
were rentals. She walked over to one chauffeur. "The
play won't break for another hour. I wonder if you'd
like—"

"Beat it, hippie!" He turned up his radio.

Her face burned. She dug into her bag, took out a ten-
dollar bill, and approached the next car. "Sir—" She
held up the money. "Could you drive me home? You'll
get back in time for the break."

"Where's home?" The driver was staring at the bill.

"The Pierre."

He nodded, took the bill and unlocked the door. "Hop
in."

As they drove uptown he said, "What happened?
Fight with your boyfriend, or did the play turn you off?"

"Both."

"They're all coming down. Just to see bare boobs,
heh? I mean, that's what they show, isn't it?"

"More," January said quietly.

"No kidding. Know something? I'm married and have

three kids. But I once wanted to be a performer. I still sing occasionally at friends' weddings in the Bronx. I do Irish ballads. I'm also great with Rodgers and Hammerstein. But they don't write songs like that no more. No more Sinatras coming up. No more Perry Comos. Now *they* were singers . . . not the stuff I hear my daughter play on her record player."

They finally pulled up in front of the Pierre. He waited until she walked in, then his car disappeared into the traffic. She was relieved to find the apartment empty. She went to her room and stood in the dark. Things didn't seem so glaringly real in the dark. She thought of Linda, transferring her personal desires for success to the magazine, making it her symbol of life. She also thought of Keith going into that dreadful show . . . of the limousine driver who once wanted to be a singer . . . of her father probably sitting in some restaurant with Dee and her friends.

She stood very still. Where did everybody go? Where was all the fun and happiness she had hoped for? All those long snow-filled days when she had worked so hard just to walk . . . for what? She snapped on the lights. The room felt so empty. The whole apartment felt empty. Then she saw the roses on her bureau.

She thought of David—and suddenly the dirty theater and the entire evening seemed far away. There still was a world with clean beautiful people. And there still were stages on Broadway with beautiful settings and talented actors.

She would get into that world, and she would make Mike proud . . . and David would be as proud to be with her as he was with Karla or the Dutch model. Because from now on she would not be just Dee's new stepdaughter—or just Mike Wayne's daughter—from now on she was January Wayne.

A lady on her own.

SIX

SAMMY TEBET'S GREETING was warm and expansive. He asked about Mike. Called him a lucky devil to be out of the rat race and said a beautiful girl like January should find a nice boy, get married and forget about show business. But if she insisted, he would do what he could.

Then he took her down the hall and introduced her to a bright young man who looked barely old enough to shave. The bright young man had his own office and sat behind a large desk. He had a telephone with five buttons, and each time one lit up a harassed secretary who looked old enough to be his grandmother poked her head in the door and pleaded, "Mr. Copeland . . . *please* pick up on two. It's the Coast." He would toss her a smile and say, "Cool it, Rhoda." Then with a bored but apologetic glance toward January he would push down the button and in a voice charged with animation launch into a multi-figured business discussion.

Between these calls he managed to set up some appointments for her. He knew of two shows that were being cast. She was too tall for the ingenue, but she might as well go and read anyway. Maybe the understudy was open. The other was a musical. Could she sing? No . . . well, go anyway. Sometimes they took a beautiful girl with no voice if they had enough dogs with strong voices to carry her. If not, nothing was lost. At least she would get to meet Merrick. He might remember her when he was doing something else. He gave her a list of producers to visit—"Just for contacts." They'd be active later in the season. He also set up an appointment at an advertising agency for a commercial. Commercials weren't his line, but it just so happened that at P.J.'s last night he had run into the director who told him they were looking for girls with great hair. When she thanked him, he held up his hand in a pontifical manner. "Cool it, sweetheart. Sammy Tebet asked me to do this. Sam's the man. Love him. Love *him*! Beautiful person. Said your father was once right up there with David Merrick. Well, let's hope you can make the old boy proud. That's part of the fun of making it. Gives them something to live for. Now you check in with me once a week and leave your phone number with Rhoda." Then he went back to his phone with the lights, and she gave her number to the hysterical Rhoda.

She followed all the leads he had given her. She read for one play. She hadn't been very good and she knew it. She was dismissed with the usual "Thank-you-very-much." She hiked over to Madison Avenue to the advertising agency and spent an hour waiting in an office along with thirty girls with hair down to their waists. When she finally met the director she learned that it was a cigarette commercial. The beautiful hair was a "must," as it was important to give the image that *young healthy* people smoked. They liked her hair, told her to learn how to inhale and come back in two days. She bought a pack of cigarettes, went back to the Pierre, locked herself in her room, and practiced. After a few puffs, the room began to spin. She lay very still and knew she was going to be sick. But after a time it passed and she tried again. This time she rushed to the bathroom and was really sick. Then she fell back on the bed and wondered why people *enjoyed* smoking.

Dee and Mike invited her to dinner. She begged off, explaining she had an audition the following morning and had to bone up on a script for a "reading." She spent the rest of the evening alternating between trying to inhale and fighting off bouts of nausea.

At eleven o'clock at night she finally stood in front of

the mirror, inhaled and managed not to feel faint. As if to punctuate her accomplishment, the phone rang!

It was David. "I expected to leave a message. I didn't think I'd find you at home."

"I've been practicing inhaling."

"Inhaling what?"

"Cigarettes."

"What kind of cigarettes?"

She looked at the pack. "True."

"Oh . . . why?"

"Why True? I just liked the name."

"No, why the inhaling?"

He listened carefully as she explained about the commercial. Then he said, "Look, try not to take it any farther than your throat. The effect will be the same. No use lousing up your lungs. And after you get the commercial—throw away the cigarettes."

She laughed. "I bet you think I'm some kind of a nut sitting here and getting sick, just for a commercial."

"No, I think you're a girl with determination. I like that in you."

"Oh . . . well . . . yes." She knew she sounded flustered.

"Are you busy tomorrow night?" he asked.

"No."

"Well, how about having dinner with me? I'll coach you while you smoke. Maybe even teach you to blow some rings."

"Oh, great! What time?"

"I'll leave a message for you during the day."

"Okay . . . Goodnight David."

She was up early the next morning. Rhoda had called telling her to be at a producer's office at eleven for a reading. She was really excited. Rhoda said that Mr. Copeland said she was a natural for the part. Maybe this was really going to be her day. She'd think positive. She was going to get the part. After all, *someone* had to get it. And tonight she was seeing David.

As she dressed she thought about the evening. She had worn the gypsy outfit with David. What should she wear tonight? The long suede skirt with boots? Or should

she wear the wet look—the black pants and jacket that
were featured in *Vogue*? The man in the Third Avenue
shop had said this was a perfect "rip-off!" Well, she had
all day to think about it.

Her sense of well-being persisted even as she sat in the
crowded office, waiting to see the producer. But Keith
was right. There was so little casting . . . and so *many*
actors. Actors who had experience. As she waited she
heard bits of their conversation. They talked about re-
siduals, unemployment insurance. And some even joked
about their experiences modeling at body-painting parlors. Nothing was demeaning if it brought in the rent
and enabled the actor to job hunt and study. She marveled at their attitude. In spite of all the rejections they
received, none of them seemed depressed. They were
actors, and all the letdowns and disappointments were
part of it. They might not have money for food all the
time, but they all managed to go to classes. She heard
snatches of conversation about Uta . . . Stella . . .
the Studio . . . And she noticed they all had picture
composites with their credits Xeroxed on the back. Another staple was the "Week-at-a-Glance" book, dog-
eared and crammed with appointments for "go-sees,"
auditions, and lessons.

She waited two hours, and was finally ushered in to
see a tired man who looked at her and sighed, "Who
sent you here?"

"Mr. Copeland."

Another sigh. "Why does Sheldon do this? I told him
yesterday—we need a tired-looking blonde in her late
twenties. It's not fair to you . . . it's not fair to me. He
thinks he's keeping you busy by sending you around, but
he's wasting your time . . . and mine. Okay, honey,
better luck on your next stop." Then he turned to his
secretary. "How many more are waiting?"

January walked out as a tall red-haired girl went in.
She wondered if Sheldon had sent her also. Did he think
just seeing a weary producer at the end of his day would
make an "impression" on him for another time? Maybe
she should tell all this to "Sheldon." She walked outside.
A little whirlpool of a wind blew some dust in her eyes.

Her mascara began to run as she dabbed at her eye. She hailed a cab, but it passed her by. Every cab she hailed seemed to have an OFF DUTY sign on it. She began to walk toward the Pierre. Mike was right. It was not the sparkling world she had seen on her weekends from Miss Haddon's. She walked up Broadway. The afternoon was ending. Prostitutes in their oversized wigs were beginning to take their positions on the corners. A blind man with a sad-looking dog shuffled along. A group of young Japanese men with cameras were taking pictures of the street. She wanted to shout, "It wasn't always like this." But maybe it was, maybe from her seat in the limousine with Mike it had just seemed different. And now, after two days of job hunting, it hit her that she really didn't give a damn about the theater—not without Mike.

It was four-thirty when she reached the Pierre. She would soak in the bathtub and wash away all the discouragement and grime of the day. Tonight she would feel fresh and wonderful for her dinner with David. She felt better just thinking about it. She wanted to go to some quiet candlelit place and talk. She wanted to learn more about him. Somehow she felt he would understand the confusion she was feeling. Mike would only say, "I told you so." Because he had been right.

There was a message in her box. She stared at it with disbelief. It was from David. He would pick her up at five-thirty. Five-thirty! Why five-thirty? Maybe it was a cocktail party. Yes, that was probably it. She dashed into the apartment, took a quick shower, and got into the long skirt. She was just putting on her lipstick when he called from the lobby.

"Come on up," she said. "I can't make a martini. But Mario is here. And Mike should be home any second."

"No. We have to hurry. You come down."

She grabbed a woolen shawl and went down to meet him. He looked at her and frowned. "I'm stupid. I should have told you to wear dungarees." She noticed he was wearing an old pair of corduroy pants and a jacket and sport shirt.

He took her arm. "There's a great espionage movie at

the Baronet. I never get to see the movies I want to see, and there's always a line for this one. So I figured if we caught the six o'clock show we'd get in. We can grab a bite afterward."

The evening had been a total disaster. She thought about it as she lay soaking in the tub. David had adored the movie, and when it was over, they had walked to a restaurant called Maxwell's Plum. It was mobbed, but David knew the captain, and they were immediately wedged into a small table against the wall. David also knew the people at the next table. He made the introductions, ordered her a hamburger, and then talked to his friends throughout dinner. At ten o'clock they left the restaurant.

"Will you come home with me?" he asked.

"What?"

"Come home with me." He held her hand as he signaled for a cab.

"Why don't you come back to the Pierre?" she said.

"Dee and Mike might be there. Besides, I'd be uncomfortable sleeping with you knowing they might be in the same apartment." The cab pulled up before she could answer and he helped her in. Then he leaned across and she heard him give the driver an address in the East Seventies.

"David, I'm not going to bed with you!" She had almost shouted it. Then in a lower voice she said, "Please take me home."

"Change of plans," he called out to the driver. "Make it the Pierre Hotel." Then he turned to her with a tight smile. "Okay. Let's talk about more important things. How'd you do on the commercial? Did you get it?"

"That's not until tomorrow. David, don't be angry. But I . . . well . . . I just can't go to bed with someone I barely know."

"Forget it," he said quietly. "It was just a suggestion."

"I do like you, David." (Why was she apologizing! After all, it wasn't as if she had turned him down for a dance.)

"Fine, January. I understand." His voice was cold.

"Oh, here we are." And when he walked her to the door and kissed her on the brow she felt as if she had been slapped across the face.

She got into bed and turned the radio to an album station. She liked David. That is, she *could* like David— if only he gave her a chance to *learn* to like him. She needed to like him, she wanted to like him, because she suddenly felt so lonely.

It seemed she had just fallen asleep when the phone rang.

"Did I wake you?" Linda said cheerfully.

"What time is it?"

"Seven-thirty in the morning . . . sixty-eight degrees . . . air quality acceptable, and I'm sitting at my desk and have already done an hour of yoga."

January switched on the lamp. "My drapes are closed. It still looks like midnight in here."

"January, I've got to see you. It's important." Linda was still cheerful but there was an urgency in her voice. "How about throwing on a pair of slacks and coming up here for breakfast? I'll send out for it."

"I can't. I have a nine o'clock appointment at the Landis agency. Hey, congratulate me. I've learned to smoke."

"Quit before it grabs you."

"Oh, I'm only doing it for the commercial. Although I must admit it helped get me through a dilly of an evening last night. When you're staring into space and your date is talking to the next table . . . a cigarette can be a girl's best friend."

"January, I've got to see you."

"Is it about the story?"

There was a split second of silence before Linda said, "Of course! Listen, you wouldn't by any chance be free for dinner?"

"Very free."

"Fine . . . then come by around five-thirty. We'll sit with Sara Kurtz and discuss the story. Then we can go to Louise's. It's a good Italian place where two ladies can go without people thinking they're trying to score. See you later. . . ."

Linda was just ending an editorial meeting when January arrived. She motioned for her to sit on the couch in the back of the room. Linda was sitting at her desk. Her editors and assistant editors sat in a semicircle surrounding her.

"I think that'll about wrap up most of the plans for the February issue," she said. There was a slight scuffling of chairs as everyone began to rise. Suddenly Linda said, "Oh, Carol, check on John Weitz. He said he might take over the Colony and give a Valentine's Day party. Find out if he is. Maybe we could simulate some shots of the decor so we could run it in the February issue. Also, if he has any idea of his guest list . . . I know it's early, but he must have about ten or twelve names that he knows he's going to invite." She stood up, signifying the meeting had come to an official end. Her hint of a weary smile conveyed that a real smile would take too much out of her. Her eyes clocked the group who were hastily disbanding. "Where's Sara Kurtz?" she demanded.

"She's on the phone with London," a young man answered. "She's trying to track down an idea she has that the Bow Bell Boys are not really English."

"That's ridiculous," Linda snapped. "They're the biggest sensation to hit the States since the Rolling Stones."

The young man nodded almost apologetically. "Yes, but Sara swears she saw the lead singer doing a disc jockey gig in Cleveland in 1965. She claims he's straight from Shaker Heights. And you know Sara—she never forgets a face."

"Well, send her in. I need her now."

Everyone left in little groups. Linda walked over to January and flopped down on the couch. "And this was an easy day," she sighed. She watched January light a cigarette. "Oh, you got the commercial, I see."

"Wrong. I was among the last three to be eliminated.

Seems I inhale like a champ . . . but my exhaling needs work."

Linda laughed and walked to her desk. She pressed an intercom buzzer. "Tell Sara Kurtz to come here immediately. I can't wait all night while she tracks down one of her neuroses."

"Do you think the boy really comes from Cleveland?"

Linda shrugged. "Sara digs disc jockeys. The boy in Cleveland probably gave her a real brush. And she won't rest until she gets even. God help him if he *is* one of the Bow Bell Boys."

"She sounds dreadful . . ."

"She is. We'll get this over with. Then we'll talk."

Within seconds, an enormously tall girl, bearing an uncanny resemblance to Tiny Tim, loped into the room. Linda introduced Sara Kurtz, who stooped over as she shook hands with January. Then she pulled a crumpled pad out of a beat-up denim bag and began scratching away. She was mostly concerned with the spelling of January's name and was amazed to learn it was spelled like the month. After a few more questions, she uncoiled herself and backed out of the room.

"She's a beast," Linda said. "Keith claims she looks as if she could play for the New York Knicks, but her father was a good newspaperman, and oddly enough she's inherited a kind of style by osmosis. We save her for our shaft pieces. She gets her orgasms doing them. I told her that this has to be an 'up' piece—that's why she looks even more miserable than usual."

"Why does she like to shaft people?" January asked. "I would think she wouldn't be able to face them afterwards."

"Maybe when you look like Sara you just naturally hate the world."

"But I thought you said being ugly was in."

"I did. But there's an 'In' ugly and an 'Out' ugly. Sara is definitely out. But don't worry. You have complete approval of the article. Here's the paper . . . all signed." She handed January an envelope. "Tell Daddy he doesn't have to worry."

January put it in her bag. Linda stared at her closely. "Hey, does losing that commercial really bug you?"

"Of course not. Why?"

"For a second there . . . you looked like it was the end of the world."

January forced a smile. "That's ridiculous. I've got everything to be happy about. I'm in New York . . . my father has a wonderful wife . . . I have a beautiful room all redecorated for me at the Pierre."

"Bullshit!"

"What?"

"I said bullshit. January, who are you trying to con? You hate living there and you can't stand seeing your father with Deirdre Milford Granger."

January shrugged. "That's not true. Besides I rarely see them. But I do feel funny about living there. I mean, it's her apartment and I feel like an interloper."

"Then move."

"He doesn't want me to."

"Look, when you try to please everyone, you wind up pleasing no one."

January stubbed out her cigarette. "Trouble is, I don't really know what I want. Probably because all my life I never really thought about anything except being with my father. And now I find when I go out on a date it's like . . . I don't know what to do . . . how to act."

Linda whistled. "Boy, do you need a shrink!"

"I had enough of that at the Clinique."

"What?"

"Oh, Linda . . . it's a long story. But look. When you grow up without a mother, it's a natural thing to make your father the major thing in your life. And when you have a father like Mike . . . why not?"

"I agree," Linda said. "Your father is damned attractive. But then, so is David Milford. Ronnie Wolfe had it in his column that you were at Raffles with him the other night. I don't dig that phony social scene. But if you have to go that route, going with David Milford is the only way to go."

"That was Dee's party. We also had a date last night.

He asked me back to his apartment, but I wouldn't go.
When he took me home he didn't even try to kiss me
goodnight."

Linda stood up. "Let's go to Louise's. We both could
use a drink."

January liked the restaurant. Louise was a warm
motherly woman who brought them a plate of her homemade chicken liver. She welcomed January to New York
and told her she looked like a movie star. The whole
atmosphere was homelike, and January began to relax.
She ordered a glass of white wine, and Linda ordered a
double Tanqueray martini on the rocks. For a few moments they both sat in silence.

Linda took a long swallow of her drink and swished
it around on the ice. Then she said, "What did you think
of Keith?"

"He's very nice."

"Have you seen him since?"

"Me? Why would I see him?"

"Well, *I* haven't," Linda snapped. Then she took
another long swallow of the martini. "Tell me, please.
Tell me the truth. Did he come on to you?"

"Did he what?"

"Make a pass . . ."

"Of course not! We went to see the show and—"

"And what?"

"I walked out on it . . . and him, I guess."

They were both silent. Then January said, "Look,
Linda, maybe I'm old-fashioned. But I was shocked
and—"

"Well, I have nothing against nudity," Linda said.
"But—" She stopped. "What is this bullshit I'm giving
you? I sound as brainwashed as Keith. Sure, we're the big
liberated generation. The body is beautiful—so show it.
Well, I went down there last night. Keith was sitting in
the audience. He didn't see me. But you tell me what's
beautiful about a bunch of ugly people rubbing their
bodies against one another in a dirty theater on a dirty
stage. Their feet were black with dirt—it was revolting.
And don't think those people with the limos come to see

art! They come to see a lot of starving actors demean themselves. God, an actor has to go through enough rejection in his life . . . at least, let him have *some* personal privacy. But no, there's no such thing as personal dignity anymore. That's for squares. We're the new generation. We're liberated. Marriage is out . . . bastards are in. . . ."

"But yesterday you said you didn't believe in marriage."

Linda shook her head. "I don't know what I believe anymore. Look, my mother has had four husbands and is working on getting her fifth. My father had three wives. Between them I have seven half-brothers and sisters, whom I hardly know. They're all off in some version of Miss Haddon's. But they were born in wedlock so everything's all very proper. At least my mother thinks so—because that's what she was taught. But now our generation is against marriage—because that's what we've been taught."

"By whom?"

"By the people we meet and care about."

"Linda, you *do* want to marry Keith, don't you?"

"Maybe. But if he thought I felt that way I'd lose him. That is, if I haven't already."

"But what's happened?"

"He never came home that night. He called and said he's decided to live at that filthy commune for a while so he can think things out. He knows I'm against his being in that play. He hadn't told me which play it was that day in the office. Look, if nudity is important to a plot, if it's realism, then okay. But the way they're doing it in that play—" She shook her head. "But I know what's really bugging Keith. It's the fact that I earn thirty-five thousand a year plus a Christmas bonus and he earns thirty-five hundred a year including his unemployment insurance. To him I'm Establishment. I'm so mixed up. Look, I've tried to do it his way. I've sat with his friends. I've drunk beer instead of martinis. I've worn dungarees instead of slacks. But there's no law that says I have to live like a pig. I pay four hundred a month for my apartment. It's in a good neighborhood, in a good building, with a doorman and elevator operators. I'm in my office every morning before eight and sometimes I don't leave until midnight. I've earned the right to have a nice place to come home to. Why should I give it up and work on some underground newspaper for fifty bucks an article?"

"Is that what he wants you to do?"

"All I know is he's always putting down me, *Gloss* and every article I dream up. But he raves about a guy he knows who sells dirty poems to newspapers that run pictures of a man's penis on the cover. He claims the man is writing because he has something to say and isn't looking for plastic glory. I tell you I'm so sick of all these phrases. But I love him and I want him. It's not that I'm forcing him to do things my way . . . but if only we could compromise. I know we could have a great life together. I want it. Oh, God, I want it!"

"It must be a good feeling to really know what you want," January said.

"Don't you? Didn't they give you any direction at that fancy Swiss University? By the way, what was the name of the school? Sara will at least want your college credits."

"Linda, I'll tell you all about it . . . after dinner."

They sat over coffee and Linda listened silently as January told her about the Clinique. She sipped some brandy and tears came to her eyes when January had finished. "Jesus," she said softly. "You really had the shit kicked out of you. Three years out of your life . . . three years of waiting to come back to Daddy Dream Man. And then to find him married . . ."

January managed a smile. "Well, it's not as if he's deserted me. He isn't my lover."

"Isn't he?"

"Linda!"

"Oh, come on, January. You didn't sleep with that divine Italian who was responsible for you breaking your skull. You rejected David Milford. Any psychiatrist

Linda raised her glass. "You also know you have to leave in ten days and you're getting panicky."

January raised her glass and smiled. "To your trip, Mr. Bailey. And to you, Linda."

Linda shook her head. "No, this one's for you. Here's to Ms. January."

SEVEN

JANUARY SAT propped up in the Castro bed, surrounded by a pile of back issues of *Gloss*. She was working on her first assignment, an article called "Breakfasts of the 'B.T.W.'" B.T.W. stood for Beautiful Thin Women. She hadn't been able to get to Babe Paley or Lee Radziwill. But Dee had given permission to quote her as saying, "*Who* gets up before lunch! Only children eat breakfast." She also had quotes from a skinny lady poet, a skinny screen starlet, and a writer who was a militant member of Women's Lib. She was still trying to contact Bess Meyerson and Barbara Walters. Did Barbara Walters eat breakfast *before* or *after* the *Today* show? Just trying to reach these people was practically a full-time assignment.

She had made a careful study of all the current articles in the leading magazines and found the stories that caught her attention had openings that hooked the reader. She had tried ten different approaches, but none of them seemed right. Of course Linda expected to put a rewrite girl on it, but January wanted to surprise her and have the article stand on its own. Working on the magazine had given her the first identity she had ever known. The little windowless cubbyhole she went to every day was *her* office. Mr. Bailey's sublet was now *her* apartment. She paid the rent with money *she* earned.

The past three weeks had been hectic. But they had

been three weeks of being on her own; making her own decisions. Getting through the first week had been the roughest. Especially breaking the news to Mike and Dee that she was moving. Dee's eyes had narrowed angrily, but before she could voice any objection, Mike had cut in and said, "I figured you'd want your own pad. Most girls do. And if that's what you really want . . . well, you sure as hell are entitled to it."

Dee insisted on looking at the apartment before January signed the lease. Edgar Bailey seemed stunned when she walked in. "Oh, Miss Granger . . . I mean Mrs. Wayne . . . Oh . . . I had no idea January was your daughter." January knew he was ready to collapse for settling for two hundred and twenty-five dollars.

"You mean it only has *one* room?" Dee asked.

"But it's so spacious," Edgar Bailey insisted. "And I'm so pleased to have someone like January live among my things in my little home."

Dee walked past him, pulled the drapes and groaned. "Good Lord, January. It's on the court!"

"A garden?" Edgar Bailey said timidly.

"No sunlight and only one room. But I suppose this is the new generation." Dee sighed. "Leave a luxury apartment for a slum."

Edgar Bailey came to life. "Mrs. Wayne, this is a very fine building."

Dee waved him off. "Well, I suppose we could make it more cheerful. Get rid of those awful drapes . . . change the rug . . . get some new throw pillows—"

"Mrs. Wayne." Mr. Bailey's voice cracked in near hysteria. "Nothing can be changed. Those drapes were made for me by—"

But Dee had already disappeared into the kitchen, and January followed her after quickly assuring Mr. Bailey that everything would stay intact and that she adored venetian blinds and his flowered drapes.

She had signed the lease and moved in October first. David sent her a Dracaena plant. Mr. Bailey had left a small bunch of rosebuds (which never did bloom), along with a little note wishing her luck. Linda sent her note-paper from Bergdorf's engraved with her name and her address. And at five o'clock, Mike arrived with a bottle of champagne. They drank it over the rocks, and Mike looked at the apartment with a smile. "Know something? I think it's great. You've been living with people all your life. In school, at the hospital. It's time you had some privacy."

Dee arrived at seven to pick him up. They were going to an exhibition at an art gallery, but she brought a basket of cocktail hors d'oeuvres. "You never know when you might need them. There are several tins of smoked oysters . . . now don't make a face. David adores them. You just put them on these little imported crackers. By the way, David also adores what I call rat cheese. Cut it in cubes and put toothpicks in it and he's happy as a clam. Which reminds me—how are you two getting on?"

"He sent that plant," January answered.

Dee smiled complacently. "Mike and I are leaving for a quick trip to Europe. There's a backgammon tournament in London that I'm entering. We'll be back soon. But we feel dreadful leaving you here with this grubby little apartment and job. Before I leave, is there anything I can do, other than reveal for your magazine that I don't eat breakfast?"

January hesitated. "Is . . . is Karla in town?"

"Why do you ask?"

"I'd love to do an interview with her."

Dee's laugh was cold. "She never does interviews. And it's not that she's pulling a Garbo or a Howard Hughes. She's just a stupid Polack. Oh, come now, January. Don't give me one of those 'everyone is equal' looks. I know Karla, and she is stupid. She's never read a book. She's never voted. She isn't aware of anything that's going on except her own creature comforts. She's in town. She called the other day. But to tell you the truth I've been too busy to see her. A little bit of Karla goes a long way. I mean, she won't lunch anywhere civilized. If she comes to dinner one must give her the entire guest list. It's ridiculous. It's not as if she's Nureyev or Princess Grace. She's just a has-been actress who

for some insane reason still attracts incredible publicity."

So much for an interview with Karla.

She had written David a note thanking him for the
plant. He had called and told her he was going out of
town on business but would call her as soon as he returned. That was ten days ago. She went to dinner with
Linda or some of the other girls at the office. But she
was perfectly content to come home and work on her
article and read. She bought a portable typewriter and
taught herself to type with two fingers. Linda saw Keith
occasionally, but they weren't officially "back together."
He stayed at her apartment most of the time but insisted on keeping his things at the "commune." "Personally, I think he only stays with me because he likes
my stall shower," Linda confided. "We're together . . .
but it's just not the same." She refused to go downtown
to see the show, but she did go along with the new
health kick Keith was on. Organic food, twenty different
vitamins a day, plus massive vitamin shots twice a week
from a new doctor Keith swore was a genius. Obviously
it worked, because Linda, who had always been enthusi-
astically energetic, was now supercharged. She never
seemed to sleep. Sometimes she'd call January at three
in the morning and shout, "Hey, don't tell me you're
asleep! There's a divine Bogart movie on Channel Nine."

Mike had sent a card announcing that Dee was in the
finals of the tournament. Somehow it didn't sit right.
Mike, the gambler of all time, standing by, watching his
wife throw the dice.

Now as she sat in the Castro bed, trying to get an
opening paragraph, she found herself wondering if it was
possible to write an amusing article without being
bitchy. She stared at the quote she had from the vapid-
faced model turned actress who had just made her first
(and last) movie. Her part had been cut to ribbons because of her flat delivery, but she didn't seem to mind.
"Oh, they were so nice to me out there. They got me
real calves' liver for breakfast and I've never been more
thinner." God, what Sara Kurtz would do with a quote
like that.

She sighed and went to her typewriter. Even Dee's quote sounded snide. Yet when she had said it in her lazy way it had been amusing.

She put a fresh piece of paper into the machine and made a stab at a new opening. Maybe if she said the model was anemic and *had* to have liver . . . or maybe if she started it with, "The reason Deirdre Wayne is so beautiful . . ." No. She tore the paper out. There had to be a better way to get into it.

She was just putting in a fresh piece of paper when the phone rang. The sound vibrated through the room. She had forgotten to turn the bell to low. Probably Linda with another flash about a Bogart picture. She couldn't believe it when she heard the familiar, "Hi, babe!"

"Daddy! Where are you?"

"P. J. Clarke's!"

"What!"

"We just got off the plane, and I had a big yen for chili. So we came here right from the airport. How about joining us? I'll send the car for you."

"Oh, I'd love to. But I'm undressed and I'm working on a story that has to be done by the end of the week."

"You really writing it?"

"Yes. And I think it's going to be all right."

"Hey, that's really great. Well, I'd better get back to Nick the Greek—that's my new name for Dee. The broad came in third and won fifteen thousand dollars. How about having lunch with me tomorrow? Just the two of us." He was shouting above the noise in the restaurant.

"Oh, Mike, I'd love it."

"Well, you dream up wherever you want to go. I'll call you at the magazine at noon. Oh, wait a second. Dee's coming over. I think she wants to say Hello."

"January . . ." It was Dee's crisp voice.

"Congratulations! I'm very impressed," January said.

"Oh, we had a marvelous time. Are you coming here?"

"No. I told Mike . . . I'll all piled up here with work."

Dee laughed. "Oh, you big career girl. Oh, Mike . . ." Dee's voice went off the phone. "Better get back to our table. Someone might grab it. Order your bloody chili and a spinach salad for me. January, are you still there?"

"Yes, and you're making me hungry."

"It's a mob scene here tonight. I don't know why everyone is suddenly staring at the door. Someone must be coming in. Probably Onassis and Jackie. Tell me, January. Are you having a marvelous time living your career-girl life?"

"I'm enjoying it, Dee. I think I can really write . . . a little."

"Well, that's nice and—" Dee's voice had suddenly trailed off. At the same time January heard a great swell of voices from the people at P.J.'s.

"Dee . . . are you still there?"

"Yes . . ." Dee's voice seemed strained.

"Are you all right?"

"Yes . . . I'm fine. Tell me, January. When was the last time you saw David?"

"Why, I—"

"There's a near riot here—he's just walked in with my old friend Karla."

"Karla at P.J.'s?"

"Oh, she does that now and then—pops up where no one would ever expect her." Dee's voice was easy. "But don't you fret, darling. Karla's no competition for you."

"I'm not fretting, Dee. Actually I'm very impressed with David."

"You go back to . . . whatever you're doing, angel. I'll take care of things. It will take me a few days to get organized now that I'm back. So why don't we plan on brunch . . . Sunday . . . around one-ish."

January hung up. She wasn't bothered about David being with Karla. But she was bothered that he was back in town and hadn't called her. She went back to her typewriter, but she couldn't concentrate on the article. She got up and went to the kitchen for a Coke. She saw the new watering can she had bought for David's Dracaena. She had just watered it yesterday. The florist said it should only be watered twice a week. She grabbed the

can and filled it. Then she marched into the living room
and poured it on the plant. "Drown, you bastard," she
said. "Drown! Drown!!"

When Dee came out of the phone booth she managed
to collide accidentally with David and Karla who were
heading toward a small table in the back of the room.

"Karla, I can't believe it. You, braving P.J.'s," Dee
said lightly.

Karla smiled. "There was a showing of *Red Shoes* at a
little movie house near here. I have seen it so many many
times, and always it is entrancing. And it was such a
beautiful night I wanted to walk. And then I got hungry." She turned and looked at Mike, who had left the
table and come to Dee's side. "And is this your handsome new husband?"

"Yes, and you are a lady I've always wanted to meet,"
Mike said.

Karla held out her hand. "And now . . . you see
how easily it has happened."

"How long are you staying in town?" Dee asked.

Karla shrugged her broad shoulders. "That is the
lovely part about not working. I stay where I like . . .
as long as I like."

"We're opening the house in Palm Beach in about ten
days. Perhaps you'd like to come down. I can give you
the east wing you had before."

Karla smiled. "That is so kind. Perhaps I shall . . .
Or perhaps I go to Gstaad to ski. Who knows? But even
ten days is so far off. Right now I can only think of my
stomach and I am very hungry." She turned to Mike. "It
was so very nice to meet you." Then she smiled and
walked off to her table with David following.

Dee sat down with Mike and rummaged through her
bag for her cigarette case. "Mike, I don't like to pry,
but do you think January has discouraged David?"

He smiled. "Karla is heavy competition."

"Ridiculous. Karla is old enough to be David's
mother." Dee sighed. "I thought David would be mad
for January. They look so perfect together."

"Dee, I learned a long time ago that looking the part doesn't always mean you can play it."

"But January should try to encourage him. After all, she's not a baby. She'll be twenty-one in a few months."

He laughed. "That's not exactly over the hill. Besides, the girls of today don't rush into marriage. Half of them don't even believe in it."

"January is not today's girl. She's caught between two worlds. The isolated one she just left . . . and the new one she doesn't quite know how to enter. If she ever really fell in love and it didn't work out, she could crack up."

"She's not going to crack up, and it seems to me she's adjusted just great. She's got a job, her own apartment. What more do you want? She's only been here a little over a month. Look, you can't wrap people up like Christmas packages. And that goes for David as well as January." He looked toward the back of the room. "Karla is one hell of an exciting woman."

"She's a stupid uneducated peasant."

He shook his head. "You dames really kill me. She's been to your place in Marbella, she's been on your yacht, you've just invited her to Palm Beach . . ."

"Darling, I always have houseguests. It's always good to have a 'live-in' celebrity. Besides, I feel sorry for Karla. She's really a very lonely lost soul."

He started to laugh. "What strikes you so funny?" Dee demanded.

"You women, the way you waste your pity. Worrying about January 'getting on,' Karla being lost and lonely. Look, my daughter will find her own way. And as for Karla, she's far from being lost. It's easy to see why David would go for her."

"Really?" Dee's voice was cold. "Then why did you ever wind up with plain old me?"

He reached out and patted her hand. "Sweetheart, I cut my teeth on the top beauties in Hollywood. And you're something special. The question is . . . why did you want me?"

"Because—" and her eyes grew distant.

"Because what?"

"Because I loved you," she said seriously. "Oh, I know we could have been together without marriage. But I think that kind of thing is grubby. I'm not old-fashioned. God, the way things are today, you're labeled archaic if you have *any* standards. If you have money you're supposed to play it down. If you have a luxurious home you're committing some kind of crime. But what's wrong with having a big estate? I keep a full staff of servants at all my places all year round. I'm giving these people work. The pilots of my plane have families. I'm responsible for their children being able to go to college. The captain of my boat gets paid fifty-two weeks a year and so does the crew. When I give big parties in Palm Beach I'm giving work to caterers, musicians, designers . . . I like to wear beautiful clothes . . . I like to see other people wearing them. I like gracious dining and pretty people. I hate this place and all places like it that people claim are so 'in.' And when I see Karla walk in here I know it's not just a casual evening with David. Even a woman like Karla gets lonely. It's no fun living alone. David could offer Karla an exciting life, sex, good companionship—all the things I want for your daughter."

Mike glanced over at Karla. David was whispering something in her ear. "Well, it looks like David has his own ideas."

Dee stared straight ahead. "It's up to January to change his ideas."

"Really?"

"Oh, Mike, don't you know that a woman can make a man think her idea was really *his*?"

"She can?"

"I bet you thought you wooed and won me," she said.

"Well, if I didn't, I sure wasted a lot of money in Marbella."

"I'll tell you a secret," she said. "I decided to marry you the second evening we spent together. I just had to let you go through the motions."

He laughed and signaled for the check. "I still don't know how I got so lucky." He leaned across the table and took her hands. "Why, Dee? I mean, why did you pick me?"

Her eyes met his and held them. "Because I wanted you. And I always try to get what I want."

David arrived at the Côte Basque at one the following day. Dee's call had come at ten that morning. "David darling, I'd love to see you. How about having lunch today?" For the rest of the morning he had definite signs of an ulcer attack.

They sat at a banquette table. He asked all the proper questions. About the backgammon tournament, about London, about the new shows she had seen in the West End. He sat there with a forced smile, waiting for the whiplash. But when they finished lunch and her conversation drifted to the current state of the market, he lit a cigarette and began to relax. Maybe she just had no luncheon date. Maybe it was just his own guilt that made him so uptight. He signaled for the check. In a few more minutes it would all be over. He'd walk through that door and out into the sunlight.

She struck just as he was signing the check. "David . . . what is this thing with you and Karla?"

He kept his hand steady as he continued to write. (Two dollars for the captain . . . four dollars for the waiter.) He felt a pulse beat in his neck and wondered if she could see it. He took longer than was necessary to put away his pen, and when he spoke he hoped his voice sounded casual and light.

"I think she's great fun to be with . . . we have a lot of laughs."

"Oh, come off it, dear boy. Karla is anything but a bundle of laughs. In fact she can be quite dreary." She shook her head. "I can understand that thing you had with that divine Dutch girl—Kim something or other— even if she does walk into Raffles with a see-through blouse. At least *she* has something to show. But when a young man is seen tagging around after an older woman . . . people do talk."

"Oh . . . what do they say?"

"That she's giving him money, that he's impotent and

is just her escort—or that he's gay." Dee's smile was almost melancholy. "I don't have to tell you, because we've all said the same thing about others."

"That's ridiculous," he said.

"*You* know it's ridiculous and *I* know it's ridiculous. But people do talk."

"We just have fun together, that's all. She likes being with me," he said doggedly.

Dee's laugh was merry, but her eyes were cold. "Don't be ridiculous. She's not capable of enjoying anyone's company. But she just might be interested in a young man who she thinks will wind up with a big inheritance." She opened her cigarette case and waited while David fumbled for a match. She exhaled the smoke slowly and stared at the cigarette. "I really should give these things up . . . I hear Nina Creopopolis has emphysema . . . which reminds me . . . what do you think of Becker, Neiman and Boyd?"

"They're a pretty fair law firm. Why?"

"I'm thinking of using them. I want to draw up a new will."

"Why? I mean, I thought Dad handled everything like that for you. Look, not just because he's my father . . . but you can't compare Becker, Neiman and Boyd to Dad's firm."

"You're prejudiced, darling." She patted his hand. "But I like that. God knows, no one is more family-oriented than I. But I should get an outside opinion. This change in my will isn't like the others. I need some very sophisticated advice. After all, I have a husband and a stepdaughter. I care about them, David. I really do. I must see that they are provided for."

"Of course." (Oh God, his voice had cracked. Now she knew he was scared. He turned to her with his best "young and earnest" look.) "Dee, you know it would break Dad's heart if you switched to another firm."

"And would it break your heart if I switched to another brokerage house?"

He didn't even try to answer. His hand shook as he lit his own cigarette. No more playing cat and mouse.

The mouse was caught and the cat was beginning the game of teasing it to death.

She leaned over and kissed his cheek. "Well, so far I'm just thinking. That's all. Just thinking."

He walked her to her car, and she pretended not to notice the photographer from *Women's Wear* who snapped her. She held her cheek for him to kiss and said, "I've enjoyed our lunch, David. It's good to keep in touch like this. I like to keep my family happy . . . and together."

He stared after her until her car disappeared into traffic. Then he went to the nearest phone booth and called January.

EIGHT

MIKE WAS MIXING Bloody Marys when January arrived at the Pierre for Sunday brunch. She had seen Mike, but this was the first time she had seen Dee since her return from London. Dee put down the *Times* crossword puzzle and held her cheek to January. "I don't know why I bother with this damn thing," she said. "I started it last night, and I actually lose sleep over it. And really there's no great achievement in getting it done. I know some of the dreariest people who whizz through it. Of course, most of them use a dictionary. But that's cheating. Now . . . sit down, and tell us all about the job. Is it fun?"

"Yes, they accepted my article. I'm really excited about it. Of course, it has to be edited—I don't punctuate too well—but Linda and the whole staff said it was really good. I hope you both like it."

Dee smiled. "I hope you aren't taking this job so seriously that you're neglecting your social life."

"Well, I do get up every morning at seven. And I rarely leave the office before seven at night."

"Why, that's slave labor," Dee said.

"You're much too skinny," Mike said as he handed her the drink. "I bet you're skipping meals."

"Oh, I eat a lot. Last night I had a fabulous meal . . . even cherries jubilee. I was with David."

Dee's reaction was merely polite interest. "And how is my handsome young cousin?"

"Fine. We went to the St. Regis to see Veronique."

"Veronique? Is she still around doing her third-rate Edith Piaf act?" Dee asked.

January shrugged. "I never saw her before. But she has a great act. She has three Russian dancers with her. Young men. And one of them had the sex change operation . . . in reverse. I mean, he *was* a girl—now she's a man."

"Now, January—" Dee's tone was a gentle reprimand. "One mustn't give lip service to dirty little rumors like that. I know they're the kind of stories your magazine likes to play up, but—"

"You're so right. I wish I could get a story on 'Nina into Nicholas.' I tried my damnedest last night!"

"Don't tell me you actually talked to this creature."

"Of course. Upstairs in Veronique's suite."

Dee put down her drink. "But how did you get to her suite? Is Veronique a friend of David's?"

"No . . . Karla's."

"Karla!" Dee's voice went up an octave.

"Yes. You see, David had a reservation for a table for two and when we got there they had us stuck behind a post. Then this young Greek man came over and introduced himself and said he and his friend were with Karla and that Karla would like us to join them. She had a wonderful table in a secluded alcove but with a perfect view of the floor. And she is so beautiful. In fact I was so busy staring at her that I almost missed seeing Nina-Nicholas. Then after the show Karla took us up to Veronique's suite and Nina-Nicholas was there. She . . . or he . . . talks about it openly. Linda says she'll raise my salary if I can get an interview for *Gloss*. But Nina-Nicholas says all the magazines have asked her . . . even offered to pay for her story."

"I think vanity might be the key," Mike said. "Tell him or her that you'll do a color photo layout by a top man and give him the pictures and the color plates. And maybe spring for some wardrobe like a Cardin outfit . . . there are a lot of ways to soften someone."

January sighed. "That's just it—we haven't got that kind of a budget."

"January," Dee cut in. "Tell me—what happened after the show?"

"Well . . . we had a drink in Veronique's suite and—"

Sadie came in and announced that brunch was served. They went into the dining room. Mario served them, and Mike insisted January take some sausage. "You can use it. I don't like you this thin."

Dee smiled with a show of good nature. Then she said, "You were telling us about Veronique."

"Oh . . . well." January swallowed the sausage. "It was as if we were suddenly transported into a foreign country. Everyone had a different accent. Veronique is French, Karla's accent is sort of Middle-European, the two Greek boys had accents, and Nina-Nicholas is Russian. So everyone used French as the common denominator, which was fine for me. Only poor David didn't understand a word."

"Where did you go after that?" Dee asked.

"Nowhere. Karla went off with the Greek boys and David took me home because he's playing squash this morning at nine."

Dee was silent for a moment. She stabbed at her eggs, then put down her fork. "I'm so furious I can't eat."

"What's wrong?" Mike went on buttering his toast.

"Your daughter being dumped before midnight so David could go off to Westport with Karla."

"What makes you say that?" Mike asked.

"I talked to Karla yesterday. She told me she was leaving for Westport last night for one last weekend in the country before it gets too cold. Don't you see . . . this was all planned. Karla never goes to a supper club. She never goes anywhere. Sure, she knows Veronique . . . but she refused to go to a party honoring Nureyev, whom she really admires, because of her fetish about crowds. But because David obviously felt he had to see January, they decided this whole thing between them— a lovely way to kill two birds with one stone. Karla would see Veronique for old times' sake, and at the same time David could take January on a date. Then January would be dumped . . . and the two of them drive off to Westport."

Mike's jaw tightened but he continued to eat. "If David wants to go off for a weekend, I think that's his business."

"And make a fool of your daughter for a woman more than twice her age."

Mike stopped eating and pushed his plate away. His voice was quiet and even. "Dee, I think you ought to let people make their own decisions and live their own lives."

January wished she could suddenly vanish. Dee was actually angry, and Mike's jaw was getting that clenched look. In an effort to break the mood, she said lightly, "Listen, both of you . . . I had a marvelous time . . . really. David and I got on just fine and—"

"Then why did you let that Polack walk off with him?" Dee demanded.

January held on to the table until her knuckles went white. She had enjoyed the evening with David . . . he had been warm and attentive. And now Dee was ruining it. It had never entered her mind that the Karla thing had been prearranged. David had seemed genuinely surprised to see her, and Karla had gone out of her way to be gracious and warm to her. She had asked about her job and given her permission to quote her as saying she ate oatmeal every morning for breakfast.

Now she suddenly had doubts. Had it all been arranged? Was David really in love with Karla? All this flashed through her mind as she watched the tension between Mike and Dee. Suddenly she knew she had to get out of there. It was dreadful enough to learn that she had been a "mercy date" with David. But to have Mike and Dee fight . . . over her! Talking about her as if she wasn't there. And how must she look to Mike? A real zero!

Her father's anger made Dee suddenly back down. Her lips trembled and she tried to manage a smile. A pleading tone crept into her voice. "Mike . . . I'm only trying to do things for her sake. Wasn't that your main concern when we got married? Didn't you tell me you wanted to be sure January had everything because of what she had gone through? All the good times she had missed?"

"That doesn't mean you have the right to run her life—to force her to date a man who obviously has other inclinations."

"Oh, good Lord. David told me that January was one of the most beautiful girls he had ever seen." She sighed. "Maybe I've tried too hard, because nothing seems to have worked. I planned that beautiful bedroom for January and she walked out on it. I had planned we'd all spend the holidays together in Palm Beach. I thought I'd send the plane for January and David and we'd have a family thing there on Thanksgiving. And then on Christmas I want to give a big ball, as I did a few years ago. Fly in someone like Peter Duchin. Invite Mayor Lindsay, Lenny, Rex . . . all the fun people. And I had hoped that January and David would announce their engagement by then—"

"That's all very nice," Mike said. "But maybe it's not what January wants."

"How can she know what she wants?" Dee's voice went cold. "She's got to be taught to want the right things."

"For three years she had to be taught just to walk and talk," Mike shouted. "From now on it's her ballgame."

Dee's eyes narrowed. "All right! Let her work at that dingy magazine. Let her live in that third-rate apartment house. I'm not going to try anymore. Why should I knock myself out when you're both such ingrates? Neither of you even knows how to enjoy the nice things in life. Let her freeze in New York this winter. I'm not going to beg her to come to Palm Beach."

"Maybe I won't go to Palm Beach either," Mike said.

"Oh really?" Dee said softly. "Tell me, Mike, what will you do? Move out of here? Find a big apartment for yourself and your daughter. Produce a hit Broadway show. Amass a fortune to leave her from all your *hits*! Go ahead. Why should I even bother to try to get her married. *You* can give her the world. Go on! Produce a show . . . a picture . . . give her back her dreams."

January saw the color drain from her father's face. She stood up. "Mike . . . you've made all my dreams come true. You don't have to do another thing. I'm a big girl now. I love my work on the magazine. And from now on, I have to make my dreams come true on my own. I'd love to come to Palm Beach on Thanksgiving. Really, I'm looking forward to it. And Dee . . . honest . . . I appreciate all you've done. I loved the room you offered me. It's just that—well—I have to be on my own now. And David is very nice. In fact, he's one of the nicest people I've ever met . . . and you both mustn't quarrel over me." She stopped. They were sitting, stiff and motionless, staring at each other. She backed away from the table. "Look, I have to run. I promised Linda I'd help on the planning of some new articles for the magazine." She kissed her father. His cheek felt as if it had turned to stone. Then she dashed out of the apartment.

Mike never looked after her. He stared at Dee, frozen with rage. When he spoke his voice was low and controlled. "You just cut off my balls in front of my daughter."

Dee laughed nervously. "Oh, stop it, Mike . . . let's not fight. We never have before."

"And never will again!"

She came to him and put her arms around him. Her voice was silky but her eyes were frightened. "Mike, you know I love you . . ."

He shoved her away and left the table. She ran after him as he headed for the bedroom. "I'll be packed and out in an hour."

"Mike!" She grabbed his arm as he pulled a suitcase from the closet. But he shook her off. "Mike—" she pleaded. "Forgive me . . . please . . . please forgive me . . . don't go. Please don't go!"

He stopped and looked at her curiously. "Tell me something, Dee . . . why *did* you marry me?"

"Because I love you." She wound her arms around his neck. "Oh, Mike . . . our first quarrel and it's my fault. Forgive me. Please, angel. It's not right for us to fight. It's because of your daughter." He pulled away but she ran after him. "Mike, I never had a child . . . I'm probably stepping out of line because of my eagerness to treat January like a daughter. I'm probably going about it all wrong . . . saying all the wrong things . . . being overbearing . . . overprotective . . . as I am with David. I never had a brother or sister . . . he's been like a son to me. And now with January . . . I guess I pushed too hard. It's just that I want her to be happy. And for us to fight is ridiculous. We both say things we don't mean. It's David and Karla I'm angry at . . . not you." Her panic mounted as he continued to throw things into his bag. "Mike . . . don't . . . please! I love you. How can I prove it? I'll call January and apologize. I'll do anything!"

He stopped and looked at her. "Anything?"

"Yes."

"Okay. I never asked you for a thing, did I? I even signed a premarital agreement that if I divorced you I wouldn't get a dime. Right?"

"I'll tear it up," she said.

"No, keep it. I don't want a cent. But from now on —cut all this talk about how you love January and how concerned you are about her future. Put your money where your mouth is!"

"What do you mean?"

"I want to know that if some day I drop dead watching you play backgammon, my daughter is going to be a rich young lady."

"I promise. I'll do it tomorrow. I'll leave her a million dollars in trust."

He stared at her and his eyes were hard. "That's chicken shit."

"What do you want?"

"Ten million."

She hesitated a moment, then nodded slowly. "All right . . . I promise. Ten million."

He smiled slightly. "And from now on, cool it on David. That's an order. If he has a thing for Karla, it will have to burn out on its own and not because you

demand it. But in any event, I'm not having January
shoved at him. Remember that!"

"I promise."

"And I don't want any cracks about her job. Goddammit, she's trying. She's got ambition, and when you
lose that, baby, you've really cashed in your chips."

"I promise, Mike." She put her arms around him and
kissed his neck. "Now come on . . . smile. Don't be
angry."

"You gonna stay out of her life and not butt in?"

"I'll never mention her name to David again."

"And the ten million you promised to lay on her is
also a deal."

She nodded.

He stared at her for a moment, then he swept her
up and tossed her on the bed. "Okay. Now that we've
had our first fight . . . let's fuck and make up."

David arrived at the Racquet Club five minutes early.
His father's voice had sounded urgent. That meant
trouble. Just when everything was going so great. Usually he hated Mondays, but he had awakened this
morning feeling he owned the world. His date with January at the St. Regis had gone off without a hitch. She
had bought the idea that running into Karla was an
accident. She was even pleased about it . . . like a
fan. And she certainly had no inkling that at midnight
he and Karla had driven to Westport. Even now, he felt
light-headed just thinking about it. It was the first time
he had ever spent an entire night with her. He'd never
get over the unbelievable sight of Karla in the kitchen
the following morning, making him bacon and eggs. It
had been the greatest twenty-four hours of his life. She
had borrowed the country place from a friend and their
privacy was perfect. The house was set back in the midst
of six acres of its own property. Even the weather had
cooperated. Sunday had been one of those rare days
when autumn lives up to all of its poetic descriptions.
To him autumn had always meant the beginning of winter. Early dusk; a gray rainy day on Wall Street; a dusty
wind and no taxis. But autumn on a country road in

Westport was an explosion of colored leaves that crunched underfoot, clear air and the feeling of complete isolation from the world.

And this had been a good Monday. The good weather had followed them into the city. Even New York's rancid air seemed cleaner. The market had closed up three points for a change, and at three o'clock she had called to tell him he could escort her to Boris Grostoff's. That meant he had really made her inner circle. Boris had been her favorite director and his small intimate dinners numbered among the few parties Karla attended.

He saw his father enter and rose to greet him. The old man waited until their drinks arrived. Then he came right to the point.

"What does January Wayne look like?"

David was startled by the question. "January? Why . . . she's beautiful."

"Really?" His father seemed surprised. He sipped his Scotch thoughtfully. "Then why is Dee so frantic about her?"

"I don't understand, sir."

"She was in my office this morning to change her will. Her main concern seems to get this stepdaughter married. I figured the girl might be awkward-looking . . . or unattractive."

David shook his head. "Actually she's one of the most beautiful girls I've ever seen."

His father reached into his pocket and took out a slim leatherbound notebook. "I jotted down some of the changes she wants in the will. It's in the process of being drawn up."

"Do they concern me?"

"Very much. You are no longer an executor of the estate."

David felt the blood rush to his face. "She cut me out!"

"I've been bruised also. Our office is now sharing the executor powers along with Yale Becker of Becker, Neiman and Boyd. But the door is still open for you, my boy—there's a provision that *if* before Dee's death, David Milford is married to someone who has met with her approval, he will then become an executor and head the foundation."

"Why, that bitch," David said softly.

"Oh, there's more," his father answered. "Her step-daughter, January Wayne, will inherit one million dollars *when* she marries, and *ten* million is to be put in trust for her, to be paid out on the occasion of her father's death—or Dee's, should she predecease him."

"I can't believe it," David said.

"I can't either," his father said. "Of course, it's not an irrevocable trust. Dee can always change it. Odd that Mike Wayne didn't think about that. Well, I guess it's obvious that the man's sophistication does not extend to the drawing up of a will. I find his faith rather childlike, especially knowing Dee. But for the moment it will probably stand because it looks to me as if she's really in love with this man. This amazing generosity toward the daughter is pretty good insurance on his staying with her. One thing for sure—Mike Wayne seems to be running this marriage. And here's the odd part—he wants nothing for himself, just this unbelievable inheritance for his daughter. It made me think the girl was totally unmarriageable and that the money was the only way to buy her a husband."

David frowned. "She's shoved January at me right from the start. She wants the girl married and out of the way. I think for the first time in her life, Dee is really in love. Also, she likes to run things, likes to feel her power. And with Mike Wayne she has no power—just through his daughter."

"And she figured by getting her married to you, that would please him?"

"No. I think she wants January married because she thinks of her as a rival for Mike's affections."

"David, what on God's earth are you talking about?"

"I can't put my finger on it," David said slowly. "But that first night—several times I caught them looking at each other. January and her father. And there was an intimacy in their eyes . . . not like a father and daughter. I was January's date, but I actually felt he was my competition. Dee must have felt it too."

"But why would she cut you out as executor of her will?"

David smiled. "It's obvious she wants me to be the one to remove her competition. The bait is there . . . in black and white."

"Good Lord. Do you have a chance? I mean, has the girl taken a shine to you?"

"I don't know. I've taken her out. But—"

"Well, would you like to bring her to the house for dinner?"

"No, let me do it my way." He sighed. "Well, I guess men have given up more for ten million dollars."

"What are you giving up?" his father asked.

"Karla."

His father stared. "Good God! I was smitten with her when I was your age. Never missed one of her films. Twenty-five years ago I used to moon over her. But now . . . good Lord . . . she has to be your mother's age."

"Karla is only fifty-two."

"Your mother won't be fifty until February."

"I don't think of age when I'm with Karla. And it's not as if I intend to marry her. Look, Dad . . . I know it has to end. I know one day I'll wake up and suddenly I'll be bored with eating steaks in her kitchen and rushing to movies that I hate. And on that day I'll break all records with a fifty-yard dash to January Wayne."

"And do you think she'll be there waiting?"

David sighed. "I try to keep my hand in. I really do. But right now I can't give up Karla. Not yet . . ."

"Do many people know about this Karla affair?"

"No. She never socializes, except on rare occasions, like tonight. I'm escorting her to a director's house for dinner."

"That's exactly how you'll be known if this affair continues. An escort . . . to an ex-movie queen." His father leaned across the table. "Suppose keeping your hand in isn't enough for January. While you're busy with Karla, suppose January meets another man, a man who meets with Dee's approval. Perhaps even a broker at another brokerage house. And would this woman—

Karla—place her money in your hands and allow you to manage her funds?"

David shook his head. "She's known to be the tightest woman in the world."

His father nodded. "Then let's say she wouldn't exactly be an asset to you at the brokerage house."

David nodded. "You've made your point. And I have the distinct feeling that if I don't start really romancing little January, Cousin Dee's next move will be to change brokerage houses, too."

His father raised his glass. "Well, hop to it, son. Hop to it."

NINE

THE DANCE FLOOR at Le Club was crowded. David held January close and inched her around the floor. He had taken her to Le Mistral for dinner. Several times he had held her hand and had been agreeably surprised at her response. Dee and Mike would be leaving for Palm Beach in less than a week, and he was determined to have January report the wonderful turn their relationship had taken. And once Dee was gone, it would be harder for her to keep track of just how *many* glowing evenings they had together. But at least she'd know he was in there pitching.

Of course a great deal depended on January's reactions. He had to make her really fall in love with him. She was no Kim Voren. To Kim he represented not only a great stud, but security and a place in society. January didn't need any of that. No, he had to come on strong with her . . . in bed. Once you hooked them in the feathers, the rest was easy. He could leave Kim alone for ten days and she'd still jump when he called.

All he needed was time. He had told Karla that Dee was forcing him to take January around occasionally. Karla understood. He had a bad moment when he hinted that he might have to go to Palm Beach over the Thanksgiving holidays. And Karla had said, "Yes, Dee invited me too."

For a moment he had panicked. He could never manage that. In Karla's presence he acted like one possessed. Dee and January would spot it immediately. "Would you come?" he had tried to make his voice sound as enthusiastic as usual.

"No. Thanksgiving is not my holiday. Even though I became a citizen, I never quite got used to it. It is such an American holiday—like the Fourth of July."

But lately he had noticed a slight restlessness in her attitude. When she spoke of Europe, which she did quite frequently now, he felt a sick feeiing of foreboding. Yet deep down he knew his only salvation would be if she suddenly disappeared off the face of the earth. Because he now realized that this affair was never going to burn itself out . . . on his part. Sometimes he even had fantasies of her death. If she was irrevocably gone—only then could he settle down to the business of living his own life.

And even now as he held this beautiful girl in his arms on the crowded dance floor, he was thinking of Karla. It was wrong . . . sick. He'd always had complete control before. No woman had ever dominated him. Even in his wildest affairs he might have been carried away for a few weeks . . that was part of the fun and excitement of a new romance, but eventually he always got the upper hand and the woman began to want him more than he wanted her, and he, in turn, cooled off. But it hadn't happened with Karla. And he knew it never would.

But he had to become all-important to January. He had to make this girl want him, and need him, and *wait* for him. He wanted a little more time. He looked at her and smiled. She was really beautiful, even more beautiful than Kim. If he made his move tonight . . . would that be rushing her? *Rushing her!* It was November. He had known her almost two months. Kim had gone to bed with him the first night. And Karla the next afternoon. He had planned it for tonight. He had even bought the albums she liked.

Suddenly he felt slightly nervous. He hadn't gone after a girl in ages. They had always come after him! Suddenly he didn't quite know how to put it. Maybe he was

out of practice. Or maybe it was because January was
a cut above the girls around town. She didn't grope for
him under the table or say, "Let's go home and make
love."

He snapped to attention. She had asked him something.

"I hear it's always sold out, but if you have any problems, Keith Winters—he's a friend of Linda's—well, he
knows a boy in *Hair* who could get us house seats."

Hair! Christ, he had promised to take her to see that
show when she first came to New York. He smiled. "I'll
get a pair for next week. Our office has a good ticket
broker. Don't worry."

He had to score with her . . . tonight. It had to be all
set by the time they went to Palm Beach. His father said
Dee's new will had been all signed and witnessed. It
was now official. Of course if he married January everything would probably be changed . . . or even if they
got engaged. He was possessed with a sudden feeling of
urgency. He took her arm and led her off the floor. "It's
impossible to talk here," he said. "Somehow we never
get to talk. We're always with people."

He helped her to her seat. Then she said, "We could
always go to Louise's."

He laughed. "No. Carmen the bartender and I are
both football nuts. We'd wind up discussing next Sunday's game. Look, why not come back to my apartment?
I have all the albums you said you like. Plenty of Sinatra
and Ella. We can have champagne and really talk."

To his amazement, she agreed without any pressure.
He signed the check and led her outside. Several people
he knew stared at her and signaled their approval to
him. Well, why not. She was goddamned beautiful! Tall
and streamlined and young and—young! He *had* to stop
thinking of Karla. Otherwise he just might not be all
that great tonight. After all, he probably had to follow
some pretty tough competition. She must have had
plenty of fancy European lovers when she was at that
Swiss college. Hell, she probably knew plenty before she
went there. Any girl who grew up around Mike Wayne
had to be a swinger. Look how fast she got a pad of her

own. And that artsy crowd she ran with at the magazine
. . . people like that reminded him of a plate of worms
—eventually everyone got around to doing it with everyone else.

Well, he'd get her hooked tonight. Then perhaps he
could manage it so they saw each other maybe two or
three nights a week. And maybe by spring become un-
officially engaged. But he had to hold her off as long as
he could . . . *why* did he have to hold her off! Karla
didn't really give a damn about his future. January *was*
his future! All right. But first things first. He'd make good
tonight. And he'd still have Karla. All he had to do was
keep his head.

January sat beside him in the cab as it sped up Park
Avenue. She knew he was going to try to make love to
her. And she was going to let him. She was curious about
the whole thing now. She was positive that once he held
her in his arms something marvelous would happen.
They'd ignite . . . and maybe she'd really fall in love.
She felt a certain attraction toward him, and Linda had
sworn that once he made love to her, everything would
be different. Linda had been stunned to learn she was a
virgin. And from the attitude of all the other girls on the
magazine, she was beginning to feel that virginity was
nothing to be proud of. It was almost like no one had
asked you to dance. She had taken her own private
poll: there was not one virgin at *Gloss*. Except the
thirty-one-year-old male theater critic; he had a German
accent and always had an eighteen-year-old girl on his
arm, but Linda had said the word was out that he was
a "self-satisfaction man."

Linda was sleeping with the art director now. Keith
hadn't called in a week and, as she put it, she had to
have a body next to her.

The cab stopped at Seventy-third Street. When they
reached his apartment, David seemed nervous as he
fitted the keys in all the safety locks on his door. Finally
he led her inside and switched on the lights. She took
off her coat and looked around. The living room was
nice enough—phony fireplace, lots of hi-fi speakers.
The bedroom door was open . . . Oh sweet Lord! A

round bed and red walls! She wanted to laugh. The jock's idea of a bordello.

He turned on the hi-fi, and the velvet voice of Nat King Cole floated through the room. Then he went to the bar and held up a bottle of Dom Perignon triumphantly. "When I heard you say you liked this, I bought a bottle the very next day. It's been waiting for you ever since." He began working with the cork. "I didn't really expect you tonight, so it isn't cold—we'll have to have it on the rocks." He walked over with the glass. "Well, what do you think of the apartment? No, don't answer. I know. The living room is Macy's version of Park Avenue and the bedroom is the socially correct young man's fantasy room." He stopped as he realized that Karla had never been to his apartment, and that the greatest fantasies of his life had been realized in Karla's bare bedroom in her prim narrow maple bed. He pushed her from his thoughts and managed a smile. "You know, when I grew up I had the typical boy's bedroom, decorated by my mother. Pennants on the wall, bunk beds until I was twelve, though God knows I was an only child and the only time the other bunk bed was occupied was when a cousin slept over."

He led her over to the couch and they sat down. Now Nat King Cole was singing "Darling, Je Vous Aime Beaucoup" softly and beguilingly. She stared at the champagne. Dom Perignon was for special occasions . . . She took a long swallow. Well, this was a damn big occasion, wasn't it? She was going to get laid!

She took another gulp from the large old-fashioned glass he had poured the champagne in. He was drinking from a smaller glass. She felt a stab of disappointment. She hadn't expected him to be so obvious . . . to try to get her drunk. No, she mustn't think like that. She wanted to fan the glimmer of attraction David held for her, not dissolve it. But Mike would never handle a woman in such an obvious way. Oh God! This was no time to think of him. She'd ruin the whole thing. She could just see his frown—"January, I wanted you to like the man but not this . . ." She wanted to run. Franco had been more attractive than David, yet when he had

touched her she had panicked. Oh, Lord. What was she
doing here? She could still leave . . . But then what?
Remain a virgin all her life? Tell Linda she had walked
out on David and Nat King Cole and Dom Perignon
and a round bed and red walls? She swallowed the rest
of the champagne. David jumped up to refill her glass.
This was crazy. Was she going to bed with David just
because Linda thought it was the thing to do? Or to
show Mike that she was a match for Karla. *Why* was she
doing this? Certainly not because she was in love with
him. But what did she know about love? What was her
basis of comparison? Linda said the kind of love she was
looking for only happened between Ingrid Bergman and
Bogie on the late show. Today that kind of love didn't
exist. Even her father had said he had never *loved*—he
loved sex. That's what it was all about. And she was *his*
daughter. She took the glass David offered her and sipped
it slowly. David was handsome. And once it got started
. . . she *would* enjoy it . . . and love him . . . and
. . . She smiled and held out her empty glass again.
Well, he wanted her to get tight, didn't he? He seemed
elated as he refilled her glass. But he still seemed slightly
nervous. He had finished his glass and now *he* was getting
a larger glass and was pouring champagne . . . to the
top.

The bottle was empty when Nat finished singing and
Dionne Warwick began purring the Bacharach-David
songs. January leaned her head back against the couch
and shut her eyes. She felt David kissing her neck.
Dionne was singing "Say a Little Prayer for Me." Yes,
Dionne. Say it for me . . . for January . . . I'm that
girl you met with my father in 1965. I was only fifteen
then and you told my father I was lovely. Tell me,
Dionne—were you in love the first time you did it? You
had to be to sing like this . . .

David was leaning over her now. He had finished with
her neck. Now he was nibbling at her ear. Oh God . . .
his tongue was in her ear. Was she supposed to like *that*!
It just felt cold and wet. Then he started on her mouth,
his tongue forcing her lips apart. She began to panic
when she realized she didn't like the sensation. His

tongue tasted rough. His hands were groping her breasts, fumbling for the buttons on her blouse. She hoped he didn't break them . . . it was her new Valentino shirt. But how do you tell a man you'll open your own blouse —you're supposed to be so carried away with passion that you're not supposed to even be noticing what he's doing.

When was she going to feel something? She tried to respond . . . she stroked his hair . . . it was stiff. He used hair spray! She mustn't think of things like that now. She opened her eyes to look at him. After all, he was good-looking. But he looked ridiculous with his eyes closed, sprawling all over the couch. Why couldn't they act sensible and walk into that horrible bedroom and get undressed and . . . and then what? Wasn't he sup- posed to hold her close and tell her he loved her instead of just biting her lips and tearing away at her best shirt? She noticed that the gold trim on his Gucci shoes had ripped his silk couch. For some reason that pleased her. Hey, she'd better get with it. . . . She closed her eyes . . . she wanted to feel romantic . . . she wanted to feel . . . oh, thank God, he had finally gotten her blouse open without breaking the buttons. Now he was fumbling with the back of her bra. He had real expertise there . . . only now it was up somewhere around her neck. Was she supposed to make some sort of a token protest—or pitch in and help him? She decided to pull away.

"Relax, little baby," David whispered as his head went to her breasts. He began licking each one gently and she felt her nipples harden . . . and the odd sensa- tion in her pelvic area. He pulled her to her feet, took off her blouse with one hand and fumbled with the zipper on her skirt with the other. Ah, he was good at that too . . . it dropped to the floor. He took off her bra. She was standing in her boots and stocking pants. He lifted her up and carried her into the bedroom. She could have walked. She would have preferred to walk. Five foot seven and weighed a hundred and ten. That was bone-thin according to fashion. But a hundred and ten plus boots must feel like a ton to a man trying to be Romeo. She tried not to think of her long silk skirt lying in a heap on the living room floor. Of her bra beside it. And her silk shirt crumpled somewhere on the couch. What did she do when it was over? Walk out there stark naked and start picking up her things? He tossed her on the bed. Then he pulled off her boots and her panty hose.

And then she was lying there completely nude and he was telling her she was beautiful. Now he was undressing. She watched him take off his pants . . . she saw the large bulge in his jockey shorts. He almost strangled himself as he tore off his tie. He took off his shirt—and then, triumphantly, his shorts. He smiled with pride and came to the bed. She stared at the huge angry penis standing erect against his stomach.

"It's a beauty, isn't it?" he asked.

She couldn't answer. It was the ugliest thing she had ever seen. All red . . . all those veins . . . it looked like it would burst.

"Kiss it . . ." He pushed it toward her face. She turned away. He laughed. "Okay . . . You'll want to kiss it before we're through . . ."

She fought off a feeling of hysteria. Where was this romantic sensation she had expected to feel? Why was she feeling only revulsion and panic?

He lay on top of her, supporting his weight on his elbows and mouthed her breasts. Then his hands began to explore between her legs. Involuntarily she clamped them together. He looked at her in surprise. "Is something wrong?"

"It's . . . it's just so light in here and . . ."

He laughed. "Don't you like to make love with the lights on?"

"No."

"The lady commands, I oblige." He went to the switch and turned off the lights. She stared at him as he walked toward her. This wasn't really happening. She wasn't lying on this bed, waiting to be taken by this . . . this stranger. Suddenly she realized she hadn't gone to the doctor Linda had suggested and gotten pills or a coil.

"David . . ." she began, but suddenly he was stabbing that throbbing thing between her legs. Pushing . . .

pushing . . . she felt his fingers everywhere . . . on her breasts . . . between her legs . . . pulling her legs apart . . . pushing into her. . . .

"David, I'm not on the pill," she said in a muffled voice as he tried to kiss her.

"Okay. I'll pull out in time," he muttered. He was breathing hard. Perspiration made his chest damp. And all the while he was trying to push that big thing into her. She felt its repeated thrust, repelled each time by its impact against a solid wall of muscle and tissue within her. Couldn't he see that it was impossible? But the thing only became more demanding . . . again and again. It was ripping her apart. Oh God, he was killing her! She bit her lips to keep from screaming and dug her nails into his back. She heard him mutter, "Great, eh, baby. Fuck me . . . Come on . . . fuck me!" Then there was a blinding pain as he finally tore through her. Unbearable pain as if he was crunching bone and muscle. Suddenly he pulled out of her and she felt a hot sticky liquid shoot onto her stomach. Then he fell on his back, holding his chest . . . gasping. The thing between his legs lay crumpled and inert like a dead bird.

Gradually his breathing came back to normal. He turned toward her and rumpled her hair. "Well . . . was it great, darling?" He reached for some Kleenex on the night table and put it on her stomach.

She was afraid to move. The pain was so intense she was frightened. Perhaps he had torn her apart. Linda had said it hurt a little in the beginning; she never said it would be agony. Like a robot she wiped her stomach. It was gooey. She longed to rush into a hot shower. But most of all she wanted to get away. He stroked her hair. "How about giving me some head, baby? Then we can do it again."

"Head?"

"Go down. . . ." He pushed her head toward the limp thing that now rested on the inside of his leg.

She jumped out of bed. "I'm going home!" Then she stopped when she saw the blood. It had made a violent blotch on the sheets and was running down her legs.

He sat up. "For God's sake, January, why didn't you tell me you had the curse!" He jumped out of bed and ripped off the sheet. "Oh, Christ . . . right through to the mattress."

She stood very still with her hand clamped between her legs. She felt that if she moved her hand, her insides would fall out. He turned and looked at her. "For God's sake, don't drip blood on the rug. There's some Tampax in the medicine closet."

She raced into the bathroom and locked the door. She took her hand away and nothing drastic happened. The bleeding had stopped. She took a towel and washed the blood off her legs. She felt sore and torn inside. The bright light over the medicine chest gave her face a yellow cast. She stared at herself in the mirror. Her eye makeup was streaked, her hair was a mess. She must dress and get out. She washed the makeup off her eyes. Then, draping another towel around her, she opened the bathroom door and dashed into the living room. He didn't even look up. He was still naked, but he had stripped the bed and was working furiously with cleaning fluid on the mattress.

She grabbed her clothes from the living room, picked up her boots and stocking pants from the bedroom, and rushed back to the bathroom. When she came out, the bed was still stripped, but he was dressed.

"Well, I'll just have to wait until it dries before I can tell," he said. "I'll probably have to call a cleaning service. Come on, I'll take you home."

He didn't speak until they were in the cab. Then he put his arm around her. Involuntarily she pulled away. He took her hand. "Look, I'm sorry if I was cross about the sheets. But they're Porthault, and you should have told me you had the curse. I know you've lived in Europe and some of those foreign characters like it. But I never wade through the red sea. Did you find the Tampax all right?"

"I don't have the curse," she said.

For a second he didn't understand. Then it hit him and he slumped in his seat. "Oh, my God! January, you aren't . . . I mean you weren't . . . oh, Christ! But whoever heard of a twenty-year-old virgin? Especially one who looks like you. I mean, you felt tight, but I figured because you were so slim and . . . oh, Jesus . . ." He wound up with a groan.

They drove for a few blocks while he sat and silently stared into space.

"Why are you so upset?" she asked.

"Because, dammit, I don't go around taking virgins."

"Unfortunately, someone has to," she said. "I remember a boy in Italy telling me that."

When they reached the corner of her street, he asked the driver to stop. "Look, let's go into that bar for a nightcap. I want to talk to you."

They both ordered a Scotch. She hated the taste of it but hoped it would make her sleepy. God, how she wanted to fall into a dead sleep tonight.

David made rings on the napkin with his glass. "I'm still in shock. But . . . look . . . I'm really proud that you selected me to be the first. And you won't be sorry. Next time I'll really make you happy. January . . . I . . . I really care for you a great deal."

"You do?"

"Yes."

"Well, that's fine. I mean I'm very flattered."

He reached over and took her hand. "Is that all you feel?"

"Well, David—I—" She stopped. She had been about to say, "I don't know you very well." That was wild. She had just gone to bed with him.

"January . . . I want to marry you. You know that, don't you?"

"No."

"No what?"

"No, I didn't know you wanted to marry me. I know that Dee wants you to marry me. But I didn't know you wanted to. I mean, this is all ridiculous, isn't it, David? We're strangers. We've been to bed together but we're strangers. We sit here trying to find things to say to one another and it shouldn't be like this. I mean, aren't you supposed to want to shout . . . to sing . . .

when you've had your first love affair? When you're in love isn't something marvelous supposed to happen?"

He looked past her and said quietly, "Tell me what you think it's supposed to feel like?"

"I don't know. But . . . well . . ."

"Like you never want the night to end?" he asked.

"Yes, I suppose so."

"And that you're afraid to leave because it's so wonderful that you want to own the person . . . be together every second."

She smiled. "Sounds like we've both been watching the same late movies on TV."

"January, will you marry me?"

She stared at her drink. Then she took a long swallow. She shook her head helplessly. "I don't know, David. I didn't feel anything for you and—"

"Look," he cut in. "Those things we both talked about. They don't really happen. Maybe for one night with kids strung out on pot . . . or people enmeshed in a clandestine love affair . . . or—"

"Or?" she asked.

"Or . . . well . . . if a teeny bopper meets her hero . . . someone she's always worshipped. I suppose every girl has her dream man . . . just as some men have dream girls. Most of us go through life never meeting or realizing our dream."

"Must we?" she asked.

He sighed. "Maybe it's better that way. Because if you ever get it, you might find it impossible to let go. And you can't hold a dream forever. You can't marry a dream. Marriage is something different—it takes two people who want the same things, two people who like one another." When she remained silent he said, "I . . . I love you, January. There . . . I've said it."

She smiled. "Saying it and meaning it are two different things."

"Don't you believe me?"

"I believe you're trying to sell yourself almost as hard as you're trying to sell me."

"Do you love me?" he asked.

"No."

"No? Then why did you come back with me tonight?"

"I wanted to fall in love with you, David. I thought maybe this would do it. But it hasn't . . ."

"Look . . . it's my fault. I didn't know you were a virgin . . . Next time it will be different. I swear."

"There won't be a next time, David."

For a moment he looked nonplussed. "You mean you don't want to see me again?"

"I'll see you . . . but I'm not going to bed with you."

He motioned for the waiter and paid the check. "Look, this is just a normal reaction after what's happened."

She stood up and he helped her into her coat. He held her arm as they walked down the street. "January, I'm not going to crowd you. I won't ask you to go to bed with me. I don't care if we wait months. Maybe you're right . . . let's get to know each other better. But I promise you—you're going to marry me. You're going to love me and want me . . . But we'll take it step by step. We'll spend Thanksgiving together in Palm Beach. We'll have four days and nights together. At least that will be a good start. And I promise—I'll never ask you to go to bed. When it happens, it will happen the way you want it. And as you fall asleep tonight . . . remember, I love you."

When she let herself into her apartment she ran the tub and tore off her clothes. She eased herself into the warm water . . . and tried to think of all the things David had said.

And it wasn't until later, as she lay in bed, trying to sleep, that she realized he had not even bothered to kiss her goodnight.

When she awoke the following morning, she found she had hemorrhaged during the night. Her first thought was to call Linda. But she realized she wasn't up to Linda at the moment. She could just see Linda's expression if she heard the story. She tore through the phone book and found the number of Dr. Davis, the gynecologist Linda had told her about. When she explained she was hemorrhaging, she was told to come right over.

Oddly enough the examination itself was easier than sitting before his desk, fully clothed, and telling him the cause of her condition. To her relief he explained that although it was rare to experience this kind of bleeding, nothing was really wrong. He gave her a prescription for the pill, and also for a sedative. Then he told her to go home and stay in bed for the rest of the day.

When she got back to her apartment there was a messenger ringing her doorbell. He had a small package from Cartier's for her. She signed for it, and went inside. It was a hand-carved ivory and gold rose attached to a heavy gold chain. The note read, "Real ones die. This will last much longer—to remind you that my feelings are also lasting. David."

She put it in her drawer. It was beautiful, but at the moment she didn't feel like thinking about David. She had stopped and gotten the prescriptions filled. The way she felt now, she had no desire to start on the pill. She put them away, beside the Cartier box. But she took one of the sedatives. Then she called Linda and said she had spent the morning at the dentist's and wouldn't be in.

She got into bed and tried to read . . . then the pill took its effect. She was in a heavy sleep when the phone rang at five o'clock. It was David. She thanked him for the necklace. "Could we have a quick drink this afternoon?" he asked.

"I'm afraid not. I'm . . . I'm piled up with assignments," she said.

He paused. "Well, there's going to be a Securities Analysts' meeting on the Coast in a few weeks, and several heads of companies are in town now. I'm afraid I'll be tied up with meetings the next few nights."

"That's all right, David."

"But I'll call you each day. And the first free night, we'll have dinner. I'm getting tickets for *Hair* next week."

"That's fine, David."

Then she hung up and lay in the semidarkness. It was a peaceful feeling of half wakefulness, half sleep. But at nine o'clock the sedative wore off and she sat up and turned on the lights. The whole night stretched out. She thought about food; but she wasn't particularly hungry.

She had made a list of subjects that might make interesting articles. She had intended to submit them to Linda today. She studied them now. Perhaps she should try to start one. She was particularly intrigued with the idea: "Is there life after thirty?"

It had come to her when Linda turned down a secretary who had top references and accepted a nineteen-year-old girl who just barely got by with shorthand. "January, I don't want a woman of forty-three to be a secretary at *Gloss*. I don't care if she was secretary to a president of an oil company for twenty years. *Gloss* is a swinging *young* magazine. I want shiny beautiful *young* people in this office."

January had noticed when she had gone for her "commercial" that most of the girls who worked as secretaries and receptionists at the advertising agency were all in the nineteen-to-twenty-nine age bracket. Of course it didn't apply to executives, or the woman who was head copywriter. Linda was pushing thirty—but for her job, she was young.

She liked Linda. But aside from their mutual enthusiasm for the magazine, they were worlds apart. At *Gloss*, Linda was "Power." When she walked through the halls, everyone snapped to attention. Linda at the weekly editorial meeting was cool and beautiful—in total command. Every editor and junior editor admired her almost classic elegance in looks and style. Yet Linda away from the office, with a man—any man—was devoid of any stature. She couldn't understand Linda's attitude about having a "body" next to her. Being able to enjoy sex with a man even if you didn't particularly like him. Last night had been dreadful . . . even before the pain. She hadn't felt any desire for David's body. Was something wrong with her?

She had to talk it out with someone. Not Linda! Linda would immediately suggest vitamins or a psychiatrist.

Suddenly she felt she had to see Mike. Maybe they could have lunch tomorrow. She couldn't really tell him what happened. But just talking to him might help. It was only nine-thirty. He wouldn't be in, but she could leave a message.

She couldn't believe it when he answered the phone. (Oh, God, maybe she had interrupted him and Dee. . . .) She tried to make her voice light. "I can call back if you're playing backgammon."

"No. As a matter of fact you woke me."

"Oh . . . I'm sorry. Apologize to Dee . . ."

"No, wait a minute. What time is it?"

"Nine-thirty."

"I'm wide awake now and I'm starving," he said. "Hey, how's about if I jump into a cab and pick you up. We'll have a hamburger."

"Where's Dee?"

"I shot her. She's hanging in the closet."

"MIKE!"

He laughed. "Be downstairs in front of your building in fifteen minutes. I'll tell you the gory details."

They went to the bar down the street and she studiously avoided the table she had sat at with David the previous night.

"Your old man is slowing up," Mike said. "Played eighteen holes of golf, came home at five, and fell into a dead sleep. Dee wanted to go to dinner and a movie, but I couldn't budge. She must have tried . . . but obviously I slept on. She left me a note that she was off to play backgammon at a girlfriend's. I guess she thought I'd sleep through the night."

"And I woke you. I'm sorry."

"No, I'm glad." The waiter brought their hamburgers. He bit into his eagerly. "I was starving . . . as you can see. My stomach would have gotten me up around midnight, but I would have missed seeing you." Suddenly his eyes narrowed. "How come you were sitting home tonight?"

"Oh . . . I had a date with David last night. Tonight he's at some kind of a meeting."

He nodded. "Translated—things aren't going right."

"He gave me a necklace from Cartier's," she said suddenly.

He pushed his beer away. He lit a cigarette and said casually, "A little early for Christmas, isn't it?"

"He wants to marry me."

His expression relaxed. Suddenly he smiled. "Well, Jesus, that's a whole different story. Why didn't you give me the bottom line right away?"

"I'm not in love with him."

"You're sure about that? I mean . . . you've known him only a short time. You're positive it's no deal?"

"Positive."

She reached out and took one of his cigarettes. His eyebrows went up. "Since when?"

"I learned when I was trying for a commercial." After a moment she said, "I'm sorry about David."

He laughed. "Tell that to him . . . not me. Hell, nothing's lost. So you dated him and he proposed. Give him back his goddamn necklace and that's it."

She stared down at her half-eaten hamburger. Suddenly she realized that he didn't want to believe there had been any intimacy between her and David. He wanted to think the necklace was just a "courting present." Mike, the sophisticate, was completely old-fashioned about her.

"Mike . . . do I have sex appeal?"

"What an insane question."

"Do I?"

"How the hell would I know? I can tell you that you're beautiful . . . that you've got a great figure . . . but sex appeal is a one-to-one relationship. A broad who would have sex appeal for me might not have it for the next guy."

"You have sex appeal for me," she said.

He looked at her. Then he shook his head. "And David doesn't."

"David doesn't."

"Oh, boy—" He whistled under his breath. "Here's a guy that every broad in New York would dig, including the most talked-about movie star in the world. And he has no sex appeal for you . . . but I have."

She tried to make her voice light. "Well, maybe I'll just have to meet someone who looks like you."

"Don't talk like that," he said roughly. "Jesus, you acted like you really dug the guy."

"I liked David," she said. "I still do *like* him. But as far as romance goes . . . he turns me off." She tried to laugh. "Maybe it's his blond hair."

He pushed his glass of beer away. "This is gonna be great! Every guy who comes along is going to lose out at the last minute on account of me . . . right?"

"Look, there's no reason to be upset just because I changed my mind about David."

"If we don't straighten this out, you'll change your mind every time. You'll get right up to the altar and change your mind. That can happen . . . hell, it has happened. And it ends up in disaster. Listen—" His voice was low. "Don't build up any false images about me. Images that other men can't follow. I'm no big deal. You only know me as Daddy . . . and Daddy is the dream man. Well, get this straight. There is no dream man. It's the woman who creates that dream image. And it's time you learned that Daddy Mike is a hell of a lot different from Mike the man."

"I see Mike the man and I love him."

"You only see what I've let you see. But now I'll give it to you straight. I was a lousy father and an even worse husband. I've never made any woman really happy. I loved sex . . . but I never loved. I still don't."

"You loved me . . . you always have."

"That's true. But I didn't hang around every night and tuck you in your crib. I lived my own life. I always have."

"That's because Mother died."

"Died? She killed herself, goddammit!"

January shook her head . . . yet somehow she knew he was telling the truth. He sipped his beer and stared at the glass. "Yep . . . she was pregnant and I was running around. So one night she got drunk and left a note saying this was her way of getting even. When I came home I found her on the bathroom floor. She had stuck a kitchen knife up her to dislodge the baby. It was there too . . . lying in the blood. It was scarcely a baby . . . maybe five months . . . a boy. I had enough clout to keep it quiet, make it look like her death came from a natural miscarriage . . . but—" He stopped and stared at her. "Now you know . . ."

"Why did you tell me this?" she asked.

"Because I want you to get a little tough. Learn how to handle yourself. Be *my* daughter. If you love me so damn much, love me for what I am. And if you accept what I really am instead of what you dream I am, then you'll find your own man and you'll fall in love with him. Hell, you'll fall in love a dozen times. But only if you learn to face reality. Go after what you want. Don't live in a dream world. Don't be a loser like your mother. She skulked around with those great brown eyes, never openly accusing me, yet damning me with every silent look. Christ, I almost respected her when I learned she had another guy. I even got a little jealous and was going to try and romance her back—then I learned she couldn't even hold him. She'd get drunk when she was with him and cry over me. And every time I looked at her there was always those sighs." He turned on her. "Don't ever sigh. That's the worst. God knows there are times right now that I want to sigh . . . But every time I start, I remember that I got into this thing for us."

"Us?" she said. "In the beginning it was just for me."

"Okay . . . Okay. Maybe it was the only way out for me, too. But I did try to give you the works. A great apartment, a maid, a car . . . Okay, so you walked away from it. But you *know* it's always there, so you're not gambling with scared money. Dee tried to give you a guy, but you don't like the color of his hair. Okay, so he's said he wants to marry you. But we both know that doesn't mean a guy is madly in love with a woman. It's a cinch he's not foaming to see you. I don't buy business meetings at night. I've used that excuse too many times myself."

"You think he's with Karla?"

He shrugged. "If he's lucky . . . maybe he is. In my book, any guy who gets a shot with Karla has to flip out over her. I know I would." He paused and looked at her thoughtfully. "Say, maybe you're not in love with

David because he doesn't want you to be . . . at the moment. Let's face it, he wouldn't want you all turned on over him while he was in the midst of making it with Karla." He grinned. "Ever think of that? Maybe he's holding you off. After all, if a guy doesn't get romantic with a girl, how *can* she be in love with him?" He seemed relieved at his new analysis. "Wait till he turns on the high voltage. I bet it'll be a whole new ballgame."

"You would flip out for Karla?" she asked.

"What?"

"You said you would flip out for Karla."

"Haven't you heard anything else I've said since then?"

She nodded. "I heard it. But I'm asking you a question."

"Sure I would." He finished his beer.

"And you really think she's too much competition for me?"

He smiled and patted her hand. "You're a girl, she's a woman. But don't worry—David asked you to marry him. That means that you're the girl he really wants —later." He was grinning. "When *he* wants."

"When *he* wants . . ." She laughed. "Oh, Mike, do you actually think David hasn't come on strong for me and . . ."

He slammed his fist on the table. "Has that sonofabitch tried anything?" His jaw tightened. "I'll kill him. Don't tell me he's tried to . . . to get intimate with you."

She couldn't believe it. Mike, who had all the women . . . Mike, who told her about Tina St. Claire and Melba . . . Mike, suddenly switching their relationship to outraged father and innocent daughter. It was crazy . . . insane . . . yet something told her not to tell him the truth.

"David has been a gentleman in every way," she said. "But I know that I could have him any way I want him."

"Any woman can have any man if she'll spread her legs," he said coldly. "But you're different. David knows that too."

"David!" She almost spit the name out. "Dee comes

up with a nice presentable cousin, and I'm supposed to act like a Barbie doll and fall in love with him and live happily ever after. And you know something? I tried . . . and I almost brainwashed myself into believing it. Tell me—is that what you wanted for me? To fall in love with a nice plastic man, wear a white bridal gown, settle down and maybe raise a daughter and find a David for her to marry? I mean—like the song says— 'Is that all there is, my friend . . . is that all there is?' "

He called for the check. Then he stood up and left some bills on the table. They walked out into the night. Two boys with long hair with red butterflies sewn on the backs of their dungarees passed. They stopped at a street light and began to kiss.

"Looks like love is everywhere these days," Mike said.

"They're Red Butterflies," January said.

"They're what?"

"It's a Communist Gay Liberation group that operates in Canada. A few of them are in town for recruits. Linda thought of doing a story on them. But it's not for *Gloss*."

Mike shook his head. "Know something? When you asked me in there, 'Is that all there is?' I can't tell you whether that's all there is or not. Because I don't know anymore. I don't know what *is*—in life, in show business . . . in anything. The whole world has changed. In my movies and all the movies of my day . . . the villain had to die. The hero won the gunfight, and ten years ago if I had a twenty-year-old daughter who was dating a David, I'd have said, 'What's your rush? The world is your oyster. And I'll give it to you.' But I'm not the way I was any more than the world is the way it was. So maybe I am looking for a quick solid soft berth for you. Because I look at this bright permissive world of today and in my book it stinks! But I can afford to turn my back on it because I'm fifty-two. I've lived a good hunk of my life. But you can't . . . because it's all you've got. And I can't turn it back to what it was. The corner suite at the Plaza belongs to someone else now. The Capitol Theater is now an office building. The

Stork Club is Paley Park. That world is gone. You can only see it on the Late Show. Unfortunately you've got to face the world as it is now. So try to enjoy it. Because suddenly one day you wake up and find you're played out. It happens overnight. So grab every brass ring you can, because when you look back, it seems like a hell of a short ride." He put his arm around her. "Look. I just saw a shooting star. Make a wish, babe."

They were standing in front of her building now. She shut her eyes, but she couldn't think of anything she really wanted. And when she opened her eyes he was gone. She watched him walk down the street. He still walked like a winner.

Later, as she lay awake in the darkness, she thought about the things her father had said. He was afraid of the world now—afraid for her . . . and afraid for himself. Well, as he said, it was her world now—the only one she had—and it was up to her to go out and squeeze it and make it fit. She would be a winner . . . and prove to him that it could be done.

She smiled as she stretched in the darkness. "Daddy," she whispered, "when Dee comes home from her backgammon game, you two better not sit up and worry about me and my future. Because, Daddy . . . I'm smiling . . . not sighing."

TEN

BUT DEE WAS NOT HOME waiting to discuss January's problems with Mike. When she saw he had fallen into a heavy sleep after his golf game, she had slipped into the study and made a quick phone call. Then she scribbled a note, propped it on the phone by his bed, explaining she had tried to awaken him but he had looked so peaceful that she left him to sleep and had gone off to play backgammon.

She got into the car and told Mario to take her to the Waldorf. "I'll be visiting a friend for several hours. Come back to the Park Avenue entrance at eleven o'clock." Then she entered the Waldorf, walked through the lobby and came out on the Lexington Avenue exit. She hailed a cab. It was only a few blocks; she could walk, but she was too eager to get there. It was only six o'clock. She had said she'd get there at six-thirty. Well, they'd have an extra half-hour together.

When she arrived at the large building, the doorman was busy piling luggage into a cab for a tenant. She walked right past him and into the elevator. The elevator operator was a new man who had never seen her before, but he merely nodded when she told him the floor. Some security in these luxury buildings nowadays!

She got off the elevator, walked to the end of the

floor and rang the buzzer. The elevator man hadn't even bothered to wait to see what apartment she was going to. She rang the buzzer again. She looked at her watch. Six-fifteen. Where could one go at an hour like this? She reached into her bag and took out a key. She entered the apartment and switched on the lamps in the living room. She lit a cigarette and made herself a drink.

Then she went to the mirror and combed her hair. Thank God she had had Ernest set it in a soft pageboy today—the Gibson-Girl style got messed up in bed. Today's girls, with their loose swinging hair—how she envied them. She looked at the new individual eyelashes Elizabeth Arden had applied. Yes, they were marvelous. She turned off one of the lamps, then went back and looked in the mirror. Yes, that was better . . .

She sat in the club chair and sipped her drink. Her heart was pounding. No matter how many times she came here, she always felt the breathless anticipation of a schoolgirl.

It was five after seven when she finally heard the key in the lock. She crushed out her freshly lit cigarette and stood up. "Where the hell have you been?" she demanded.

Karla dropped her shoulder bag to the chair and took off her raincoat. "Am I late?" she said easily.

"You know damn well you're late. Where have you been?"

Karla smiled. "Just walking. I always like to walk at dusk. Besides, I did only two hours at the bar today. I needed the exercise."

"You didn't need to walk. You did it intentionally . . . just so I would be sitting here waiting!" She paused because she knew her voice had risen. "Oh, Karla! Why do you do everything to bring out the worst in me!"

With a slow smile Karla held out her arms. Dee hesitated for a second, then rushed to her. And Karla's kiss silenced any further protests.

Later, when they were locked in one another's arms in the cool dark of the bedroom, Dee clung to Karla

and said, "Oh God, if we could only be together forever."

"Only death is forever," Karla said. She pulled away
and reached for one of Dee's cigarettes. She snapped
open the gold case and stared at it. "Very beautiful."

"Mike gave it to me . . . or I'd give it to you. But
I've given you three cases. And you always lose them."

Karla shrugged as she exhaled the smoke. "Perhaps
it is some inner instinct that is trying to tell me I must
stop smoking. I am down to ten a day . . ."

"You're such a health fiend. All that walking and
those ballet exercises—" Dee paused as she lit a cigarette. "Oh, by the way—I made out a new will."

Karla laughed. "Dee, you're not ever going to die.
You're too mean to die."

"I also put ten thousand dollars into your savings
account today."

Karla laughed. "The joint savings account of Connie
and Ronnie Smith. Connie puts in . . . Ronnie takes it
out. I'm sure everyone in the bank is onto it."

"They don't recognize me," Dee said quickly.

Karla jumped out of bed and did an arabesque. "But
can I help it if I am so magnificent that everyone rec-
ognizes me!" she said, mocking her own fame.

"You nut." Dee laughed. "Come back here."

Karla slipped into a dressing gown and switched on
the television set. She climbed back on the bed, sat
cross-legged, and worked the remote control, clicking
the channels until she came to a movie. It was *Grand
Hotel* starring Garbo, Barrymore, and Joan Crawford.

"What time do you have to be home, Dee?" she said.

Dee snuggled against Karla. "No time, especially. He
played eighteen holes of golf and will probably sleep
through the night. Just in case, I left a note saying I
was playing backgammon with Joyce."

"Who is Joyce?"

"Someone I invented. This way he can never check."

"Mike Wayne is very attractive," Karla said slowly.

"I only married him because of you."

Karla leaned back and laughed. "Oh, Dee, I know
the press thinks I am not very bright because I will

not give interviews. But you know better than to think I really believe that."

"It's true! I told you before I married Mike . . . before I ever met him, that I was going to get married. That I *had* to get married. All last spring when I had David take us around . . . I knew people were beginning to wonder . . . not about you . . . but me . . . like why was I tagging along? You're famous for wanting to live your own life. Everyone knows how you fight for your privacy. But they're accustomed to seeing me in all the newspapers—at the opening of the opera season, the ballet, opening nights of certain Broadway shows, especially when there's a charity benefit. Then there're the Balls . . . I'm on the boards of three big charity organizations . . . and there are my business affiliations. I'm chairman of the board of two corporations. There are dinners I must attend. I need a presentable escort. I need to make appearances at the proper places with a *man*. A hospital is being dedicated in my name in Spain. Next spring, when I go there, the Monsignor will officiate. Can't you see? I can't risk any scandal."

"Why not donate the money and stay away from all these public functions?" Karla suggested.

"Turn away from the world? The way you try to do?" Dee looked at her. "If I did . . . would you promise to move in with me and stay with me forever?"

Karla's laugh was low. "Unfortunately, the only person I must be with forever is myself."

"But you don't mind being alone. I'm terrified. I've always hated it. But it didn't turn into terror until you came into my life. The first time you disappeared I swallowed a whole bottle of Seconals. I'll still suffer when you go off . . . but at least I'm not alone."

"This kind of fear I cannot understand," Karla said, as she watched the movie.

"Maybe it's because loneliness is something I grew up with. My parents died so early and I grew up with just banks and trustees and the knowledge that I wasn't a beautiful little girl, but it wouldn't matter because I was so very very rich. Do you know what that's like? To feel that every man you meet only flatters you and acts as if he cares about you because of your money."

"Dee, that is ridiculous. You are very beautiful."

Dee smiled. "I have the kind of beauty that comes with money, grooming and dieting. I wasn't born beautiful like Jackie Onassis or Babe Paley."

"I think you are." Karla stared at the close-up of Joan Crawford.

Dee stared at the television screen. "She's beautiful," she said. "And her beauty got her money, and men who loved her. While my money got me beauty and men who professed to love me. But I've always known it . . . and I never really let myself feel anything for any man. Basically I hate men. Women are different. And I've always picked women who had plenty of money so I would know they wanted me for myself. They all did. But I never really loved any of them. I didn't think I was capable of really being in love until I met you. Karla . . . do you realize you're the only person I've ever loved in my whole life?"

"You know, this picture still holds up," Karla said.

"For God's sake, will you turn that damn thing off?"

Karla turned down the sound and smiled at Dee. "Now, are you happy?"

Dee looked at her. "Know something? I don't think I've actually had a happy day since we met."

"But I thought you said you loved me." Karla was watching the movie without sound.

"That's why I'm so unhappy! Oh, Karla, can't you understand? As close as we are . . . like right now . . ." Her hand went under Karla's robe and stroked her body. "Right now, touching you where I am touching you now—I don't feel as if you really belong to me, or that I'm really reaching you in anything I say . . . or do."

"You are making me feel very sexy right now . . . and I think maybe I better take my robe off and we make love."

And once again Dee felt the indescribable perfection of their physical intimacy. And when it was over she clung to her and she said, "Karla, I worship you. Please . . . please . . . don't make me unhappy."

"I thought I had just made you very happy."

Dee turned away. "I'm not talking about just sex. Can't you understand what you do to me! The times you disappear—"

"But now you know I always come back," Karla said.

"How can I *know* that for sure . . . any more than I can know when you are going to pick up and go off again? Karla, do you realize that I've loved you for almost nine years and yet if we added up all the times we've been together, it would be no more than a few months?"

Karla turned up the sound. Garbo was in the midst of her love scene with Barrymore. "You'd get tired of me if I stayed too long," Karla said.

"Never."

Karla kept her eyes on the screen. "My sweet little Dee, just as you cannot be alone, there are times Karla *must* go off alone."

Dee reached over and grabbed the remote control and switched it off. "Karla . . . you know about the sleeping pills I took the first time. Well, I swore to myself that would never happen again. I suffered each time you took off . . . but each time I told myself I was getting stronger . . . that you would come back . . . But last spring, after you took off again, I . . . I cut my wrists. Oh, it was kept quiet. I was in Marbella and I have several friends there who are doctors. But that's when I knew . . . I had to get married . . . to save my sanity."

Karla's large gray eyes looked at her with compassion. "You say things like that—it makes me very sad. Perhaps I should go out of your life for good."

"Oh, God! Don't you understand?" Dee clung to her. "I can't live without you. And I also know that if I cause too many scenes like this, you'll leave me. That's another reason I married Mike Wayne. He's not like the others. I can't walk all over him, or push him around. I have to play the game of being his wife. I must answer to him. And the discipline of it will keep

me from going off the deep end over you. And I know
that as long as I act like a wife, he'll stay . . . because he has no money . . . and because I just created a ten-million-dollar trust fund for his daughter."

"Isn't that unlike you?" Karla asked. "Usually you
hold strings over someone's head."

Dee smiled. "It's not an irrevocable trust. I can always change it." Then she looked at Karla pleadingly.
"You must come to Palm Beach. Mike will play golf
all day . . . we can be together . . . and we'll even
have nights together . . . like this. The place is so huge
he'd never find us—"

Karla laughed. "What was all that talk about appearances? For me to houseguest with a newlywed couple
would most certainly cause talk."

"Not if you come down during the holidays. Everyone has houseguests then . . . and if you stayed on
. . . no one would talk."

"We shall see." Karla took the remote control from
Dee, and walked over and turned on the set. Then she
got into bed and clicked the channels. She came in on
the middle of a Cary Grant picture. She settled back
happily. "A wonderful man . . . I almost did a picture with him. We couldn't get together on terms."

Dee lay back and watched Karla's perfect profile.
She saw the fresh scars behind Karla's ears and suddenly she wondered why Karla had done it. Dee had
gone through a face-lift seven years ago. But she had
done it to stay beautiful for Karla. She had gone
through another a year ago. Again, just to hold Karla.
And last spring when she had seen the beginning of
the tiny lines under Karla's eyes . . . the slight slack
along her jaw . . . she found herself praying it would
happen fast . . . that the magnificent face would fall
apart so no one else would want her. And now—during
this last disappearance, Karla had gone and done it.
Why? She wasn't interested in going back to work.
Every time anyone came to her with an offer she turned
it down. Then *why* had she done it? Suddenly she felt
weak inside. Could Karla really be serious about David?
Until this very moment, she had thought it just flat-

tered her ego to have David hanging around. But now the fear began to take hold, because suddenly she realized it was possible. Karla was a homosexual . . . she had told that to Dee. Once she had said she knew it when she was a little girl. She never elaborated on it . . . but Dee assumed it must have happened in some ballet company. But Karla had also had some well-publicized love affairs with men. And Karla had admitted she had felt genuine attraction toward the men. Dee closed her eyes as a wave of despair hit her. Twenty years ago in Hollywood, Christopher Kelly, the actor Karla almost eloped with, looked very much like David. Maybe there was a certain type man who turned her on. She looked at Karla. Karla tossed her a bright smile and returned her attention to the TV set. She wanted to scream. Here they were . . . lying together . . . yet she didn't dare ask or pry into Karla's personal emotions. She had learned that no amount of physical intimacy gave her permission to invade Karla's privacy. The part of herself she held remote could not be penetrated by tears, threats, or even money. Long ago she had discovered Karla's pathological stinginess. The woman was a millionaire . . . yet the nearest thing to a display of devotion came when Karla was the recipient of a large amount of money. But tonight even the ten thousand hadn't brought more than a polite smile. She seemed preoccupied. Maybe Karla was really in love with David. Her panic suddenly made her forget all rules but she kept her voice even.

"Karla, have you been seeing much of David?"

Karla kept watching the television screen. "Yes."

"I think he likes my stepdaughter."

Karla smiled. "I think you would like him to like your stepdaughter."

"Well, he doesn't really mean anything to you, does he?"

"Of course he does. Why else would I see him?"

Dee jumped out of bed. "You bitch!"

Karla lay back and smiled. "You will catch cold if you stand without your clothes. And, Dee, you really should take ballet exercises. You need it in your thighs."

Dee dashed into the bathroom and Karla turned up the sound on the television. She seemed completely engrossed in the picture when Dee came out of the bathroom. Dee dressed in silence. Then she walked over to the bed. "Karla, why do you do these things to torment me?"

"How do I torment you?" Karla's voice was cold. "You have a husband . . . and so very very much money. You enjoy running people's lives, controlling them and frightening them with your money. But you cannot control or frighten Karla."

Dee sank down on the edge of the bed. "Do you know how rotten it is to have my kind of money?"

Karla sighed. "Oh, my poor Dee. You suffer because you wonder whether people really care for *you*. You say that has left a deep scar within you. But we all have scars." Karla turned off the television set. "Unfortunately—or fortunately—you have never known the scars of working to get to become a star . . . and the harder work of staying there . . . remembering all the time what it was like *not* to have money—"

"But that was a challenge and fun—"

"Fun?" Karla smiled.

"You don't talk about your early days. But I've read everything that was ever written about you. Sure, you were growing up in Europe during the war. It must have been dreadful. I remember I was about twenty when Pearl Harbor happened. I joined committees and knitted for the English, the Russians—yes, they were our allies then—but we only read about the fighting. There was no TV that brought the war into our living room as it does today. It's horrible." She shuddered.

Karla stared into space. "You shudder because TV brings it into your living room. But in Poland we had it walk right into our living room."

"In your living room?"

Karla smiled. "I was twenty when Germany and Russia were allies. In 1939 Hitler invaded Poland and divided it between them."

"Is that when you went to London?"

"No . . . first Sweden . . . then London. . . .

But this is not bedtime conversation and I am suddenly very tired."

Dee knew she was expected to leave. Karla was dismissing her. She hesitated. She could walk out and threaten to never see her again. But she'd only crawl back. They both knew that.

"Karla, we're leaving for Palm Beach next week. Please come down."

"Perhaps."

"Shall I send the plane for you?"

Karla stretched out. "I'll let you know." (Dee realized she was actually falling asleep.)

Dee leaned down. "I'll call you tomorrow. And Karla . . . I love you."

When Dee reached the Pierre, Mike was just coming in. He threw his arm around her shoulder. "I went for a hamburger. Did you have a good game?"

He opened the door of the apartment and she tossed her coat on the couch. He came to her and put his arms around her. "Sorry the old man fell asleep." He grinned. "But I'm up now . . . in every way."

She pulled away. "No . . . not tonight, Mike . . . please!"

He stood very still for a moment. Then he forced a smile. "What happened? Did you lose in backgammon?"

"Yes. A little. But I'll get it back. I've got to—" She turned to him with a tight smile. "You see, it's a matter of pride."

ELEVEN

AT MIDNIGHT, on the Tuesday before Thanksgiving, Linda sat in the middle of her bed (with January as her captive audience), damning the hypocrisy of the holiday. "Just what are we celebrating?" she demanded. "The fact that some emotionally disturbed people, who called themselves 'Settlers,' came here, met some friendly Indians, and then proceeded to take the whole country away from them."

"Oh, Linda, they were friendly with the Indians. The fighting came later. In fact, Thanksgiving was to celebrate a year of good crops and friendship with the Indians."

"Bullshit. And besides, what smartass settler decided to make the celebration come on a Thursday and screw up a whole business week? It'd be different if it was summer and you could go to the Hamptons. But what am I going to do with a long weekend in November?"

"What about your family?" January asked.

"What about them? My father's new wife is like twenty-five and she just had another baby and the last thing he wants around is a daughter who is older than his wife. Might remind him how old he is. And my mother is on the verge of splitting with her husband. She caught him at a cocktail party groping her best friend in the powder room—so she's not exactly hanging over a turkey. You're lucky . . . four glorious

days at Palm Beach in a beach-front palace . . . going
there in your own jet . . . with two guys in attend-
ance as you soak up the sun . . . Daddy and David. Or
is it still just Daddy and will David be in the way?"

January walked to the window. She had been ready
to go to bed when Linda called and insisted that she
come up to her apartment. She had said it was urgent,
but for the last twenty minutes, she had been holding
forth on Thanksgiving.

Actually January was looking forward to the trip.
Mike had been gone ten days. David had taken her out
twice since the dreadful night. They had gone to see
Hair (he had loathed it . . . she adored it). The next
time they had done the early movie and Maxwell's
Plum evening. And both times he had taken her home,
held the cab, and said goodnight with that *"I'll*-wait-
until-*you*-ask-*me"* smile.

She realized the remark about David and Daddy had
stemmed from Linda's own loneliness. Linda was wearing an old pajama top that had belonged to Keith. Suddenly she realized January was staring at it. She smiled.
"Every girl has an ex-lover's old pajama top, that she
wears on special occasions . . . to remind her that, at
heart, every man is a shit heel."

"Oh, come on—" January tried to change her mood.
"With Keith it's a career problem."

"I'm not talking about Keith," Linda said. "I am
talking about Leon . . . *the* asshole of all time. At
exactly five o'clock this afternoon he announced that
he was going back to his wife. He loves me, but his
psychiatrist thinks I'm castrating him. Also, it seems
he can't afford the alimony he would have to pay her,
along with the occasional dinners he bought me. And,
of course, he's got his psychiatrist three times a week."
She shrugged. "It's just as well—he never really ap-
pealed to me."

"Then why did you sleep with him?"

"Darling, Leon is a brilliant art director. He could
get much more at another magazine. . . ."

"You mean he's staying on?"

"Of course. We'll still be friends. Maybe even sleep

together occasionally. Look, one of the main reasons I started the relationship, was to keep him on the job. This way, *he's* walked out on me to go back to his wife. And I've had enough therapy myself to know just how to handle it. I cried . . . told him I really loved him . . . made him promise me he'd enjoy his Thanksgiving . . . that I understood . . . he had a wife and a kid . . . In short, I laid such a guilt trip on him—he'll *never* leave the magazine."

"Is that all that matters to you—the magazine?"

Linda lit a cigarette. "When I was at Miss Haddon's, all the girls there adored me because I was always on, always with it, right? And the boys dated me because I went all the way. But even by going all the way, I was never sure they'd call again, or for how long I'd hold them. Because I guess I knew there would always be someone they'd meet who would go all the way better than I. And when I got out of Miss Haddon's and had the nose job and tried to be an actress, I saw how girls humiliated themselves auditioning. And I was one of them—singing your guts out on a dark empty stage and then hearing a disembodied voice call out, 'Thank you very much.' And even if you were lucky enough to get a job . . . the following season you were back, groveling, begging, walking, trying . . . praying . . . for another chance to stand on some dark stage and hear 'Thank you very much.' But when I got hired on at *Gloss,* I knew I'd only have to jump, run, fetch and carry, *once*—on my way up. And if I made it, *Gloss* would always be there. Not like a show that closed after a season . . . not like a man who leaves your bed and doesn't come back. There will be plenty of Leons . . . maybe even a few more Keiths."

"Keith . . . wasn't he the big love?"

Linda smiled. "Oh, come on, January. Do you think he's the first man I almost died over? I just cared for him in a different way from Leon."

"But you told me you wanted to marry him. That Keith was—"

"Was important then," Linda cut in. "Look, I'll be twenty-nine next week. That's a shitty age. Because when you say it no one believes you. Like, twenty-seven they'll believe. But twenty-eight and twenty-nine both sound phony. And twenty-nine is over the hill to have not even had a *bad* marriage. But it isn't over the hill when you're editor-in-chief of *Gloss*. When you're the youngest editor-in-chief in New York. So you don't cry yourself to sleep when you realize Keith is gone forever."

"But how do you know he is?"

"He's shacked up with an older woman. I mean a really older woman. Would you believe Christina Spencer?" When she saw no sign of recognition on January's face, she said, "She's rich . . . Oh, not in Dee's class, she never gets full pages in *Vogue* like Dee. This one's the type that sometimes makes the centerfold of *Women's Wear,* in one of those tiny pictures coming out of restaurant X, Y, or Z. But she's got a few million—" Linda put out her cigarette. "God, these women with money. They buy themselves younger faces, younger boyfriends . . . A few days ago I saw a picture of Keith in a new Cardin jacket, escorting her to a Save the Children ball at the Plaza. There they were, right in the centerfold of *Women's Wear,* only Keith was half cut off and *Women's Wear* called him an unidentified escort."

"But what would he want with her?" January asked.

"Christina Spencer's been taking pieces of Broadway shows for the past ten years. This morning I read in the *Times* that she was a major backer of the new rock musical *Caterpillar* and that Keith Winters has been signed for a featured role."

"Do you feel bad?" January asked softly.

Linda shook her head. "I haven't really felt bad since Tony."

"Tony?"

"Yes, he was the big one. When he split, I took five red dolls and two yellow jackets. I was twenty and thought our love was forever. Well, I survived. Both Tony and the pills. Then there were a lot of quickies. You know—you latch on to someone because he's available, because you want to show Tony that you aren't dying, you want to show yourself that it's 'Right on, baby . . . all the way.' But it never becomes a meaningful relationship, because no matter how attractive he is, he isn't Tony. Oh, it can last several months. Sometimes a year. But something's wrong with it—maybe it's because you generate a negative reaction because suddenly he stops calling. He even forgets he's got three shirts at your place all nice and fresh from the laundry that *you've* paid for. I guess that was when I began picking people who could help the magazine. And most of the time, there isn't even any sex involved. Like right now, a big advertising agency buys full-page color ads for their clients. The president of this agency, Jerry Moss, lives in Darien, has a lovely wife and two children and has been a closet queen all of his life. But a year ago he fell in love with Ted Grant, a male model I know. And I'm their beard. Sometimes I go out with the two of them. Naturally the wife thinks it's business. I even went to their house in Darien on Christmas Eve with Ted as *my* date and sat with the wife in the living room making small talk for forty minutes while they did their number in the upstairs john. Then there's a designer and his wife—they're both gay. She has her girl, he has his boy, and I'm there to make it a fivesome—confusing to everyone but the principals involved. The designer has been a big help, and his wife gives lovely dinner parties and I go and meet all the best people. Yes . . . I love *Gloss.* It's been good to me. I can hold its sales growth in my hand better than a penis that goes limp on me. Oh, that's happened too. When they can't get it up and the guy just lies there with his limp cock and looks at you like *you're* the one who's made him impotent. He lies there and defies you to make him hard. You get a bellyful of them. And then along comes a Keith and you begin to think maybe . . . and you con yourself that it *can* happen. But you know it can't. And when he splits . . . you don't really cry."

"Well . . . I'm sorry." January started for the door.

"Sit down, you idiot. I didn't get you here to talk about my sex life. Or to torch over Keith. I'm resilient. And besides, I read my own Tarot cards the other day and they said something big was going to happen in 1971. So tonight when Leon gave me the news, I came home, took a lamb chop out of the freezer, and while I was waiting for it to thaw, I started reading the galleys of Tom Colt's new novel."

"Is it as good as some of his others?"

"Better. More commercial. His last few were too good. I mean he went literary. No one but the critics dug him. They didn't sell at all. But this one is going to be a rocket. That's why I'm a fatalist. If Leon had been here, we would have had sex and I wouldn't have gotten to the galleys."

"What do you want to do?" January asked. "Bid for serial rights?"

"Are you kidding? I hear *Ladies' Home Journal* has bid up to twenty-five thousand just for two excerpts. We can't get his book, but we can get him. Understand?"

"Linda, I'm tired and I haven't packed yet. Let's not play games. No, I don't understand."

Linda's eyes narrowed. "Listen, you've been acting spooky lately. I'm telling you, you better make it with someone or the next thing you know . . . your skin will go."

"That's a fallacy, and—" January stopped.

"And what?" She looked at January. "Hey . . . you're blushing. You've made it with David! Well, thank God! Are you on the pill? Is everything divine? No wonder you're so thrilled about Palm Beach—four long days and nights of sand and love and—"

"Linda! We did it only once, and it was awful."

Linda paused. "You mean he couldn't get it up?"

"No . . . he . . . well . . . he was fine . . . I guess. It was awful for me."

Linda laughed in relief. "It always is . . . the first time. For the woman that is . . . but never for the man. From what I hear, those bastards come like crazy the first time, even if they're thirteen and do it in a dark hallway with the local 'bad girl.' *She* may not come— and they may come before they even get it into her bird —but goddamn it . . . *they come*! And that's something Women's Liberation is never going to be able to change. A virgin lady is all tight inside even if she's been finger-fucked. A virgin lady hurts when the glorious prick enters. And a virgin lady—whether you call her Ms., Miss, or Mrs.—rarely comes until she's properly stretched and oiled with passion. Thank God you're no longer a virgin lady . . . Only it's a shame you lost it with David."

January nodded. "That's the way I feel . . . I think maybe I should have waited."

"Sure. I could have fixed you up with someone . . . even Leon."

"Are you insane!"

"Never do it the first time with someone you care about. As I said, the first fuck is usually awful and you can lose the guy. Did you turn David off completely?"

"I don't think so, really . . . He says he loves me and wants to marry me."

Linda stared at her. "Then why are we sitting here having a wake for your lost hymen? You sneaky elegant ones—you're always the wild women in the kip. Now look—congratulations and all that. But let's get back to Tom Colt. From what I hear, he needs money and he's consented to do the grand tour."

"But he's very rich," January insisted. "I met him when I was little. He had a town house here with one of his wives and my father was buying one of his books for a picture. He's written about fifteen big novels . . . he has plenty of money."

"So did your father once. Maybe the dice got cold for Tom Colt too. He's married . . . pays alimony to three ex-wives . . . gave the fourth a huge settlement. His new wife just presented him with a baby boy. Imagine, at his age . . . he's never had kids till now. But as I said, his last few books didn't do well. And when you live in a big home in Beverly Hills, with a Rolls, servants, a projection room—the works—you can't have three non-selling books and still be solvent. Not with all the upkeep he's got. He also hasn't had a picture sale since 1964—and that's where the big money is, that and paperback. But on this new one he's back to his old hard-hitting style. Claims he stopped writing for the critics and wants to reach the people again. There was that interview in *Paris Review* a few months ago where he said he doesn't care if the artsy crowd says he sold out—he wants to be number one, and he wants a big picture sale, so . . ."

"So?"

"So he will need all the publicity he can get. And he may ask big money for an excerpt from his book. But he could come absolutely free if we offer to do a cover story on him."

"And what's to keep Helen Gurley Brown from getting the same idea, if she hasn't already?" January asked.

"Oh, she probably has . . . but *we* have *you!*"

"Me?"

"*You* know Tom Colt."

"Oh, Linda . . . I met him when I was about five years old. What do I do? Send him my baby pictures and say, 'Guess who?' and let's get together for old time's sake. Besides, you said he lives in Beverly Hills."

"If necessary, I'll send you there. First class. Look, the book doesn't come out until February or March. All you have to do is ask him for an interview . . . for Daddy's sake."

January stood up. "I'm tired, Linda. And I have to pack . . ."

"Okay. Have a marvelous time. And while you're basking in the sun and making love, see if you can't frame up a good letter to send to Tom Colt. Maybe you could even get Daddy to add a few lines . . ."

TWELVE

MIKE WAS WAITING at the airport when the Grumman jet landed. He watched January come down the steps, with David at her elbow. She hadn't spotted him yet, and for a brief moment he reveled in the pleasure of watching her unobserved. Each time he saw her, there was some almost imperceptible change. A new facet of beauty seemed to emerge. He approved of her casual "today" look. The wide slacks, floppy hat, and long straight hair. She looked like one of those new breed fashion models. And then she saw him, and raced toward him, shouting, "Daddy . . . oh, Daddy . . . I'm so glad to see you." He smiled when he realized that in an emotional moment she always reverted to *Daddy* instead of *Mike*.

"I left Mario making drinks. I'm your chauffeur," he explained as David sat in the back of the convertible, wedged in between the luggage.

"How many houseguests this time?" David asked.

"Maybe about eight or ten. But you lose count because she gives those lunches for thirty or forty every day. I go off for golf at nine and when I get back at four, half of them are still here. And then at seven the cocktail group arrives. But Dee has decided that the Thanksgiving dinner itself will be an intimate affair. Just two tables of twelve. Meanwhile let's hope we stay lucky with the sun. You both could use some color."

The good weather held throughout the weekend. There

were always two or three backgammon games going at poolside. Hot and cold buffets were wheeled out by an endless stream of servants. Mike and January sat together; soaked up the sun; walked on the beach and swam together. And when she played tennis with David, Mike watched with amazement as she outwitted him on every volley. Where had she learned to play so well? And then like flash bulbs . . . the memory of all those tennis tournaments he had never attended flashed through his mind. All those scrawled little notes he had received in Los Angeles, Madrid, or London! "Am playing for the Junior Cup. Wish you could come." "Am representing Miss Haddon's in the Eastern division. Wish you could be here." "I won." "Am sending cup to the Plaza." "I won." "Sending cup to Plaza." "I came in second." "I won." "Did you get trophy? This one is real silver." "I won." "I won!"

God, how little of himself he had actually given her. And suddenly he found himself wondering what had become of all those cups and trophies. She had never asked him about them. They were probably in some storage place along with the typewriters, the piano, the filing cabinets, and the office furniture he had collected on all those "Comebacks." And he didn't even know where the storage slips were.

How much of her childhood he had missed. And how much of her teens *she* had missed. And now she was hitting her best years and he had to miss them too. He was married . . . only this was one flop he couldn't just close the office and walk away from.

And suddenly as he sat watching his daughter playing tennis, he was hit with panic at the thought that had just slipped through his subconscious. He had thought of his marriage as a flop. Yet actually nothing had changed. Dee still smiled at him across the table each night. She still slipped her arm through his when they greeted guests. He still went to bed with her twice a week . . . There! That was it! He had just touched the exposed nerve. *He* went to bed with *her*. Lately, he had the feeling that she was accommodating him, putting up with him. She wasn't "acting" anymore. When was the

last time she had moaned and clung to him and told him
how wonderful it all was? But maybe it was his fault.
Maybe because he felt he was accommodating her . . .
she sensed it. Things like that can be felt. Yes, it was his
fault. The poor broad probably resented that he spent
so much time at the club. God knows he certainly wasn't
paying much attention to her. Golf all morning, gin
games in the afternoon (he had found a few good pigeons) . . . Sure, he got back only in time to join her
in the martini bit. And the evenings were always filled
with dinner parties.

Well, from now on things were going to be different.
The moment January left, he'd give Dee the old razzle-
dazzle. And he'd cut down on the gin games every afternoon. Nothing wrong in spending a few afternoons with
her. But he wouldn't be *with* her. He'd be hanging around
having lunch with all those friends of hers, watching
them play backgammon. No, he'd stick to the golf club.
Besides, so far he had won close to five thousand bucks
at gin. He had opened a savings account. Five thousand
was a joke, of course. But it was *his* money, money *he*
had earned, or won. What the hell, when you earn it in
gin, you shoot the same kind of adrenalin you shoot
when you earn it anywhere else! But he had to pay more
attention to her in the kip. Maybe he was being too
perfunctory about it. Well, Sunday, after January and
all the houseguests left, the new romantic regime would
begin. Suddenly he felt better. It was necessary to take
stock of things like this every now and then. Here he
had been sitting around thinking something was missing
in their relationship when actually he was the one at
fault. Hell, she had the same crowds hanging around at
Marbella, and she'd have them in Greece next August—
and wherever else she decided to go. In London there
were never fewer than twenty for cocktails, at the Dorchester. This was her way of life. He knew it when he
went into it. He was supposed to supply the romance.
That's what he had done when they first met, and she
had flipped out for him, and that's what he would do
now—starting Sunday.

But for the next few days he concentrated on enjoying

his daughter. He watched her turn golden brown, watched the marvelous body in the bikini (Dee was so goddamned white), the way her hair swung, the way Dee's was always in place. Her crazy denims—Dee's perfect white sharkskin pants. The little silver rings on all of her fingers—Dee's David Webb jewelry. They were such wild opposites. Dee was a beauty. Yet he was glad his daughter looked the way she did.

There was something so clean and sparkling about her. And he liked her keen interest in everything. Vital interest in *Gloss* magazine. Casual interest in David. "Pretended" interest in Dee's small talk about the current romantic affiliations of some of the local socialites. The names all had to be a maze to her, but she listened attentively.

It was hard for him to evaluate David. He was always there . . . smiling . . . the perfect escort. You could tell he and Dee were first cousins. They were cut from the same cloth. The aristocracy was all there. The excellent manners—the way he tirelessly played backgammon with Dee's guests, his proper clothes for every occasion. His tennis shorts were just the right cut, his sweater was casual and right, even his perspiration was classy, just a little on the brow, the better to make his suntan glisten. But wasn't that what he wanted for January? Long before he had ever met Dee, he knew he wanted something better than a show business life for his daughter. That's why he had chosen the fancy school in Connecticut. That had been on advice from his business manager: "She'll get to know classy girls, meet their brothers—that's how it all happens. That's what good schools are for."

Well, the only thing she had gotten out of that school was a lot of tennis trophies and a job on a magazine. Of all the girls there, she had to tie up with Linda, a real barracuda, the kind that leaped in and out of a different bed each night. But then, wasn't that part of the new permissiveness of today? He stared at his daughter on the tennis court. Had she? Nah! Not that he expected her to remain a virgin forever. But she was the kind who would probably do it with a guy after they got engaged.

Or maybe just before . . . just to make sure. Right now she was all involved with the magazine. But like Dee said, she'd probably play around with being the career girl for a short time and then marry David.

He wondered why he felt depressed. This was what he wanted for her, wasn't it? But did he want her to turn into a young Dee? Well, why not? It would be a hell of a lot better than having her go the route some of the other kids went. Moving in with some guy, going funky and East Village. Or suppose she had been more like him—intent on becoming a superstar. Then what? Suppose she made it. She'd catch herself a few hot years on Cloud Nine, but the eventual end for any superstar, including himself, was loneliness and defeat. If a man had money, he lasted a little longer. But for a woman, even with money, the loneliness came quicker. Age was a woman's defeat. Even a legend like Karla—what kind of a life did she have? Still with the ballet exercises! But without them, where else would she have to go each day? And most of the superstars weren't lucky enough to be born stupid like Karla, content to go walking and practicing ballet. The more emotional ones—they were the bleeders, sitting home alone in a mansion in Beverly Hills, taking sleeping pills or booze. Anything to get rid of the night so they could wake up to an endless day that stretched before them, to meals served on a tray while they sat alone watching daytime soap operas on television. No, it was turning out right for January. She had learned all the basic things at Miss Haddon's—and now he had supplied the rest. A place like this to come to—sun in the winter, snow in the summer. Anything she wanted.

And he had gotten it for her. He watched her walk off the tennis court with David. She had beaten him again. That was his daughter—a champion. But David was also a champion. Losing gracefully was a hard art to come by. And David had mastered it. The way he leaped over the net to congratulate her, the way he put his arm around her shoulders while the other guests applauded. But most of all, Mike admired the charm and enthusiasm he engendered at all the endless parties they attended each night.

But January had seemed to enjoy the weekend too. Maybe he had done it all right. Maybe it was all working out as he had hoped it would. Maybe when they came back to Palm Beach for the Christmas holidays they'd be really serious about each other. Dee would like that. But hell . . . not yet. She wouldn't be twenty-one until January. She deserved some free time.

Free time for what? She was a girl . . . he was thinking of her subjectively. Girls didn't need to play the field. They were content to settle for one man for life. She wasn't one of those half-baked Women's Liberationists. Anyhow, he didn't even believe them. Sometimes when he saw them on TV, he'd talk back to the screen. "Yeah, baby . . . just one good fuck and you'd sing a different tune." That's all they were—broads without a guy. And his daughter would never have to worry about that.

He got up early on Sunday. He had promised to have an early breakfast with her at the pool. She was leaving around four. Then he and Dee would be alone. And he was determined to keep his vow. He hadn't been to bed with Dee in a week. He wondered if she noticed it. They both had their own rooms here. Rooms! His bedroom was forty feet by thirty-five, facing the ocean. He also had a sauna, a shower and a black marble bathroom with a sunken tub. His bedroom adjoined hers, but as he put it, it was a sleeper jump to get there. First he had to walk through her dressing room . . . and her bathroom— a huge white and gold marble affair with a real tree growing in it and one whole wall filled with tropical fish. That wall was also a wall of her bedroom; it was slightly smaller than his, but its ocean-front terrace was almost the size of a ballroom. They breakfasted there occasionally under an umbrella.

Today he started his training—no Bloody Marys at lunch, no martinis at cocktails . . . Tonight he'd make love to her with his old passion.

He spent the morning with January. She glanced

through the magazine section of the *Times,* and he went
for the sports pages. That was another great thing they
had together—they didn't feel conversation was necessary for communication. It wasn't until he had finished
the sports section and the theatrical section that he noticed she was reading a set of galleys.

"Any good?" he asked.

"Very good." She looked up and pushed her sunglasses
up into her hair. "Tom Colt . . . remember him?"

"How could I forget?" he said. "I made a three-million-
dollar profit on the picture I did of his book."

"I meant, do you remember the time you took me to
his house?"

"I did? Oh, of course. A brownstone in the East
Sixties, wasn't it?"

"*Gloss* may do an article on him. What's he like?"

"He was having a love affair with himself in those
days. He had won a Pulitzer Prize with his first novel,
but instead of being impressed with it, he blandly told
me he was after the big one. The Nobel. He had written
only about six books when he told me that, and the way
he figured it, ten more prolific years would do it. But I
guess all those marriages and bar fights killed that
dream." Mike looked thoughtful. "I know his last books
haven't been selling well. But I still didn't think he'd
panic enough to go for an interview with a magazine
like *Gloss.*"

"Mike! Have you ever read *Gloss*?"

"From cover to cover, when you said you were going
to work there. And it's not for Tom Colt. Look, babe,
remember about six years ago when all the newspapers
carried the story of how he had a dogfight with a shark?
When the fishing boat he was on capsized, he had been
the one to swim under water and actually punch the
sharks on their snouts and kept them at bay until help
arrived for the others."

"He did?"

"He also fought a bull in Spain. Knocked out a professional fighter in a bar. When his plane crashed, he
walked a mile into town with a broken leg. He can also

drink any man under the table and he can knock out Muhammad Ali with one hand tied behind him."

"He can?"

Mike laughed. "No . . . but that's the kind of publicity he wants. He did knock out a lot of guys in barroom fights, only no one knows if he knocked out a fighter. The shark story is true . . . so is the bull. Everyone says it was a tired bull, but the fact is, he did go in the ring and try it. And what I'm getting to is . . . *that's* the kind of publicity he goes after. And I can't see him holding still for a story in *Gloss*."

"Well, we're hoping to get one."

"Oh, you mean you haven't really got it?"

January stared at her tanned legs. "I'm supposed to write him a letter."

"And casually mention that I'm your father?"

"Yeah . . . real casual. Like have you write a P.S. at the bottom."

"No way," he said. "It's not that I wouldn't do it for you. Hell, I'd crawl on my belly if it would help you in any way. But your best chance of getting an interview with him is *not* to mention that I'm your father."

"Why?"

"Well, like I said, when I knew him, he was thinking 'Nobel.' And to make a big commercial hit picture out of his book, I had to leave out a lot of key scenes and characters; otherwise we'd have had a six-hour picture. He never forgave me for it."

"But if the picture made money—"

"It did—for me and the studio. He had just gotten a flat fee—like two hundred thousand—but no percentage. So he was looking at it artistically. Let's say . . . we're not enemies but we're really not exactly buddy chum pals."

"How old is he?"

Mike wrinkled his brow. "About five or six years older than me . . . maybe fifty-seven or fifty-eight. But from what I hear, he's still boozing and making the scene with young broads." He sighed. "Know something? There's nothing worse than an overaged stud.

It's like a forty-year-old woman trying to look like a
teeny bopper."

"What would you suggest I do about getting the interview?"

"Forget it . . ."

And then the butler announced lunch was being
served, guests began arriving at the pool, Dee made her
entrance in flowing pajamas and a large hat, and the
ornate buffet lunch had officially begun.

After that he didn't get too much chance to talk to
January. There were at least fifty guests. Several of the
young men gave David rough competition for her attention. Mike noticed this. And he also noticed David's
confident attitude. Why not? The bum was gonna have
her all to himself on the plane ride home. But Mike was
beginning to like him better. The few times they had
talked during the week, he had detected a warmth that
the boy hadn't shown before. Probably being with January had drawn him out, made him loose. Or maybe just
because he felt that David might become a permanent
fixture, he was *looking* to like him. Anyway, he wasn't
in the mood to analyze his thoughts. She was leaving
soon, the whole caboodle would soon leave—and he'd
be alone with Dee tonight. Tomorrow the luncheons
would begin again . . . And then there would be the
start of parties before the final Christmas rush. She had
said something about going to Palm Springs for a week in
January—a backgammon tournament—and they would
be houseguesting with friends. Maybe after that they
could go back to New York. He liked the sun and golf
—but enough was enough. Even though he just played
gin and goofed in New York, it was different. There was
something invigorating about New York, about the cold
weather. It was his town. He could still walk down Fifth
Avenue and run into someone he knew . . . talk shop
at the Friars Club . . . see the Broadway shows . . .
go to Danny's Hide-a-Way for dinner with January when
Dee played backgammon. He remembered the old days
when Danny's was his second home. He'd sit at that front
table with the girl of the moment—and most of the
time he knew everyone in the room. But lately . . . he

didn't see the same faces anywhere. Where did everyone go? At "21" and at Danny's, new faces sat at the front tables . . . TV stars, recording artists, Society Charlies. But he still wanted to get back to New York. And tonight he'd ball Dee, make her happy, dependent on him—and then suggest a stopover in New York for a few weeks after Palm Springs.

He drove January and David to the airport and watched them climb into the plane. He walked back to his car. They looked so young and beautiful. When did he get so old? He stared at himself in the rear view mirror as he drove. He was going to be fifty-three. Hell, that wasn't old. He was in his prime. And he looked good. He didn't have an extra ounce of flesh on him. Dames still gave him the look. Of course they were Dee's friends—all in their forties—but at the club some of the younger women who played golf gave him the eye. But he always kept his smile open and friendly, nothing more, even though there were a few he would have liked . . . that daughter of Dee's banker friend . . . Monica. Yeah, Monica was about thirty-two, a divorcee. She was suddenly taking golf lessons every day. One of his gin-playing friends said it was because of him. Monica . . . yeah . . . That'd be real nice. But he wouldn't. He had made a deal with himself—if he married Dee and if she laid enough money on January, he'd play it straight. Besides, there was nothing wrong with Dee's looks. She was slim. A little soft in spots . . . but good-looking. Hell, plenty of men would give anything to be able to have her whenever they wanted . . . and he had only "wanted" twice a week lately. That was all wrong. She couldn't come to him and ask. She wasn't like Tina St. Claire, who would say, "Hey, lover, let's fuck." No. The Dees waited. And they didn't fuck . . . they made love. And you courted them. He had let it get cut and dried, he had to change all that. If this was the life he was stuck with, he could at least make it interesting.

It was almost six o'clock when he got back to the house. Everyone had gone. One of the butlers was restocking the bar on the terrace. "Where is Mrs. Wayne?" he asked. For a moment the butler stared at him vacantly. Mike swore softly—the dumb sonofabitch was one of the help who still thought of her as *Miss Granger* —well, he wasn't going to say it, he'd never say, "Where is Miss Granger?" Not if they stood all day and had a staring contest. The old butler blinked a moment—then a happy smile spread across his features as his memory rewarded him. "Madam is upstairs resting, I believe."

Mike nodded and started toward the massive flight of stairs. He looked at them for a moment, turned around, took the elevator down to the wine cellar. He selected a bottle of champagne and took it to the kitchen and waited while the maid set it up with glasses and put caviar on an iced dish.

She was lying on the chaise longue when he came in carrying the tray. Her phone book was in her lap and he realized she was setting her appointments for the following week. He walked over with the tray and set it on a table.

"What's the occasion?" she asked.

"Us . . . we're alone . . . and I dig you." He walked over and took the phone book out of her lap. He sat on the edge of the chaise. "We have no dates tonight, have we?"

"Several parties we can drop in on if you like. Vera is in town and the Arnold Ardens are giving a party for her. Then there's—"

He leaned over and kissed her. "How's about blowing them all. . . ." His hand went under her dressing gown. She pushed him away. "Mike, it's only six o'clock."

He laughed. "Where is there a rule that sex has to happen on specific hours? Now, let's get a little high . . . and make love right over there on that big bed where we see the ocean and maybe if we're lucky . . . the moon will come up. Twilight fucking is just great, Dee."

"Mike!" She jumped up and walked across the room. "Who do you think you're talking to . . . one of those chorus girls you used to date?"

He came to her. "Oh, Dee . . . that's part of love talk. I meant no harm."

"Well, it's vulgar."

He grinned. "Come on. I've said that word when we were in bed."

"That's different. I mean, when you're actually doing it, well, I can't stop you from saying those words, but . . . well, I don't like them. Oh, I know some men get a kick out of using them . . . but why? Does it excite them, does it make them feel more of a man? One of my husbands couldn't even get an erection until he forced me to say that word, to say I wanted him to . . . you know."

He managed to force a smile. "All right. I'll try and watch my language in the kip . . ." He came to her but she turned away. "Now what?"

"Oh, Mike, don't be ridiculous. This is not the time for—" She turned away.

He stared at her back for a moment. Then he picked up the champagne and started for the door.

She turned around. "Now, Mike . . . don't be angry. It's just that I'm not in the mood."

"Okay. I understand." He saluted her with the bottle. "I think I'll have this all by myself. Because it is an occasion, you know . . . It's the first time I ever got a turn-down. But like they say—there's always a first . . ." He closed the door.

Dee stood very still when he left the room. That had been a wrong move. She should have given in . . . but she just couldn't. She was exhausted. Exhausted from smiling and floating from party to party, playing the role of the beautiful cool Dee Milford Granger Wayne. Lucky Dee Milford Granger Wayne, married to such an attractive man. Poor, poor Dee Milford Granger Wayne, heartbroken because that slob of a Polack didn't show up. Karla had practically promised that she would come. Oh, God, how she had wanted Karla to be there. She had especially wanted Karla to see January and David together. To see them swimming together, dancing together, playing tennis together . . . to see that they were young and belonged together. And when she had spoken to Karla on Tuesday, Karla had said "perhaps." She had even promised that if she decided to

come she'd be at the airport at four. Dee had told the
pilot to wait until four-thirty.

She had masked her disappointment when she saw
David and January arrive alone. She was delighted they
were getting on so well. That had been the only bright
spot of the weekend. David seemed to really like January. If only Karla had been there to see it. Why *hadn't*
she come! Just plain perverseness. After all, everyone in
New York had gone away. What would Karla do with
herself during the long weekend?

David had also thought about Karla. He had thought
about her the entire weekend. And he was thinking
about her now as he sat in the plane watching it make
its approach to Butler Jetport, the private field at La
Guardia. He suddenly realized he had barely talked to
January during the flight. But she had been reading
some galleys, and when she had put them away she had
just sat staring out the window. He wondered what she
was thinking about. But he didn't really care.

Actually January was thinking about David. She had
finished the book and had decided to send Tom Colt a
letter on her own as assistant editor of *Gloss*. She
wouldn't tell Linda that Mike would be no help to them.
She watched David's tanned face staring out his window at the bright lights below. He had been so nice
during the holiday. Always ready to play tennis or go for
a swim. That faint glimmer of something she had begun
to feel for him had been snuffed out after their awful
night together. Perhaps it could be fanned back to life.
Perhaps if they had a drink together, talked a bit—
maybe they might even make love again. And this time
it might be all right. But she couldn't face that horrible
red bedroom of his . . . ever.

David had ordered a car. It was waiting on the airfield. They piled their suitcases in the trunk and headed
toward January's building. David helped the chauffeur
give her bags to her doorman. She smiled. "I've enjoyed
the four days together," she said. "Really enjoyed it."

"I have too . . ."

She looked at her watch. "It's only nine o'clock. Want to come up for a drink? You've never seen my sumptuous apartment."

He smiled. "Will you promise me one thing? Give me a raincheck the very next time. I have so many business calls to make when I get home . . . and I know my service is jammed with messages. I'll phone you tomorrow. First thing."

She stared after him as he got back into the car. Wow! Now she knew how Linda felt . . . what a turn-down.

David had no idea he was turning her down. He thought her invitation had been extended out of politeness. And he had no intention of wasting an hour sitting around having a drink with her. He got home, dismissed the car, and checked with his service immediately. There were a few messages. Kim was at a party at Monique's —please come . . . Princess Delmanio had called— she was having a backgammon party . . . His maid had called—she couldn't come in on Monday, but would Tuesday be all right . . . there was a number to call her. There were a few more messages, but none that he cared about. Nothing from Karla. Well, why should there be? She knew he wasn't coming back until tonight. She'd call him tomorrow at his office.

Suddenly he kicked the wastebasket near him. This was ridiculous. It was only nine-thirty. Karla was the woman he loved. He had the whole evening free— they could be together. Yet he had no way of calling her. He couldn't go on like this, sitting around like a girl, waiting to be called. He grabbed his coat, raced out of his building and hailed a cab. He would go to her . . . bang on her door and demand that she give him her phone number. He didn't care if she was asleep. He was going to assert himself. If he wanted her to treat him like a man, he'd better start acting like one. He would stand his ground tonight, even if it meant their first fight. But more than anything he wanted to take her in his arms . . . to look into her eyes . . . feel her strong arms around him . . . listen to the husky laugh.

The cab pulled up. David paid the driver and sprang

out. Ernest, the cheerful and polite doorman, was on.
He gave him the usual friendly nod, but instead of say-
ing, "Good evening to you, Mr. Milford," he said,
"Where are you going, Mr. Milford?"

"To see Miss Karla."

"But she left Friday morning."

"Left!"

"That she did . . . with two suitcases."

"Where? I mean . . . she didn't move . . . or—"

The doorman saw the panic on David's face. "Now
come on, son . . . nothing to be so upset about. Of
course she didn't move. You know Miss Karla. She
always takes off on a moment's notice. None of us here
knew she intended to leave. But on Friday morning down
she comes at nine, huddled in that big fur coat and dark
glasses, only instead of taking her usual walk to her dancing studio, she asks for a cab. And like I said, she's got
them suitcases. She tells me she left word for them to hold
her mail and stop her *Wall Street Journal*. That's the
only newspaper she ever reads . . . but she told me to
check on it and make sure. Then she told the driver Kennedy Airport. That's all I know."

"I . . . I was away myself," David said in an attempt at recovery. He couldn't bear the sympathetic
look in the doorman's eyes. "I was in Palm Beach . . .
you can see by my tan . . . and I haven't checked with
my service. Afraid I took off without giving Miss Karla
any notice myself and I called from the airport and when
her phone didn't answer . . . well, you know how
phones are today . . . you never can tell . . . so I
thought I'd come around. But I'll probably find a message from her on my service."

"Of course you will, my lad."

David turned and walked away. She was gone. No
more of those "Good evenings to you," from the doorman. God, they had been such *good* evenings! Those
evenings when he sailed in, confident and happy, smiling
at the doorman who knew he was expected, nodding to
the elevator man who also knew he was expected. And
now she was gone again. For how long? And why? The
lights of the street were blurring now . . . he began to

run. She was gone . . . without even saying goodbye. He kept running . . . it was the only way to keep from cracking up. He ran all the way to his apartment. And when he let himself in, he called out to the empty walls: "OH GOD . . . KARLA! WHY?"

And then he stood there and sobbed . . . great dry sobs . . . the first time he had sobbed since the day he was cut from the football squad at Andover.

THIRTEEN

Karla sat huddled in the front seat of the jet. After calling all the airlines she had settled on TWA's eleven o'clock flight to London when they had assured her that no one would share her seat.

She was still wearing her oversized dark glasses. So far the young stewardesses had not recognized her. Some of them were only children when she had retired. But these same children were members of the new cult who had discovered her on the Late Show. She watched them giggling together, preparing hors d'oeuvres and drinks, always smiling as they flashed up and down the aisle serving people. They were so young. And so very happy. Had she ever been that young or giggled like that? No . . . it was not possible. Not when you grew up in a village near Wilno.

WILNO. A mistake of migration by her father . . . a mistake made by so many Poles. In 1920, Poland had launched a successful attack on Russia and seized Wilno, the capital of Lithuania. And to this new state came farmers eager for new acres. In 1921, Andrzej Karlowski, his wife, his baby daughter, and their two small sons arrived. He came from a village near Bialystok hoping to make his fortune in Wilno; to send his sons to the university when they were grown. Instead he found a land that was scourged. His neighbors were Ukranians and Ruthenians who retained their national characteristics. There was a small Catholic church in the nearest village, a state school where the nuns taught, and Andrzej and his wife had no choice but to work fifteen hours a day to farm their barren land. There was no time to miss the old life or friends. The farm took all their energy—that and the dream of the university for their sons. And it was in this desolate atmosphere that Natalia Maria Karlowski was raised.

It was a placid unemotional childhood. She grew up with no laughter, no imagination, no dreams, and no ambitions other than to marry a boy with a nice piece of land.

The Karlowskis were good Catholics, and the only day she could remember seeing her mother sitting without peeling potatoes was Sunday, when she attended Mass. On that day her mother exchanged the babushka for the black hat with the large hatpin, the apron for the shiny black dress, and the rosary replaced the paring knife in her rough calloused hands. Her father wore his one black suit, the suit he wore to church, weddings, and funerals.

She attended the state school, and her first few years were as calm and as unemotional as her days on the farm. She was nine when Sister Thérèse arrived, bringing the first bit of beauty and excitement into the lives of the drab little students.

Sister Thérèse was from Warsaw. She had been to Moscow and Paris. She had studied for the ballet and had suddenly gotten the "calling." She gave it all up and entered a convent. The little school had been her first assignment. She told this to her spellbound pupils in a quiet direct way. They stared like mutes—it was the first time any of them had seen a beautiful woman, a woman without weather-beaten skin and red hands. The hard Polish winter robbed young women of their beauty before it blossomed.

All of the girls worshipped Sister Thérèse. But little Natalia was enraptured. And when Sister Thérèse offered to teach some ballet exercises in the gym class, Natalia worked with demoniac energy. At home she spent hours in her small room practicing every exercise because she noticed how pleased Sister Thérèse was when any of the girls displayed the least bit of grace. And a word of praise from Sister Thérèse sent her home with vaguely disquieting, yet hauntingly wonderful daydreams. And then one afternoon, Sister Thérèse asked her to wait after class. Her palms were wet and her heart seemed to be beating in her neck and throat as she waited. Sister Thérèse came to her with a smile. "Natalia, I think you have the makings of a real ballerina. I have talked with the Mother Superior, and if it meets with your family's approval, I would like to try to get you a scholarship at the Prasinski School of Ballet. You will have to live there, and your school work will continue there, but you will receive five hours of ballet a day."

Her mother and father agreed immediately. They knew nothing about ballet; but if a nun had suggested it . . . then it was right. Natalia was torn. She realized it was a great opportunity, except it would mean leaving Sister Thérèse. But when the Sister told her she would visit the school and watch her progress, Natalia felt better. All of the students picked names to use when they danced in the school recitals. Natalia had no imagination. She was enrolled as Natalia Karlowski and that was her name.

For the next seven years her entire life was centered around the ballet and Sister Thérèse. Every Saturday afternoon the students performed a ballet in the little theater in the school. The money for the tickets helped toward running the company. During the first few years of recital, Natalia helped with scenery, makeup, and sewing costumes for the girls who performed. When she was twelve she made the corps de ballet. And each week Sister Thérèse would sit in the audience, and Natalia would dance her heart out to her.

Her mother and father had come to the first recital in their church clothes, looking uncomfortable and warm in the auditorium. Her father fell asleep during the second act and her mother had to pinch him to stop his snoring. They never came again—too long a trip, too much work to be done at home . . .

When Natalia got her first solo, and all the girls insisted she pick a name, it was Sister Thérèse who suggested "Karla." And after the performance when she flung herself into the nun's arms and Sister Thérèse whispered, "Congratulations . . . Karla," she never thought of herself as anything but Karla again. She had been rechristened and reborn.

One day after a recital, Sister Thérèse requested to visit her parents. "You are nineteen. It is time to talk about your future. May I come next Sunday . . . after Mass?"

She would never forget that Sunday. She had left ballet school on an early train. When she reached the house, her parents were still at church, but she smelled the goose and the apple pie. She stood in the small living room. Suddenly it looked so shoddy. It was immaculate . . . but so very poor. It was June, and she rushed outside and picked some spring flowers. She put them around the room and tried to cover the worn spots on the chairs with the doilies. But when Sister Thérèse arrived she seemed unaware of the poverty. She admired the andirons at the fireplace . . . the pewter mugs . . . she moved about like a beautiful porcelain goddess. Sister Thérèse praised the goose and red cabbage and knedlicky. Her mother's round face beamed, and it was the first time Karla realized her mother had dimples . . . or that her father's gray eyes were so beautiful when he smiled. She sat in silence as Sister Thérèse explained to her family that she would like to send Natalia to Warsaw.

"My family is very wealthy," Sister Thérèse said softly. "And my mother's brother, my Uncle Otto, lives in London. He is also a big merchant. They will do for Natalia what they hoped to do for me. She could stay with my family in Warsaw while she auditions for the ballet. Later perhaps she could stay with Uncle Otto if she tries out for the Sadlers Wells in London . . . but do I have your permission?"

Her parents nodded in unison. It was too much for

them to fathom. Warsaw . . . London . . . anything the Sister wished was acceptable—only there was no way they could repay her.

Later Natalia and Sister Thérèse had taken a walk. The moment they were outside, Natalia said, "I am not going to Warsaw. I am not leaving you."

Sister Thérèse had laughed. "In time you will be very happy there. Very shortly our little Prasinski Ballet will not be able to teach you anything more. You are almost ready." Suddenly she pointed toward a tree. "And what is that?"

Karla blushed. "I made that for you when I was nine."

Sister Thérèse walked over to it. Some planks were built around a tree forming a seat, and a crude picket fence surrounded the tree. Karla laughed with embarrassment. "You brought not only dancing, but poetry into my life. One day at school you talked about a beautiful gazebo . . . you made it so real . . . I could almost see you sitting in it. So I came home and built it. I used to dream that one day I would show it to you— and now I see how very ugly it is."

Sister Thérèse entered and sat down. "It's lovely, my little Karla. Come sit with me." Sister Thérèse smelled of clean soap and violets. Suddenly Karla threw her arms around the Sister and said, "I love you. I have loved you since I first saw you."

Sister Thérèse disengaged herself carefully. "I love you, too."

"You do! Oh, then let me kiss you and hold you and—" She reached out and touched the Sister's cheek . . . and held her hand.

But once again Sister Thérèse calmly extricated herself from the girl's embrace. "You must not touch me. It is wrong."

"It is wrong to love?"

"Love is never wrong," Sister Thérèse said. "But physical love between us is wrong. You cannot kiss me or touch me."

"But I want to. Can't you understand? Oh, Sister, I know nothing about the ways of making love. I talk very little to the girls at school. But sometimes at night as I lie in bed in my cubicle, I hear them sneak into bed with one another and I know they are caressing. I have been approached . . . but I turn away. No one matters but you. I lie there alone and dream that you are in a nightgown and coming to me and taking me in your arms and then—"

"And then?" Sister Thérèse asked.

"And then I hold you close and kiss you . . . and touch you—" She paused. "Oh, Sister, I want you close to me. Is that really wrong?"

Sister Thérèse fingered the rosary that hung from her habit. "Yes, Karla, it is wrong. You see, when I studied ballet in Warsaw, I too paired off at night with other girls. It is something that happens . . . girls reach puberty . . . they only have one another . . . there is no time to meet young men. So they love one another. I did it, but I knew it was wrong . . . and it tormented me. And I also knew I was not as fine a dancer as some of the others, that I had been accepted because of my family's money and prestige. And one day after I had just been given a role that another girl had tried out for, I heard someone whisper, 'It is her face that got her the role . . . not her feet.' And the girl who did not get the role ran off sobbing, saying my beauty was evil—that it got me things I did not deserve." Sister Thérèse's face was drawn as she forced the unpleasant memory into words. "That night I fell to my knees and prayed for help. And suddenly it was as if I had been released from a prison. I realized I didn't want to be a great ballerina. I found I wanted only to serve and love *Him* . . . my sweet Jesus. I spent days meditating. I read the lives of all the Saints, read about how *they* had gotten the calling, and suddenly when I read the life of the Little Flower—Saint Thérèse who just wanted to do 'little things'—I knew then that I must become a nun. I knew I could never bring about any big miracles . . . but I could make people happy by doing little things. And the first little thing happened when I left the ballet. The girl who had run off sobbing got my part. And believe me, Karla, it was the first genuine happiness I had known. And when I came here, and saw all the serious little faces,

I knew that the years of study had not been in vain
. . . not if they could bring some little bit of happiness
to the children of Wilno . . . and to you, my little
Karla. And you must work hard at your dancing . . .
and always remember *He* is watching and that it is a
mortal sin to make love with a woman. One day a man
will come along . . . and then you will understand true
love."

"Why didn't that man come along for you?"

"He did. His name is Jesus."

Then they left the gazebo, and they never spoke about
love again. As the summer drew to an end, Sister
Thérèse changed the plans about the Warsaw trip.
"We must arrange for you to go to England. . . ."

"When?"

"Immediately. I have written to Uncle Otto in London
about you. Today I received an answer. He and Tante
Bosha will be delighted to have you stay with them
while you audition for the Sadlers Wells."

Karla tried to put her off. "Not for a while. Next year
perhaps."

But Sister Thérèse was insistent. "You must make
your plans to leave in ten days. Here is your plane ticket
to London."

Karla stared at the ticket Sister Thérèse had placed
in her hand. She shook her head. "No . . . no . . . I
don't want to go."

"Karla, you must listen to me. War is just seconds
away. Germany has signed the nonaggression pact with
Russia. Von Ribbentrop went to Moscow last week. Why
do you think I said you must not go to Warsaw? You
will only be safe in London."

"But what about you? If it is so dangerous . . . why
are you staying?"

"I am protected. I am in the church. Even in wars,
the church is not molested. God will protect me. Jesus
watches over us all."

"Then let Him watch over me."

"No. You have your own calling."

The following day there were no classes as all the

students and teachers huddled around the radio and listened to the news that Hitler had served notice on England and France that Germany wanted Danzig and the Polish Corridor. There was talk . . . groups huddled together—how would war affect the ballet? But the following day all the students were back to their bar work and rehearsals went on as usual. But reality and fear hit the Prasinski Ballet on August 31, when Hitler offered Poland sixteen conditions of peace and Poland rejected the terms. Suddenly there was frenzied activity at Prasinski. Classes ended. Suitcases were dragged out. Instructors tried to get train reservations to get back to their homes. That night everyone gathered in nervous little groups, whispering together. Students who had to part to return to homes in distant cities sat together, their arms around each other, openly professing their love. Karla sat alone and thought about Sister Thérèse. What was she doing? Praying with the other nuns? Was she thinking about her?

The following morning at dawn, without any formal notice of war, Germany invaded Poland. Students no longer waited for proper trains. They left on foot. They sat at railroad stations waiting for any train. Karla was fortunate. She managed to get a lift from a milk farmer who had land near her parents.

When she finally reached the farm, she found her parents sitting in front of the radio in a somnambulistic stupor. Their sons had left the university to join the army . . . everything they had worked for was gone. Karla had never read newspapers, but now she went to the village to buy the daily paper. She read about things she couldn't understand. She suddenly realized she knew so little about anything other than ballet. She knew all about Nijinsky—his wife, his manager, his instructors. But she knew nothing of the world she lived in. She had been aware of the peril of Hitler . . . but the full impact of war had never permeated the Prasinski Ballet.

Now the most important moments were the broadcasts from Radio Warsaw—listening to it sign on with the first few notes of the Chopin Polonaise in A Major. When she learned German mechanized units had reached the outskirts of the capital and had opened fire on Warsaw, she knew it was time to leave. She must get to London and Uncle Otto. She packed her bag, kissed her parents goodbye, and walked the two miles to the convent to tell Sister Thérèse.

When she arrived, Sister Thérèse was sitting at the radio, fingering her rosary, her eyes staring into space. All night she had tried to get through to her parents in Warsaw, but the lines were down. When she saw Natalia's bag and heard she planned to go to London, she shook her head with a sad smile. "It is too late for that. No planes . . . no trains . . . no more ballet . . . the dream has ended."

Secretly, Karla was relieved that she would not have to leave Wilno and Sister Thérèse. For the next week she alternated between visiting the convent and sitting with her mother and father at the farm, listening to the radio. The radio became a way of life. Her family couldn't get through to their relatives in Bialystok . . . obviously they had fled. The escape route was through Rumania. In the village a mass exodus had begun. A constant flow of people carrying bundles, bits of valuable furniture, and even some livestock, were trying to make their way to Rumania. The Polish army was fighting valiantly, but on the seventeenth of September the Russians began to invade from the east. Andrzej told his wife and daughter to seek refuge at the convent. Maria, fear turning the blue eyes glassy in her round weather-beaten face, refused to leave her husband and their land. But she insisted Karla must go. She stared at the girl as if seeing her for the first time. "You are tall . . . you will be a strong beautiful woman. Go to the convent. Even the Russians will not harm the church."

Somehow Karla knew it was the end of the only life she had known. These two strangers were her parents . . . yet she didn't know them. She clung to them, but they barely responded. They stood like petrified images of people. They did not know how to give affection . . . or to accept it. They raised their children because they were there. They farmed the barren land because it was there. And now the two sons had vanished from the university . . . and with them went all hope of any tomorrow. Nothing was left but the land.

Sister Thérèse welcomed Karla into the convent. As people fled they left their dogs, cats and even baby lambs on the street. Each day Karla went out and collected the homeless animals. She took them all into the convent. But as the days passed and the Russians drew closer, the Mother Superior said they must be turned out. They were running low on supplies themselves . . . they were God's creatures, she claimed, and the Lord would take care of them. Karla had pleaded . . . she had grown to love the kittens and the dogs. She begged to be allowed to keep the smallest, but the Mother Superior was adamant. Another nun collected them and turned them out. When Sister Thérèse came to her room, she found Karla sobbing. She looked up and shouted, "I am never going to love anyone . . . not even an animal. It hurts too much when it's taken away from you."

Sister Thérèse stroked her hair. "Love the Lord. He will never desert you or be taken away from you. He will be with you throughout eternity."

"He'll never leave me?"

"Never. This life is just something to get through as well as we can. But it is only the preparation for the real world—the life we have after death—when we go to Him."

"Perhaps I could become a nun," Karla suggested.

Sister Thérèse looked at the girl seriously. "It is too big a decision to make in such a short time. I do not feel you have the calling. You are coming to this decision from fear. But pray to Him . . . ask Him to show you the way."

And so Karla spent the long days with the Sisters, ate with them, and went to early Mass and evening Chapel with them while the Polish army fought on. After nineteen days of unbelievable resistance to the bombardment of Germany's superior forces, the battered and heroic

defenders of Warsaw surrendered to the Germans. Until
the last hour, Radio Warsaw continued to identify itself
with the first three notes of the Polonaise.

A few days later several Russian officers arrived at
the convent and informed them that they were now living in Russian-occupied territory. Schools were closed,
and the remaining citizens were notified that an immediate Sovietization of the Russian occupied areas had
begun. Tales began to trickle into the convent of midnight arrests by the Soviet officers. At first they were
made on the charge of subversiveness to the new government. By September 30, President Moxcicki had crossed
the border into Rumania with the entire government,
and the exiles formed a provisional government in exile
in Paris.

General Sikorsky, also in exile, acted through some
high-ranking Polish officers who had remained in the
country, and gradually the Polish Underground began.
It was a ground swell that grew larger and larger despite
cruel and barbaric reprisals. It became known as the
Polish home army—ARMIA KRAJOWS, whispered among
the Poles as the A.K.

No one bothered the nuns, but for safety's sake, after
hearing rumors of rape by drunken army privates, the
Mother Superior allowed Karla to wear the habit. Each
weekend Karla drove the battered convent car to her
parents' farm and brought them any news that she heard.
And she would return to the convent with fresh eggs,
which her parents insisted she give to the Sisters. The
Soviets had reopened elementary and secondary schools.
Nuns were no longer allowed to teach, and the Polish
universities at Lwow and Wilno were transformed into
centers designated to convert the population to the
Soviet order. Although the convents and churches were
not desecrated, religion was frowned upon.

One weekend, just before Christmas, she drove to
the farm, just as her mother and father were being
herded into a jeep by two Russian officers. She was wearing her nun's habit and was about to rush to them, but
her mother merely nodded and said distantly, "Hello,

Sister. Take the eggs for the convent. They are in the kitchen." She started toward them, but the fear in her father's eyes also shot her a warning not to speak. The Russian soldiers ignored her, made some jokes among themselves about the ugly black habit, and drove away in the jeep with her parents. She felt helpless. But if she rushed after them and declared they were her parents . . . then what? Be taken off with them and shipped to a labor camp.

She drove back to the convent, and as she got out of the car, she noticed a good-looking young Russian officer turn to stare at her on the street. She rushed inside and bolted the door, and that night when she looked at herself in the small bathroom mirror she realized that although the coif hid her hair, it only served to make her prominent cheekbones and large eyes more effective. She stared at herself from every angle. Yes . . . she was beautiful . . . not petitely beautiful like Sister Thérèse . . . but the way the Russian officer had stared . . . she knew a man would find her desirable. But she was now serious about becoming a nun, and in her daily prayers she asked guidance and pleaded for the Lord to make her love Him more and Sister Thérèse less. But as arrests grew more frequent, her days became too busy for daydreams about Sister Thérèse. Half of the chapel had now been converted into bed-space for the children found wandering in the streets . . . children whose parents had been taken off in the night. And the library which had been the Mother Superior's office held cribs with five infants. Mothers who knew they were being taken away hid their children in closets and warned them against crying out. They often bundled up their infants and hid them in the yard, praying a more fortunate neighbor would care for them. The neighbors invariably brought them to the convent. And as the days passed, more children streamed into the convents. People who had been arrested as "political" prisoners were now arrested for being nothing other than Poles and were forced into slave labor.

As the stories of rape grew, women began to wear

thick glasses to make themselves unattractive to the Russian soldiers. Some carried a handkerchief and a small penknife. If a soldier approached, they cut their finger and let the fresh blood stain the handkerchief. Then if the soldier reached for them, they'd pretend to cough into the handkerchief, show the fresh blood, and say "Tuberculosis." It was an effective ruse, and it forced many soldiers into an abrupt change of mind.

Both Sister Thérèse and Karla had acquired thick glasses brought to them by the children. They came with their pitiful possessions. A lock of the mother's hair . . . the father's glasses . . . the family Bible.

Winter came early the year of 1939. By October there was snow on the ground, and when dusk came they could hear the soldiers singing songs of their homeland. But when they were drunk, their songs were raucous and often they loitered near the convent. Many nuns grew frightened, but Sister Thérèse would constantly remind them, "They are God's children too. It is a war between countries . . . not *people*. Remember, they are in a strange land . . . away from their loved ones. Conquerors can be the loneliest of all."

A few weeks later, Karla was in the children's dormitory, hearing the children's prayers. She was about to turn out the lights when she heard the thundering noise downstairs at the front door of the convent. The children began to scream when they heard the sounds of Russian voices and heavy boots. She quickly put on her thick glasses and commanded the children to be quiet. She slipped out of the dormitory and tiptoed down the stairs. The sight in the reception room turned her rigid with terror. A surge of nausea ripped through her, and she clamped her hand over her mouth to kill the scream that started in her throat. She wanted to run, but she was paralyzed as she clung to the wall in the safe darkness. She wanted to cover her eyes but her horror held her transfixed.

The Mother Superior was naked. She had always seemed such a powerful and domineering figure as she marched into Chapel, shrouded in the thick black habit with the massive silver cross hanging down her ample front. But stripped of her habit, she had diminished into a skinny old woman, with long flat hanging breasts, blue-veined legs, a quivering object of ridicule to the drunken soldiers who laughed every time they glanced her way. She stood huddled in a corner, praying, as the Russian soldiers boisterously and methodically raped all the other nuns who were lying nude on the floor, their helpless arms and legs flapping under the weight of their merciless captors.

And then Karla saw Sister Thérèse. Blood was smeared between her thighs as one Russian got off her. Another picked her up by the neck and kissed her violently. Then his mouth began to ravage her body, beginning at the breasts as he chewed away on each of them, his dirty fingers groping between her legs. While he was enjoying himself, slobbering down her body, an-other soldier approached her from the back, spread her buttocks apart and rammed into her. At the same moment, the soldier in front opened his pants and also rammed into her. Karla couldn't believe it—two men tearing at her insides . . . one from the front . . . one inside her back! Mercifully, Sister Thérèse passed out.

Karla stood crouched in the darkness for half an hour. She counted ten of them who had attacked Sister Thérèse alone. Suddenly she heard footsteps behind her. It was Eva, the thirteen-year-old who helped her with the smaller children. Karla tried to motion her away, but it was too late. The child saw the nude bodies on the floor and screamed. The soldiers looked toward the dark hall. "Run, Eva," Karla commanded. "Run and get into bed." But the child stood frozen as the soldier approached.

He grabbed Karla and Eva by the arms and shoved them into the room. One soldier looked up at Karla and saw the thick glasses. He shrugged with distaste, but snatched off the white starched bib and pulled her habit apart. He looked at her flat chest, and at the glasses, and pushed her away and reached out for the screaming

Eva. Karla rushed over to protect the child, but she was thrown across the room where she fell against the naked and shivering Mother Superior mumbling bits of prayers. Karla adjusted her habit, stood in front of the older nun, and clenched her teeth as the tormented Eva's screams filled the room. Sister Thérèse was still mercifully unconscious.

The bedlam began to abate after another half hour. The soldiers were satisfied. They adjusted their belts and pants and stared at the limp naked bodies on the floor like diners who have eaten their fill at a banquet but are still loath to leave food on a table. One who was obviously in command pointed at Sister Thérèse, Eva, and three other nuns and shouted a command. Blankets were thrown around them, and the soldiers threw them over their shoulders like potato sacks and carried them outside. Karla broke away from the icy grip of the Mother Superior. "Where are you taking them?"

One soldier who spoke Polish said, "To our camp. Do not worry, ugly one. We only want the beauties. We leave you and the others to stay and take care of the children."

She stood at the door helplessly as the jeeps rolled away into the cold night. As the last sounds of the raucous laughter faded away, the Mother Superior began to move like a sleepwalker. She groped around the floor for parts of her habit as other nuns picked up broken rosary beads that were strewn across the room. Prayer books that had been torn from the nuns' hands lay abandoned on the floor. Karla saw Sister Thérèse's prayer book and rosary near the spot where she had lain. She knelt down and touched the blood. She put her fingers to it and touched her lips. She pressed the prayer book to her cheek. Then she set about helping the other ravaged nuns. She ran baths for them, put ice on swollen lips, prayed with them and for them. By dawn some semblance of order was restored. Shrouded in a new habit, the Mother Superior seemed to take on at least a shadow of her old strength.

A week later the same soldiers returned. They were

more raucous than before. And this time Karla did not escape. They pulled off her glasses and her clothes. She was thrown on the floor and her head struck against a chair. She prayed for unconsciousness but was jolted into awareness with the knifelike pain as her legs were forced apart and the soldier ripped into her. Rhythmically, roughly, they rode her, one after another—five, six, seven, eight . . . her blood mixed with their orgasms . . . their wet mouths biting at her lips, her breasts.

And then she saw the heaviest man coming toward her. He looked like a giant. He fell on top of her . . . his breath was foul and he slopped some kisses on her lips . . . she prayed for death . . . then she heard the door open and more voices. Oh, God . . . more soldiers. But suddenly the man was dragged off her. There were angry voices . . . the soldiers were scrambling to their feet. And then, almost gently, an officer was helping her up. It was the same young Russian captain she had seen on the street. Blond and brown-eyed . . . and it seemed as if there was sadness in his eyes as he handed her part of her torn habit to cover herself. Then he snapped orders at the men . . . another officer herded them off. He spoke to Karla in Polish. "I am sorry for what these men have done. They will be punished. We are soldiers, not animals. I shall return tomorrow and see what reparation can be done."

When they were gone, Karla and the other sisters gradually got to their feet. They moved slowly . . . silently . . . and hopelessly. Some of the sisters went to a small chapel they had erected in one of the rooms and prayed. Karla went to her bed and lay very still. She thought about taking her life . . . but then she would spend the rest of eternity in Purgatory. She thought about Sister Thérèse. And for the first time in her fear and loneliness, she found herself thinking of her mother, and as she listened in the darkness of the night, she heard muffled sobs coming from many of the other small cubicles . . . only they were calling for Jesus . . . and suddenly she realized she had no one.

The following morning, the blond young captain arrived and apologized again and promised complete protection for the convent. His name was Gregory Sokoyen. His father was General Alexis Sokoyen . . . and he had just married a beautiful girl whose father was an important government official. He was lonesome for his young wife and took to visiting Karla several nights a week. He would sit in the reception parlor while she sewed and tell her stories of his boyhood, of the children he and his young wife hoped to have.

She listened politely. He was attractive and he was also the first young man she had ever known. He made no improper advances and always brought the nuns provisions along with candy for the children.

It was toward the end of November when Karla noticed her waist was growing thick. She had never been too regular with her periods, but suddenly she realized she was overdue. She was terrified, but she methodically went about her work. When the children went outdoors to play and she noticed some soldiers look with interest toward the ten- and eleven-year-old girls, she immediately cut off their hair and bound their chests and had them dress like boys. And every night, in the secrecy of her bedroom, she did the most strenuous ballet exercises, hoping to dislodge the baby that was forming inside. After a time she realized it was hopeless. Her waist was thick and her stomach was taut.

One morning the young captain arrived unexpectedly with some provisions. He had warm blankets and several pounds of cereal. She helped him unload them and was suddenly seized with an attack of nausea. She rushed to the sink and he held her head as she threw up. "You are sick. You must go to bed," he said.

She managed a smile as she sat down. "I am all right —it has passed."

"What causes your illness?" he asked.

"The Russian soldiers," she said tonelessly.

His eyes shot to her stomach which was hidden by the voluminous folds of her habit. "A baby?" He paused. "Do you want it?"

"Want it . . . how can I want it . . . knowing it came from one of those beasts?"

"But it is also yours. It is your body that is forming it . . . your blood . . . it might be a little girl who would look just like you."

She wrung her hands. "And then what could I do for her? How could I raise her? And besides, how do I know it would not be a boy who would look like Rudolph or Leopold or Nicholas or Igor or Sversky or—"

"You know all their names?"

"When you are lying on the floor and they are calling out to one another . . . you remember. You remember the bad breath, the hairs on their noses, the decayed teeth . . . and their names. Oh God—if there is a God—how can I rid myself of this thing growing in me?"

He colored slightly. "I know of a way that might work. I . . . I saw it happen one night last week. Some soldiers were searching some homes . . . looking for some escaped prisoners from work camps. Suddenly I heard a scream . . . I rushed upstairs . . . one of the soldiers had raped a woman—" He sighed. "You must understand, some of these men are peasants . . . they are lonely . . . they have never been away from the farm . . . they have never had much to drink . . . suddenly they have Polish vodka . . . there are pretty women. And—" He shrugged. "They rape. This man . . . he raped a girl in your condition. Only it was a baby she wanted . . . from her husband. She had pleaded with him . . . told him she was three months' pregnant . . . that she might lose it." He shuddered. "I heard her begging . . . but when I got to the room it was too late . . . and she lost the baby . . . or what was the beginning of the baby. I shot him." Then he stood up. "Think about it . . . I shall come by tonight at eleven. You can give me your decision then."

When he arrived, the convent was dark, but she was waiting at the door. She led him quietly to her small bedroom. With a sense of urgency and no shame, she

took off her robe. He undressed quickly. In the dim
light she saw his young body, he said, "Sister Karla,
are you sure? It could be a little boy with gray eyes
like yours."

"Let us get it done," she said.

He lay beside her on the bed and stroked her body.
She was rigid. When his lips went to her breast she
pushed him away. "Please . . . do your business and
be done with it."

"No . . . first I make love to you." And against her
will he gently caressed her . . . kissed her lips . . .
her neck . . . her breasts . . . And soon she found
herself relaxing. And when he lay on top of her and
took her smoothly, rhythmically and fiercely, she suddenly felt an odd sensation. She held him close, and
when the unbelievable explosion shot through her, she
cried out in agonized delight because she knew she had
lost the baby. When he fell off her, she jumped out of
bed and hid in the corner, covering her eyes. "Don't
tell me what it was . . . just clean it up and take it
away before I see it," she begged.

"There is nothing . . . come look."

"No . . . because if it looks human I will feel that
I have done murder."

"Come, Sister . . . obviously God intends for you to
have it as there is nothing there. The baby is still inside
of you."

"But I felt . . . my whole insides had turned upside
down."

He smiled. "You had an orgasm, my sweet Karla."

Later, as they lay beside one another, he said, "You
must think of your future now . . . you and the child."

"There must be others like me. What are they doing?"

"The mothers are sent to Russian labor camps. Doctors deliver their babies and they are sent to an orphanage. The children will be raised by the state. Si-
beria needs young settlers . . . eventually the orphans
will be sent there when they come of age."

"And what about the children here in the convent?"

He sighed. "As long as I am here they will be safe.
But any day my orders can change. And how long will

our peace with Germany last? Already there are rumblings—"

"Then I must try and reach the A.K."

He put his hand over her lips. "I do not want to know
anything. But I will get you some money. What you plan
to do . . . I must not know."

"I must get the children out of the country first."

"Please, Karla, do not tell me."

Each day he arrived with money. She never asked
where he got it, and he never asked what she did with
it. If he noticed there were fewer children at the convent each time, he never mentioned it. Until one night
when he arrived and she was alone. She had candles
on the table and had cooked the meal herself. She had
discarded the habit and was wearing a dress. He stared
in disbelief as she handed him a glass of wine.

"Are you allowed not to wear the habit?" he asked.

"I am not a nun," she said. "Sit down, Gregory.
There are so many things I want to tell you."

Throughout dinner, she told him the events that had
led to her coming to the convent. It seemed such a
short uneventful life in the telling . . . so little had actually happened to her . . . and now, she sat alone in
the convent with the handsome young Russian soldier
and there was a baby growing inside.

"What about the baby?" he asked.

"The A.K. will take care of it. I will manage to get
to Sweden, I hope . . . have it there . . . and put it
with a family."

"And then?" he asked.

"And then, I will get to London. Sister Thérèse
had an uncle there. Uncle Otto. I have his address."

"And the baby?"

She shrugged. "It will be placed with a family. Somehow I shall send money back to support the child."

"But why go to all that trouble for a bastard you
don't want? If you have it here, it can always be placed
in an orphanage."

Karla's eyes flashed. "Because it will still be half
mine. And it is such a cruel world. I must give it some
kind of a chance. But I would never want the child to

know that I was its mother. I would just send money for its support."

"Then eventually you will send for the child?"

She shook her head. "I am going to be a ballerina. It is hard work. I will give the child money . . . not love. In that way he cannot ever miss what he has never had." She touched her stomach wistfully. "It is not good to grow up knowing someone does not want you. It is better to think the parents are dead."

He held her close that night. And she looked at him intently, as if trying to imprint his image on her mind.

"I shall never forget you, Karla," he said as they made love.

She clung to him, because although she knew she could never really love a man, she was grateful for all he had done . . . and his body felt so young and strong.

Karla closed her eyes as the plane began its descent to Heathrow Airport in London. She had sent Jeremy a cable. But would he be there? He was getting so old. Each time she saw him, he seemed to have shrunk a little more. What would she ever do when the day came that Jeremy would not be there?

The plane landed. . . . There were photographers on the airfield. Karla covered her face and followed the waiting airline official who led her to the limousine. Jeremy Haskins was waiting inside the car. She sat beside him and squeezed his hand. "It was nice of you to come and meet me."

The old man managed a smile. "I'll be eighty next month, Karla. As long as there's a breath inside of me, I shall consider it an honor to meet any plane, boat, or train that you choose to take."

She sat back in the car and closed her eyes. "We've traveled a long road together, Jeremy."

He nodded. "The moment I met you, I felt that we would. . . ."

They had met in a bomb shelter. She had been terrified. She had just arrived that day, and was met by a

smiling Uncle Otto who welcomed her to his home. She
had a nice room. Tante Bosha was warm and jolly and
for the entire morning they had sat and talked about
Poland, about the hazards of her escape. She tried not
to dwell on it, even though they were anxious for details. She omitted the gory parts—the rape, the Russian
soldiers, her own pregnancy. She just spoke glowingly
of the A.K. Uncle Otto had heard nothing from Sister
Thérèse or her family, and without actually saying
it, Karla insinuated that Sister Thérèse and the other
nuns, along with the orphans, were safe.

At dusk she had gone for a walk. Uncle Otto had
warned her not to go far. At any time the air raids
might begin. London was in the midst of Germany's
blitz, and the British people were growing accustomed
to spending many a night in an air raid shelter. The
Nazis had given up daylight raids the past October when
the RAF in an enormous counterattack took too big a
toll on their Luftwaffe invaders. But they still continued
their night attacks on London, which spread panic and
destruction but had little military value.

She had walked about ten blocks when she heard
the first siren. She stood rooted to the spot as people
came pouring from their homes heading for the nearest
Underground. She started back toward the house but
stopped when she realized she'd never make it in time,
and that Uncle Otto and Tante Bosha were probably in
a shelter themselves. So she turned and followed the
stream of people. She found a spot and sat with her
hands over her ears as she heard the sounds of destruction overhead.

"Child, you act as if this is your first air raid."

She looked up at the smiling man. She found herself
smiling back. "It is in a way."

"Where are you from?"

"Wilno . . . Poland. Is my English that bad?"

"Dreadful. But then, I don't even speak a word of
Polish so you're way ahead of me. What's your name?
I'm Jeremy Haskins."

He forced her to talk as the bombs fell and she told
him about Uncle Otto and Tante Bosha . . . and how

she intended to try out for the Sadlers Wells Ballet. Of
course that would not be for some time . . . it was
so long since she had practiced . . . she would have
to get a job in a factory or something first . . . and
work out each day to get into shape.

"I can't really see you in the darkness," he said. "Are
you beautiful?"

"I am a fine dancer," she said.

When the All Clear sounded they came outside. He
walked her home and told her about himself. He was a
publicist for J. Arthur Rank films. His wife was an
invalid and his daughter had been killed in a bombing
raid. They reached the block Uncle Otto's house was on
and for a moment she thought they had come to the
wrong place. A street that had held a row of houses
an hour ago was now just a smoldering ruin. Fire trucks
were still hosing down some charcoaled skeletons of
buildings. There were moans of people who were being
taken to ambulances . . . cries of young babies . . .
and the muted sobs of the women as they plowed among
the ruins of their homes, searching for things dear to
them.

Suddenly she saw Uncle Otto, holding Tante Bosha's
hand. She dashed after them. Tears were streaming
down his face. "Our money . . . so much of it . . .
we had in there. All burned . . . gone. Bosha's pearls
. . . everything is gone." He looked at Jeremy in a
daze. "Such beautiful things we had from the old
country . . . things I was hoping to sell to give my relatives in Poland a chance when all this is over. Tapestry
. . . fine laces . . . paintings . . . all gone. A Goya
. . . gone! No money can replace that." He looked toward the sky. "Why? This is no military target . . .
this is plain vandalism . . . destruction without reason." Suddenly he seemed to remember Karla. "Your
clothes . . . they are all gone. I will get some money
from the bank tomorrow . . . tonight we are to stay
with a neighbor in the next block . . . they have no
extra room for you, but perhaps if I ask around someone will put you up."

"She can come stay with us . . . in our daughter's room," Jeremy Haskins said quickly.

Uncle Otto frowned. He looked at Jeremy Haskins as if suddenly seeing him for the first time. Then he stared toward the charred ruins of his house, and heaved a lumbering sigh, a sigh that signified he felt too old, too tired, and too despondent to take on the added responsibility of the morals of a strange Polish girl. He nodded with a vague relief, and Karla found herself meekly following Jeremy Haskins to the Underground. They got into a crowded train and rode in silence. After a time she felt he was staring at her. Her face flushed and she looked down at her plain hands.

He reached over and patted them. "They could do with a little manicuring. But you know, you are really quite beautiful."

She kept staring at her hands. This nice man who had comforted her during the air raid, who had convinced Uncle Otto he was sincere—who was he really, and where were they going? There probably never had been a daughter who died . . . or a sick wife. He was probably taking her off to some dreadful little room and . . . she stared down at her mud-spattered shoes. Did it really matter? Where did she have to go? And after the Russians . . . what could this poor little Englishman do? Force her to spread her legs . . . what did it matter?

Suddenly he spoke. "Look, my girl, there's a part in a film that a friend of mine is producing. It's not a large part, but it would put you over. It's a Nazi spy, and I was just thinking—your accent would be perfect. Can you act at all?"

"I don't know . . . my English is bad."

"Of course. But it will be perfect for the role. Tomorrow we shall have you meet him. And look, old girl —it may not be Sadlers Wells, but it's certainly better than the factory."

He had a nice little house and she met the invalid wife, a lovely tissue-paper-looking lady named Helen, who looked at her husband as he made the tea, her eyes filled with gratitude and death. She was delighted that Karla had come to stay. Her pride was mingled with sadness as she offered her their daughter's room. Karla had never had such a nice room, and as she fell asleep, she felt safe . . . and knew that once again she had found someone who would think for her.

She had gotten the part . . . and suddenly the acceleration of the pace of her life was like a movie running in double time. Makeup tests, costume fittings, nights of working on her heavy accent . . . and the final discussion . . . the argument over her name. She insisted on being called Karla . . . just one name. Karla. Arnold Malcolm, the producer, finally agreed. He also sensed the stubborn Polish girl had something that would register on the screen. And as Arnold Malcolm predicted, it happened. The newspapers all singled out the new foreign discovery. She caused a small sensation when the picture came out, and the only thing that made her sad was Helen's death, which occurred a week before the picture was finished. Once again Karla realized the danger of growing attached to someone. She had cared about the delicate woman who bore her suffering so silently, who had helped her with her English, and encouraged her each day. They buried her silently and without tears. And that same day she took the Underground back to work at the studio. Karla sat stoically, and when she got off she said, "I hate movie making. I hate the English language which I will never be able to learn. I hate the waiting, the lights—but most of all, I hate this train."

And Jeremy had managed a tight smile and said, "One day you will understand English with ease and you shall ride in a limousine."

Jeremy had sold the house and taken a flat for himself and Karla in Kensington. He gave up his job with J. Arthur Rank and became her manager. The newspapers all hinted that he was her lover, but actually they had only gone to bed once. She had done it out of gratitude and he had realized it. "I was silly to hope . . . I am too old for you." He sighed.

"No," she said, looking at him directly. "It is not your fault. You see, I am a lesbian."

Her tone was so matter-of-fact that he found himself accepting it as just another fragment of information about her life. And then, as they lay in the darkness, holding hands like two good friends, she told him everything about herself. About the men who had raped her . . . about Gregory . . . about the baby, who was living with a Swedish couple. She sent money to them every month now. And when he asked why the baby was never to know she was its mother, she had answered, "What you never have, you cannot lose. It was still such a little baby when I left—it didn't know me, I didn't know it. Neither of us will feel pain or disappointment in one another this way. Why should my child wonder which bastard was the father—or feel neglected because I am not there?"

When he tried to probe her about Gregory—or force her to admit she really cared for him—she shrugged. "Perhaps I did. I will never know. I was so filled with hate for what the Russians had done to Sister Thérèse, to the others . . . I never let myself feel." And then she went on to tell of a short but tender love affair she had had with a woman resistance worker in the A.K. A woman who had been beautiful, considerate and kind, who had helped her with her escape, helped her get the baby to Sweden. No, it was the tenderness of a woman that she loved. She could never really love a man.

So they became good friends. Together they worked on her English, on the parts she played. In her fourth picture she received star billing. Each day she'd sit with Jeremy in the darkened studio and stare at the daily rushes on the screen. She couldn't believe that she was that exciting woman on the screen.

It was Jeremy who decided against interviews. "We shall not allow any. Your English is not good enough, you might not understand some of their questions, you would be misquoted, and—"

"And I am stupid and dull."

"No, that isn't true. You are still very young. On the screen you come across worldly . . . as a woman of mystery. But to know you . . . is to know a child."

"No, Jeremy. I am stupid. I know it. You do not have to pretend. I hear other actresses talking. They speak of Shakespeare . . . they can quote him. They talk about books written by Maugham, Colette, even American writers like Hemingway. Some of them ask me about Polish writers. I know none of them . . . but *they* do. They speak of art . . . I know nothing."

"You may lack education," he said. "But you are not stupid. To realize there are things you don't know only proves you are most intelligent. If you like, I can help you learn about these things."

"Will they help me make more money?"

"No . . . but they—"

"Forget it," she said.

Karla was terrified about going to California, but Jeremy had signed the contract with Century. And then, on the day she was supposed to leave for Hollywood, the Swedish couple had cabled that they didn't want to take care of the child any longer. Jeremy sent her to California alone, in spite of her protests, while he remained and arranged to have the child brought to London. He hated to trust her away from him for the six weeks it took to get things settled with the child and bring it to London. When he got to California, he found his premonitions had not been groundless. She was living in a huge partially furnished mansion the studio had found for her and was enmeshed in an ecstatic love affair with Heidi Lanz.

"Karla, you cannot afford this kind of gossip. It could ruin you. Heidi is a big star with a husband and three children. The public would never believe it of her."

"Tell me about my child."

"Everything is fine. I have found a perfectly marvelous couple—John and Mary. They think the child is a distant relative of mine and your interest is due to our relationship. The child is a little slow—the doctors say it has something to do with not getting enough oxygen at birth—but I think it was the Swedish couple. They scarcely ever spoke. John and Mary are marvelous. Everything will be fine. Naturally they think we are lovers."

"Wait until you meet Heidi . . ."

"Karla, you must be more discreet."

"I will be a star after this picture in America. An international star. Already they compare me with Garbo and Dietrich . . . they say I am bringing back the lost glamor. Here, look at my pictures—on *Photoplay, Modern Screen, Movie Mirror* . . . all of them. Wonderful stories about the great Karla. So do not worry—my publicity has been excellent. I have obeyed you to the letter. No interviews, closed set, lunch alone in my dressing room. No one can see me except Heidi."

He sighed. "Karla, already in London there have been pictures of the two of you in pants, ducking cameramen."

Karla shrugged. "Out here everyone wears pants . . . and many people duck cameramen."

"Are you saving money—remember—for your child? You want the best schools . . . everything you missed—"

"Am I saving?" She threw back her head and the throaty laugh filled the room. "I have been here almost seven weeks and have only cashed one paycheck. Heidi pays for everything!"

The romance between Karla and the German star didn't last long. But Jeremy was amazed at how the top lesbians of the film colony came after her. He wondered if there was some sort of radar that passed among them —like a neon sign lighting on their forehead that only they could see. But Karla refused to mingle with them.

Byron Masters was cast opposite her in her third picture. He was dashing, handsome, did his own stunts, had been married three times, and was bisexual. And to Karla his resemblance to Gregory was startling. She suddenly grew coy. And when she learned he was currently living with another male star, the challenge ap-pealed to her. Suddenly she wanted a young man's strong body in her arms.

They began filming, and after the first week, Byron moved out on his roommate . . . fell insanely in love with her . . . to the extent that he allowed her to dominate the entire picture. She emerged a full-fledged star, and stories of their romance flooded every movie magazine.

For a few months she reveled in her love affair with Byron. She had him come to dinner at her sparsely furnished home. They cooked steaks and ate in the kitchen. Jeremy had discreetly moved to a furnished apartment and grown interested in a divorced real estate lady.

But Byron loved the excitement of Hollywood—the large parties, the klieg-light openings. Karla refused to attend them. In her own home when she picked up the steak with her fingers, he laughed—they were two kids on a picnic. But she knew her table manners were bad (Jeremy had given up on pleading with her about the slurping noises she made with soup or tea), and she was terrified of crowds, and of the brittle small talk that went with big parties. She was afraid they would laugh at her accent. So gradually her affair with Byron ended, and he fell in love with his new leading lady.

Karla took it very philosophically. There was always an ingenue who went into raptures at the idea of coming to the great Karla's home. On the set Karla never even acknowledged the girl . . . so if the girl did talk about her "romance" with the great Karla, there would be no credence to her stories. And every so often there was a young man who reminded her of Gregory, and she allowed him to come and make love to her and eat steak in the kitchen. The press always lunged at these romances and blew them up. Fan magazines were screaming for stories on Karla . . . but the romances were usually over before the story got into print.

And then in 1952, Karla co-starred with Christopher Kelly. He was of Dutch and French extraction and had the combination of blond hair and brown eyes that always attracted her. Christopher's popularity was also at its crest. He ate steak in her kitchen the first week they worked together. And throughout the three months it took to film the picture, the romance grew in intensity.

She learned she was pregnant the last week of shooting. She thought about it coldly and unemotionally. Theoretically, the practical thing would be to rid herself of it *and* Christopher. But for the first time she found she couldn't just walk away. It caught her by surprise. She had never become involved with a man to the extent that she didn't want him to leave her. Oddly enough she found it easier to handle her romances with women. She could make all the rules. She felt no fear of being hurt with women. They loved her. With women her problem was to ease them out of her life and cause as little pain as possible to the girl she was rejecting. And most men had also fallen into line, becoming almost effeminate in their desire to please . . . to acquiesce . . . to hold her.

But Christopher was different. He had actually dragged her to his palatial house with all the servants and taught her to swim. He tried to teach her tennis but she never got further than volleying the ball across the net.

And now the picture was almost over. In six weeks she was to start another. She could have him as her leading man if she wished. Century had already signed someone else—a newcomer. They didn't feel the need of paying out two star salaries. Karla could carry a picture alone. But if she demanded Christopher, they would get him.

Christopher didn't care one way or another. He was one of the new breed of stars who worked without a studio contract. His fee was two hundred thousand a picture, and he'd work for Twentieth, Metro, Century —any studio that gave him his fee, and offered a starring role and co-star billing.

She waited until the picture was finished. Then one night as they were taking a drive she told him about her pregnancy. "I am seven weeks late," she said. He almost veered off the road. "Karla . . . it's fabulous! We'll head right now for Tia Juana . . . we'll get married . . . keep it secret . . . then in about a week we'll tell everyone we got married before the picture. Your little man Jeremy can fix everything."

She agreed and watched him turn the car around and whip down from the mountains. "It will be great. We'll give up both our homes . . . get a huge showcase . . . maybe have it built. There's a great piece of property up on Crescent. I've got two alimonies to pay. But what the hell . . . I make two hundred thousand a picture, and with what you make we can live like royalty. We'll call our home Karl-Kel . . . we'll be the new royalty . . . we'll entertain. Karl-Kel will be like Pickfair was in the old days, and we'll be the new royal couple. We'll live to the hilt!"

Live to the hilt!

"Turn back," she said harshly.

"What's the matter?"

"Turn back. I am not going to Mexico. If you dare to take me there I'll accuse you of kidnapping me."

They drove back to her house in silence. Live to the hilt! Have another baby! How had she allowed herself to think that way? She already had one child to support . . . one huge obligation. She could never live his way—sit back and watch people coming in and drinking *her* liquor . . . eating *her* food. It would be like seeing them take *her* money . . . when she had worked so hard to earn it.

The next day Jeremy arranged for an abortion, and she changed her phone number. A week later Christopher Kelly attempted suicide. He recovered . . . but even this dramatic act could not get Karla to answer his telegrams.

She spent a great deal of money trying to trace Sister Thérèse. But there was no sign of her . . . or of her family. Finally she gave up and concentrated only on her work.

In the middle fifties, Karla was now firmly entrenched

as "Karla, the living legend!" But her salary in no way matched her fame. Her contract with Century had originally started at five hundred a week. With raises and "holdouts" she had worked up to three thousand during the last two years. She knew she was underpaid, but in 1960 the contract would expire, and Jeremy said then they would make their real money.

Jeremy was rich. He had invested in the market and had tripled his money several times over. He had begged and pleaded with Karla to be allowed to invest her money or put her with an investment counselor. But she clung to it and deposited it in savings accounts, never allowing one to exceed ten thousand in any given bank.

She ran into a bad cycle of pictures in 1957 and 1958. But her personal publicity carried her through. The legend grew, and her isolation from the studio heads kept her totally unaware of the box-office receipts. Jeremy saw to it that the public was also unaware of any slip in Karla's popularity. The announcement of her retirement in 1960 caused headlines and shock waves throughout the motion picture industry—throughout the world. Neither Karla nor Jeremy had intended the retirement to become permanent. It began when Jeremy went to renegotiate her contract with the head of Century.

"I hear Elizabeth Taylor is getting a million dollars for *Cleopatra*," Karla said. "I want a million one hundred thousand. Tell the Head I will give him a three-picture deal at three million, three hundred thousand."

While Jeremy was negotiating with the studio, a negotiation that took several weeks, she busied herself building a ballet bar in one of the empty rooms of her house, doing four hours a day of bar exercises, and taking long walks.

Then one night Jeremy came to her house for dinner. He told her he had a deal, but that they would discuss it after dinner. She nodded with her usual detachment. They sat in the kitchen, and he watched her plough into the steak, the gravy running down the chin of the magnificent face so many people worshipped. "Karla, you know the book *The Emperor*?" He sighed as he said it. How could she know it? He knew and she knew that she never read books. "It's number one on all the lists," he went on. "And the Head is trying to get Marlon Brando or Tony Quinn to play the Emperor."

"So . . . ?" She gnawed at the bone of the steak.

"They want you for the Empress."

"So? Is it a right kind of part for Karla?"

"Marvelous."

"And the money?"

"Very little."

She stopped eating. "I thought we were getting a million."

And then in the brightly lit kitchen he explained the facts—how her last few pictures had died at the box office. But her legend was so strong that no one except the top people in the industry realized it. She was to get a hundred thousand for the picture, and, after the break-even point, 2½ percent of the profits . . . which could only mean something after the picture grossed ten million dollars.

She was silent.. Then he said, "We have no alternative."

She pushed away her plate. "If I take so little money, then *everyone* will know I have fallen. But if I retire, no one will know."

Jeremy stared. "You're forty-two years old . . . at your peak."

"Oh, I retire . . . but only for a year. Then they come after me. You'll see. And each offer will get bigger."

He stared at her. It was a brilliant move . . . but could she hold out financially? "You only have two hundred and fifty thousand dollars," he said.

"Invest it in bonds at six percent. I will not touch it."

"But what will you live on?"

Karla crossed the room and stared out at the stone fence she had erected around the house. "It's damp out tonight. But I think I will take a walk." She threw on a coat and left.

Jeremy was in the living room watching the news on television when she came in.

He clicked off the set. "Have you made your decision?"

She nodded. "Have you ever heard of a woman named Blinky Giles?"

"Yes . . she's a millionaire from Texas or somewhere."

"She is also a big bull dyke. For a year now she has let it be known among the girls that she'd drop a hundred thousand dollars at my feet if I would let her be my lover for one night. I will tell Sonya Kinella . . . she has those Sunday brunches that all the gay set attend. I shall tell her to allow Blinky to visit me this weekend."

Blinky Giles . . . the fat heavy-breathing bull dyke. But she had entered the house and tossed the money at her feet. One hundred thousand tax-free dollars. It had been unbelievable. She thought of it now as Jeremy sat at her side. And after Blinky there had been the Countess. . . .

And as her retirement continued, the legend grew. And the offers also grew until one day, three years after her retirement, Jeremy came to her with a contract . . . one million dollars against 10 percent of the gross.

To his amazement, she refused. She openly admitted she was frightened about coming back. She had just met Dee Milford Granger, the "sixth richest woman in the world." Dee was in love with Karla, the legend. What would happen if the picture failed? The legend would be smashed! Why chance it by making a comeback? By remaining a legend, there would always be women like Dee who would offer anything just to be with her. In the last three years she had managed to save almost half a million dollars *without* working. Dee had her own plane, a yacht, and a fag husband who didn't care what she did. Dee wasn't as generous as the others. She had that "prove-you-really-love-me-for-myself" attitude that

some rich people get. But at least Dee was beautiful and
Dee was security. So she refused the million-dollar
offer. And all the ensuing offers. Because she felt secure
in the knowledge that she controlled Dee . . . and
could have her as long as she wished, on any terms that
she wished. And everything had gone just as she had
planned . . . until Dee's fag husband got killed in an
automobile race, which forced Dee to drag out David
as their escort.

David . . . she had thought she was too old for all
that. David with the blond hair and brown eyes. David,
as young as Gregory . . . and she was so old. But a
woman never gets old. It's only the years that mount up.
Inside she is still eternally eighteen . . . and she felt
young and foolish and wonderful when she was with
David.

*The car was approaching Park Lane. Jeremy was
talking about her latest offer. (They still filtered in, no
longer for a million dollars, but big money for a cameo
"starring" role.) The latest was for half a million, two
weeks' work, and a thousand dollars a day expenses.
She smiled as she shook her head. Why bother? What
was she trying to prove? She had never really believed
in herself as an actress . . . She had never even really
believed in herself as a dancer. She had done that just
to incur Sister Thérèse's favor. Perhaps that was why
she kept up with the ballet exercises—somehow she felt
as if she was paying off a debt when she did them. She
was not a religious person—she never went to Mass—
yet each night she got on her knees and said a prayer
in Polish that she had said since she had learned to talk.
And often in the darkness, she felt God about her . . .
and she hid her head under the pillow and silently told
Him she was doing her best.*

*She entered the Dorchester Hotel and huddled her
face in the sable coat that Dee had given her. She knew
her future was with Dee . . . and that the affair with
David had grown too important. It was time to leave,
time to settle some business . . . And thank God for
Jeremy.*

But that night, long after Jeremy had left, she sat staring out at Hyde Park. She knew that Jeremy had noticed her unlined face. When she had left David to have her face done, she had prayed David would be waiting. Because for the first time, she had known that she wasn't really a lesbian. In his arms she felt safe and happy. Each time they were together, it made it more difficult to be with Dee. A woman's soft body after David's strong lean one suddenly was beginning to repel her. And when she got on her knees to say her prayers, she found herself also praying that David would be waiting again. . . .

FOURTEEN

JANUARY SAT in Linda's office drinking lukewarm coffee from a plastic container. Linda was in one of her down moods. Linda was always morose on Mondays. But a rainy Monday in February was, as she put it, the "mother of them all." January was cheerful in spite of the weather. After all, February only had twenty-eight days. And the twenty-first of March was officially spring. So once you cracked February, winter was practically over.

She had always hated winter. Winter had meant school. Summer and holidays had meant Mike. But now holidays meant Palm Beach. She had gone there Christmas Eve and stayed through New Year's. But before Palm Beach there had been . . .

THAT WEEK BEFORE CHRISTMAS IN NEW YORK!

Holly and fake Christmas trees at the office even though everyone is working on the layout for the April issue.

The sudden change of attitude of all the employees at the apartment building. The doorman springing to open the door. The elevator man's newly acquired talent of leveling the car with the floor. The fifteen names of hitherto invisible employees that suddenly crop up on the "Christmas list" the super slides under the door.

Sloshing through the rain. People on every corner

252

weighted with shopping bags, futilely signaling at the empty taxis that flashed by flaunting their OFF DUTY signs. Dismal men in Santa outfits, their arms jerking with a spastic reflex as they rang their tinny bells. "Merry Christmas. Help the needy."

Fighting through Saks—a madhouse encased with silver decorations. A cashmere scarf for David; squashing into the elevator to the third floor to get a Pucci bag for Linda, which Linda promptly returned. ("January, I've told you a million times . . . it's *Gucci* that's *in* . . . *Pucci* is *out!*")

At least Mike had been easy. Two dozen golf balls with his name engraved on them. But Dee! What can you buy for a Dee? (And this was before she learned that the crystal icicles on Dee's Christmas tree were from Steuben.) You couldn't get Dee perfume. She had a closet full. At Palm Beach *and* the Pierre. Probably in Marbella, too. The salesgirl at Bonwit's recommended a "Fun" present, like red flannel booties. She finally wound up buying some imported linen handkerchiefs at a shop on Madison Avenue. Dee could always give them to someone else as a gift.

CHRISTMAS IN PALM BEACH!

The twelve-foot Christmas tree! Massive and shimmering with its silver balls and crystal icicles. A displaced giant in a glass-encased room overlooking the swimming pool. It stood like an angry sentry. Uprooted, disoriented, its cold silver silence protesting the tropical atmosphere.

And there was Mike, tan and beautiful. Dee, white and beautiful. Parties . . . backgammon . . . gossip. A ten-day extension of the Thanksgiving holiday. Going to the track with Mike and wanting to sob at his indifference as he walked to the ten-dollar window to place a bet. Because she could remember the old days when he'd pick up a phone and bet five thousand on one race. Yes, she could remember. And so could he. After the first party, every other party seemed like an instant replay. And then there was the surprise party Dee threw for her twenty-first birthday. Five thousand dollars in floral arrangements, a dance floor covering the Olympic-sized swimming pool. Two orchestras—one indoors, one outdoors. David arriving to celebrate. Both of them dancing together, playing the "Hello, Young Lovers" bit for Dee. The guests were all the same people she had seen throughout the week. There were just more of them. They all brought "just a teensy remembrance" from their own Christmas surplus. (She was now set for life with silk scarves.) Some came towing lantern-jawed daughters or an uncommunicative son. And always the omnipresent photographers, shooting the same people they had shot at the last party . . . and the same people they'd shoot in the parties to come.

AFTER CHRISTMAS IN NEW YORK!

Finding the first cockroach in the sink. Sure, it's dead, but what about its brothers and sisters? It couldn't be a lone spinster roach.

A frantic call to Linda. "Relax, January. They're everywhere in New York. Call the super. You gave him a generous Christmas present. He'll get the exterminator."

The super thanked her for the twenty dollars but explained that the exterminator had gone to Puerto Rico for the holidays and couldn't be reached for another ten days.

David took her out several times. Each time they joined another couple or a group at Raffles or Le Club where the music was too loud for any real conversation, so everyone danced, smiled, and waved at people across the room. And then one evening he took her home and dismissed the cab. For a moment they both stood in front of her apartment building. After an uneasy silence, he said, "Aren't you going to at least ask me up to look at the plant I gave you?"

"Oh, it's doing fine. They say I should prune it in the spring."

Her breath smoked the cold air. There was another awkward silence. Then she said, "Look, David, I like you. I really do. But what happened between us that

one night was a mistake. So as they say in the movies—
'Let's be friends.'"

He smiled. "I'm not going to rape you. I like you too,
I more than like you. I . . . I . . . well at the moment, I happen to be freezing . . . and we haven't had
a chance to talk all evening."

January wondered why this evening should be different from all the other evenings. "Okay, but it's really
just one large room." Once again there was an uncomfortable silence as they went up in the elevator. She
suddenly realized they had nothing to say to one another. Absolutely nothing. And for some insane reason
she felt off balance. She found herself chattering nervously as she opened the door. "It's not too neat. Linda
and I share a maid who has a violent love life. Half the
time she comes in sniveling with a black eye. But that's
when things are good. When things are bad, she just
doesn't show. Linda says that means he is gone and she
is sitting home drinking and waiting for him." She knew
he didn't give a damn about her maid. "Well . . . this
is it. And look at your tree. It's grown two inches and
has three new branches."

"Why don't you get rid of her?" he said as he stood
standing stiffly in the center of the room.

"Get rid of what?"

"The maid." He unbuttoned his coat and took off the
scarf she had given him.

"Oh, well, Linda has empathy for anyone who is a
loser in love. And I have empathy for anyone who sur-
vives all those black eyes." She sat on the couch. He
sat on the club chair near her, and stared at the floor,
his hands folded between his knees.

"January . . . I want to talk to you about—" He
looked up. "Do we have to have that thing on?"

"You mean you don't like Mr. Edgar Bailey's Tiffany-
type lamp?"

"I feel as if I'm in a bowling alley with all these lights."

She jumped up and put off the overhead light. "Can I
get you some wine . . . or a Coke? That's all I have."

"January . . . sit down. I don't want anything. I
want to talk about us."

"Okay, David." She sat quietly and waited.

"I guess you've been wondering about me . . . about us," he began. "Well, I've had some personal problems and . . ."

She smiled. "David, I told you before—we're friends. You don't owe me any explanations."

He stood up and fished for a cigarette in his pocket. Suddenly he spun around and faced her. "We're not friends. I . . . I love you. I meant everything I said that night. We *are* going to get married. But not . . . not for a while. I've got something I have to work out . . . business-wise. I'd appreciate it if you didn't mention it to Dee. She gets worried if she thinks I have any problems with my work." He attempted to smile and shrug it off. "She actually tries to mother me. I love her for it, but I want her to enjoy herself with your father. He's really a great guy, and I can work out my own problems. So just trust in me, January . . . trust in me and be patient. We're going to get married . . . eventually. Will you remember that . . . even if there are times I don't call?"

She looked at him and shook her head slowly. "Wow! You blow my mind. You really do! I mean, how many ways do I have to put it to you that *I* have no intention of marrying *you?* But if it will make you feel any better, I'll let Dee and my father assume that we're seeing a great deal of one another."

He turned on her angrily. "What makes you think I care about their opinion?"

"Because you do. And, look, it will be easier for me too. As long as we do see one another occasionally, and they think it's . . . well, like steady . . . why not?"

He dropped into the club chair and stared into space. He looked like a giant rubber toy that had suddenly sprung a leak. She could almost see his body deflating. "It's such rotten timing," he sighed. "I mean, ordinarily we'd have been so great together." He stared at the floor for a moment, then looked up and managed a smile. "Know something? You're a good kid, January. Okay. We'll let them think we're dating a lot, if it will help you.

And when you grow up a little, I think we'll be just fine together. Just fine."

He called her at the end of the week to announce that he was going to California to attend the Securities Analysts meeting he had been telling her about. She wasn't quite sure there really was such a thing as a Securities Analysts meeting in California . . . but she did know that Karla had arrived in Los Angeles from Europe via the Polar route. The newspapers had carried the usual pictures of her, holding a magazine in front of her face as she tried to avoid the photographers. One of the columnists reported she had come to visit Sonya Kinella, the wealthy Italian socialite and dilettante poet. They were old friends from Karla's early picture days.

But January had no time to wonder about David or Karla. Thomas Colt was due in town February 5 to attend a big publication day party his publishers were giving him. That was less than a week away, and as January sat drinking the lukewarm coffee on the bleak Monday in February, Linda was fuming at the impertinence of a Ms. Rita Lewis who had not answered any of her calls.

"I've put in five in the last three days," she said as she slammed down the phone. "I even talked to Mr. Lawrence's secretary."

"Who's he?"

"The publisher himself. I said that *Gloss* had not received its invitation to the party at the St. Regis and was it an oversight? She gave me the real private 'secretary to the President voice' and said, 'Well, really, Miss Riggs, it's not actually a press party: Oh, no doubt some of the press will be there, but actually it's more of a welcome to New York party for Mr. Colt. The Mayor will be there . . . all of the top celebrities.' I got the distinct impression that *Gloss* just isn't chic enough to rate. It wound up with her promising to give Rita my message."

"Well, we still have four more days," January said optimistically. "Maybe she'll call."

Four days passed and there was still no word. January sat in Linda's office trying to cheer her. "Come on, Linda. He's going to be in New York for quite a time. There must be another way to get to him."

Linda sighed. She glanced at the gray window. "Is it still raining?"

"No, it's snowing," January said.

"Good!" Linda said cheerfully. "I hope it turns into a blizzard. Then maybe half the people won't show . . . and the other half will be all wet and in a lousy mood. Honestly, January, everyone I know who has ever met your father says he was divine to work with . . . how colorful he was . . . everyone adored him—except Tom Colt!"

"Maybe they were both too strong for each other. Or maybe it was just Tom Colt being Tom Colt. Look, I sent in my first team. I wrote him a letter in November. I didn't say I was related to Mike, because I knew that would kill any chance we had. So I just signed it J. Wayne. Then I followed it up with another letter two weeks later. When I didn't hear, I called Jay Allen, his press agent in Los Angeles. Jay had done some work for my father, so he was real nice and gave me Tom Colt's beach house address. I wrote a letter there. Nothing! Then I followed it up with a Christmas card, with a 'Hope to see you when you get to New York' little note on it. Then three weeks later I wrote another glowing letter telling him I had read the galleys and knew he had a big hit." January leaned forward. "Linda . . . be realistic. Tom Colt wouldn't attend the Oscar ceremonies of the picture my father made of his book. It won in five categories. Of course he didn't write the screenplay . . . he felt that was beneath him. So you start out knowing what kind of a snob he is. Mike told me how everyone had pleaded with him to attend. But he refused. Know why? Because he said he was a serious writer, not part of a circus. He also said he had nothing to do with the crummy commercial picture Hollywood made of his book. So why on earth should we even think he'd do a story for us?"

Linda nodded slowly. "Everything you say is right. But then, who would have believed he'd consent to do a publicity tour? That's a real circus. He probably doesn't know what he's getting into. And as for magazine publicity, he probably never heard of it in connection with a serious novel. Oh, I'm sure he expects *Life* to do a story on him. And *Time*. And *Newsweek*. But *Gloss*? He probably never heard of it. Or thinks it's some new kind of toothpaste. But I won't give up. If I have to be a panzer division. I did that with Dr. Blowacek from Yugoslavia. I hounded him and actually got him before anyone else. That was the story that helped get me promoted to editor-in-chief. January—*Gloss* is my life! As it grows, so do I! And I've got to get Tom Colt for *Gloss*! I've got to!" Her expression was grim. The blood seemed to drain from her face. Then she sighed. "The Dr. Blowacek story elevated me in the eyes of my publisher. And since then I've been running stories geared for circulation and advertising. Now it's time for me to go after stories to elevate *Gloss* in the eyes of the trade. If I get an interview or story on Tom Colt, that would help turn *Gloss* into something pretty heavy. That's why I can't take no for an answer. Sure he'll be in New York for some time, but *Gloss* has to get him first. And getting to his cocktail party would have been a big help. He digs beautiful girls. That's why Rita Lewis hasn't invited me. She doesn't want him to do a story for *Gloss*. She's very into the literary thing . . . like she'd rather get him a paragraph in *The New York Review of Books* than a cover story with us. That's why I wanted to go to the party. I figured if we could just see him . . . we could convince him."

"Then let's go," January said.

"You mean crash?"

"Why not?"

Linda shook her head. "Too important a party. With this kind of an 'A' list, they'll have people at the door, checking off every name."

"Let's try it anyway," January insisted. "We'll dress our best, hire a limo, and go—"

"Hire a limo? January, what a smashing idea!"

"It's the only way. With this weather there won't be a cab in sight. Everyone will arrive as you predicted

. . . wet and looking slightly beat. If we're going to crash, we're going to crash with style."

Linda laughed nervously. "Do you really think a limo will give us enough style to bring it off?"

"Well, Ernest Hemingway once defined style as grace under pressure. And arriving in a limousine is certainly a step in the right direction."

The party was held in a small ballroom. Judging from the noise of the crowd, the weather had been no deterrent. People spilled out into the hallway, forming their own small noisy cliques. A long sheet of paper with guests listed in alphabetical order lay deserted on a table outside the door. Linda's theory about arriving late had been right. Once the V.I.P.'s were checked in, the people at the door would duck inside to mingle with the celebrities and grab free drinks.

They pushed their way into the main room. January recognized several authors, some press, several Broadway stars, a few Hollywood personalities, and the usual inveterate party-goers.

There was a bar at the end of the room. They spotted Tom Colt immediately. He was much better looking than the picture on his jacket cover. He had a strong face, dark hair, pugilistic features. A man who looked as if he had lived through much of the violence and action he wrote about.

"He scares me," January whispered. "You go up to him if you like. . . . I'll just stand back here and watch."

"He's gorgeous," Linda whispered.

"Sure he is. But so is a rattlesnake if it's in a glass cage. I mean . . . Linda, you can't mention *Gloss* magazine to a man like that."

"Well, I'm going to . . . and you're going with me. Come on." She grabbed January's arm and pulled her through the crowd toward the bar.

Tom Colt was encircled by an admiring group that seemed to be trying to close in on him. But he stood erect, with a bottle of Jack Daniel's in front of him, pouring his own drinks. He took a long swallow as he stared at the plump little man who had written a best seller five years ago. He hadn't written anything since, but he was making a career out of going on talk shows and attending celebrity parties. He had also turned into a lush. Suddenly he clamped his pudgy hand on Tom Colt's arm. "I read everything you write," he squeaked. He smacked his lips in ecstasy and rolled his eyes heavenward. "My God, but I adore your work. But be careful about getting caught up in the rat race of television." He giggled. "Look what a whore it's made out of me."

Tom Colt pulled his arm away and looked at the damp-looking group around him. His dark eyes seemed angry as they quickly surveyed the crowd. Suddenly they rested on January and Linda. "Excuse me," he said to the plump little writer, "but my two cousins from Iowa just walked in. And they've come all the way by bus." He took the stunned girls by their arms and led them across the room. "Thank God for the pair of you . . . whoever you are. I was stuck with that bore for twenty minutes and no one came to rescue me because they thought I was being amused."

Linda was staring at him in a glazed way. January found him completely overpowering. She managed to loosen his grip on her arm and said, "I'm glad if we were able to help you, and—"

Linda suddenly came to life. "And now you can help us."

His eyes narrowed. "I've got a feeling that maybe I should have stayed at the bar."

"I'm Linda Riggs, editor-in-chief of *Gloss* magazine, and this is my assistant editor, January Wayne. She's written to you several times about an interview."

He turned to January. "Holy Christ! Are you the J. Wayne with the letters and the Christmas card?"

She nodded and for some strange reason found herself blushing. He laughed, as if it was some private joke. "So you're J. Wayne." He laughed again. "And all the time I kept thinking the letters were from some skinny fag. Well, glad to meet you, J. Wayne. I'm glad you're not a fag . . . but it's *no* on the interview. My publisher has too many lined up as it is." He turned and looked at her again. "But why the J. Wayne? Is that part of this Ms. business? At least I might have answered you if I had known you were a girl."

"Well, January Wayne wouldn't have given you any lead on my sex either."

"No, it wouldn't. It's a crazy name, it's—" He stopped. Then he pointed a finger at her accusingly. "You wouldn't by any chance be the daughter of that sonofabitch Mike Wayne!"

She started to walk away but he yanked her back by the arm. "Listen, he fucked up one of my best books."

"Don't you dare use that language when you're talking about my father! He got an Academy Award with that picture."

"January . . ." Linda's voice was a whispered plea.

"Let her rave on." Tom Colt laughed. "I have a six-month-old son. One day when someone pans his old man's book, he'll hit out for me." He smiled and held out his hand. "Truce?"

January looked at him and held out her hand. Then he locked his arms through theirs. "Okay, now that we're all friends, let's the three of us cut out. Where can we go for a few quiet blasts?"

"There's Elaine's," Linda said. "A lot of writers go there and—"

"Yeah, I heard about it. But not tonight. The little capon at the bar told me he's winding up at Elaine's. Let's go to Toots'!"

"Where?" Linda asked.

"Toots Shor's—the only place to go for some serious drinking." Still holding them by the arms he started for the door. A harassed young woman with long stringy hair rushed to him. "Mr. Colt, where are you going?"

"Out."

"But you can't leave. Ronnie Wolfe hasn't gotten here yet, and—"

He patted her on the head. "Relax, press lady. You've done a fine job. The booze is flowing. I've been here for two hours and talked to everyone you put with me. My deal was that I'd attend a press party. No one said how long I'd have to stay. Oh, by the way . . . do you know my cousins from Iowa?"

"I know Rita Lewis," Linda said, not able to hide her delight. "We've never actually been introduced. But no doubt she's seen some of my messages this week."

"I told my secretary to send you the invitation," Rita said, rising to the occasion. "I see you got it."

"No, we crashed," January said happily.

"But you can make it up," Linda added. "All we want is an in-depth interview with Mr. Colt. We'd give you the cover for that."

"No way," Rita Lewis said. "Mr. Colt is lined up with interviews all next week. All the major magazines, plus the A.P., U.P.I.—"

"But our story would be different," Linda pleaded.

"Yes," January added. "We'd sit in on some of his other interviews, like the talk shows; we'd cover the Green Room backstage; we'd even go to some of the other cities."

"Forget it," Rita said. "I don't want him to be in *Gloss*." She looked at Linda and added, "And don't start harassing him with phone calls."

Tom Colt, who had been watching the cross-talk like a tennis match, cut in. "Wait a minute! What are you, some kind of a Nazi general? Telling people it's off limits to phone me?"

"Of course not, Mr. Colt. I didn't mean it that way. But I know how persistent Linda can be. And I'm sure she's trained January well. It's just that our schedule is set . . . and *Gloss* is out. I don't care what you do in your personal life with either of them . . . but you can't give them any interview. I've made commitments that might be endangered if you did their story."

His eyes grew cruel as he looked at the publicist. "Look, baby. Let's get things set from the very beginning. You can make appointments for me . . . and like a nice little trained dog, I'll go through all the paces. I made a deal. And I always keep my word. But don't

ever tell me what I *can't* do." He put his arm around
January protectively. "I've known this little girl since
she was a baby. Her father's my buddy chum pal. He
made a hell of a picture out of one of my books. And
you're going to stand there and tell me I can't do an
interview for her magazine!"

Rita Lewis looked at Linda pleadingly. "Well . . .
make it a small one, Linda . . . please. Otherwise I'll
lose *McCall's* and *Esquire*. No in-depth thing, no following him around—"

"They can follow me into the can if they want," he
stormed. "But right now, we're going out to booze a
little." Then he took each girl by the arm and propelled
them through the room.

January opened her eyes slowly. She was asleep in
the club chair. Why hadn't she opened the bed? Why
was she sleeping with her clothes on? She stood up, but
the floor began to slant crazily. She fell back on the
chair. It was seven o'clock in the morning! She had only
been asleep two hours.

She stood up and struggled to get out of her clothes.
Several times she had to grab the chair for support. She
managed to pull out the bed, then rushed to the bathroom and threw up. She came back and fell across the
bed. The events of the entire evening floated back to
her. The abrupt change of heart Tom Colt had about
her father . . . the three of them leaving the St. Regis
while the bewildered Rita Lewis stood by, glaring helplessly. His amazement at their having their *own* limousine. He liked that . . . said it was the first time he
had ever heard of gate-crashers coming in a limo. Then
there had been his entrance in Toots Shor's . . . Toots
back-slapping him . . . sitting with them at the front
table. Only no one mentioned food. It was Jack Daniel's
all the way. When he had stated that no one could really
be his friend unless he drank Jack Daniel's, she and Linda
had hesitated for a split second, and then instantly announced they adored bourbon.

She had found the first drink heavy going, but the
second went down much easier. And the third brought a

strange lightness to her head along with a marvelous sense of good will. And when Tom Colt leaned over and kissed each of them on the cheek and called them his Chocolate and Vanilla girls (January still had her Palm Beach tan and Linda had streaked her hair blonde this month), January felt they were a hilarious threesome. People drifted over to the table. There was much back-slapping—"Sit down, you crum bum" (this was Toots); sports writers who knew her father joined them; Tom kept refilling everyone's glass. At midnight, Tom insisted on stopping off at "21" for a nightcap. They closed "21" and went to P.J. Clarke's. At four in the morning they had all stumbled out of P.J.'s—she could remember that. She remembered weaving into the lobby with Linda, both of them giggling . . . But everything that was said or done from P.J.'s on was a haze.

She stumbled into the bathroom and took some aspi-rin. Then she made it back to the bed. When she closed her eyes the room began to spin. She opened her eyes and tried to fix her attention on a stationary object. Mr. Bailey's Tiffany lamp. She must have finally fallen asleep, because suddenly she was in the middle of a dream. She was aware that she was dreaming. She was enough awake to know it was a dream, but enough asleep to allow the dream to propel itself. A man was bending over her. He was about to take her. Any mo-ment he would enter her, yet she experienced no panic. She wanted him, even though his face was a blur . . . She looked closer . . . it was Mike. But then as his lips touched hers she realized it was Tom Colt. Only his eyes weren't black like Tom's . . . they were blue. But not blue like Mike's . . . they were aquamarine! She reached out for him . . . and then she woke up. She lay back against the pillows trying to determine whose face it was—Mike's or Tom's—but all she could remem-ber was the color of those amazing eyes.

She forced herself back to sleep, searching for those eyes. But it was a soft dreamless sleep, dissolved sud-denly by the telephone. It was Linda. "January, are you up?"

There was a throbbing in the back of her head but

her stomach had settled some. "What time is it?" she asked slowly, afraid of any sudden movement.

"Eleven o'clock and I have a godawful hangover."

"Is that what it is?" January asked. "I thought I was dying."

"Take some milk."

"Oh my God . . ." January suddenly felt a wave of nausea.

"Look, eat a piece of bread and take some milk. Right now! It will absorb any liquor left. Do that and call me back. We have to make our plans."

"What plans?"

"To go on with Thomas Colt."

"Oh, God . . . must we?"

"Last night you told me you adored him."

"That was probably after I met his friend, Jack Daniel's."

"We're not going to do that tonight," Linda said.

"Do what?"

"Drink when we go with him. We take a firm stand. We'll sip Scotch. He can drink all he wants to. But if we want to write this story we have to stay sober. We don't tell him that. We just don't try to match him drink for drink."

"Is that what we did?"

"We damn well tried."

"Linda . . . I'm going to be sick."

"Eat the bread. I'll throw on some slacks and come to your apartment and we can plan our strategy."

She managed to get down half a glass of milk, and she watched Linda make the coffee. Linda finally settled in the club chair and smiled happily. "Now sit up . . . come to life . . . you've got to make the call to Tom Colt."

"Why me?"

"Because even though I intend to sleep with this man tonight, I have a distinct feeling that this morning he will not remember my name. But your name will strike a bell. It has to after that big love he suddenly developed for Daddy."

"I still feel he's not exactly wild about Mike. He was just furious at Rita Lewis for giving him orders."

Linda lit a cigarette and sipped her coffee. "January, this instant stuff is awful. You've got to learn to make real coffee."

January shrugged. "It suits me."

Linda shook her head. "But it won't suit your man."

"What man?"

"Any man who stays over. That's the one thing they usually demand the next morning—decent coffee."

"You mean you have to make coffee for them too?"

"Sometimes even eggs. And if you have a health freak like Keith used to be, it's Granola or one of those nutsy raisiny cereals and Vitamin E and . . . oh, Lord, thank God that's all out of my life."

"Don't you ever think of Keith or miss him?"

Linda shook her head. "When *Caterpillar* opened I almost sent him a wire. But I figured the hell with it. It's over. I'm glad for Keith the show's a hit, because he sure has to pay big dues sleeping with Christina. Besides, it takes a man like Tom Colt to make you realize that Keith is just a boy."

"But Linda . . . he's married, he has a six-month-old baby."

"But his wife and baby are on the Coast . . . and I'm here. Besides I'm not looking to take him away from his wife or child."

"Then why are you after him?"

"Because he turns me on . . . he's beautiful . . . I want to go to bed with him. And so do you. At least you acted that way last night."

"I did?"

"January, your sign should be Gemini instead of Capricorn—you really are twins. I mean, when you drink, you really become another person. Last night he was kissing us both at P.J.'s . . . like taking turns . . . real deep kisses . . . calling me Vanilla . . . and you Chocolate."

"He was kissing us at P.J.'s?"

"That he was."

"Really kissing?"

"Well, he had his tongue down my throat. I don't know about you."

"Oh, my God."

"And what about going home?" Linda asked.

"What about going home?" January sat up straight.

"He reached over, slipped his hand under your top, and said, 'Tiny buds. But I like them.'"

January buried her head in the pillow. "Linda . . . I don't believe it."

"Sure . . . then he kissed my boobs and said they were really wild."

"What was the driver doing?"

"Watching the rear view mirror like mad, I suppose. But they're used to everything, including actual rape, I'm told."

"Linda—" January's voice was weak. "It's all gradually coming back to me. I remember thinking as he slipped his hand under my blouse that it was the most natural thing in the world. Oh, good Lord . . . how could I?"

"Because you're finally turning into a nice normal girl."

"Is that what being normal is . . . to have a man you've just met touch you, in front of another girl?"

"Oh, come on. I've never played the three-way scene in my life. When I'm in bed with a man I've always felt anything goes as long as there's just the two of us in that bed. And last night was all in fun. It was nothing to get uptight about."

January got out of bed and wobbled across the room to get a cigarette. She lit it slowly, inhaled deeply, then she turned to Linda. "Okay, I know I've been away from it all, and I know things have changed. Like, you don't have to be married to love someone . . . or to go to bed with someone. I know that's the way everyone thinks. But there's no rule that says I have to think that way. I thought of myself as some kind of freak because I was a virgin. I literally talked myself into thinking I was stuck on David. And it was awful—" She shuddered as she ground out the freshly lit cigarette. "Linda, I want to fall in love. Oh God, how I want to fall in love. And I'll even go along that marriage isn't necessary right off. But when I'm in love, and the man I love . . . touches me . . . I want it to be something wonderful between *us* . . . and not just 'all in fun.' "

"January, when people get high—whether it's on bourbon, wine, or pot—the things they do . . . or feel . . . are usually true. Drinking just releases the inhibitions. If you let Tom Colt touch you and if as you say you thought it was so natural at the time, then it means deep down, you *wanted* him to touch you."

January lit another cigarette. "That's not true. I admire his work . . . I admire his strength . . . but Holy God, what must he think of us? Two gate-crashers, coming after a man in our own limousine . . . allowing him to—" She stopped as she stubbed out her cigarette. "Oh, Linda, what *can* he think of us?"

"January, stop torturing yourself about what he thinks of us. Do you realize how many bourbons he had and how many breasts he's fondled? He probably doesn't even remember those little gems of yours. Now, for God's sake, it's almost noon. Call him."

"No."

"Please . . . for my sake. Let him take us both out and in the middle of the evening you can say you're not feeling well . . . and leave. But please make the call. I really want him. I mean, there's no one around quite like him, is there? He looks so mean at times. Yet when he smiles or looks you in the eye, you could die."

"You mean you want to go to bed with Tom Colt, knowing there's no future in it? Knowing that he has a good marriage—"

"What are you trying to do to my head? Lay a guilt trip on me? If I dig Tom Colt and he digs me, what's wrong with us having a few marvelous evenings together? Who is it going to hurt? There are no next-door neighbors who are going to laugh at the poor unsuspecting wife as she hangs out the wash. *His* wife is young and gorgeous and is roughing it at Malibu with a nurse for the baby and probably some big Hollywood celebrities as neighbors. What am I taking from her!

She isn't here, is she? Now. . . will you call him?"

"No. And even if he didn't have a wife, I wouldn't call him."

"Why?"

January walked over to the window and rolled up the blinds. "Looks like snow again. Thank goodness last night's stuff didn't stick."

"Why wouldn't you call him even if he didn't have a wife?" Linda demanded.

"Because . . . well . . . you don't just go calling men. They should call you."

"Oh, my God . . . I don't believe it. You sound like something out of a Priscilla Lane movie. Like Saturday night dates, and little gardenia corsages. Today women don't have to sit around and wait for a man to call. Besides, Tom Colt isn't just a man—he's a superstar— and we're doing a story on him." Linda picked up the phone and dialed the Plaza. "I know eventually we'll have to put that beast Sara Kurtz with him a few times, so she can catch his style . . . Hello . . . Oh, Mr. Tom Colt, please . . ."

"Why Sara Kurtz?" January asked.

"Because this is just about the most important story *Gloss* has ever done. And she is the best writer I've got . . . Hello . . . what? . . . Oh . . . Miss January Wayne calling! Yes . . . January . . . like the month."

"Linda!"

"Hello, Mr. Colt . . . No, this isn't January. It's Linda Riggs . . . But January's sitting right here beside me . . . Yes, we're fine . . . Well, a little . . . Oh well, we both want to see you. . . . who? *Hugh Robertson*. Honestly? . . . Oh, great. We'd adore it. . . . Fine. Your place at seven . . . the tenth floor . . ." She scribbled down the suite number on a pad. "We'll be there." Linda hung up with a beautiful smile. "Hugh Robertson is coming up to his suite for drinks this afternoon. And we're all to have dinner together. And Tom is sending *his* limousine for us."

"Why did you call him Mr. Colt on the phone?" January asked.

"Isn't that wild? But I suddenly got scared. He

sounded so cold at first. But after two drinks tonight, it'll be Tommy. And imagine having Hugh Robertson along as an added starter. I wonder what it would be like to make love to an astronaut."

"Looks like you're going to have your chance," January said. "At least he's divorced."

"*You* take Hugh . . . I want Tom."

"Why are you dismissing Hugh?" January asked. "He's a superstar in his own right. I mean he has made the cover of *Time* and *Newsweek*."

"Look, January, I am not a superstar groupie . . . in fact I've never balled a star, let alone a superstar. Keith got into *Caterpillar after* we broke up, and he's still no star. He never even got mentioned in the notices. So when I say I want Tom Colt, it's because he has something special . . . I mean, he'd turn me on even if he were an out-of-work accountant. He's so strong . . . so completely his own . . . Yet at times, there's something gentle and melancholy about him. Haven't you noticed it?"

"No. Unfortunately I got involved with Jack Daniel's, and after that I couldn't see anyone's eyes. But I'll look tonight."

"No, tonight you look into Hugh Robertson's eyes. *I'm* with Tom. Just think . . . tomorrow at this time, I'll probably be having breakfast in bed with him at the Plaza."

FIFTEEN

THEY ARRIVED at the Plaza at five after seven, looking like two eager schoolgirls on an outing. When they
walked into the lobby, January suddenly stood motionless. The place held so many memories. Linda pulled
her toward the elevator. "Come on. We'll be late."

"Linda, I haven't been here since—".

"January, this is not back-to-daddy time. This is now!
Tom Colt . . . Hugh Robertson . . . Remember?" She
dragged January into the elevator.

Hugh Robertson opened the door. January recognized him from his pictures. He introduced himself and
invited them in. "Tom is on the phone in the bedroom
talking to his agent in Munich about foreign sales. I'm
supposed to make the drinks. I can't ask what will you
have because all we seem to have is Jack Daniel's."

Linda took a drink but January "passed." She walked
over to the window. It was unbelievable . . . Tom
Colt in *this* suite. The suite Mike had kept on a year-
round basis. Even the same table near the windows. She
touched it lightly, almost expecting some kind of a
vision to materialize. How many times she had sat
there, watching him wheeling and dealing. Sometimes
all the phones would ring at once. She turned away.
It was spooky, because now all the phones were ringing at once and Tom Colt walked into the room and said,
"To hell with them . . . let them ring . . . it's Satur-

day and I don't have to work." Then he walked over to her and took her hands. "Hello, Princess. Feel okay after last night?"

"Yes." She suddenly felt self-conscious and off balance as she watched him cross the room to greet Linda.

They went to "21." Tom remained reasonably sober. When he noticed January wasn't drinking the bourbon he had ordered for her, he sent for a wine list. "White wine, I bet. Is that it?"

"But you said last night—" Linda began.

"This is tonight," Tom said. "I say different things every night."

It was a relaxed evening, but January suddenly found herself unable to direct any conversation to Tom. She weighed everything before she said it, then rephrased it in her mind, and then the moment had passed so she didn't say it. She felt like an idiot. Linda was chattering so easily, telling them about how she had started at *Gloss,* about the miracle she had wrought. January tried to think of something to say. Why did she suddenly feel shy and look away whenever he looked at her? Maybe she should tell him she enjoyed his book. How should she phrase it: "Mr. Colt, I think . . ." *No* . . . "Tom, I adored your book . . ." No, that sounded inane. "Tom, your book has to make number one on the list . . ."—too presumptuous. Who was she to tell him how it would rate with the public? How about . . .

"Oh, Tom," Linda said. "I must get you to autograph your book for me. It's so sensational."

(Well, that polished off the book as conversational opener.)

Tom was promising to get them each a copy at Doubleday's. "They're open at night. I'm glad you like it. Lawrence and Company tell me it makes *The New York Times* list in number six spot next week. Actually this book isn't half as good as some of the others that bombed. But it's commercial . . . and today that's the name of the game." Then, dismissing his book, he turned to Hugh and demanded to know what he was doing holed up in Westhampton. "Has to be a lady involved," Tom said.

"It's a very big lady," Hugh said. "Mother Nature."

"You mean the ecology thing?" Linda asked.

"No, I'm worried about dear old Mother's body. She's liable to fall apart in spots from shock. It's the faults of our earth I'm interested in. The San Andreas is the best-known, what with all the mystics predicting that California might sink under the ocean this year. I think Los Angeles is long overdue for an earthquake, but I don't believe tidal waves will turn it into another Atlantis. It's the other faults I'm interested in—we have so damn many in our earth. I'm especially interested in finding out whether any new ones have been created. So I've gotten a grant, and I'm trying to prove a few theories that in the end might make our tiny little world last a few years longer."

"Well, if we don't use the bomb or foul up the air, won't the world just keep going?" Linda asked.

Hugh smiled. "Linda, the other night when I lay out on the dunes in my sleeping bag and—"

"You lie out on the dunes in February?" Linda asked.

"I have a one-bedroom house smack dab on the beach," Hugh said. "But I don't think I spend more than a few hours a day inside. I have my thermal underwear, my sleeping bag . . . I get myself nestled between a couple of dunes to protect me from the wind. Of course it's much nicer in the summer, but the sky is fascinating in all seasons . . . kind of cuts you down to size. Especially when you realize that in the theory of the universe, our world is just one little cinder. Just think—there are millions of suns out there, maybe breeding the same kind of life. And when you look up there, you realize that there may be worlds fifty million years ahead of us."

"I was in my second year at Miss Haddon's when I first learned the stars were huge and could be other worlds," January said. "Until then I had always thought of them as tiny, warm, comforting . . . God's lights—" She paused. "I can't remember who told me that, but

I do recall the terrible shock I had when I learned the truth. I lived in constant terror that they might drop on us, crush us. When I told my father about it, he told me every star had its special spot. And that when people died they went on other stars to live."

"Nice theory," said Hugh. "He sounds like a good man. I mean, it's a good story to tell a little girl. Makes her believe in eternal life and takes away the fear of the unknown." Then he went on to explain about the solar systems and his firm belief that one day there would be interstellar communication.

Tom seemed fascinated with Hugh's theory and kept throwing questions at him. January listened with interest, but Linda was bored. After making several attempts to get the conversation on a more personal level, Linda gave up and sat back. She shot a murderous glance at January when she asked Hugh a question that set him off on another long explanation.

But January was genuinely interested. Also she found it easy to talk to Hugh. And when she talked to Hugh, she felt she was also communicating with Tom. She was even able to make them both laugh—as long as she directed her conversation toward Hugh. The one time Tom said something directly to her, she found herself tightening up, choosing words, withdrawing.

She watched Tom covertly as Hugh explained something about the moon and the tides. He looked so intense, like a man molded in granite. Yet she felt there was a vulnerability about him, a quality Mike never had. Mike was always a winner. You knew when you looked at Mike that no one could ever hurt him. Yet oddly enough, you felt that with all of his toughness, Tom had been hurt. Tom wasn't as strong as Mike. Yet, perhaps in some ways he was stronger. He admitted that some of his best books had bombed, the last four . . . Yet he had sat down and written another. Mike had quit because he was positive the dice had grown cold. Tom Colt obviously didn't believe in dice.

"Are you a gambler?" she asked suddenly.

Both men stopped speaking and looked at her. She

wanted to dive under the table. The question had just slipped out. Tom stared at her for a second and then said, "Only if the odds are in my favor. Why?"

"No real reason. I . . . you remind me of someone."

"A long-lost love?" Tom asked.

"Yes . . . her father!" Linda snapped.

Tom laughed. "Well, that's a pretty good bringdown for any man. And when a guy is in his late fifties and thinks he can entertain two beautiful young girls, he should be brought back to reality."

"You can't be in your late fifties," Linda said.

"Don't try to make it up to me," Tom said with a smile. "Yep, I'm fifty-seven, a few years older than Mike Wayne. Right, January? And Hugh, you're young enough to know we've been boring these ladies with all the talk about stars. The only stars they're interested in are Paul Newman, or Steve McQueen."

"I wasn't bored at all," Linda insisted. "It was fascinating."

They left "21" at eleven. The weather was clear and there was very little wind. "Let's walk the girls home," he said. "They share a pad."

"We live in the same apartment building, but we each have our own apartment," Linda said pointedly.

Tom dismissed the car and they walked to Doubleday's. The sales people all greeted him; he bought books for January and Linda, autographed them, and grudgingly autographed a few for the store, then quickly cut out. They walked east. Linda tried to steer January and Hugh up front as she held on to Tom's arm, but he kept talking to Hugh, and when they could, the foursome walked abreast. They finally reached a narrow block and were forced to separate into couples. Linda and Tom walked ahead. January noticed he was holding Linda's hand. Suddenly she realized Hugh had asked her a question.

"I'm sorry . . . I didn't hear you," she said. "That taxi was making so much noise . . . I . . ."

He smiled. "Don't let your girlfriend bug you. Tom is married . . . and you don't look to be the type for a quickie romance."

"I'm not bugged. What makes you think I am?"

"The way you've been staring at them holding hands while I was talking. No cab was making any noise."

"Actually . . . I suppose I was daydreaming. That's a bad habit of mine. And really, Hugh, I'm delighted to be walking with you."

"We're both deadbeats . . . romance-wise . . . me and Tom. Me, I've got the stars and the ocean . . . and Tom's got himself a new wife and a new baby. He never had a baby before . . . you realize that? Four marriages and gets his first baby at fifty-seven. So if your little friend has any serious ideas beyond—"

"No, Linda knows the score."

"That kind of talk doesn't sound like you," he said.

"How do you know what I sound like?"

"Because I know who you are and what you are. Just like I know what Linda is. Tom always winds up with the Lindas. He even married a couple of them. Know why? Because he doesn't go after any girl. He's a lazy sonofabitch—he takes the ones that come after him. It's easier that way. Besides, I don't think he's capable of being in love . . . except maybe with the characters he creates in his books. So to him, it's whichever girl chooses *him*. Only now that he's got a son . . . he'll stick with this new little wife forever."

"What's she like?" January asked.

"Beautiful . . . red hair . . . had a kind of a career going in pictures for a few years. Didn't ever get beyond doing bits. But she was pretty. And she met Tom . . . went after him . . . gave up her career and gave him a son."

"What was her name . . . I mean as an actress."

He stopped in the darkness and stared at her. "January," he said softly. "Lady, want some advice? Leave him to the Lindas. You'll get hurt."

Before she could answer, Tom suddenly called out, "Hey, Hugh, you still want me to come out and spend the day at the beach tomorrow?"

"Sure, all set. The freezer is loaded with steaks."

"Well, how about inviting the girls to come along and cook the steaks?"

"We'd adore it," Linda said quickly. "I've never been to the beach in February."

They had reached the apartment building. Linda looked at Tom. "Can I invite you all up for a nightcap? I have no bourbon, but I've got rye—"

"No, we want to start early," Tom said. "I dig the beach in gray weather . . . even in cold weather. It belongs to you then. At Malibu I do my best writing when it's cold and the fog rolls in."

Sunday was cold, and rain was predicted, but they all left for the beach at ten-thirty in the morning. Everyone wore heavy slacks and sweaters and old jackets. Tom Colt looked truly relaxed for the first time.

It did rain, but the house was warm and they kept the fireplace going all day. January felt at times that they were the only people left in the world as they sat before the fire. It was a strong little house. A large living room, a big kitchen, a big bedroom upstairs with its own sundeck. "Perfect for a bachelor," Hugh said.

"Perfect for a couple in love," Linda said, gazing at Tom. "Do you like our beaches in New York as much as Malibu, Tommy?"

He smiled and yanked at her hair. "Linda, you can call me shit heel . . . sonofabitch . . . or whatever—but never call me Tommy."

The limousine returned at ten o'clock to take them back to the city. Hugh was remaining behind. As they left, Tom reached out and grabbed a bottle of bourbon. "Provisions for the road."

Linda tucked her arm through Tom's as they walked down the path to the car. Hugh walked the short distance with January. A light rain whipped their faces. "Looks like the match has been made," he said. "So now it's up to you to watch out over them on the tour."

"Tour?"

"Linda says you both are going with him to write the story. And this tour . . . it's not for Tom. He'll drink too much. Basically he's very shy. I've only known him for six years, so I don't know what his private demon is. God knows women love him and men are equally attracted to him. But it seems as though he has to prove something every second. Maybe that's what the drinking is all about. Maybe after each book he feels he's said all he has to say. Yet he knows he has to do it again. This tour could hurt him—his psyche, that is. That's why I say watch out over him. He needs someone who will help make it all not seem too honky-tonk."

January smiled. Linda and Tom had already gotten into the car. "I like you, Mr. Hugh Robertson," she said.

"I like you, too, January Wayne. I think you're very special."

"Thank you."

He took her hand. "I mean that· . . . in the best of ways. I'm a friend."

She nodded and held out her hand. "Friend."

They both smiled and she climbed into the car. Tom opened the bottle and took a long swallow. He handed it to Linda. She managed to take a big gulp. Then he offered it to January. She hesitated . . . their eyes met and held in the semi-darkness . . . for a moment everything seemed suspended . . . like a motion picture when the frame suddenly freezes. She reached for the bottle slowly . . . their eyes still together . . . and suddenly with a quick movement he pulled it away. "No. I've changed my mind. No more refreshments on the way home. Tomorrow is a working day."

The moment was gone. He discussed the interviews that were set up—the appearances he was to make on the *Today* show, the Johnny Carson show, the quick trips he would take to Boston, Philadelphia, and Washington before starting on the tour across country.

"I guess we better stay away from your interviews," Linda said. "Rita would really do a number if we showed up for any of them. But if it's all right we'll cover your TV appearances and some of the out-of-town shows and press conferences."

"Come along. But I can't see why it will make that interesting a story."

"Have you ever been on a tour?"

"Of course not."

Linda smiled. "It will be very interesting. I promise you."

When the car pulled up in front of their apartment, he got out and walked them to the door. He leaned down and kissed them both on the cheek and started toward his car. For a split second, Linda was speechless . . . then through her teeth she hissed, "Go on in, January . . . now." She pushed January through the door and rushed back to the limousine just as Tom was getting in. "Tom . . . I know you're doing the *Life* thing tomorrow . . . but what time does . . ."

January didn't hear the rest. She went directly to the elevator and went to her apartment. Her emotions were scrambled. . . .

She undressed and got into bed. She wondered if Linda had made it back to the Plaza . . . to the bedroom that once belonged to Mike. She tried not to think about it.

If Linda wanted to have a romance with Tom Colt, why not? She punched up the pillow and tried to will herself to sleep. Everything seemed too quiet. She could hear the clock . . . the television set next door . . . a couple arguing across the court. . . . Then the phone rang.

It was so unexpected that she jumped when she heard it. She picked it up on the second ring.

"I didn't wake you, did I?"

She stared into the phone dumbly. It was Tom Colt.

"January . . . are you there?"

"No . . . I mean yes, I'm here . . . no, you didn't wake me."

"Good," he said. "I was just about to leave my wake-up call and I suddenly realized I'm free tomorrow night. Have you seen *Gingerbread Lady*?"

"No."

"Well, I'm a big fan of Maureen Stapleton, so I'll get three tickets and we can go tomorrow. You tell Linda."

"She might have seen it," January said.

"So what? We haven't. That makes it two out of three. That's the way we'll have to work things between the three of us. Majority rule. I'll pick you both up at seven. Goodnight."

She stared into the phone for a moment, after she heard the click. Then she hung up slowly. Linda wasn't with him. She lay in the darkness and thought about it . . . Linda wasn't with him! But why was she so happy about it? *Because she wanted him herself*! She lay very still, almost in shock at this sudden revelation. But it was true . . . She was falling in love with a man older than her father. A man who had a wife and a baby! And he felt something for her!

Otherwise, why had he called her and not Linda about *Gingerbread Lady*? Could he feel something for her? But hadn't Hugh said he was lazy . . . that he allowed the girl to pick him . . . rather than make the effort to go after the girl. And hadn't Linda very definitely picked him? Yet he had called *her*. She stretched out and allowed herself the freedom of a dream, like suppose his wife suddenly came to him and wanted a divorce, or suppose . . . suppose she suddenly died and . . . no . . . that wasn't right . . . she couldn't kill her off. . . . Well, suppose he did fall really in love and wanted a divorce . . . no . . . he wouldn't give up his son . . . Tom Colt, Jr., was a big thing to him. . . . Well, suppose the beautiful young wife came to him and said it wasn't really his baby . . . that it belonged to some beachboy . . . and she wanted a divorce. And then he'd have no guilt . . . he would support the child . . . because it had his name . . . and then he could marry January . . . and they could live in the beach house together . . . and she'd type his manuscripts and . . . it would be wonderful . . . and . . .

IT WAS INSANE!

Yes . . . it was insane . . . but she hugged the pillow and went to sleep thinking about the way he had looked at her for that one instant in the car.

SIXTEEN

SHE DIDN'T SLEEP well. But when the alarm went off, she sprang out of bed, eager for the day to begin. She stood under the shower and found herself singing, "I'm in love, I'm in love, I'm in love with a wonderful guy!" Then she remembered another Rodgers and Hammerstein song: "The gentleman is a dope, he's not my cup of tea, but why am I crying my eyes out, he doesn't belong to me." Only she wasn't crying her eyes out. She was standing in the shower like an idiot, singing old show tunes . . . and she never felt better in her life.

But he *was* married. She thought about it as she dressed. Where was her conscience? Look how her mother had suffered when her father had affairs with women. But she wasn't going to go to bed with Tom Colt. It was just so wonderful to feel something for a man . . . other than Mike. To want to *be* with another man . . . to want his admiration. Could that be so wrong? Just wanting to be with him. Especially if no one ever knew how she felt . . .

It had been murder trying to be casual with Linda. "What do you mean *we're* going to see *Gingerbread Lady*!" she had screamed. "I'd much rather see *No, No, Nanette*. Besides, why did he call *you*?"

"I don't know. . . . Maybe because there's always

been the three of us. Maybe he thought it would look better if he was impartial."

"Well, this threesome is going to split into a twosome . . . like after tonight!"

"What about us working together on the article?"

"That's all changed. As of now, you are off it."

"But why?"

"Look, January, Sara Kurtz will do all the rewriting anyhow. And when it gets time to go on the road, only two of us are going—Tom and me. I'll tell him that when the time comes . . . and explain I had to put you on something else. I'll even introduce him to Sara and tell him I'll be sending tapes back to her. I'm sure one look at Sara and he won't want her to go on the road."

January hesitated. "Linda, let me try to write the story. I really feel I can do it. Let me just go along with you on the tour. I won't be in the way. I promise."

"Darling, you're in the way right now. Unfortunately there's nothing I can do about it tonight . . . but enjoy it for all it's worth. Because suddenly three is getting to be quite a crowd."

They sat in the darkness of the theater. Tom had told them that Maureen Stapleton was his idea of the best actress around. She had seen Maureen in several shows and agreed with him. But this was the first time in her life she couldn't concentrate on what was happening on the stage. She was too acutely conscious of the man sitting beside her. Although his entire attention was focused on the play, she felt a peculiar sense of intimacy, sitting beside him in the darkness of a theater. Several times when his arm accidentally brushed hers, she had an insane urge to reach out and touch him. His hands were so strong . . . and clean . . . she liked the shape of his fingers. He smelled of something faintly reminiscent. She sniffed, trying to place it. He turned to her. "It's Chanel Number Five cologne," he said. "I always use it after shaving. Some people get the wrong idea."

"No, I like it," she said.

"Good. I'll get you some." Then he returned his attention to the stage.

They went backstage after the show and visited Miss Stapleton, who joined them at Sardi's. Tom told her that if he ever took a crack at writing for the stage, he'd write something for her. They began talking about shows . . . past and present . . . making comparisons. January came up with the names of some shows that amazed Tom. "But you couldn't have been around then," he said. "That was probably before you were born." She nodded. "It was . . . but from the time I was eight, I not only saw every show on Broadway, but I used to sit in this restaurant and listen to talk about shows from the forties."

She realized they were all into a world that Linda couldn't enter. January tried to pull her into the conversation. "Linda and I went to school together. She was our star. You should have seen her in *Annie Get Your Gun.*"

Linda began to spark a bit, and before the evening was over she was talking to Maureen Stapleton about doing an interview for *Gloss.*

When Tom Colt dropped Linda and January off together, Linda made no attempt to invite him up. "I've decided to save it all for the road tour. I think he feels the same way. It'll all be so natural then."

The doorbell rang just as the alarm was going off the following morning. January slipped into a robe and looked through the peephole in the door. It was a messenger with a package. She opened the door cautiously, keeping the safety chain on. She signed for it, gave him a tip, told him to leave the package on the floor. She didn't remove the chain until the messenger had gone down in the elevator. (This was a rule Mike had forced on her—part of the survival kit of a girl living alone in New York.) The moment the elevator door closed, she opened the door and grabbed the package. She took it inside and opened it carefully. It was the largest bottle of Chanel No. 5 she had ever seen. There was no note.

She held the bottle to her cheek—he had actually thought of her—and where had he gotten a bottle this size at eight-thirty in the morning? Had he sent two of them? Was the messenger on his way to Linda's right now?

She arrived at the office reeking of perfume. Linda smelled it immediately. "What have you got on?"

"Chanel Number Five." January waited for Linda's answer.

She merely shrugged. "I left a short story on your desk. Read it . . . I like it. Let me know what you think. I may be too close to it. It's about a girl who has her nose done to hold her boyfriend . . . comes out looking gorgeous . . . and loses him to a girl who looked like she did *before* the nose job. It's a funny story . . . and it came in over the transom."

"Over the transom?"

"Unsolicited . . . no agent . . . by an author I've never heard of . . . with a self-addressed return envelope to the Bronx. It's a pretty dog-eared script, so I gather Ms. Debbie Mallon has gathered a lot of rejection slips . . . it doesn't figure she'd send it to us before *Ladies' Home Journal, Cosmo, Redbook* or the others. See what you think."

January took the manuscript into her office. She sat down and lit a cigarette and began to read the manuscript.

He hadn't sent Linda any Chanel . . .

She re-read the first paragraph of the manuscript. She couldn't concentrate. She went back and read it again.

But maybe he also felt three was a crowd . . . and this was like a "kiss-off" present.

She went back to the first paragraph of the story. She glanced at her watch. Yesterday Tom had called her at home . . . in the morning. It was almost ten o'clock now . . . maybe he had called her again. She should get an answering service. But until now, there just hadn't been any need for one. Mike always knew where to find her. He usually called her at the office every day after golf. Even David knew how to find her.

So if Tom Colt wanted to find her, he certainly would
know enough to look up *Gloss* magazine. He had found
her home number and she wasn't listed yet in the phone
book. That meant he had to call Information to get it.
Maybe he had called Linda . . . and Linda was telling
him that January was on another story and too tied up
to go along with them.

She stared at the manuscript, "Nose Job" by Debbie
Mallon. Probably the girl's own story. Had to be . . .
poor Debbie Mallon . . . poor Debbie Mallon's unsolicited manuscript . . . being given to her to read. She
felt a jolt of conscience. She *must* read about Debbie's
nose or else God wouldn't be on her side . . . He
wouldn't make Tom call. This was ridiculous! Of course
God wasn't on her side. Why should He be? Why should
He help her by making a married man call her? "But
it's just to be with him," she whispered as she stared
toward the ceiling. "Just to maybe hold his hand . . ."
Would that be wrong? . . . She forced herself to read
the manuscript . . . "I looked like a parrot but Charlie
loved me. And Charlie looked like Warren Beatty.
That's enough to give any girl a complex. . . ."

She forced herself to read on. Debbie was being very
clinical about the whole operation. Even to getting all
those needles jabbed in her nose. She shuddered. And
the chin . . . they were adding something to her chin
. . . All this and she was going to lose Charlie at the
end of page ten. She stopped in the middle of the operation. Ten-fifteen. Maybe he had called Linda. Well, she
couldn't go back to Linda's office until she got through
with Debbie's nose.

At ten-thirty she had finished the story. She was un-
decided. But why not give Debbie a break? She put the
manuscript back into the manila envelope and walked
down the hall to Linda's office.

"It's good," she told Linda as she handed her the story.

Linda nodded. "I think so too. Sara's got the biggest
nose in town, so if it gets by her, we'll use 'Nose Job'
in the August issue. We can use a piece of short fiction
from an unknown, because that will be the issue we use
the story on Tom Colt. I intend to get a lot of good

pictures of him on tour . . . Shit, if only Keith weren't in *Caterpillar* . . ."

"You would want him on tour with you and Tom Colt!"

"Yes . . . but only because I could afford him. Any other photographer is going to be expensive, real expensive. Oh, I know. I'll call Jerry Coulson. He's great and he doesn't know just how good he is yet. I probably can make a good deal with him."

"Has Tom okayed the pictures?"

"I haven't asked him. And I don't intend to. Look, by then we'll be a big hot romance. Last night in the theater he kept pressing his leg against mine. And he did the same thing in Sardi's while you all were talking theater."

"Oh . . . well . . . I guess I'll go back to my office . . ."

"Sit down. The coffee wagon is due."

"No. I've got the article on Celebrity Cats to do. Do you realize how few celebrities have cats? They all seem to have dogs."

"That's ridiculous. Pam Mason has a thousand cats."

"But she's in California! Say, do you think Maureen Stapleton has a cat?" (January knew she was talking too fast.)

"I don't know . . ." The phone rang on Linda's desk. "Maybe that's Tom. I'll get Maureen's number from him." She pressed the button. "Hello . . . What? . . . Sure, Sherry . . . You're kidding! I want to hear. Come to my office and tell me." She hung up. "Don't leave, January. This will be some real dirt. Sherry said Rita is splitting a gut over something. I've put two calls in for Tom already, but his suite doesn't answer."

Sherry Margolis, an attractive girl who headed the magazine's Public Relations, came in. Linda motioned her to sit. "You said Rita Lewis is blowing a fuse over me?" Linda's smile was almost unctuously complacent.

Sherry nodded. "She asked if you had heard from Tom Colt. She's a wreck. Seems she arrived at the Plaza to pick him up at seven for the *Today* show and he was still asleep. And he was due on it at eight. He claimed he didn't know it was for *this* Tuesday. She sat in the lobby almost having a fainting spell until he calmly walked down at ten minutes to eight. She had a car, so they just about made it. After the show, he was talking to Barbara Walters, so she took time out to go to the john. And when she came out he was gone. Someone said he was in the News Room. There was a big commotion going on. She saw Tom using their telephone. She figured he was talking to you. Then he bolted out. She called . . . ran after him, but the elevator door closed just as she got there. She didn't panic because she assumed he had gone back to his hotel. He knew she had a ten o'clock breakfast interview. But he's not there, and she's been cooling it for half an hour with a guy from *Playboy* who's on his third Bloody Mary. One more and he won't be able to do an interview if Tom Colt *does* show. His suite doesn't answer and she even went up and banged on the door. The maid said she had just made up the room and no one was there. Rita kind of intimated that he wound up with you over the weekend and figured *you* might know where he is. . . ."

Linda smiled again. "That's exactly right. Only tell Rita that I left him safe and sound at the Plaza last night . . . all tucked in."

Sherry stared with open admiration. "Well, that beats Group Therapy . . . and that's where Rita Lewis spends four nights a week. I'll be delighted to give her the message."

When Sherry left the room Linda looked at January and winked. "This will kill Rita. She's had her eye on Tom from the beginning. Wait until she gets to Group Therapy tonight and they start telling her she's not rejected . . . that *they* love her and she's to be happy with *their* love . . ."

"How do you know?"

"Because I've played that scene myself. Thank God I was able to afford my own private shrink three times a week."

January shook her head. "Honestly, Linda, I just don't understand. Why would you want Sherry to think you went to bed with someone when you didn't? I mean, is there some kind of an honor in having a high score? Is it like a batting average?"

Linda yawned. "When you go to bed with a Leon, you keep it a private matter. But with a Tom Colt you make it a headline."

Suddenly Sherry came dashing back. "Linda, turn on the television set. There's an earthquake in California. A real one!"

"Did you call Rita and tell her what I told you?" Linda asked.

"Yes, and she took it beautifully—three gasps and a choked sob." Sherry had turned on the set. People were pouring in from the other offices.

Within seconds everyone was huddled around the set. They sat stupefied as the newscaster announced that the first violent tremor had hit forty miles away from the downtown area of Los Angeles at five fifty-nine Pacific Coast time . . . eight fifty-nine New York time. It registered 6.5 on the Richter scale and was felt over a three-hundred-mile area from Fresno to the Mexican border and as far east as Las Vegas. News reports stated that the initial shock was equivalent to an explosion of a million tons of TNT.

They switched to all the stations. Bulletins were interrupting regular shows . . . announcements of new tremors . . . fires. In New York, Kennedy Airport was a madhouse. A roving reporter went around . . . asking questions . . . one man said his house had collapsed but thank God his wife and children were unharmed.

Suddenly Sherry screamed. "There's Tom Colt!"

The reporter had seen him too. He pushed through the crowd and shoved a hand mike in Tom Colt's face. "Why are you rushing back to Los Angeles, Mr. Colt?"

"To be with my wife and baby." He turned away.

"Are they all right?" the reporter asked.

Tom Colt nodded. "Yes, I called her right after I did the *Today* show. The big shot had just hit, and there was another while I was talking to her."

"Aren't you here in the east to publicize your new book?"

"Book?" Tom Colt looked vague. "Look, right now there's an earthquake going on. I have a wife and son, and all I'm interested in is making sure they're safe." Then he pushed past the reporter and got on the plane.

Linda suddenly stood up and snapped off the set. "Well . . . we've got to get back to work. The worst is over. Los Angeles may have its problems with property damage, but at least it's not going to sink under the sea and disappear." Everyone quickly dispersed. There were murmurings. "Come to my office . . . I have a radio." "We can always catch it during lunch hour at a bar!" When they were alone, Linda looked out the window and whispered, "I can't believe it!" Then she spun her chair around and said, "I mean, I really can't believe it. My love life is doomed. Even nature is against me. It's hard enough to hold a man against the usual competition. But *I* have to have an earthquake!" She sighed. "Well, as long as I'm obviously free tonight, how about going to Louise's for dinner?"

"No, I think I'll stay in and work on the cat article." Then January dashed back to her office. He was gone. Friday, Saturday, Sunday and Monday. Four nights of her life . . . four nights with Tom Colt. And even though nothing had happened between them, it had been wonderful . . . And it was still wonderful to have someone to think about. Even if he never came back. . . .

The next day she got an answering service. But when a week passed without word from him, even Linda grew discouraged. "I guess I blew it. His book is up to number four spot in *Time*. I guess he'll do his shows from out there. Why not? Johnny Carson goes out there enough. Merv Griffin is there . . . Steve Allen . . . He's got enough to keep him busy for a month. But the least the man could have done was call and tell me that."

January decided to try to put Tom Colt out of her thoughts. She told herself it was a sign. Maybe God was telling her, "Stop before anything happens." Maybe it was His way of telling her He disapproved. She wasn't particularly religious. But at times she found herself

speaking to the God of her childhood, the wonderful old
man with the long white beard who presided over all
the heavens with his big book, like a ledger—keeping
score, marking down the good deeds on one page, the
sins on the other.

But each day she checked with her answering service
and found excuses to duck going to dinner with Linda.
She spent another dreary evening at Le Club with
David. Everyone was talking about the upcoming backgammon tournament at Gstaad. Dee was going . . . it
was a three-day affair . . . David couldn't take the
time off from work . . . but he envied Mike . . .
Gstaad was great at this time of the year . . . everyone would be at the Palace Hotel . . . then the Eagle
Club.

David dropped her home at eleven-thirty and didn't
even ask to come up for a nightcap. But she was excited. If Dee and Mike were going to Gstaad, they'd
come through to New York first. She'd see Mike. It was
just what she needed—a long lunch with him, a good
long talk . . . She'd tell him about her mixed-up feelings about Tom Colt. He'd help set her straight, and he'd
understand. After all, he had been there so many times
himself.

She called Palm Beach the following morning. When
the butler said Mr. and Mrs. Granger had left for Gstaad
three days ago, she hung up and sat staring dumbly at
the phone. He had been in New York and hadn't called.
There had to be some explanation. She had talked to
Mike just a few days ago . . . Suddenly she began to
panic. Maybe something had happened. But that was
ridiculous. Nothing could have happened. It would be
in the newspapers. Unless he was sick . . . Maybe
he was lying in a hospital with a heart attack or something. And Dee was playing backgammon. She placed
a call to the Palace Hotel. Then she dressed and sat
waiting for the call to be completed. Ten minutes later
Mike's voice sounded as if it were in the next room.

"How are you?" she yelled.

"Just great. Anything wrong! You okay?"

"Yes . . ." She sighed. "Oh, Mike, I was frightened."

"About what?"

"Well, last night David told me where you were. And I knew you'd have to come through to New York. And I called Palm Beach and they told me you had gone . . . and I thought that . . ."

"Hold it." He laughed. "First, we arrived at the airport at five in the morning. Stayed just long enough for the plane to be refueled. I didn't want to wake you. And I figured we'd stop over a few days on the way back. Listen, I've got great news—I finally broke the back of this idiotic game. I won a few bucks the last few weeks in Palm Beach. I'm not up to playing in *this* yet. But at the Calcutta auction, I'll buy me a player. It's a great game, babe . . . wait till you get the hang of it."

"Yes, Mike . . ."

"Listen, you're paying for this. Jiggle the operator, tell her to reverse the charges to me."

"No, Mike. It's my nickel. I want it that way."

"Okay. Listen, I got to run. I've got me a pigeon for gin. While we were waiting for the plane to be refueled, I beat Freddie out of three big ones . . . in one hour. And he's come on this trip with us, and I got him eager to play every day."

"Who's Freddie?"

"Oh, some young schmuck married to a rich broad. I thought you met him in Palm Beach . . . sure you did."

"Okay, Mike. Good luck with Freddie."

"Bye, baby. See you soon."

That night she accepted an invitation to go to dinner with Linda and a friend of hers who was bringing along a "friend." They went to a small restaurant on Fifty-sixth Street and Linda warned her to pick the cheapest thing on the menu. "Mine is paying two alimonies and yours is paying alimony plus shrink fees for his son."

January decided her date looked like a long skinny pig. He was tall and thin, but from there on all resemblance to a man ended. His face was pink and his nose was absolutely a snout. He had wisps of pink hair that barely covered his scalp, and patchy little sideburns that refused to grow. He talked about his squash game and his jogging and the ulcerous work of Madison Avenue. Both men worked at the same advertising agency and during the better part of the evening they discussed their accounts and inside gossip at the office. It was obvious from their conversation that they lunched together every day. Why talk about it now? But she realized they were nervous . . . and they were, as Mike would put it, born losers. They were with two girls they hoped to impress, and somehow they felt "big business" talk was the key. She marveled at the unreality of it all. Didn't they look in the mirror when they shaved? If the pig (who answered to the name of Wally) *owned* the advertising agency, he couldn't impress her. She was sorry she had accepted the date. At the moment she would rather be home eating a TV dinner and reading a good book. At ten-thirty the dinner finally dragged to a finish. It was freezing, but the pig said he hadn't done all of his jogging so they walked home. Linda immediately invited everyone up for a nightcap, but January said she was tired.

The pig insisted on going into the building and escorting her to her door. When she put the key in the lock and turned to say goodnight, he stared at her. "You must be kidding."

"No. Goodnight and thanks for a very nice dinner."

"But what about us?"

"Well . . . what about us?" she asked.

"Don't tell me you're one of those frigid types?"

"No . . . right now, I'm just a tired type."

"Well, let's fix that." He leaned over and immediately his tongue was pushing its way down her throat and his hands were all over her body . . . groping under her coat . . . trying to slide up her blouse. In a burst of anger she lifted her knee and it made its mark. He leaped away with a groan. For a split second his little pig eyes smarted with tears of pain. Then his mouth went ugly. She was frightened now and tried to open the door and get inside, but he pulled her around and slapped her across the face. "You lousy little cunt! You stone-assed virgin types kill me. Well, I'll show you." He grabbed for her. She was now more angry than frightened, and with a sudden surge of strength, she shoved him away, pushed open the door, slipped inside and slammed it in his face. For a moment she stood trembling from anger and shock. He had expected her to go to bed with him for a $3.95 table d'hôte dinner.

She undressed slowly and turned on the bath. She needed a lot of bubbles and perfume to wash away the ugly evening. She was just about to get into the tub when the phone rang. It was Linda in a muffled voice. "January . . . is Wally there?"

"Of course not!"

"Oh. Well, listen. Steve is in the bathroom. I just checked with my service. And guess what. Tom Colt called!"

"He did!"

"Yes. He's in town. My service said he called at ten-thirty. Call him now. He's at the Plaza."

"Me? But he called you."

"January . . . I can't. I'm in bed with Steve—that is, I will be when he gets out of the bathroom. Look, tell him you're calling for me . . . that I'm having a late conference . . . you know . . . but find out if he plans to see me tomorrow."

"I can't. Honestly, Linda."

"Do it. Come on, now. I'll tell you what . . . you can even cut yourself in on the date."

"No."

"Please! Oh, hi . . . Steve . . . I was just checking with my service." There was a pause, then Linda said in an impersonal tone, "All right, Miss Green. Thank you for my messages, and *please* make that call for me."

January sat on the bed. The water in the bath had cooled. Twenty minutes had passed and she still hadn't made the call. She couldn't. How *could* she call him? But then she owed it to Linda. She was letting her own feelings hold her back. She picked up the phone.

The night operator at the Plaza said Mr. Colt had left a DO NOT DISTURB. She left a message that Miss Linda

Riggs had returned his call. Then she hung up and wondered whether she was disappointed at not being able to talk to him . . . or grateful that he'd never know she had called.

Linda's call came before the alarm went off. "January . . . wake up. I only have a second. Steve's in the john. Then he's going to give me an early morning fuck. Tell me . . . did you talk to Tom?"

"Oh, my God. What time is it?"

"Seven o'clock. Did you talk to him?"

"No, he had his phone turned off, but I left a message saying you had returned his call."

"Good girrrl! Talk to you later."

At eleven-thirty Linda summoned January into her office. "I just spoke to him," she said. "And I'm keeping my word. We're all going to see *No, No, Nanette* tonight."

"Oh . . ."

"Aren't you going to thank me?"

"Linda, I don't have to go really. In fact I think I'd rather not."

"No. It's all right. He said, 'Last time *I* picked the show . . . now what do you want to see?' And when I said *No, No, Nanette,* he said, great, because Patsy Kelly has always been a favorite of his. Then he said, 'Do you want to ask January along?' and I said, 'Yes, I think it looks better. After all, you are married. On the road it won't matter because everyone will know I'm there to do the story.' So that's how we left it. Only tonight, I think I want to clinch it. So let's not do the Sardi's bit. Let's make it some place where he'll really drink. Then at the proper time you can cut out. Or if I get him to come up to my place for a nightcap . . . you don't come."

"Linda, maybe he'll invite Patsy to Sardi's . . ."

"Oh shit. That means we sit and talk theater and everyone is very proper like last time."

"He obviously likes the theater."

"Well, let's play it by ear. We're to meet in his suite

at six. He said he'd have some hors d'oeuvres and a drink to hold us until after the show. Now if I can just get him drinking on an empty stomach . . . I'll score . . ."

They arrived at the Plaza at six. Rita Lewis was there, along with a subdued young man from *Life* magazine. Tom was holding a glass of bourbon and made the introductions. Rita went into a state of shock when she saw Linda and January. Tom fixed them a drink and they both sat quietly while the interview continued. January noticed that Tom looked at the clock on the mantle several times. At six-thirty, the young man was still asking questions. At quarter to seven, Tom said, "How much longer will this take? We have tickets for a show."

"Mr. Colt," Rita's voice veered on quiet hysteria. "This is for *Life* magazine. Mr. Harvey will be here for quite some time. I mean . . . there is no time limit. And a photographer is coming at eight-thirty."

"Looks like we'll have to postpone the session," Tom said. He turned to the reporter. "I'm sorry, young man, but—"

Rita jumped up. "Mr. Colt . . . you can't do this. You've already upset our schedule by two weeks. I had to change all the bookings—the Mike Douglas show, Kup in Chicago . . ."

"Well, next time when you say I have a five o'clock interview, don't spring any surprises on me."

"But I left an envelope with your schedule for you last night. It distinctly said, '*Life* reporter and pictures at five . . . first session.' Anyone knows that a session means several hours. And a photographer can't be rushed either. We've got Rocco Garazzo—he's one of the best."

"Sorry, kid . . ." Tom said. "We'll do it another time. Look, the booze is all set up over there. Enjoy yourself."

"Mr. Colt . . ." Rita's voice broke. Her eyes were glassy with tears "You're going to make me lose my job. They'll say I goofed. And it would keep me from getting other jobs because the word would go out that I wasn't competent enough to handle a star author. I'll also blow all my personal contacts . . . like with *Life* magazine . . . because what you're doing is insulting to the reporter. He's a writer . . . doing his best, and—"

"Cut it," he said quietly. "You've made your point." He turned to Linda. "The tickets are in my name. You kids go see the show. Come back here when it's over. Use my car. It's out front." Then he took off his jacket, poured himself a stiff drink and said to the reporter, "Okay, Mr. Harvey. I'm sorry about the misunderstanding. Let's have a few blasts together, and take all the time you want."

As they drove to the theater, Linda rhapsodized over the turn of events. "He's drinking. And now there's no chance of Sardi's. But I'm going back alone. I feel the timing is right."

After the show, Linda lost some of her nerve. "Maybe Rita and the *Life* people are still with him. You better come back. If he's alone, stay for one drink, and then split. I'll give you the cue. When I say, 'January, I think your cat article is going to be great,' then you can say, 'That reminds me, I have some work I need to do on it tonight. I'd better go.' Okay?"

"Okay. But Linda, aren't you? . . ." She stopped.

"Aren't I what?"

"Aren't you kind of going after him like a man should go after a girl?"

Linda laughed. "January, I bet if you balled a man, you'd expect him to send you flowers the next morning."

"Well . . . yes . . . David did."

"Maybe that's why David only comes around every ten days. But I happen to know that model whom he balls quite often not only doesn't get flowers from him, but she makes him breakfast and brings it to him in bed. And considering that Kim only eats maybe one stalk of celery every other day to keep nice and consumptive-looking . . . it's not easy to watch a guy eat bacon and eggs when you are starving."

"Meaning what?"

"Meaning, there is no boy-girl thing anymore. The

girl can be as aggressive as she wants. She can call the man. She can ask him to go to bed. That's the way it is today. This is the seventies. *Not* the fifties."

"There's one thing I'm curious about—if you dig Tom Colt this much, why would you go to bed with Steve last night?"

"Last night, I didn't know that Tom was coming back until after I had already told Steve I wanted him. I couldn't throw him out, could I? Besides, he's very good in bed and I hadn't had sex for quite a while."

"But don't you have to *feel* something to go to bed with a man?"

"Yes . . . horny."

"Linda!"

Linda stared at her in the darkness of the limousine. "Know something, January? Tom Colt is fifty-seven, but he's with it. *You* are the generation gap."

Rita Lewis and the reporter were just leaving when January and Linda returned. Tom greeted both girls expansively, asked about the show, and insisted everyone, including the harassed Rita Lewis, have a drink. Rita had to leave. The *Life* journalist stayed for one nightcap. Then he said, "I've really got to go. I told my wife I'd be home by ten. She's holding some food for me."

Tom shook his head sadly. "Why didn't you speak up, man? Just because I forget about food when I'm drinking. Christ, I starved you . . . and that poor P.R. lady from the publishers. Where do you live?"

"Down near Gramercy Park."

"Well, the car is outside. Take it. Then send it back and it can take the girls home."

"January, I just love that cat article you're working on," Linda said.

January started for the door. "It needs work. In fact, I had intended to work on it a bit tonight . . . I'll leave with Mr. Harvey . . . he can drop me."

"The poor guy is starving," Tom said. "And he goes in the opposite direction. You gonna make him go uptown first, then backtrack downtown just for a cat story. Can't it wait until tomorrow?"

"Well, I really should—"

"January does some of her best work at night," Linda said quickly.

"Don't we all. But this time her genius will have to wait. Go on, Bob."

The young man hesitated. "It's really all right. I don't mind . . ."

"Beat it," Tom said good-naturedly. "Get home to your wife and dinner." Then he turned to Linda and held out his glass. "Want to freshen up this one, baby? And pour some ginger ale for our cat girl."

Tom had two quick drinks. Then he noticed an envelope on the table. He picked it up. "Tomorrow's instructions from the Press Lady."

"You'd better read them," January said. "I mean . . you might have an early call."

"Oh, I know about the call. It's Philadelphia . . . the Mike Douglas show. Then Washington."

"You're leaving?" Linda asked.

"Just for two days. Then I'm back here for a week. Then Chicago, Cleveland, Detroit . . . Then back here for another few days. Then Los Angeles."

"What time are you leaving tomorrow?" Linda asked.

He nodded toward the envelope. "Open it and see."

Linda ripped it open. "You don't leave until noon. It says the limo will pick you up then. But you have a nine o'clock breakfast date with Donald Zec."

"Yes. He's from London . . . doing a story on me for the London *Daily Mirror*." He stood up. "I'd better get to bed. I want to be awake for Donald. He's a buddy of mine." He started for the bedroom.

"January, I think your cat story is—"

"I've got to leave. I can take a cab," January said.

He turned on them. "You'll both leave together with the car. I'm going to get undressed, and when I call, you both can come and tuck me in, and we'll have one for the road together."

He disappeared into the bedroom. January looked at Linda and shrugged helplessly. Linda was furious. "I've got to find out when he leaves for the Chicago, Cleveland, Detroit tour. Because I'm going to be on it with him. I can't go to Philadelphia and Washington . . . it's too late to make reservations for hotels and all. Besides, I think he'll probably have the *Life* people with him." Suddenly she looked at January. "Look . . . get out . . . now."

"You mean, just leave?"

"Yes. And when I go in I'll say you really wanted to split."

"But Linda, that's so rude . . ."

"He doesn't really want you. He's just being polite. And you never really insisted on going. Bob Harvey was willing to go the few blocks out of his way, but you certainly didn't fight very hard."

"Well, holy smoke, Linda. I don't want Tom Colt to think I hate him. If I accept a theater invitation from him, I can't act as if he's suddenly contaminated. He'll think I'm rude."

"What do you care what he thinks? After he's in bed with me, he won't be doing any thinking. Come on, January—get your coat and go."

Suddenly Tom's voice bellowed from the bedroom. "Hey, girls, bring in the bottle and three glasses."

"Go on," Linda hissed.

"Linda, will you really tell him I *had* to work? Please."

"Yes . . . For God's sake, just get going!"

Suddenly he walked into the room. He was in a dressing gown. It was obvious he had nothing under it. "Hey, why are you both standing there like bookends? Get the booze and come on in."

Linda glared at January and took the bottle. They both went into the bedroom. Tom Colt propped himself up on the bed on top of the covers. "Now, we'll all have one for the road. Then you both can tiptoe out and put off the lights." When he saw Linda had only two glasses, he pointed toward the bathroom. "There's a glass in there. I want you to have a drink this time, January. To toast my road tour."

She went into the bathroom and obediently returned with the glass. He poured a good shot for each of them, and then poured half a glass full of straight bourbon for himself.

"Now . . . sit on each side of me." He patted the

bed. Both girls sat down. He rumpled Linda's hair teasingly. "Now, we drink to the big author who is about to go out and sell himself like breakfast food. Step right this way, folks . . . come see the writer . . . laugh at him . . . hiss at him . . . do anything . . . as long as you *buy* him." He tossed half the drink down in one gulp. Linda finished hers in one swallow and stared at Tom for approval.

He winked, and refilled her glass. He freshened his own, then looked toward January. She had taken a sip . . . suddenly she bolted it down. He grinned and refilled her glass. Her throat was burning. For one second she thought this is how people must feel when they swallow poison. Then the burning gave way to a slight glow in her chest. She sipped the second drink . . . and once again, found the second went down easier. She kept taking small sips. It was better than burning her throat with one big gulp. She wondered if Tom realized that she and Linda also had not eaten any dinner. She felt giddy, as if she were outside, watching herself. She edged toward the end of the bed. Linda had put her head on Tom's chest. Almost absent-mindedly, he was stroking her hair. He lifted her chin. Their eyes were close. January wondered how she could slip out. He leaned over and kissed Linda's brow. "You're a beautiful girl," he said slowly.

January knew she should leave . . . but she was paralyzed. Linda was staring into Tom's eyes. She looked as if she were about to dissolve.

"Linda," he said slowly. "You've got to help me."

Linda nodded dumbly.

He stroked her hair. "Linda . . . I'm kind of crazy about January. What shall I do?" For a moment the room was very still. It was as if time had suddenly stopped . . . like a wax museum with everyone frozen into position. Linda was still leaning close, staring into his eyes. January was sitting at the foot of the bed, still holding her glass. Seconds passed. Then she snapped into action. She jumped off the bed.

"The bathroom," she said suddenly. "I have to go." She dashed in and sank to the floor, resting her head in her arm on the bathtub. The whole tableau was unreal. Was Linda still sitting there gazing at Tom? How could he have said that? Or was it a gag . . . a private joke between them? Of course! That was it! Right now they were probably in each other's arms laughing at the way she had fallen for it. Well . . . she hadn't fallen for it. She'd pretend to go along with it. Pretend she really had to go to the bathroom. She flushed the toilet several times. She let the water run in the sink and made a good deal of noise washing her hands. Then she opened the door and walked resolutely into the room.

Tom was sitting propped up against the pillows, staring at her. There was no sign of Linda. For a moment they both looked at one another. Then with almost a sad smile, he motioned her over. She moved slowly and gingerly sat on the edge of the bed.

"Where's Linda?" she asked.

"I sent her home."

She started to rise but he pulled her hand gently and she sat down again. "Don't be so uptight. I'm not going to rape you. I don't usually go around falling for a girl who has a father younger than I am. I can get all the girls I want . . . uncomplicated girls. I even marry them. Too often . . . That's my trouble. I think the kids today have the right idea about abolishing marriage. People should be together as long as they care about one another, not because it's a law, like a prison sentence. Now, here's the answers up front. No, I'm not wildly in love with my wife. I never really was, except she gave me a child and that was something I wanted. If I left her, she'd keep the baby. So I'll never let that happen. It's crazy . . . my wanting you. Linda would have been easier. No questions . . . just balling together. I tried to want Linda . . . but you got in the way. I found myself thinking about you all the time. I really didn't have to come back here and do the eastern part of the tour. The book is selling great—over fifty thousand copies so far and going into another twenty-five thousand printing. But I came here and agreed to go on with the tour because of you." He pulled her to him and kissed her on the lips gently. "Nothing is going to happen tonight, January. In fact nothing is going to happen until you feel the same way about me . . ."

"Tom. I . . . Oh, Tom I do care for you . . . and I was horrified when I realized it . . . because you do have a wife and a child."

"But what we feel for one another has nothing to do with my child. I've already told you how I feel about my wife."

"Tom, I couldn't take it for just a week . . . or just for now . . . don't you understand?"

"January . . . love is never forever. Thank the fates and take it wherever you find it."

She looked at him steadily. "Do you love me, Tom?"

He looked thoughtful. "That's a heavy word. And I have to admit I've used it many times and never really meant it. But I kind of get the idea that if I use it with you, it'll have to be for real."

"Yes . . . it's the only way I could . . ." She tried desperately to find the right words. "You see I'd feel so guilty . . . I mean, I even feel guilty sitting here talking like this with you, knowing you are married, that you have a child. What we are doing is wrong . . . completely wrong . . . But if I felt you really loved me . . . and that no one could get hurt . . . except us . . . well, that's the only way we'd have a chance for anything at all. I'd figure maybe God wouldn't be too angry because we both are really in love—" She knew she was blushing and looked down at her hands. "I know I must sound like an idiot to you . . . and . . . ."

He lifted her face and his eyes were gentle. "January, you're even more wonderful than I thought you'd be." Then he took her in his arms and stroked her hair as if he were comforting a child. After a few moments, he broke the embrace gently and got off the bed and led her into the living room. He picked up her coat and suddenly she flung herself into his arms. The coat dropped to the floor as he held her close and kissed her. And for the first time she understood the intimacy of a real kiss. Their bodies were close. She pressed against him, wanting to become part of him . . . Suddenly the phone jangled. It was the driver announcing he had returned.

"Time for you to go," he said as he picked up her coat.

"Oh God, Tom, I wish you weren't leaving."

"It's just for a few days. Maybe it's for the best . . . it will give us both a chance to think." Then he kissed her lightly and watched her go down the hall until she reached the elevator.

She felt elation . . . fear and excitement. It couldn't be wrong. It had to be Fate . . . to have Tom live in Mike's suite. She would have her first real love affair in Mike's bed.

She sat back in the limousine and thought about it. She relived every event of the evening . . . everything he said. Then something bothered her. At first it was just a nagging thought that cut into her happiness. But by the time she got home, she was almost in panic. What had he meant when he said the two days would give them both a chance to think? Oh God, did that mean he was going to change his mind? Had she scared him off, talking about love and guilt? Would he come back and say, "I've thought about it, January . . . And we'd better not let anything happen." No, he wouldn't do that. He cared about her. And then in the darkness of the limousine, it suddenly occurred to her that when their bodies had been pressed together . . . he hadn't even had the slightest erection. Absolutely nothing! Oh God, maybe she didn't really turn him on . . . maybe she had really frightened him away!

SEVENTEEN

SHE DIDN'T SLEEP all night. In some ways it was a more tormented night than the night she had learned Mike was married. That night she had just sat by the window in a stupor, unable to feel any distinct emotion other than a sense of loss. This sleepless night had been different. She had smoked an entire pack of cigarettes. *"It's just for a few days . . . Maybe it's for the best . . . It will give us both a chance to think."* The words haunted her. *Think about what?* Think about ending it before it really started. How could she have been so stupid? Demanding that he love her . . . What was it he had said? He had lied about love many times, but with her it would be a heavy word. Of course—she had scared him off. You don't go asking a man if he really loves you right off, not if you're cool. But she wasn't cool. She didn't want to play games with Tom. If they had anything between them, it would be rough enough because of his marriage . . . let alone playing games. She wanted an honest relationship with him, she wanted to be able to tell him how she felt, how much she loved him. . . .

At nine o'clock she dragged herself to the office. She had toyed with the idea of calling in sick to avoid the confrontation with Linda. But Linda had to be faced . . . sooner or later. She decided to get it over with and went directly to Linda's office.

To her amazement, Linda was smiling when she walked in. "Sit down. Have some coffee and give me the fabulous details."

"Linda . . about last night . . . I—"

"January, I'm not upset," Linda said cheerfully. "At least, not now. I must admit that I did contemplate various forms of suicide last night. But this morning I was back at my shrink's, sitting out in front of his office, at seven-thirty, waiting for him to come and open shop. I made him give me twenty minutes, even though there was a hysterical menopausal lady waiting in the outer office. And I told him everything. And by the time I finished I was sobbing louder than the menopausal lady. Then he said, 'Linda, I usually wait for you to find your own solutions. But for now, I will tell you that Tom Colt is not in love with you or January. For a man his age to have had so many women means he has to constantly prove something to himself. And for him to choose January definitely relates to her father.' Then he explained how in taking you, Tom Colt is getting back at your father."

"Wow," January said softly. "Remind me never to get involved with a shrink."

"You had one at that Clinique in Switzerland, didn't you?"

"Yes, but, we never talked about anything personal. I mean he would just talk to give me confidence that I would walk and get back into the world and be with my father again. But that was all. I mean, how can you sit there and tell your innermost thoughts to a strange man, even if he is a psychiatrist?"

"Dr. Galens is not a strange man. He's a Freudian analyst, but he does believe in therapy for situational problems. Like me getting tossed out of bed for you. Later on, he'll still deal with it in a Freudian way and prove how it all relates back to my past. You see, even with my nose job and all, inside there is still an ugly little girl screaming to get out. That's why I need sex—to prove I'm attractive. And with you . . . everything relates to your father. Like even in the accident on the

motorcycle. You got on the damn thing just to punish
your father for going with Melba."

"You mean you told him about me!"

"Yes. He said you had an Electra complex. That's why
you can't dig David. He's too young and handsome."

"Linda, you didn't tell him about that too!"

"Of course. He's my shrink, and he not only has to
know everything about me, but also about the people I
associate with. And as you can see, he's just great. You
see, basically I'm a very shallow person . . . Oh, don't
look shocked. I know I am. I have a superstar complex.
Unfortunately, I can't sing as well as Barbra Streisand.
As an actress, I'm not exactly Glenda Jackson. And
Ann-Margret doesn't have to worry about me crowding
her as a sex symbol. So how do I go about becoming a
superstar? With *Gloss* magazine. Dr. Galens forced me
to admit that my dedication to the magazine is not because I believe in it . . . but because I AM *Gloss*. And
if *Gloss* makes it, so do I. I'm not a Democrat or a
Republican. But in Seventy-two, no matter what the
publisher says, *Gloss* will go all-out for the Democratic
candidate, because I want to be part of the political
picture. I don't know whether it's going to be Muskie,
Lindsay, Humphrey, or Ted Kennedy. But nothing is
going to stop me."

Then she smiled. "But the hell with that. I pay Dr.
Galens to put my head in order. Tell me about last night.
Was it great?"

"We didn't do anything. I mean . . . we just talked."

"You what?"

"Because—Linda, I'd rather not talk about it."

Linda nodded good-naturedly. "Don't feel bad. He
was probably too drunk." Her voice changed and became all business. "Look, do you know how to work a
tape recorder?"

"Yes."

"Okay. Take this." She handed January a small com-
pact machine. "I guess it's obvious who is going to tour
with Tom Colt. So each night, or each morning, or whatever . . . talk into it and tell about the tour. Tell every-

thing as you see it. And from your tapes, Sara will write
the story. Talk into the machine as if it were a diary.
Don't leave anything out—"

"Linda, I can't."

"I don't mean your sex life. I just want you to tell
me about that. Although from your track record, it
could be a total disaster."

"What do you mean?"

"Look what happened with David."

"But I didn't love him. I . . . I care about Tom Colt."

Linda sighed. "Look, loving a guy, or caring about
him, doesn't necessarily mean you're going to be great in
the kip. Some of the biggest courtesans in the world were
lesbians, yet they made men go out of their minds. It
takes finesse, not just love. And this isn't just a man.
This is Tom Colt—a legend in his own lifetime and all
that jazz."

"I've lived with a legend. And they're human."

"Oh, is that it? So that's why you've fallen for him.
Because your father has shown his cracks you're looking for someone who is bigger and better. Your own private superman. Right?"

"Linda . . . know what? I think you're over-analyzed."

"Okay. But take this tape machine. And maybe in the
end when we play them back, we'll not only find out what
Tom Colt is like . . . but maybe we'll find the real
January Wayne."

She tried talking into the tape—about Tom . . . her
first impressions of him . . . the cocktail party . . .
his strength . . . his gentleness. But when she played it
back, it sounded like a high school girl's diary.

She spent a murderous day. Suppose Tom never called
again. Suppose he decided he wanted out. Had she really
bungled it? At four o'clock she left the office. Maybe if
she tried to write about it, if she faced a typewriter and
a blank piece of paper she might be able to write dis-
passionately of her meeting with Tom . . . and then
read it off to the tape machine. She decided to walk
home to clear her head. She tried to tell herself every-

thing would be all right. But she kept hearing the words
—*Perhaps it's for the best. It will give us both time to
think things over.*

"Think things over." What did that mean? It had to
mean that he wanted to pull out. Oh God, if only Mike
were here, if only there was someone she could talk
to . . .

She got home and checked with her message service.
Nothing. Suddenly the room seemed to close in on her.
Empty Coke bottles, littered ashtrays . . . Remnants
of last night's ordeal were strewn around the apartment.
She began to clean up. Suddenly she felt she had to get
out of that room. She had to talk to someone.

She rushed to the phone and called David. He answered on the second ring. "January, this is a nice surprise. It goes down with all of the big firsts in my life.
This is the first time you've called me."

"I . . . well . . . I've been working hard on a
story, and I'm afraid I'm stumped. I need a man's
point of view. David . . . could you take me to dinner
tonight? I need to talk things out with someone."

"Oh, my poor angel . . . of all nights. I have a seven-
thirty dinner date with a client. But look . . . I'm free
until then. Want me to come up for a drink? It's only
five-thirty."

"No, let me meet you somewhere. I've got to get out
of here."

"January . . . is anything wrong?"

"No, it's just that I've been cooped up in the apartment writing."

He laughed. "I'm very impressed. Look, I have to
be somewhere on the East Side at seven-thirty. Could
we meet at the Unicorn? That way it will give us more
time."

"Yes, David. I can be there in ten minutes."

"Make it fifteen," he laughed. "I just got home and
I want to give my face a fast runover with the electric
shaver."

They sat in the Unicorn at a small table. David stared

in amazement when she ordered a Jack Daniel's. She hated the drink, but somehow it made her feel close to Tom.

"All right." He smiled. "Now, tell me what's the big hang-up with America's newest and most beautiful writer."

"Well, it's a short story I'm trying my hand at. And I just realized I'm writing it all from the woman's angle and I've got to get the man's point of view."

He nodded seriously. "Good thinking." He looked at his watch. "Go ahead. Tell me about it."

"Well, I have my heroine in love with a married man, a man much older than she is . . ."

"Oh, he's got grandchildren and all that?"

"No, he has a baby . . . and a wife. No grandchildren."

"How old is he?"

"In his late fifties."

"Then you're writing it wrong. A man in his late fifties should have grandchildren, not a baby. Make it grandchildren . . . more pathos already."

"That's not important. The crux of my story is the relationship between the man and the girl."

"How old is the girl?"

She took a good swallow of the bourbon. "She's . . . I haven't really decided."

"Make her around thirty-two. A man in his fifties rarely marries anyone younger. Otherwise it won't work. And if he has a baby with the other woman . . . well, she has to be in her thirties, too."

"Why couldn't the girl be in her twenties?"

"Well, only if the man is an unmitigated louse. Then you could even make her fourteen. But if he has a wife and baby and falls in love with another woman—she has to be a woman, not a girl."

"All right, suppose she is in her thirties, and they fall in love and she has a guilt feeling about the wife and baby . . . and refuses to go along with it for like a one-night stand. But she's mad about him, and tells

him she doesn't expect to break up his marriage or anything like that, but if they have a relationship it has
to be love . . ."

"So, what's your problem?"

"Do you think she would be wrong in telling him
that?"

He looked at his drink. "Why would she be wrong?
Every girl says that, even if it's a one-night stand."

"I don't mean it that way, David. I mean, what if
they were together for several days . . . no sex . . .
just thrown together . . . then separated. And when
he came back, he told her he wanted her, and she said,
'You'll have to say you love me, and—' "

"Oh, no," he groaned. "January, what are you writing for, *Screen Romances*? A girl knows better than to
demand that a guy says he loves her."

"She does?"

"Of course. That's the quickest way to scare him off."

"Okay. The girl in my story is kind of an idiot. And
what's more, she says it just before he goes off on a
business trip. She tells him she won't settle for less than
love, and also that she'll miss him the few days that
he's gone. And he says, 'It's just for a few days. Maybe
it's for the best. It will give us both a chance to think.' "

He was silent for a second. Then he smiled. "Beautiful!"

"What?"

"January, maybe you can really write at that. What
a finish. I can see it. That's your last line, followed by
dot dot dot. And then you leave it to your reader. Does
he . . . or doesn't he come back!"

She took another sip of the bourbon. "As a reader,
what would you think?"

He laughed as he waved for the check. "She's blown
it. She'll never see him again."

"Will everyone feel that way?"

He scribbled his name on the check and shook his
head. "No, that's why it's great. Women will probably
feel he will, but a man will understand. It's the biggest

cop-out line in the world. That 'Give us both a chance to think' bit."

"You make it all seem so final," she said.

He stood up and helped her with her coat.

"Well, honey, you're the one who wrote it."

EIGHTEEN

THE FOLLOWING NIGHT she accepted a date from Ned Crane, a dull but attractive young man she had met with David. He had called her several times, and she had always refused. But suddenly anything seemed preferable to another long, sleepless night. They went to Le Club, joined up with a group of his friends, and for a short time she almost welcomed the noise and frenzied activity. She sipped white wine, allowed herself to be pushed around the floor, and even tried to join in the conversation. By eleven o'clock, she suddenly felt drained. She fought to hide her yawns and wondered how she could break away. She was saved at eleven-thirty when someone suggested going over to Vera's for backgammon. January said she didn't know Vera and she didn't play backgammon, and she finally convinced Ned that she would be perfectly safe taking a cab home.

She fell into bed at midnight and was so exhausted that she slept. She was still asleep when her phone service rang her at eight-thirty.

"Miss Wayne, I just came on duty and I notice you didn't call in and get your messages last night."

"Oh. Holy smoke. I was so tired . . . I even forgot to set the alarm. Thanks for calling. I've got to get up anyway."

"Don't you want your messages?"

"Oh . . . oh, sure . . . yes."

313

"Sara Kurtz called. Said she expects some tapes by this afternoon. That you would understand."

"Oh, yes. Thank you."

"And a Mr. Colt called from Washington."

"What?"

"A Mr. Colt called from Washington at eight-thirty P.M., and again at ten. He wanted you to call him at the Shoreham Hotel."

"Oh, thank you. Thank you!"

"I'm sorry if I woke you."

"No . . . no, it's wonderful. I . . . I should be up anyhow. Thank you so much!"

She caught Tom at the Shoreham just as he was leaving. "Oh, Tom . . . I came home at twelve and forgot all about checking with my service. I'm so sorry."

"Wait a minute." He laughed. "First . . . how are you?"

"I'm fine . . . no, I'm not . . . I miss you. How are you? Do you miss me?"

"Yes . . . to everything."

"When will you be back?"

"Friday night. Will you have dinner with me?"

"Will I . . . oh wow . . . I mean . . . yes, I'd adore it."

"Okay. I'll call you as soon as I get in."

"Okay. Look, Tom. Maybe I should call you . . . you know . . . I could keep checking at the Plaza . . . because you might miss me between the office and my apartment."

"I'll find you, January. Don't worry." And then he hung up.

She spent the morning trying to tape an unemotional account of the cocktail party for Tom Colt. His attitude, the people who were there, the trapped feeling an author has when he's spotlighted as guest of honor.

Linda played it and nodded. "Sounds okay. I'll give it to Sara." Then she stared at January. "What's the matter with you? You look awful."

She was silent for a moment, then she said, "Linda, I don't know what to do . . . I'm so scared."

"Of what?"

"Well, Tom gets in tomorrow—"

"Don't tell me you're still going to play the virgin queen."

"No . . . I . . . I want to go to bed with him. But suppose I don't arouse him."

"A man like Tom Colt will be aroused. Don't worry."

January stared at her hands in her lap. "Linda, when he held me close that night at the Plaza . . . he . . . he wasn't wearing anything under the robe . . . and . . ."

"And?"

"There was nothing," January said.

Linda whistled. "I forgot. Sure. He's in his late fifties and he drinks. That combination is murder. You'll have to start right off by giving him head."

"I don't think I could. I . . . I don't even know how."

"Pretend it's a popsicle—pretend—oh, hell . . . that's something that takes practice. If I say so myself, I give the best head in town. Every man says that. But you've got to get started. Part of it is instinctive. And a man like Tom will guide you . . ."

"But . . . what happens if he comes?"

"You swallow it."

"*What!*"

Linda groaned. "January, when you're making love with someone you really care about, it's the ultimate fulfillment and expression of love. The man ejaculating it . . . you taking it . . . and swallowing it. Swallowing part of him."

"Linda, I may throw up! That's the most revolting thing I've ever heard."

Linda laughed. "Listen, stone-age lady. It's also very good for you. It's loaded with hormones. It's also great for your skin. I use it as a facial mask whenever I can."

"*You what!*"

"I use it as a mask. When Keith was living with me and we were doing it every night, I'd do the hand bit maybe three times a week, and just before the explo-

sion came, I'd be ready with a glass. Then I poured it
into a bottle and put it in the refrigerator. It's great
for a facial mask. It's like egg white . . . only better.
You leave it on ten minutes until it stiffens, then wash
it off with cold water. Why do you think I let that jerk
from the advertising agency stay . . . I got half a glass
from him."

"Linda, that's the most awful thing I ever heard. I
just couldn't. I'm nauseous. It's—"

"Well, when you go down on Tom, if you can't get
yourself to swallow it, let it come all over your face
. . . rub it into your skin and . . ."

January jumped up. "Linda, I can't listen! I—"

"Sit down! Jesus, I realize you spent three years
away from everyone and everybody in Switzerland.
And Miss Haddon's wasn't exactly a place Masters and
Johnson would go for research. No one is telling you
that you *have* to do any of the things I tell you. But
it's time you learned people who do these things are not
degenerates . . . and the least you can do is listen!"

"All right. But I don't want to rub, swallow, or package any of that stuff."

"Okay. But you also can't just lie back and give him
the pleasure of allowing him to enter you. It *is* a two-
way thing."

"But what do I do?"

"Respond!"

"How?"

"Oh Jesus!" Linda got up and paced the room. Then
she leaned over the desk, her eyes level with January's.
"You did kiss back when he kissed you, didn't you?"

"Yes."

"And then what! Did you respond?"

"Yes."

"Good girrrl! Now, when you're in bed with him and
when he kisses your boobs, start feeling him."

"Where?"

"Oh God, January . . . anywhere. Start rubbing the
back of his head. Kiss his neck . . . his ears, . . . his
cheek . . . just to let him know you're alive. That you

like what he's doing. Move and groan in pleasure, bite him—"

"Bite him?"

"Oh, not to draw blood . . . playful bites . . . like a kitten . . . scratch his back . . . then let your hands travel . . . then later your tongue . . ."

"Oh my God—" January leaned back in the chair. "Linda, suppose I can't. Suppose I suddenly get uptight when I actually am in bed with him."

Linda stared at her for a moment. "I know." She snapped her fingers. "What time are you seeing him to-morrow?"

"When he gets back from Washington. For dinner."

"Then at four, you take a vitamin shot."

"A vitamin shot?"

Linda was spinning her rolodex. She stopped at a card and scribbled down a name and address. "Here. Dr. Simon Alpert. He and his brother Preston are fantastic. Keith took me to him a few times when he was on the health kick. He's still on it, I guess. He has to be to get it up for Christina Spencer."

"But how will vitamin shots make me feel sexy about Tom Colt?"

"Look, all I know is that when Keith made me take one of those shots, the whole world exploded . . . everything became technicolor. I worked twenty hours a day. I had orgasms with Keith that seemed to last an hour. I was great in bed without being too aggressive. Keith always said I was too aggressive because I was always directing him. That's his male chauvinism. I mean, when he's going down on me, what's wrong if I say . . . go more to the left . . . or harder . . . or lighter. Some men feel that if they dive, we're supposed to be grateful. The ones who make a token dive are the ones who kill me. You know . . . touch it with their tongues for one second and then look at you as if they have given you the Kohinoor diamond. And for that, you are then supposed to flip out and go down on them for hours . . . even if their dingle is like spaghetti. But, anyway, when I had a vitamin shot it seems I adored everything he did without once being a stage manager. They're really fabulous. It's some kind of a combination of the Vitamin B's plus some E. Dr. Alpert mixes it in front of you. Try to get Dr. Simon Alpert rather than Preston—he's got a gentler touch with the needle. But they're dynamite. Listen, they have to be great—they cost twenty-five bucks a shot. And if Keith shelled out that kind of money . . . well, you know. I took about three of them . . . I think they also have some appetite depressant in them because I didn't even want to touch food. A lot of women who are overweight go there. In fact, a lot of doctors give them. There's one who's supposed to give them to big stars, some Washington big shots, a big composer, and several Hollywood producers."

"Why didn't you keep taking them?"

"At twenty-five a shot? They last about three days. One woman I met in the waiting room told me she took four shots a week. But then I broke up with Keith, so I didn't need all that energy. Certainly not for the Leons who come into my life."

"But isn't it dangerous?"

"Listen, January, you're twenty-one, you've had one affair that you hated. With a dreamy guy . . . that you didn't dig. So David went down the drain. Now you've got a shot at Tom Colt . . . and you sit here and tell me you're afraid of failing. God, if I had a date with him coming up, I'd be rushing up Madison Avenue to find some divine outfit, not sitting and wondering how I was going to make him get a hard on. *That's* the only thing I'd be sure of . . ."

January smiled. "You make me sound like I'm retarded . . . sexually."

Linda laughed. "Listen, there's nothing wrong with you that a good fuck won't cure. Now call Dr. Alpert and make the appointment for this afternoon. You'll never get out of bed. Oh . . . and stop into Leon's office and ask him to get you a popper."

"What's that?"

"Ammies. You put it in a Benzedrex inhaler and

leave it on the night table. Then you each take a sniff just as you are about to come. It's wild!"

"Linda, can I ask you something? Tell me. Doesn't anyone just go to bed with someone they care about and have a real good old-fashioned affair?"

"Of course, darling—that's what you had with David!"

She left the office at five and rushed home. She took a long bath. Then she doused herself with perfume. She laid out two outfits. Slacks and a shirt; a long skirt and silk blouse—depending on where he wanted to go. She put on her new Pucci bra; she wondered if Linda would say Pucci bras were out. But then Linda said all bras were out.

At seven, she was still sitting in her bra staring at the phone. She smoked half a pack of cigarettes and had taken a sip of Jack Daniels. She had bought a bottle in case he came over. She had also bought real coffee and some eggs. She didn't know what she expected—but she just wanted to be prepared.

By eight o'clock she had called the Plaza three times. Each time, the operator confirmed: Yes, they were holding a reservation for Mr. Colt, but he had not checked in.

His call came at nine. "January . . . forgive me. The planes weren't going because of weather. So I had to take the train. It was supposed to get in at six. That's why I didn't call. But there was an hour wait in Baltimore. And would you believe it? We had to stop in Trenton for half an hour because a woman was in labor—"

"Oh, Tom . . . no!" She was so relieved to hear from him that she was actually laughing.

"Look, I'm beat . . ." (Her heart dropped.) "Would it be all right with you if we just had some room service here at the Plaza?"

"Look, Tom . . . if you're too tired to see me, I understand." (What was she saying!)

"No, I've got to eat. And I'm starving . . . unless it's too late for you."

"I'll be right there."

"Good. You'll find my car in front of your place."

"You mean . . . you knew I would come."

"Of course. Weren't you the one who said . . . no games?"

He was waiting at the door when she came down the hall. She flung herself into his arms and he kissed her lightly. "God, you look great," he said. "Come on in . . . the steaks are on their way. I figured a girl in love wouldn't care what she ate."

He was full of his trip. He had hated every minute of it. He felt like a trained monkey, especially on TV. The performers all told him they were his fans, yet he admired the ease with which they went on, their cool as they sat under the lights and ad-libbed with one another. When he came on, he felt like a prehistoric animal—oversized, out of context, out of place. But the hosts of the shows had all helped him, and somehow he had gotten through. "You earn every book you sell," he said. Then he added that he had hit number three on *The New York Times* Best Seller list.

They had dinner, and then they sat together on the couch watching the late news as he drank bourbon. She sipped at hers slowly. Tom seemed surprised that she wanted one. But she knew that if they were going into that bedroom she had to feel relaxed. Suddenly he turned to her and said, "Listen . . . how would you feel about the beach?"

"Westhampton?"

"Yes. Hugh invited me up. We can stay over. He sleeps out on the beach half the night anyway. And he said he'd bunk down on the couch if he wanted to come in."

"When?" she asked.

"Tomorrow. We could leave at three. I have two interviews in the morning."

"I'd love it," she said.

He stood up and took her into his arms and kissed her gently. His hands slipped under her shirt and under the bra. She remembered what Linda had said—"Do something. Show him you care!" Tentatively she let her hand roam . . . down his back . . . toward the front.

Suddenly he pulled away. "Look, it's late and I'm beat. We'll have the weekend together."

He got her coat and walked her to the door. "January," he said, "you haven't mentioned it once all evening."

"Mentioned what?"

"Love." He smiled. "Do you still love me?"

"Oh God, Tom . . . you know I do."

He smiled and kissed her lips lightly. She wondered why he had said that. Suddenly she looked up at him. "Tom . . . do you love me?"

He nodded slowly. "I think I do . . . I really think I do."

She was at Dr. Alpert's office at nine o'clock the following morning. She filled out the card the receptionist gave her. She was a bit apprehensive. But she realized she needed something. Last night Tom had broken the embrace . . . because he had not had an erection. He had pulled away because he hadn't wanted her to know. She had not aroused him. All the Fracas perfume, the Pucci bra—a waste.

She had called Linda at midnight. And when Linda yelled, "What happened?" and she had answered, "Nothing," Linda advised her to get to Dr. Alpert's unless she wanted to blow the whole weekend.

"But is it possible for a man to love you and not get an erection?"

"Oh Jesus, January, do you know how many guys come to me in wild heat, leap on me, and then their cock turns to rubber and we practically have to fold it in."

"Linda!"

"Will you stop yelling 'Linda' and get with it. This man has had every kind of woman in the world. He's also fifty-seven and slightly weary. You've got to turn him on. The sight of that nymphet body of yours isn't going to turn him on. *You've* got to do it."

She sat in Dr. Alpert's office and filled out all the questions on the card. Then the receptionist took her to a private cubicle equipped with just an examining table.

There were at least seven cubicles in the office. And they were all filled. The waiting room had already begun to get crowded when she left it. The receptionist pointed to the paper coat and said, "Take everything off and then go to the end of the hall." She wrapped the crinkly examining robe around her and went to the room down the hall. A nurse was waiting with a cardiograph machine. She motioned for January to lie on the couch. Then she attached the electrodes.

When the test was over, the nurse led her to another room. "And now, Miss Wayne, we'll take some blood samples."

"But I'm just here for a vitamin shot. I told that to Dr. Alpert on the phone this morning."

"Dr. Alpert always wants a complete examination on the first visit."

January held out her arm. She winced as the nurse took the blood. And even more when she pricked her finger. But it gave her a sense of confidence. This was really a doctor to be reckoned with. He was thorough. No wonder his shots were good.

Finally she was led back to her cubicle. She sat on the edge of the examining table and waited. His office had been crowded. But she had purposely come early, explaining, as Linda had told her to say, that she was making a plane and had to be out by noon.

After about fifteen minutes a middle-aged man with a stethoscope hanging around his neck, entered the room. His smile was warm. "I'm Dr. Simon Alpert. Now, what's your problem? Feel listless? I noted your blood count is only ten. That's slightly anemic. Nothing to worry about. But you should be twelve."

She noticed his collar was frayed and his fingernails were dirty. It seemed impossible that this man was responsible for the beautiful Park Avenue office, the efficient antiseptic nurse and receptionist. Perhaps he was like Einstein who never combed his hair and walked around in sneakers. His teeth were tartar-stained, and since his smile was perpetual, she found herself studying the discolored teeth. His gums weren't good either. He certainly looked as if he could use some vitamins.

"Now just exactly what is it that brings you here? I understand Miss Riggs, a former patient, recommended you."

She looked away, then studied her own immaculate nails. "Well . . . I . . . there's a man I've been seeing and—"

"We don't handle abortions here . . . and we don't give the pill."

"No, it's nothing like that. You see this man is divine, every woman finds him attractive, and I—"

"Say no more." He smiled knowingly. "I get the picture. He's walked out on you. You're depressed. Uptight. Stay there." He waddled out of the room.

In less than five minutes he returned with a syringe. "This will make you feel like a new woman. You'll get him back. I know." He was adjusting the needle. She hoped he had washed his hands. "Young things like you, you fall in love, give too much of yourselves. The man gets bored, and then you start phoning him . . . right?" He went on before she could answer. "Sure, it's the same story . . . phoning him . . . begging him . . . pleading . . . driving him farther away. It's the same story all the time."

He untied the string of her examing robe. It fell to her waist, but he barely noticed her nudity. He put the stethoscope between her breasts, listened, seemed content with what he heard. Then he swabbed the vein of her arm. "Listen, don't call him. Promise Uncle Simon . . . don't call the bastard." She felt the needle go into her vein. She looked away. Amazingly enough he did have a light touch . . . no real pain. She turned and saw her own blood floating back into the syringe . . . then watched it gradually return to her arm along with the contents of the syringe. He smiled. "Now, hold your arm up like this." He placed a piece of cotton on the needle mark. "Just hold it like that for a second. You have beautiful veins."

She couldn't believe it. But she felt an instant reaction. A slight sense of floating . . . light-headed . . . but a nice feeling. Then suddenly a wonderful feeling of warmth shot through her . . . like when she got sodium

pentothal in Rome . . . that amazing fluidity that went
through her entire body. Only instead of the nothingness
and sleep the pentothal caused, she felt crackling with
life. She had a wild urge to touch herself between her
legs because that's where she was vibrating with a pulsing
sensation.

Dr. Alpert smiled. "Feel better?" He tweaked the tip
of one of her breasts and she laughed. Because it wasn't
the gesture of a dirty old man. It was just a nice gesture
of friendship by Uncle Simon.

"You'll be fine," he said. "We'll have your blood up
to twelve or thirteen in no time. Maybe you'll want a
shot a week . . . or sign up for a series. Take that up
with Miss Sutton, my receptionist. Some people like them
twice a week . . . or milder forms every day. I have a
man whose blood is fifteen, but he takes one every day.
He's a famous composer and he works eighteen hours a
day. He pours energy into his work so he needs them
often. And so do you skinny little things who make love
all night and work all day." Then he tweaked her breast
again and waddled out of the room.

She leaped off the examining table and the white robe
fell to the floor. She ran her fingers down her breasts. She
did it again. The nipples hardened. She felt that divine
unbelievable feeling between her legs. She touched herself. Oh, how glorious. Oh, beautiful Dr. Alpert with the
dirty fingernails and the wonderful vitamins. She realized
with a new clarity that she had probably only been half
functioning until now. Maybe she had been anemic all
her life. That is, since the accident. Of course . . .
before that . . . she always felt alive like this when she
was with Mike. And now, she felt alive again . . .
aware. The world was waiting to belong to her!

She dressed quickly and wrote a check for one hundred and twenty dollars for the cardiogram and blood
tests and the shot. The receptionist explained from here
on the shot would cost twenty-five dollars unless she
wanted a series of twenty; then it would cost four hundred dollars payable in advance. January smiled. She'd
take them as she needed them and pay twenty-five.

She stopped off at Saks and bought Tom a tie. She

went to Gucci's and sent Linda a belt she had admired, and wrote on the note, "Thank you for Dr. Alpert." Then she rushed home and packed. And when the buzzer rang at three and the chauffeur announced the car was waiting, she floated down in the elevator eager for the weekend ahead.

She couldn't wait to see Tom. And she also looked forward to seeing Hugh . . . he was wonderful, too! The whole world was wonderful!

NINETEEN

Tom loved the tie. "I'll wear it on all my TV appearances," he said. He had a bottle in the car and offered her a drink. She shook her head. "You're my high," she insisted. And when they arrived at Westhampton, she flung herself into Hugh Robertson's arms. If he was surprised at the exuberance of her greeting, he did not show it. But she had thought about that day they had all spent at Westhampton so many times that her return felt like a homecoming. The oversized couch and fireplace were exactly as she remembered them. The sound of the surf seemed far away, even though she could see the ocean through the picture window in the living room. They sat around the fire. Tom sipped at his drink and Hugh cooked the steaks. She cuddled against Tom on the huge sofa, leaping up now and then to help Hugh with the food.

At ten o'clock, Hugh stood up. "Well, it's time for me to hit the dunes."

"You'll freeze," January said.

"Oh, I won't stay long tonight. I've got a workroom behind the kitchen with a studio bed in there. I often sleep there. Sometimes I just don't feel like going to all the trouble of climbing the stairs to go to bed. So you both enjoy the room with a clear conscience."

After Hugh left, January and Tom sat watching the crackling of the logs on the fire and listening to the rumble of the waves lapping at the shore. January never grew tired of watching the waves—there was something stubborn in the way they would rise in strength, dissipate themselves against the beach, and then regroup and try again. They reminded her of mischievous little children, scampering to the beach, only to be dragged back by their mother.

She snuggled closer to Tom and traced his profile with her fingertips. He leaned over and kissed her. Then he picked up the bottle of bourbon, took her by the hand, and led her upstairs.

The room was a reconverted attic. The owner was obviously very patriotic. It was painted white and the furniture was bright blue and red enamel. A huge feather bed dominated the center of the room. January flopped on it, kicked off her shoes, and jumped up and down. "Tom . . . come on in . . . wow . . . no springs. It's like floating." Then she leaped off the bed and came to him. "I love you," she said as she unbuttoned her blouse. Their eyes met and held as she dropped her jeans to the floor. Slowly she unhooked her bra and stepped out of her pants. "Here I am," she said softly.

He stared at her for a moment with a slow smile. She put her arms around his neck. "Come on, lazy," she whispered as she unbuttoned his shirt. "Let's go to bed."

He turned toward the bureau and poured himself a drink. He swallowed it quickly, then reached out and switched off the light. She lay on the bed and watched him undress in the darkness. She could see the contrast of his buttocks against his tanned shoulders and back. His thighs were strong . . . then he turned and jumped on the bed with such force that it creaked. They both laughed and hugged one another. He was on top of her, resting his weight on his arms. He stroked her hair and in the darkness he whispered, "Oh, baby, I want to make you happy."

"I am happy, Tom." She put her arms around his neck and pulled him down to kiss her. He rolled to his side and held her close as they kissed. She ran her fingers down his back. She felt relaxed and at ease, as if their bodies had always been close like this. She was eager to

touch him . . . to be taken by him . . . to belong to
him.

Then he eased away and she felt his tongue streaking
across her body . . . on her breasts . . . her stomach
. . . she clutched his head . . . the feeling was so
warm and wonderful. But she wanted to please *him*
. . . to do anything he wished . . . his tongue was on
her thigh . . . his fingers were exploring her . . .
every nerve of her body was responding . . . his tongue
seemed everywhere . . . and then she felt an insane
sensation . . . so unbearably wonderful. She couldn't
believe what was happening . . . she had never felt
anything like it. She moaned. Her entire body was dis-
solving into an explosion of ecstasy . . . she held his
head and shivered . . . and finally fell back wrung out
and exhausted. He came up and lay beside her and
stroked her breasts. "Did I make you happy?"

"Oh God, Tom . . . I never felt anything like that
. . . but . . . we didn't do it . . . I mean . . .
you—"

"I wanted to make you happy," he said.

"And now—" Her strength was returning. Now he
would enter her.

"And now we'll just hold one another in our arms."

She lay very still. Something was wrong. He held her
close . . . but she felt sick with panic. She hadn't
aroused him. She began kissing his neck . . . stroking
his body. She wasn't quite sure how to go about it . . .
but perhaps if she imitated him. She got on top of him
and began kissing his chest. Then she slid down. But
there was no big throbbing thing like David had thrust
at her . . . something inert lay between his legs. It was
about the size of a man's thumb. She couldn't believe it.
How could a man Tom Colt's size—a man as virile as
Tom—have such a tiny penis? She began to stroke it,
but there was no reaction. Then she put her lips to it.
She felt a sudden surge of protective tenderness toward
him. Tom Colt, whose fiction exploded with volatile sex
. . . Tom Colt, the man women worshipped, the man
other men looked up to . . . Tom Colt, the living sym-

bol of man—with a boy's penis! God, how this must have haunted him throughout his life. She had worried at school when her breasts didn't grow large enough . . . but at least she had something. But for a man to have nothing . . . the penis was his entire sex object. Oh God, so this was the reason for all the prizefights . . . the scuba diving . . . the championship golf and tennis . . . the barroom brawls. She made love to him with an added tenderness. Poor, poor Tom . . . to have to write his sex fantasies because he couldn't live them.

He suddenly pulled her up to him. "January . . . don't feel you've failed me. My pleasure is in making you happy."

She lay very still. She wondered how many other women he had said the same thing to. And suddenly she was determined to make him feel like a man. She began to stroke him. She let her tongue run up and down his arm . . . his hips . . . She tantalized him . . . coming closer to him . . . then stroking him and pulling away . . . and she saw the small penis begin to stiffen . . . she kept playing the game . . . letting her lips brush against it . . . then darting off to another part of his body . . . her fingers explored him . . . suddenly he rolled her over and got on top of her . . . he began to move steadily . . . faster . . . and with urgency . . . and then she heard him moan and felt his body go limp. He stayed on top of her for a few seconds. Then he looked into her eyes and said, "Thank you, January."

"Thank you, Tom."

He pulled away from her and took her into his arms. "January . . . I love you."

"And I love you," she whispered.

He stroked her hair. "Do you know what you've done for me?" he said. "This is the first time I've made it in ten years."

"I'm so glad, Tom." She kissed his cheek and it was wet. Then she saw the tears in his eyes. "Tom . . . is anything wrong?" He buried his head against her neck and she held him close and comforted him as she would a child. After a few minutes, he got out of bed and walked to the bureau. He took a long swig of bourbon and kept his back to her. "January, I'm sorry—I—"

She jumped out of bed and went to him. "Tom . . . I love you."

He turned and looked at her. "I'm sorry about letting go like that. I don't think I've shed a tear in twenty years."

"Did I do anything to cause it?" she asked.

He stroked her head. "No, baby . . ." He led her back to bed and they lay beside one another. He held her close and said, "You've made me very happy, January. I think the tears were for both of us. For me because I've found a girl with such class . . . and for you because you're only getting the remnants of Tom Colt. Not that my equipment was any better . . . a man can only use what he's got . . . but at least it was always workable. For the last ten years it's been call girls, aphrodisiacs . . . you name it—nothing worked. Until tonight . . . with you."

"But Tom . . . You have a baby."

"I want you to know the truth. You see, all my life women went along with me . . . accepted the fact that I wasn't built like a stallion. But they wanted to be seen with me. And hell, I could satisfy them in other ways. But a few years ago I got to thinking . . . all the years of writing, all my body of work . . . who was I leaving it to . . . who would care? I had no one. I lost two brothers in World War Two. I have an older sister who has no children. And suddenly I realized I wanted a kid. So I decided to adopt one. But you have to be married to adopt a child. So I started casing all the women I knew, trying to figure out which one would make the best mother. None of them fit. Either they had kids of their own from another husband . . . or they frankly stated they hated kids. There was just no one around who fit the bill. Then about a year and a half ago I ran into Nina Lou Brown, a little starlet type at a party at Malibu. She was slightly over the hill for a starlet . . . twenty-seven at the time . . . and she had just about given up.

She was doing some TV commercials. She came on strong and we got to talking. She told me she was from Georgia and had twelve brothers and sisters and hadn't worn shoes until she was twelve. She loved kids and said she was even thinking of marrying a cameraman she knew because she wanted kids and at twenty-seven she felt she was getting on. At first it all sounded too good to be true . . . but I realized it was no put on because she didn't know I wanted a kid. Our host had two little boys and later in the afternoon, the youngest one, he was about five, got a splinter in his foot. A big angry-looking thing from some driftwood. He wouldn't let his mother touch him. Suddenly Nina Lou moved in. She began to play a game with him. Told him she bet he could help her get it out. She asked for a glass of Scotch. She made him stick the needle into the Scotch to sterilize it. But she told him she was going to get his foot drunk. Well, believe it or not, he allowed her to pick that damn thing out . . . and it was wedged in there deep as hell. When it was over, he kissed her. And I knew right then that she would be the mother of my kid.

"We dated for about a month. And I never went to bed with her. But I asked her to marry me and I explained about my problem. And it was Nina Lou who came up with the idea. Artificial insemination. It had never occurred to me. We got married . . . went straight to a doctor . . . it took several months . . . but it worked. And six months ago she bore me a son."

January lay very still. Tom lit a cigarette and handed it to her. "Now you know the story of my life."

"Wow," January said softly. "Then you really must be in love with her."

"Grateful is the word. I was never in love with her. But I love her for what she gave me. In exchange, I've given her sexual freedom . . . as long as she's discreet. She's got a young actor type who comes and services her now and then. But she's a hell of a mother to Tom, Junior. And she likes being Mrs. Tom Colt—she likes the prestige, the parties she's invited to, the house at Malibu . . . And the marriage is working, if you can call it a marriage. But hell, I can't expect a girl of twenty-nine to give up normal sex for the rest of her life. She loves the baby and——"

"Tom . . . it happened with us tonight. Did you ever really try with her? It seems to me you weren't even going to try with me."

He shook his head. "Of course I tried. She was positive she could work miracles. I suffered the humiliation of letting her try . . . night after night . . . until we finally agreed there was no chance. I never expected anything to happen with us tonight . . . but I cared for you enough to let you know the score——" He held her closer. "January, you can see what you've done for me. Even if it never happens again . . . I'll be grateful for the rest of my life."

"It will happen again."

"January, I can't get a divorce. Nina Lou would never give it to me . . . and I can't give up my son. I want him to have everything. That's why I agreed to do the tour bit. I have enough money to live fine for the rest of my life. But I want to leave a bundle to her and my son." He got off the bed and brought the bottle back. "Shall we have a nightcap?"

She shook her head. "I'm happy this way," she whispered.

He took a long drink. "I don't know how to put it in words . . . I love you . . . like I've never loved any woman. I never leveled with any woman except you and Nina Lou. I had to with her, but I wanted to with you. I've been a heel with most women. I just tell them *they* don't turn me on. I act like maybe with the right woman my pecker grows six feet. Look, I don't know how long you'll want me, but as long as you do . . . it's going to be your way . . . no games. I'll love you all the way . . . and if you want what there is of me . . . then . . . I belong to you."

She held him close. "Oh, Tom . . . I love you. And I want you . . . and I'll be with you whenever you want me . . . and for as long as you want me . . . forever . . . we *are* forever. I swear it."

They lay together for a while, and after a time his even

breathing told her he was asleep. She was still wide awake and longed for a cigarette. She also wanted to think things out. She loved him—the size of a man's penis wasn't a barometer for love. She had to convince him of this. She slid out of bed, careful not to disturb him, put on her robe and tiptoed down the steps. The living room was deserted and the fire was just about dying. She put some newspaper on it and added another log. Soon it was crackling and warm. She sat on the couch, her legs curled under her, and stared into the fire and thought about Tom. She had always thought all men were built pretty much alike. Oh, she knew some were larger than others . . . but she never knew anyone could be like Tom. Suddenly she wondered about her father. Was he a stallion like David? Of course. He would have to be. But poor Tom. Her emotions were confused. She thought of him protectively, yet with tenderness and desire. It was the desire to be in his arms . . . to feel his bare chest against her breasts . . . to feel the closeness of him . . . to feel his lips on hers—that was what love was all about.

She heard the door open and she knew Hugh was standing behind her. He came around and stared at her. Then he glanced upstairs.

"He's asleep," she said. "He's finished the bottle of Jack Daniel's."

He went to the wooden table that served as the bar and poured himself a Scotch. "Want one?"

She shook her head. "I'll take a Coke though."

He handed her the drink. "Want some cold steak? You must be starving. You didn't eat a thing at dinner."

She stretched. "I feel marvelous. Just marvelous. I don't need food."

He looked concerned. "January, I don't know how good his marriage is, but he loves that baby and—"

"Hugh, I know he'll never marry me. Don't worry about it."

"You're in love with him?"

"Yes."

He sat beside her. "I've seen girls fall in love with him before. And they all say they can handle it. But when he decided to walk . . . several of them reached for the pills."

"Hugh . . . how well do you know Tom?"

"Does anyone really know Tom? I've known him for six years. We met when he was writing something about space in one of his novels. He came to Houston for research. We buddy-buddied together. And when I came to Los Angeles, he was just getting a divorce, so I shacked up with him. He fixed me up with some of his rejects and I had me quite a time. My own marriage was coming apart, but I had that thing about divorce . . . you know the bit . . . wait until the kids can understand. Hell, they never really understand . . . even when they're grown and have kids of their own. My daughter, God love her, has a three-year-old, and she says, 'Dad, why are you and Mother splitting . . . after all these years!' Well, hell—" he stopped suddenly. "What am I doing, rambling on like this? You ask me a simple question and I give you my life's story . . . when it's really Tom's you want. Okay. How well do I know Tom? I don't. It's not easy to know Tom. We're friends, good friends—I know if I ever needed him, I could call on him. And he knows the same about me. We're a lot alike in some ways. A man like Tom gets lost in his writing, the characters become him, or vice versa. I get lost in my work . . . I never even got to really know my kids . . ."

Then he began talking about his children, about his early days of flying. She listened carefully, realizing he was unburdening his own guilts—his wrecked marriage, the loss of contact with his children. She told him not to feel guilty, that he was only following his destiny. "You really think that people should do their own thing?" he asked. She nodded, and it never once struck her as odd that she was offering Hugh Robertson advice, because at that moment she felt she could solve anything. They talked about the mystery of life . . . the solar system . . . infinity. He explained that the concept of intelligent life existing beyond our own solar system was now an accepted fact. He felt that in centuries to come there would be communication between solar systems. There

would be telstars and satellite planets . . . chains of
them . . . stretching out into space like a giant bridge
connecting the planets and the solar systems.

"But how will we communicate with the little green
men?" she asked.

"What makes you think they'll be green? If a planet
is adjacent to another sun in the same position earth is
to our sun, it has to breed the same kind of being."

"You mean there could be another earth? With a
superior race?"

"Millions of them. Some, billions of years ahead of us
. . . and of course some, billions of years behind."

They were both silent after that. Then she smiled sadly.
"It makes everything we do or think about seem awfully
small in comparison. I mean, when you think that on all
those other worlds there are people like us, praying to
God. Like when I think of how I used to pray to Him to
help me to walk . . ."

"Walk?"

They both turned, and it was Tom coming down the
steps. He had on a robe and he was carrying an empty
bottle. "I woke up and found both my girl and my booze
gone." He came and sat beside January. "Did I hear
you two say something about a walk? It's almost two in
the morning."

"No," Hugh said. "January was saying how she
prayed to God to learn to walk."

"I couldn't sleep," she said as she snuggled against
him. "Hugh and I have been talking about the stars."

"What about the walking?" Hugh asked.

"It's a long story."

"It seems to me I've told you some pretty long stories
tonight," Tom said. "Now it's your turn."

She began to talk, hesitantly at first. And then she
found herself reliving those long hopeless months. The
fire died out, but neither of the men seemed to notice.
And as she talked Tom's dark eyes held her, offering
silent compassion and admiration. She realized she had
never told anyone how much she had really endured.
She had told Linda just the facts. Even Mike never knew
the total desolation she had felt, because she always put

on a brave front with him. But sitting in the darkness with Tom's arm around her, all the suffering and loneliness she had known suddenly spilled out. When she finished, neither man spoke. Then Tom stood up. "I think we all need a drink now."

Hugh poured himself a Scotch. "Can you use this? We're clean out of bourbon."

"I came prepared," Tom said. "I had the driver put a case in the kitchen. I'll be right back."

Hugh watched him leave the room. Then he raised his glass to January who was still huddled on the couch. "I get a whole new picture of you now. You know, I think everything's going to be fine with you and Tom. Looks like he found himself a real hunk of woman in a skinny little girl."

The front door opened so quietly that neither of them heard the two men enter. January turned just as a hand clamped over her mouth. She saw the gleam of the knife that was held at her throat. At the same moment, the other man flashed a light in Hugh's face. "Okay, Mister . . . if you don't want your old lady killed, give us your jewelry and the money. If you shout or try to get help, your old lady gets her throat slashed."

"There is no money or jewelry," Hugh said hoarsely.

"Come on, Mister . . ." The man towered over Hugh. He was close to seven feet. "Last week we hit someone down on the beach. A weekend couple like you. Had to threaten to cut his balls off before his old lady coughed over her rings. You people who come out for weekends on the beach . . . you always got cash and jewelry."

"She's got no rings or anything," whispered the one with the knife at January's throat.

Hugh emptied his pockets. Some change . . . two fives . . . a few singles and keys came spilling out.

"That's chicken shit, man," the giant said. Then he glanced at the stairs. "You hold the girl," he called out. "I'll take him upstairs. Maybe I can convince him to show me where he keeps things."

January was left alone with the man with the knife. Where was Tom! The kitchen was behind the workroom. Unless she screamed he wouldn't be able to hear her. She stared at the man, who was breathing heavily and smirking at her. He was a little man, he hardly reached her shoulder. But he had a knife and it was at her throat.

One of his hands reached out and untied the sash of her robe. It fell open, and he stared at her nude body. His smirk became an evil grin. "Oh . . . Caught you and the old man ready for a little action."

She shut her eyes and tried not to scream as his rough hand touched her breasts. Then he unzipped his pants and exposed himself. "Pretty good for a little guy like me. But like I always say, you got to have your weight somewhere. Now my friend up there"—he nodded toward the steps—"he's all business. But me, I like to combine business with pleasure. So you and me is gonna have ourselves a little fuck." He wrenched the robe off her. "Turn around!"

"Please . . ." she begged.

"Oh. Maybe you'd like it all romantic. On the nice soft couch over there with me on top of you. Sure, and give you a chance to grab for the knife. Oh, no, sister. You're gonna take it doggie style. That way I got you in no position to fight. Now turn around and bend over!" he snarled.

"Please . . . I won't take your knife. Please . . ."

"You bet your ass you won't. And because you gave me some lip—I'm gonna make you use it. Your lips. Hey, that's a joke. Get it? Now before I give it to you, you do a little ground work." He pushed her to her knees and shoved his penis in her face. Her revulsion made her forget fear, and she suddenly jumped away and raced across the room. In an instant he had her by the arm and slapped her across the face. Then he pushed her on the floor. "Get on your knees, you cunt. No more games. I'm gonna ram my joint so far up your ass it'll come out through your throat!"

As he leaned close to her, she screamed. His reflexes caused him to jump away. Then she felt the cold blade of the knife at the back of her neck. "Trying to wake the neighbors? Well, nobody's home . . . on both sides of you. We hit them for some transistor radios. Nothing worthwhile. But don't try any more screaming. It would take the enjoyment out of it all for me and might make me cut you up before I fuck you."

But she continued to struggle as he pushed her into a kneeling position on the floor. Then she saw Tom's shadow in the doorway. He had heard her scream! With one last burst of strength, she twisted and managed to pull away. But the little man grabbed her. He was breathing hard, and she felt him against her as he made a futile attempt to penetrate her. She knew Tom was creeping around the room. She made one final effort and wrenched herself from his grasp. He clawed at her breast in anger as he tried to pull her toward him. Tom was behind the man now. And then she heard the thump as the bottle hit his head. The man gasped, released her, and slipped to the floor. Tom pulled her into his arms. She was sobbing hysterically. "Oh, Tom! He was trying to . . . Oh, God! If you hadn't come in time . . ."

He picked up her robe and helped her into it. Her teeth were chattering, but she pointed upstairs. "There's another one. A giant. And he's with Hugh . . ."

Tom looked at the unconscious man on the floor. He handed her the bottle. "Now, look, if the bastard even stirs, hit him with this. Don't spare him. Just remember what he wanted to do to you."

Then he started for the stairs. There were sounds of a scuffle. Obviously the giant was beginning to rough up Hugh. Tom crept up the stairs, one at a time. A board creaked. She held her breath. The little man on the floor stirred slightly. January wavered as she held the bottle. But the man merely moaned and slipped back into unconsciousness. She was relieved. Somehow she felt she couldn't have hit him. Not with him lying there like that. If he was attacking her it would have been different. She stared at him. He was an ugly little man with two days' growth of beard. There was a smell of decay about him. Yet with his eyes shut and his mouth open there was something oddly pathetic and innocent about him.

She turned and watched Tom inch his way up the

stairs. There was another sound of scuffling in the room. Furniture scraped, and it seemed as if the ceiling would come down. Tom took two steps at a time. He had just reached the top when the door opened and the giant appeared. He stood there for a split second, taken off guard at seeing another man. His eyes went from Tom to his unconscious accomplice on the floor. With a guttural curse he leaped at Tom and they both rolled down the steps. Tom was the first to scramble to his feet, but the huge man lumbered after him. "I left your friend half dead in the bedroom," he snarled. "But with you, I'm gonna finish the job." His fist crashed into Tom's stomach. Tom doubled over but staggered to his feet. This time the man lunged for his jaw. Tom ducked. He was stalling for time to get his breath back. But the huge man gave him no chance. He came at him with another smashing blow to the stomach, and Tom went down. January stood riveted in one spot as he approached her. Then she saw the knife lying on the floor. She grabbed it and raced across the room. The giant laughed. "Oh, want to play games? Want Big Henry to try and get the knifey away from the little girl?"

He started toward her. She leaped behind the couch. He came after her and she ran to the other side. "TOM . . . HUGH . . . HELP!" she screamed.

The man laughed. "No one awake but just us chickens." Then he laughed heartily at his joke. He was coming closer. She hesitated. If she stabbed at him and missed, it would be all over for everyone. She had to stall for time. She ran around to the other side of the couch. The giant was laughing. "Come on. You're a cute piece. Wish I had the time to give it to you." He came closer. She backed away and almost tripped over the man on the floor. She heard Tom begin to stir. The giant heard it too. His smile disappeared. "Okay, you bitch. No more fun and games." He jumped across the couch and grabbed her. She tried to slash at him with the knife, but he twisted her arm. She cried out in pain as the knife fell to the floor. He picked it up, shoved her across the room, and started toward Tom, who was standing now.

"Okay, Mister. This is one time you're gonna wish you never woke up." He lunged at Tom to slash at his throat, but Tom ducked. Then Tom connected with a punch on his jaw. But the man seemed to barely feel it. He came at Tom, grinning, stalking. Tom kept backing away. Then he crouched like a cat, waiting. The man approached, brandishing the knife. Tom didn't move. The man came closer. And suddenly Tom leaped up like a panther, smashing the side of his hand against the man's windpipe, following with his fist to the man's jaw. It all happened so quickly that January couldn't believe her eyes as the huge man crumpled to the floor like a paper bag. Then Tom raced up the stairs for Hugh. January followed. Hugh was on the floor, just beginning to regain consciousness. His jaw was beginning to swell. One eye was shut, but he forced a slight smile. "I'm gonna live . . . guess I wasn't much help . . . I'm not in very good fighting shape these days."

They went downstairs. The little man was beginning to come around. Hugh went to the phone. Tom stopped him. "What do you think you're doing?"

"Calling the police. They're junkies. Look at that one's arm—loaded with needle marks."

"Put that phone down," Tom commanded. "We'll get some rope and tie them together and I'll drive them a mile off and dump them. If we have the police, then January gets involved. You know how the papers will play that up."

Hugh went to get the rope while Tom tried to slap some life into the face of the bigger man. When Hugh came back Tom was still working feverishly on the man, massaging the back of his neck. But he lay like a rag doll. "We can't dump them," Tom said. "They'd never make it. They'd freeze to death."

"They'll make it," Hugh said as he bound them together. "They're junkies . . . junkies don't feel weather."

"Hugh, I think this man is dead." Tom stood up and stared at the limp figure of the huge man.

Hugh leaned over him, felt his wrists, his neck. "I feel a slight pulse."

"Then we've got to get him to the hospital. Hugh, you're going to drive January back to New York. January, get dressed immediately." It was a command and January ran up the stairs.

"But what will you do?" Hugh asked.

"As soon as you both get out, I'll call the police and tell them to send an ambulance. I'll say I wanted to do some writing and you loaned me the place. Then I'll tell it like it was—that I was out in the kitchen . . . I surprised them. . . ."

"Why don't you drive January back to New York? I'll call the ambulance and give the same story. I think January would prefer it that way."

"I would, too," Tom said. "But look, man. You're five foot ten. There's no way you could have hit that guy in the windpipe or on the jaw unless he bent down to let you." He looked at his raw fist. "And I've got the skinned knuckles to prove I did it."

January came down with her bag. Her face was white and she clung to Tom while Hugh went out to start the car. "I heard your plans. But what if the men talk? What if they say there were three people here?"

"They're junkies, so they saw double, or triple—it's my word against theirs. Don't worry." They heard Hugh's horn. He led her to the door. "Oh, Tom." She clung to him. "I thought we'd have the whole weekend together. Not just one night."

He looked at her and managed a wry smile. "I know. But you have to admit . . . it's been one hell of a night."

TWENTY

JANUARY AND HUGH had been silent on the drive back,
both immersed in their own thoughts. The night had
faded into a slate-colored dawn when they reached New
York. The heater in the car was uncomfortably warm,
but January suddenly shivered. Everything about New
York seemed so dismal and gray. Westhampton and the
violence that had occurred suddenly seemed unreal.
Hugh pulled up in front of her apartment building. The
streets were empty. A chill wind sent small bits of paper
skimming across the sidewalk. Her mood was as heavy
as the soot-stained canopies of the unattended apartment buildings along the street. "Buildings look dead
without doormen," she said.

Hugh smiled and patted her hand. "Go grab yourself
some rest, January." He helped her out of the car and
they stood in front of her building. Her teeth chattered
from the early morning cold. "You must be tired and
stiff from driving," she said. "I make lousy instant coffee . . . but if you want some—"

"No. The police at Westhampton are very polite but
also very thorough. Tom can handle just about anything, but I think he'd feel better if I was there." He
leaned over and kissed her cheek. "Look, I want to take
back a lot of the warnings I handed out so freely in the
beginning. There's something that's clicked between
you and Tom that's never happened with any other girl

before. I'm not just saying this because you're a woman in love. I'm saying it from watching Tom, the way he looked at you tonight, his attitude—it's a whole different thing. Now you get some rest and we'll call you as soon as everything is settled."

When she entered her apartment it was as if time had stood still. Remnants of her packing lay strewn about. Slacks across the chair, shirt on the bed—inert signs of a distant past. A lifetime had happened in twenty-four hours.

She went to the refrigerator and poured herself a Coke. It suddenly occurred to her that she hadn't eaten anything. Hugh had teased her about not liking his cooking. Perhaps she should scramble some eggs. But for some reason the thought of food repelled her. She felt crystal clear . . . wide awake . . . charged with energy. She longed to go out into the lonely morning and walk. She leaned out the window. A heavy mist coated the air. She felt that if she walked . . . she could dispel it . . . like a magic genie . . . wave her arms and scatter sunshine everywhere. She was stronger than the mist . . . stronger than any element . . . Because as Hugh had put it, she was a woman in love. But she couldn't leave, she had to wait for Tom's call.

She chain-smoked, drank another Coke . . . It was still too early to call Linda, and besides she didn't want to keep her phone busy in case Tom called. She turned on the television set. There was a sermon on one channel. She switched to another channel—a children's cartoon. Then there was an early movie, an old Van Johnson picture with the sound so bad on the print that she couldn't listen—she couldn't listen to anything. She turned off the set. Suddenly she thought of her answering service. She had forgotten to check. Not that anyone important would call.

The woman on the service was disgruntled. "Miss Wayne, you must remember to check in with us. Or at least leave a number if you're going away for a long stretch of time. Your father was very angry. He acted as if it was our fault that we couldn't find you. After all, we're just an answering service, not a—"

"When did he call?" January asked.

"Friday night at ten. He had checked into the Plaza and wanted you to call." *(Friday night at ten . . . she was at the Plaza . . . and of course she had forgotten to check in with her service.)* "And then again Saturday morning at nine-thirty," the woman continued. "He wanted you to have lunch with him." *(She had been at Dr. Alpert's.)* "Then again at noon." *(She was at Saks on her shopping spree.)* "And then at five . . . at seven . . . and finally at ten o'clock last night. He left for Palm Beach and wants you to call him there."

She looked at the clock. Eight-ten. She waited until nine, then called Palm Beach.

"Where in hell have you been?" Mike demanded.

She managed to laugh. "Mike, you won't believe it, but I keep forgetting about checking with the answering service. I was out in the morning . . . shopping. I forgot to check. I went out again in the afternoon, and must have just missed your call, and then I was out for dinner. It's awful . . . I'm so sorry. But how was Gstaad?"

"Great. Dee came in second in the tournament. She flew right back to Palm Beach, but I stopped off in New York to see you. And instead of going to our place at the Pierre, I checked into the Plaza because I thought you'd get a kick out of it. I couldn't get my old suite . . . Hey, guess who has it . . . Tom Colt. But I got an identical one on a lower floor. And there I sat—like a groom left at the altar—waiting for my girl."

"Oh, Mike . . ."

He laughed. "It was okay. Listen, I didn't tell Dee. I said we saw each other. I didn't want to look like a damn fool."

"Of course, Mike."

"Now listen, we're staying here until Easter. And we expect you and David to come down for that weekend. That's when Dee gives her last big bash. Then . . . I have a real surprise for you."

"What?"

"The Cannes film festival."

"The what?"

"Remember how we talked about it in Switzerland, how you dreamed of going? Well, there's a backgammon tournament in Monte Carlo just about that time, so I've convinced Dee to go. We'll stay at the Carlton Hotel in Cannes—you're twenty-one now, so I can take you to the Casino, teach you Chemin de Fer, Baccarat . . . We'll see all the pictures . . . all my old friends . . . And I may just have a few other surprises for you, too."

"Mike, when is all this?"

"It starts in May. But I figure if we hit it around the fifteenth, we'll get all the action we want. That'll give Dee a chance to come back to New York from Palm Beach, open the suite at the Pierre—I think it's probably all covered with sheets and stuff. And I'll catch up on the shows. Maybe you'll go with me if David can spare you. But I've got to teach you backgammon. I'm on a hot streak with it, and eventually I'll play big. Right now I'm still playing for five bucks a point. But it's just a matter of time . . ."

"You're happy, aren't you, Mike?"

"I'm gambling, and I'm hot, and that's what it's all about—for me anyway."

"I'm glad."

"How is it with you and David?"

"He's really a very nice man."

"That's it."

"I'm afraid it is . . ."

"Anyone else on the scene?"

"Yes . . . Mike . . ." Suddenly she knew she was going to tell him. He would understand. "Mike . . . I met someone . . . I think . . . I mean I know—"

"Who is he?"

"Mike, he's married."

"Go on." His voice was suddenly hard and ugly.

"Don't tell me that shocks you?"

"It disgusts me. When I played around, I played around with bums. That's exactly what I thought of them, even if they were stars, because they all started off knowing I was married and had a kid. So when you . . . at twenty-one . . . a girl who has everything . . . who has a guy like David in love with you—"

"Love has to be a two-way deal, Mike."

"You mean to tell me with all the guys you could meet, you could only hook up with a married one. And, of course, he has kids."

"He has one."

"Can he get a divorce?"

"I don't know. He's—"

"Don't tell me. I can see the scene. An advertising guy . . . maybe in his thirties . . . tired of the girl he married on the way up . . . has her stashed in Westchester . . ."

"Mike . . . it's nothing like that."

"January, tell me one thing. Have you . . . have you been intimate with this man?"

She stared at the phone. She couldn't believe it. She couldn't believe the phrase—"have you been intimate" —or the faltering way he asked. He sounded like a preacher . . . not like Mike. She *couldn't* tell him. He really wouldn't understand. It was awful—to have to hide this from Mike—but she heard herself saying, "Now, Mike, it's not that serious. I just said I met someone and—"

"January, have I ever steered you wrong? Now listen to me . . . please. Don't see him again. He can't respect you if he thinks you'll go with him when he's married . . ."

"Mike, you're talking like . . . well . . . like three generation gaps . . ."

"I'm talking to my daughter. And I don't give a damn about how things have changed. Sure there's more sexual freedom. I wouldn't be shocked if you told me you went to bed with David . . . say . . . a few months before you married him. Or that you had gone to bed with him already and he left you cold. That's Today. That's the new freedom. That's the big change. But men don't change as far as their emotions go, and let me tell you, they don't respect a broad who goes to bed with them when they have a wife. Because no matter what kind of a story they give you . . . how the wife is a wife in name only . . . or that they have separate

bedrooms . . . or an arrangement—you better believe
that the nights they don't see you and have to go home,
they're still going to bed with their wives. Even if it's a
mercy hump. I know . . . because I've been there. And
they still respect their wives because of their guilt. In
fact, she almost gets to be a madonna because of it.
And the better the lay the girl is, the more guilt they
feel toward their wives. And when the guilt gets too
heavy and when the girl wants more than a few nights a
week . . . or a stolen trip . . . or gets too demanding
—they drop her and go back to their wives for a few
weeks until they find a new girl. Don't give me this liberated jazz. A married man is a married man—in nineteen fifty . . . sixty . . . or seventy. Laws and morals
might change, but emotions remain the same."

"Okay, Mike. Please. Cool it. I'm fine . . ."

"All right. Now get back to David or some guy like
him. Make your old man happy. I'll talk to you later in
the week. I've got to run off for golf. I'm playing that
game for big money—because like I said, when your
luck is good, you've got to push it." He clicked the
phone.

She hung up and walked to the window and stared
aimlessly at the barren courtyard. She had been insane
to think Mike would understand. Even if he hadn't
sounded off on it, she could never have told him the
entire story. And unless he knew about Tom's problem,
there would be no way she could convince Mike that
Tom really loved her, that their love was different from
the affairs he had had. She thought of Tom . . . and the
love and tenderness she felt constricted her chest. This
great strong wonder of a man . . . and she had been
able to make him happy.

The phone jangled. She almost turned her ankle rushing to it. "Hello—" She stopped. She had been about to
say, "Hello, Tom." But it was Mike.

"Listen, I can't go off to play golf leaving it like this
between us. Look, if this joker you say you like is really
a good Joe and wants to get a divorce and you really
love him and—"

"Oh, Mike, it's not anything like that . . . really."

"I have a hell of a nerve sounding off like that. I'm sorry."

"It's all right, Mike."

"I love you, babe. And remember—there's nothing you can't tell your old man. You know that, don't you?"

"Yes, Mike."

"Love me?"

"Of course."

"Okay. Call you in a few days."

She sat by the phone the rest of the day. Tom's call finally came at five o'clock. "I've sent the car for you. Will you come to the Plaza?"

"Of course, Tom. Are you all right?"

"I will be . . . as soon as I see you."

The traffic was heavy and she felt jittery as the car inched its way toward the Plaza. When she reached the hotel she actually ran down the hall to his suite.

He looked drawn and weary, but his smile was bright as he took her in his arms. He sat on the couch and sipped bourbon as he told her how everything stood. The man was in a coma, but no charges would be filed. The man had a long record of arrests. The police were still checking on his accomplice.

"I don't know how you did it," she said. "You were drinking a good bit."

His smile was sad. "I fight for blood when I fight."

"Have you ever lost?"

"A few teeth at times. But there's a killer instinct in me that always makes me win. It worries me at times, because I could kill. That was a karate chop I gave the big guy. I tried to miss his windpipe. Thank God I did. Otherwise he'd have been dead. I once promised myself I'd never do it unless my life was threatened."

"But it was."

"No, I could have beat him with my fists. The karate thing"—he showed her the motion with the side of his hand—"you hit a man in the right place with that . . . it's over."

She spent the night with him and once again she managed to arouse him into actual intercourse. His gratitude was overwhelming, and when he held her and told her he loved her, she knew he meant it.

The next day he was deluged with reporters. The story at Westhampton broke in all the papers. It was the kind of story the press associated with Tom Colt. At noon, the police got a "make" on the little man. He was wanted in Chicago for raping and killing three women. Now the story took on national importance. The Chicago police had arrived. The phones were going. The suite was cluttered with police and reporters.

Rita Lewis was ecstatic as she directed the traffic of the news media. January had slipped out at eight-thirty in the morning just before his first scheduled interview . . . before the news had broken. That afternoon he called her at the office and said, "The place is a madhouse. Now the FBI is in on it. I may have to go to Washington tomorrow—something about testimony on the little guy—and added to everything, his accomplice, the big guy, his name is Henry Morse. Well, Henry has a common-law wife and two kids and she's got herself a lawyer who's slapped me with a million-dollar assault charge."

"She can't do anything to you, can she?" January asked.

"No. Just take up my time. In the end, she'll settle for a few hundred bucks."

"But why should you have to pay her anything? That man was out to kill us all."

"It's easier than going through pre-trial examinations. Her lawyer knows that. Unfortunately, that's the way it works. The people who have plenty of time and nothing to lose figure their nuisance value will make you pay off . . . and you do."

"Oh, Tom . . . how awful."

"Anyway, you better play a low profile as far as I'm concerned for the next few days. The little guy—his name is Buck Brown—he's already mumbling about a girl with long brown hair being there. No one believes him. But it's just as well that no one see me with you until this blows over."

"Well, how long will it be?"

"Just for a few days. My publisher is jubilant. He acts as if I planned this whole setup just to help the book. We had over eight thousand reorders in the last twenty-four hours. They're going into another big printing. Everyone seems to think I'm a cinch for number one."

"Oh, Tom, how wonderful!"

"I was getting there on my own." His voice was grim. "Number three this week. I'd hate to think a fist fight could put me to the top."

"If the book wasn't there, all the fights in the world couldn't make it sell. You know that."

"January, tell me something—how did I ever live without you?"

"I'm just wondering how I'm going to get through today without you."

"I'll keep in touch by phone. And the first chance I get, we'll be together."

He left for Washington that afternoon and called her at midnight. "I'll be here for a few days. I'm also doing some book stuff, so it works out fine. That little Buck Brown—the one that was holding the knife at your throat—he would have killed you. That's his pattern. Rape, then kill. He just hooked up with the big guy a few weeks ago on a dope score. They're both involved with drugs. They're pushers and users. But the little guy is paranoid. Now it seems he's killed six women, and the list seems to be growing—once he rapes, he must kill, he's admitted that." His voice went low. "Know something, baby? I may just give up drinking. Suppose I had been more sloshed . . . and had slept through it all . . . You'd be—" He stopped. "Look, I'll be back at the end of the week. You get some rest. Then we'll spend the weekend together."

"Not at Westhampton," she said.

"No. At the Plaza. All safe and sound in Fun City. And, January, for God's sake, never let on to Linda that you were there when all this happened. After all . . . I am under oath."

It hadn't been easy. When the story broke, Linda had turned into a Torquemada.

"Where were you when all this happened? I thought you were spending the weekend at Westhampton with him?"

"No, I just went for the day. He sent me back so he could work."

"And nothing happened?"

"Well, it looks like plenty happened after I left."

"I mean . . . with the bed department."

"Linda, everything is fine."

"January, are you leveling with me?"

"Yes."

"But when did you do it?"

"Linda, for heaven's sake! I didn't leave there until around ten."

"Was he great?"

"Yes . . ."

"You don't sound very enthusiastic."

"I'm just tired . . . I haven't slept very much."

"You look awful. You're getting too thin, January."

"I know. I'm going to eat a big dinner and go to bed early."

But she hadn't eaten. And after she had talked to Tom, she hadn't been able to sleep either. A whole week without him . . . suddenly all of her sense of well-being vanished. The following morning she woke up stiff and her neck was sore. She went to the office, and at three o'clock she was positive she was coming down with a virus. Linda told her to go home. "Honestly, January. Most girls who are in love bloom . . . you wilt!"

She got into bed. But she had chills and began to shake. She didn't know any doctor and she didn't want to bother Linda. Then she thought of Dr. Alpert. Of course. He certainly was a good doctor. Look at all the tests she had gone through before he gave her the shot. She phoned him, but his receptionist told her he didn't make any house calls and advised her to come over immediately.

The office was crowded, but the receptionist slipped her into a small examining room. "I'll get him to you," she promised.

Five minutes later Dr. Alpert shuffled in. He looked

at her, nodded, shuffled out and returned with the syringe.

"Shouldn't you take my temperature?" she asked. "I mean . . . I know vitamins help everyone. But I feel sick. Like I'm coming down with something."

He felt her brow. "No sleep . . . no food . . . too much energy. When did you eat last?"

"Why I . . ." She tried to think. Tom had berated her for leaving her steak the night before, and she had barely gotten a piece of toast down this morning. "Not since . . . well . . . maybe Friday. I've been nibbling. But I'm not hungry."

He nodded. "This will set you right, I promise."

She was sitting in dungarees and a shirt. She rolled up the sleeve and extended her arm, but he shook his head. "Take off the pants . . . this is an intramuscular shot."

She pulled down her dungarees and lay on her side. The needle went into her buttock with ease. But there was no rush of exhilaration. She sat up and pulled on her pants. "I don't feel anything," she said.

"You didn't come here to feel something. You came here because you were sick," he said gruffly.

"Yes, but last time the vitamin shot made me feel marvelous."

"When you feel good, the shot makes you feel marvelous. When you feel sick, it makes you feel better."

She sat on the edge of the table and stared at him. She had to admit that the stiffness had left her neck. But there was no sign of that glorious euphoria she had experienced before. She walked into the outer office and paid the receptionist twenty-five dollars. As she walked home, she realized the shivering had stopped. She was feeling stronger and the pains in her back and neck were gone. But she didn't have that "go out and conquer the world" feeling.

Tom returned Friday afternoon, and she rushed to the Plaza to meet him. He looked strong and somewhat less harassed. And when he opened the bottle of Jack Daniel's, he insisted she join him. "I know I said I might give it up, and I have cut down . . . but we have to celebrate. I just got the news—a week from Sunday, I'm number one. And it looks as if I'm making a big picture sale. Right now Columbia, Metro, Century, and Twentieth are all bidding, plus a few good independent producers. And the best news of all—the big guy is going to make it, he's out of the coma—so I won't have to carry that guilt on my back." Then he reached into his pocket and handed her a gift-wrapped box. "It's not really a present. It's just something I saw in a window and couldn't resist getting for you."

She opened the package. It was a beautiful silk scarf emblazoned with the word Capricorn. "Oh, Tom . . . I love it . . . But more than that . . . I love the idea that you thought of it."

But that night when they went to bed, she was unable to arouse him. He held her close and tried to pass it off. "I'm over-tired," he said. "And maybe I didn't cut down on the drinking like I promised. Let's both get a good night's sleep. Tomorrow will be different."

The following morning she told him she had a dentist appointment. He told her to cancel it, but she promised to be back in the early afternoon.

She rushed directly to Dr. Alpert's office without calling for an appointment. Fortunately the office was not crowded, and Dr. Alpert was smiling again. He told her she looked better, and she told him she had eaten and kept regular hours. Almost as if she were reporting to a teacher for good marks. (See how good I am. *Now* will you give me the real vitamin shot?) She waited hopefully while he went out to get the needle. Her heart beat fast when she saw him shuffle back with the big syringe. She had not changed into the examining gown, but in a flash she had taken off her blouse and held out her arm. "You promise to eat . . . even if you aren't hungry?" She nodded eagerly as he tied the rubber tubing around her upper arm. She watched the needle go into the vein. Once again she saw the rush of her own blood fill the syringe . . . then pump back into her arm. And once again the fantastic surge of electric excitement charged through her. She felt reborn. Fully alive for the first time . . . her senses were alert to colors . . . to

smells . . . And above all there was the sense of power
. . . there was nothing she couldn't accomplish . . .
her body tingled . . . suddenly she felt as if she was
having an orgasm. She longed to get back to Tom. She
threw on her blouse . . . hugged the doctor, scribbled
a check for the receptionist, and rushed outside. It was
cold again; but she knew spring was coming. She felt
it. Everything good was coming . . . The Plaza was only
a few blocks away, but she hailed a cab. She couldn't
wait until she was in Tom's arms.

He was on the phone when she arrived. It was a long-
distance interview, and she sat patiently as he answered
the usual questions. Occasionally he'd look over at her
and smile. Then he sighed; the man was going into questions about context against literary quality of today's
novel. Tom tried to be polite. "Look, I don't think I want
to get into that area. I don't ever criticize any other
writers. Hell, it's even hard work to write a bad novel."
But the man was persistent. January got up and put her
arms around him. He was still in his robe. She began
kissing his neck. Then she swung around and got on his
lap and cradled herself in his arms under the phone.
Her hands slid under his robe. He grinned but grabbed
her with one hand and tried to continue his interview.
She began to kiss his cheek. Finally he said, "Look, I
think we've covered everything and I've got another appointment. In fact it's kind of urgent, so if you don't
mind, let's cut it off here." Then he hung up and held
her in his arms. "You have just destroyed an interview."
He laughed.

"You were trying to end it."

"I tried . . . but you finished it."

She encircled his bare waist . . . then she opened
her blouse and unhooked her bra . . . she pressed her
breasts against him. "I love you, Tom. I really do." Then
she stood up and led him into the bedroom.

Later when they were lying together, he said, "How
do I thank you?"

She snuggled against him. "For what?"

"For not giving me a chance to worry about last night.
For turning me on this morning . . . right now . . .

and having it turn out to be the best we've had so far."

She kissed him violently. "Oh God! It was wonderful!"

"Was it for you? It was for me because I functioned normally . . . but nothing happened with you."

"Yes, it did, Tom."

"January—" He leaned over her, and his eyes were stern. "Wasn't that part of our deal? Complete honesty. Don't ever lie to me . . ."

She held him close. "Tom, a woman isn't like a man. I don't have to come all the time. Just holding you in my arms and knowing I make you happy makes me more of a woman than I've ever felt before."

His dark eyes glowed in the semidarkness of the bedroom. "January, I can never be without you again . . . never."

"You won't have to be, Tom. I'll always be waiting . . . whenever you want me."

Then he smacked her across the bottom. "Okay. Let's take a shower together. Hey, do you bike?"

"Do I what?"

"Ride a bike?"

"I don't know . . . no . . . I never rode one."

"Well, today, you're going to learn."

They rented bicycles and spent the afternoon in Central Park. She caught on immediately. Her balance was good, and soon she was whizzing past him on the bicycle lanes. They went to a movie on Third Avenue . . . ate pizza . . . and went back to the Plaza. And when they made love again, it was perfect, and Tom insisted on satisfying her until she had to cry out.

The following day they rode downtown on their bicycles. He took her to Irving Place and showed her where Mark Twain had lived. He pointed out the brownstone house where Oscar Wilde had lived when he was in this country. They went to a little French restaurant and he told her stories about Sinclair Lewis—he had been a young man then, and "Red" Lewis had been on an acting kick—he told her about meeting Hemingway . . . how he had met Tom Wolfe when he was teaching at N.Y.U. He told her about his early days. He was born in St. Louis and came to New York and got a job

on the *Sun*. Then a short stint in Hollywood. He had met
them all out there—when writers were looked down
upon by the movie industry. "That's why I never do a
screen treatment of any of my books no matter what
they offer me. I wrote too many pieces of junk tailored
to fit the stars during the forties, and I promised myself
—if I ever got to be a novelist, I'd never write a movie
script again."

During the next two weeks, time and days fused into
a meaningless maze for January. She forced herself to
try to concentrate at the office. But her life only had
content when she was with Tom. Mornings of waking
up in his arms, having a quick breakfast together, es-
caping just before Rita Lewis arrived, rushing to her
apartment to change, running to Dr. Alpert's for shots
every third day, returning to the magazine and accom-
plishing a day's work in two hours. She did five tapes
in one day after a vitamin shot, and even Sara Kurtz
had to admit they were good. She told about the loneliness of a writer like Tom Colt . . . the demands on
his time . . . his feelings about the circus atmosphere
of today's promotional efforts for a book. How he
understood that the media had changed—New York
had only three newspapers. She drew a fine impersonal
picture of Tom Colt—she called it "Echo of a Lion"—
and compared him to the lion coming out of the jungle
to face civilization. At the end of the two weeks Sara
said she had enough for a good story.

But it was at night that she really came alive. Bursting with this new incredible energy, she'd tear back to
her apartment, shower and change, and rush to the
Plaza. Sometimes they'd go to a show and stop off at
Sardi's. Once he took her to Danny's Hide-a-Way for
dinner and they sat at the front table . . . Mike's old
table. And sometimes if he'd had a rough day, they'd
just stay in and have room service and she'd listen to
his gripes about the interviews . . . the television
shows . . . his agents . . . and then there would always be the wonderful tenderness of his arms when
they lay in bed together. There were some nights they
didn't make love, when he said, "I'm fifty-seven, baby.

And I'm tired. But I want you to be with me." Those were some of the best nights. And when she got the curse and told him, and asked if she should sleep home, he had looked at her in amazement. "I want you in my arms at night, not just to hump you . . . but because I love you. I want to wake up and find you there, to reach out during the night and be able to hold you— isn't that what it's all about?"

Then there were nights when he wanted only to satisfy her . . . when he made love to her until she was limp with exhaustion.

And then there was always Linda. Always questioning. Always watchful. Growing slightly resentful because January had developed an expertise in evading personal questions.

At the end of March, Tom had to leave for another short promotional trip. Detroit, Chicago, Cleveland. "I don't think you should come," he said. "Why cause a lot of talk? I don't care for myself. It's you I'm concerned about. It'll only be for five days."

When he saw the tears in her eyes, he grabbed her in his arms. "January, for God's sake, of course you can come. Please, baby, don't cry."

She shook her head. "It isn't that. Of course you're right. It's only five days. And you will come back. But it just suddenly hit me that there will be a time when you'll have to leave for much longer than five days, when you won't be coming back . . ."

"I've thought about that, too," he said slowly. "Much more than you would believe. It's something I've got to think out while I'm gone. I told you once—I can never be without you. I mean it. I've also been thinking about the next book I want to write. The idea finally crystallized in my mind. And when that happens I can't wait until I go off to write. Only it's not quite happening that way now. I think of the book . . . and you come through. Before, a new book always took precedence over anything. I'd lock out the world and the book became my new mistress. But it's not like that now."

"That's wrong, Tom. You've got to write."

"I know . . . and I'll have to figure it out. Look, we'll talk about it when I get back."

When he was gone, it was as if all the oxygen had been taken out of the air. She skipped her usual appointment with Dr. Alpert. After two days she felt nervous and listless, but she forced herself to have dinner with Linda, who was now in love with one Donald Oakland, a newscaster on a local television show. They went to Louise's, and January listened while Linda gave explicit details of her sex life with Donald. "He doesn't give good head . . . but that's because he's Jewish. Jewish boys never really think it's proper to give head. But he's learning. I've assigned Sara to do a story on him," she said as she chewed on a piece of celery. "He's on local news right now, but when the story comes out and he gets a taste of real fame and realizes what I can do for him, he'll unload his wife and stick with me. I can't stand this three-evenings-and-one-afternoon-a-week scene."

"Do you want to get married?"

Linda shrugged. "I'm pushing thirty . . . so why not? Or at least I'd like him to live with me. And I'm also learning a lot from him. His I.Q. is 155—that's near genius. And I've just realized how little I know about politics. He's been explaining things to me. I don't dare tell him I've never voted. He's given me a lot of books to read. He's a big hot Democrat. I want to be able to hold my own with him and his friends so I'm reading *The New Republic* and *The Nation* like they're *Cosmo* or *Vogue*. Until now I was always busy watching my competition and trying to make *Gloss* as good. But I suddenly realize that while *Gloss* has grown, I haven't. I mean, like I don't know anything except things that concern the magazine. Donald thinks Women's Lib is great, so maybe I'll join one of the groups . . ." She laughed. "Except when he stays over he forgets all about Women's Lib and even expects me to wash out his underwear."

"Do you?" January asked.

"Of course. I even bought him a toothbrush and his favorite mouthwash to keep at my place. I make him breakfast when he stays over . . . a good breakfast, better than that wife of his makes. She wants to be a poet, so she's up writing half the night and is always asleep when he leaves Riverdale. And some nights I cook dinner—almost cordon bleu type because he really can't afford to take me out each time. I mean he's paying for his house in Riverdale . . . and his wife just put in a pool . . . and he's puttting his brother through college and—"

"Linda, can't you ever find a nice available man?"

"No. Can you?"

TWENTY-ONE

TOM CALLED every night. They discussed the shows he had done, the hassle he had gotten into with a critic on Kup's show, the endless interviews he had given, the mixed reviews his book had received. He was still number one, but he was concerned about the new books coming out on the spring list. He mentioned nothing about his future plans.

By the middle of the week January began to feel unstrung, physically and emotionally. Tom was due back Friday night. He had said he could never be without her. But he was without her now. And he had admitted that his work had always come first. Had this brief separation given him time to have second thoughts?

The following morning she was at Dr. Alpert's office before he arrived. Once again the receptionist slipped her into a booth without an appointment, and once again Dr. Alpert came shuffling in, and when that needle went into her vein, every doubt about her future with Tom vanished, and she floated out of the office with a golden feeling of confidence.

He returned Friday night and stopped off at her apartment without calling her. She let out a shriek of delight and fell into his arms. They clung together, both talking at once, both insisting each had missed the other more. And as he held her, she knew that her worries had been groundless. He would never leave her.

When he broke the embrace, he turned and looked at the apartment. He was so massive; the room seemed to shrink.

"How long is your lease?"

"It's a sublet. I have it until August. But Mr. Bailey wrote and said that if I wanted it for another year, he would stay on in Europe."

"Get rid of it. I'm going to buy us an apartment. You're going to pick it out. I want it to be on the river, with a wood-burning fireplace, a bedroom, a living room, and another room for me to work in, because that's where I'm going to write my new book."

"But what about California?"

"What about it?"

"Don't you have to go there?"

"Yes. We're leaving next week."

"We?"

He looked at her earnestly. "Look, I don't know about you . . . But these last five days seemed like five years. I did a lot of thinking. In a couple of years I'll be sixty. You'll be—well, you'll still be a child. So we've only got now. I don't know how long 'now' will last. But let's grab it. I love you. I want you with me. I've got a final two-week blast of publicity to do out on the Coast. I can't afford to be separated from you for that long. I called Nina Lou and told her about you. I didn't tell her your name, but I leveled with her and explained how it was with us. I told her I was bringing you out . . . and that as long as you'd have me, I was going to be with you. I told her I'd check into a bungalow at the Beverly Hills Hotel—the publisher is paying for that. And to make things look okay, I'll get you a room at the hotel which you won't use. And for all concerned, you are out there to do the story on me for your magazine. I'll go to the beach to see my kid. But that's the extent of it. Nina Lou says it's fine. She's pretty hung up on some actor, so as long as I don't make her look bad to her friends, she couldn't care less."

It was all going too fast for January. But she was light-headed with the knowledge that she hadn't lost him.

"We'll be in New York for another week now," he went on. "So your job will be to find the apartment. Get one all set, so we can move into it when we come back. I know it's short notice. But a good renting agent should be able to swing it. You go see them all. Then when you've narrowed it down to maybe two or three that you like, I'll come and see them. And we'll decide together."

"But Tom, if you live in New York with me . . . what about seeing your son?"

"I'll fly to the Coast every other weekend. Don't worry. It'll work out. I just know I can't be without you."

She spent eight hours a day looking at apartments. Linda was carried away with the idea. She was so expansive she told January to count the trip to the Coast as a paid vacation. "It's a bonus. You rate it. And remember . . . don't worry about a thing, just keep the genius happy. And we've got to find you the greatest apartment in New York. January, just think—as Tom Colt's girl, you can run a salon. With his muscle, all the 'In' people will come. We can start a whole new thing. Like maybe Sunday brunches. I'll write them up for *Gloss*. Wow! It's out of sight! We'll be the new 'A' group in town. *We'll* make the news . . . set the pace. And will I have muscle with Mr. Donald Oakland! He's impressed as it is that I know Tom Colt. But when he comes to your salon and sees all the important men I'll be able to meet . . . January, the timing is perfect. New York is ready for something like this. Now, it has to have a huge living room, one that opens on a dining room preferably, and . . ."

She was amused at Linda's enthusiasm and felt it was best just to let her ramble on. The apartment was going to be a fortress. Just for Tom. No guests, no parties—just the two of them. But she allowed Linda to come along and visit some of the apartments because she was slightly terrified of the efficient real estate lady who took them around. After four days, January was positive she had been in every great building in New York, and the search had finally narrowed down to an apartment at the U.N. Plaza or a ground floor apartment with a huge terrace hanging over the river on Sutton Place. Linda liked the U.N. building, but Tom was enthusiastic about the Sutton Place apartment.

It was a co-op, and the price of one hundred and ten thousand didn't seem to bother him. He was pleased with the relatively low monthly maintenance, the ninety-year ground lease—he kept nodding as the woman reeled off all the selling points of the apartment. Finally he said, "It's a deal. Draw up the contract and send it to my lawyer on the Coast. He'll send the check." He gave the ecstatic real estate lady all the necessary addresses and phone numbers. Then he took January to the nearest bar. He toasted their new apartment with a sad smile. "I like her talk about the ninety-year lease. January, for a man my age to expect this thing to last with a child like you—" He shook his head. "I know I'm crazy . . . but let's give it a real try. And no matter how long it lasts . . . let's make it a happy time."

"Tom, it will last forever."

He raised his glass. "To forever. I'll settle for five good years."

She spent the rest of the days buying clothes for California, cleaning up last-minute things at the office . . . And each night she rushed to the Plaza exhilarated. Her energy was boundless.

They were due to leave for California on a Wednesday afternoon. That morning she visited Dr. Alpert. When he saw her, he seemed surprised. "You were here just two days ago . . . you're not due until tomorrow."

"I'm leaving for Los Angeles today," she said as she watched him fix the syringe. "Dr. Alpert, I'm going to be away for a week at least. Can you give me some long-lasting shot?"

"Where will you be in Los Angeles?"

"The Beverly Hills Hotel."

He smiled. "You are a lucky girl. My brother, Dr. Preston Alpert, flew out there a week ago. An important singer is out there to make a comeback at some big club, and he must have a vitamin shot every day, so my brother is staying with him throughout the engagement. You call him at the Beverly Hills Hotel."

"Dr. Alpert . . ." She felt a sudden rush of fear. "Are these injections addictive?"

"Why should they be?"

"I mean, if the singer has to have them every day . . ."

"He drinks two quarts of brandy a day . . . doesn't eat . . . sleeps with a lady every night—of course he needs vitamin shots. You also have a great need for vitamins. Tell me, before you came to me . . . was there some traumatic thing in your life?"

She smiled. "Like three years of trauma . . . and then a kind of shock. But that was back in September. And everything worked out fine."

He shook his head. "Delayed reaction. Look, my little girl. There are doctors who treat the head. And why? Because something that happened twenty years ago hurts the mind today. So why do patients feel that things that happened to them some months ago can't hurt the body? If you're run down, what's wrong with taking vitamin shots three times a week if they make you function and feel good? Don't you have your teeth cleaned every few months . . . don't you brush them three times a day . . . don't you use eye lotion at night? Why not help your tired young blood? Today with the food you girls eat . . . or better yet, don't eat . . ."

He was right. This dear sweet man, taking all this time explaining things to her when he had an office filled with patients. His smile was benevolent. "Have a good time . . . call my brother. And when you get back, make your next appointment in advance."

She walked home. She knew she would be able to pack in no time at all. It was one of those rare April days— clear and cool, no smog, a Wedgwood sky. She wondered why the New Year always began in the middle of winter when everything was dead. The new year should start in April, on a day like this when new young life was just beginning. She saw it everywhere—a lady walking a tiny puppy, wobbly with its training leash; tiny buds breaking through the bare branches of the new young trees propped up with sticks and braces, burlap around their slim bodies to help them survive in a small patch of earth on a New York City street. Then she saw an old woman, the stockings slipping down her frail legs, walking an arthritic dog—the two of them inching down the street. Tears came to her eyes. She felt sorry for anyone who wasn't young. In fact, she felt sorry for everyone who wasn't going to California and for everyone who didn't know a man like Tom Colt.

As the day progressed her state of euphoria grew. She had never felt so complete and aware of everything around her. She sat beside Tom on the 747. The ride was smooth, the service perfect. Everything was perfect! Until the hostess placed the small glacéed Easter eggs on their dessert plates.

Easter eggs!

This was Wednesday.

Sunday was Easter!

And tomorrow Dee's plane would be waiting to take her to Palm Beach for the Easter weekend.

She wired her father the moment she reached the hotel. "AM IN LOS ANGELES AT THE BEVERLY HILLS HOTEL DOING A STORY ON TOM COLT. WILL HAVE TO MISS EASTER. LOVE, YOUR CAREER GIRL."

She hoped that by keeping it light, it would sound like a last-minute assignment rather than complete thoughtlessness on her part. She had checked into her "own room" in the main building, but her luggage went to Tom's bungalow. "I'll go there each day and muss up the bed for appearance's sake," she said. He laughed and shook his head. "With everyone living together, stars publicly having babies out of wedlock . . . do you really think anyone gives a damn about where you sleep?"

"I do," she said.

The publisher had set up a tight schedule for the next two days. Breakfast interviews, luncheon interviews, the Merv Griffin show, a news show, and a seven o'clock morning show. She accompanied him everywhere, carrying a notebook and playing Girl Reporter from *Gloss* magazine.

On Saturday Tom sent her to sit at the pool while he went to Malibu to visit his son. Sven, the attractive young man who managed the cabanas, offered her a comfortable chair in the sun. He gave her suntan lotion and brought her some magazines. But she couldn't relax. After an hour she began to feel nervous. She forced herself to stay at the pool; she could use some sun. Tom had admired her tan when they first met. She clenched her hands and gripped the arms of the chair. She felt she had to hold on. It was as if she was coming unhinged. She told herself she was just restless because Tom was away. But soon she was forced to admit that the pains in her neck were very real and she had the beginnings of a blinding headache. All of the unmistakable signs . . . it was time to call Dr. Alpert's brother.

She left the pool and went to her own room. It was a nice room, but even with the nightgown and robe she had hung in the bathroom, it was still obvious that no one used it. She wondered what the maid thought. She lit a cigarette and picked up the phone and asked for Dr. Preston Alpert. The operator said he was expected back at six. He was at Malibu. God, was everyone at Malibu!

It was only three o'clock. How was she going to get through the rest of the afternoon! She lay back on the bed to ease the hammering inside her head. By four o'clock she was hanging over the sink, letting cold water fall on the back of her neck. Two more hours to go. She left the room and went to the bungalow. She changed into slacks and a shirt. Her hands were shaking as she poured some bourbon into a glass. She almost gagged but forced some down. It always seemed to do so much for Tom; maybe it would help her head. She took another swallow. Her throat burned, but the headache didn't seem quite as intense. She slipped the bottle into her pouch bag and returned to her room. She stretched out on the bed and began drinking the bourbon. It was a restful room. It was sad to keep it and not use it. "I'm sorry, room," she said aloud. "It's nothing personal . . . just that my man lives in a bungalow."

She continued to sip the bourbon. It dulled the head-ache, but she knew she was getting drunk. She didn't want Tom to come home and find her that way. Maybe a warm bath would help. At least it would pass the time. She forced herself to stay in the tub until the skin of her fingers began to crinkle. Then she fixed her makeup and looked at her watch. Five-fifteen. She checked Dr. Alpert's room again. The message was the same. Dr. Alpert was expected back at six.

Her head was aching again, even worse than before. Her neck felt as if it were packed with swollen glands. Oh God. She was probably really anemic now. She hadn't eaten a thing today, just coffee with Tom in the morning. Dr. Alpert had warned her she must eat. And she had lost more weight. Even her hip-huggers were slipping down.

The next half hour was interminable. She felt warm and turned on the air-conditioning. Then she felt cold and turned it off. At five forty-five she left another message for Dr. Alpert, adding that it was urgent. At six-fifteen he still hadn't returned. Oh, God . . . suppose he didn't get back at all. Suppose he decided to spend the whole weekend at Malibu. She had run out of cigarettes and began smoking the butts. Tom was due back at seven. She wanted to feel great when she saw him. After all, his wife was probably very beautiful. She had to be if she had been a starlet. There weren't any starlets anymore! She poured herself another drink. She was a bit player! That's what she was. Just a girl who did extra work, an overaged bit player. So there was no reason to get uptight about her. But even an overaged bit player could be attractive. Look at how many were becoming stars on television. But this was silly . . . Tom had gone to see the baby. But how could you spend a whole day with an eight-month-old baby? It had to sleep a lot, didn't it?

It was six-thirty and she had gone through the last decent butt. The drugstore was just downstairs, but she was afraid to leave her room, afraid of missing the call. She sent for a pack and tipped the bellman a dollar. At quarter to seven she tried Dr. Alpert again. His line was busy! She sat by the phone, drumming her fingers on the table. Why was his wire busy? Hadn't she left word that her call was urgent? Five minutes later she tried again. A calm lethargic voice said, "Yesssss?"

"Is this Dr. Preston Alpert?"

"Who is calling?" the quiet drawl asked.

"January Wayne."

"What is it in reference to?"

"Oh, for God's sake! Are you Dr. Alpert?"

"I asked, what is this call in reference to?"

"I'm a patient of Dr. Simon Alpert. He told me you would be here, taking care of—"

"Never mind." The voice suddenly became firm and clipped. "What do you want?"

"A vitamin shot."

"When did you have the last one?"

"Wednesday morning."

"And you need another so soon?"

"I do . . . Honestly, Doctor, I do . . ."

He paused. "I'll be speaking to my brother later this evening. Suppose you call me tomorrow at noon."

"Oh no! Please . . . not then . . . I need it now. Look, I write for *Gloss* magazine. I'm here doing an in-depth piece on Tom Colt, and—"

"Tom Colt?" The voice was impressed.

"Yes. And you see I have to be alert all the time and watch everything and remember . . . because I don't take shorthand."

"Oh . . . I see . . . well . . . I'll check with my brother and find out what vitamins you take. Mr. Colt is in Bungalow Five, isn't he?"

"Yes . . . but I'm not there . . . I'm in room one twenty-three."

"Oh, then you're not the girl who's staying with him?"

"No girl is staying with him!"

"My dear girl, if you're really interviewing him, you must know he has a beautiful young girl with him . . . young enough to be his daughter. Everyone at the hotel knows it."

She paused. Then she said, "Thanks. But she won't be young and beautiful if you don't get here pretty soon. For God's sake . . . it's five of seven now."

"I'll be right there."

Ten minutes later he knocked at the door. She hated him on sight. He was tall, with heavy sandy hair and a hawk-like nose. His skin was bad and his long skinny fingers were clean but bloodless-looking. She preferred his brother. At least there was some warmth about Dr. Simon Alpert. He might not be as sanitary-looking, but he was warm and friendly. This one was like an immaculate antiseptic fish. She rolled up her sleeve as he fixed the syringe. Then without looking at her, he said, "Lie down on your side and take down your pants."

"I take it I.V."

He seemed surprised but wrapped the rubber tubing around her arm and proceeded to mix the solution. She winced when the needle went in. She fell back against the pillow. She had never had a shot like this one. She felt dizzy, as if she were rocketing to the sky. Her heart was pounding . . . her throat closed . . . she kept going up . . . up . . . Then she felt as if she were falling through an enormous air shaft . . . with no bottom. . . . For a moment she panicked. Then everything leveled off, and she felt nothing but a golden glow of life flowing through her entire body. She rolled down her sleeve after he had placed a bandaid on her arm. "How much do I owe you?" she asked.

"It's a gift."

"What?"

"Any girl who attracts a man like Tom Colt deserves a free vitamin shot."

"Well, thanks . . . thanks a lot."

"How long are you both going to be here?" he asked.

"For another week. He's been working very hard. He has a few more interviews next week, then two days in San Francisco, then back to New York and he—" She paused.

"And he goes back to his wife?"

She had been about to tell this dreadful man that they were going to sign the lease for their apartment. That was the danger of the shot—you felt so good you wanted to talk to everyone . . . trust everyone.

"I think I'd better get back to the bungalow," she said.

He nodded. "A man like Mr. Colt . . . with all that work . . . he certainly could use a series of shots."

She smiled faintly. "He doesn't need them. He has Jack Daniels."

"You know about the singer I'm treating?"

She walked to the bureau and pretended to comb her hair. His unctuous manner bothered her. Yet she couldn't afford to completely alienate him . . . she might need him again.

"I also treat a very famous composer; he takes a shot every day. And then there are several TV personalities that have started their injections. A man Tom Colt's age —granted he is a very virile-looking man—but he certainly could use some vitamins. Any man going at his pace—writing a book, promoting it, making love to a young girl." His gray eyes were glassy with what was supposed to be sexual innuendo.

It was all she could do to keep from throwing him out, but she turned and managed a faint smile. "I'll suggest it to him," she said. "And now . . . I've really got to dress."

He packed his case and left the room. She waited until he was gone, and then dashed to the bungalow. Tom hadn't returned. She felt wonderful. Dr. Preston Alpert's shot was much more powerful than his brother's. She poured herself another glass of bourbon. Tom would be pleased if he found her drinking it. Good Lord, the bottle was almost empty. It had been three-quarters full when she took it to her room.

She walked to the bar and opened another bottle. She thought of Tom and suddenly put the bottle to her mouth and took a long swallow. She gagged a bit, but it went down. She tried it again. Suddenly the entire room began to float. She realized she was very drunk. Roaring drunk. It struck her as very funny. She began to laugh. She kept laughing until the tears rolled down her face. Until her stomach actually ached. She wanted to stop . . . but she couldn't. Her body felt lighter than air. She was still laughing when the phone rang.

She looked at the clock. Almost eight o'clock. It had to be Tom . . . offering some explanation for being so late. She reached for it but changed her mind. No. She had waited all day. Let Tom and the operator have a little trouble finding her. She knew how it worked. Now they'd try the Polo Lounge, then page the lobby . . . Okay. Now she'd let them find her. She picked up the phone. "Hello . . . Operator, this is Miss Wayne. You have a call for me?" She began to laugh again. The whole thing seemed so terribly funny.

There was a pause while the operator connected the call. Then she heard Mike's voice. "January . . ."

"Mike." She began to laugh harder. It was Mike . . . not Tom. She kept laughing. But it wasn't funny . . . only she couldn't stop laughing. She wanted to stop . . .

"January, what is it? What's the big joke?"

"Nothing . . ." She was doubled over now. "Nothing. It's just that I had a shot and some bourbon and I . . . I feel . . . so marvelous . . . and . . ." She broke into spasms of laughter again.

"What kind of a shot?"

"Vitamins. They're . . . heaven—ly . . ." Now she had stopped laughing and felt she was drifting on a cloud. The vitamins had conquered the bourbon. She felt silken inside . . . the bed was a cloud floating in space . . .

"January, are you all right?"

"Oh, my beloved father . . . I've never been better. Never . . . never . . . never . . ."

"Who are you with right now?"

"No one. I'm just waiting for Tom."

"Tell me something," he said. "How come the magazine sent *you* to do this interview? Since when did you become their star reporter?"

She began to laugh again. Mike sounded so serious. So stern. If he only knew how happy she was. How happy everyone should be. She wanted him to be happy. She wanted him to know how it felt to float. "Mike . . . are you happy?" she asked.

"What are you talking about?"

"Happiness. It's the only thing that matters. Are you happy with Dee?"

"Never mind about me. What are you doing there? What are these shots you're talking about?"

"Just vitamins. Heavenly wonderful vitamins. Oh, Mike, there're palm trees out here, better than the palm trees in Florida. And Bungalow Five is like my own private home. Did you ever stay at Bungalow Five when you were here? I bet you did . . . because you and he are a lot alike. After all, he even had our suite at the Plaza."

His voice was hard. "I want you to leave Los Angeles immediately."

"No way. And after Los Angeles I go to my big new apartment with a garden terrace on the river and—" She suddenly couldn't remember what she had been talking about. "What was I just saying?" she said.

"Too much. Goodbye, January."

"Goodbye, my magnificent father . . . my lord . . . my handsome one . . . my . . ." But he had hung up.

She was stretched out on the bed without any clothes when Tom came in at nine. He stared at her for a moment, then smiled. "Now this is what I call a real greeting." She held out her arms but he shook his head as he sat on the edge of the bed. "I'm too weary. It's been a rough trip. And today was another ball-breaker."

"You mean you're tired from playing with the baby?"

He laughed. "Actually, I held the baby for exactly twenty minutes. Then he threw up and the nurse gave me a dirty look and whisked him off. I got to see him once again after his bath."

"Then what did you do all this time?"

He stood up and took off his jacket. "You're making noises like a jealous wife. And you have no cause to be. I told you it was part of my deal to keep up a semblance of a marriage. So today I had to be nice to a lot of people that Nina Lou had in for brunch, cocktails and . . . well . . . the whole deal was like a twenty-four-hour open house—welcoming the big author bit."

"I feel shut out," she said suddenly. "Like you have a whole other life going for you. And to me, you're my whole life."

He sat down on the edge of the bed again. "Look, baby, writing is my life. Right now you've come into it in a very big way and you can stay as long as you like. I love you. But no woman can be my whole life. Except for now while I'm on this circus of promoting. Because through all this you're the only thing that is real. But once I start writing—you're going to have to accept the fact that the writing comes first."

"But no other woman."

"No other woman. I swear to that."

She grinned happily and jumped off the bed. "I accept those terms and now you must accept mine . . . for tonight." She pulled him to his feet and began unbuttoning his shirt. "And now that you've done your husbandly duties, your loving geisha girl awaits." She stroked his chest and ran her fingers up his back. He took her hands and held them.

"Baby . . . I'm not up to it. I'm just too tired. But if you want, I'll make love to you."

"No . . . Let's just stay up all night and talk and be together in each other's arms."

"Fine. But I think I'd better order some dinner for you."

"I don't need food . . . I've got you."

He smiled. "I wish I knew what you were sniffing. I'd like some too."

"Vitamins," she said. "You should try them."

He laughed. "God, it's wonderful to be young. You can turn on and recharge yourself. I could do it too when I was your age." He sighed heavily. "It's rotten getting old. I never thought it would happen to me. I felt I'd always be strong . . . always be young . . . able to get by with too much booze and too little sleep. Health and stamina were just things I took for granted. But it creeps up on you—" He sighed again. "It's hell to know you're creeping up to sixty."

"You're not old," she said. "And I do take vitamins. Shots . . . here . . . look at my arm." She held it out and pulled off the adhesive. He saw the tiny prick on her arm. "What the hell are you doing?" he demanded.

"It's a vitamin shot."

"You get them in the ass."

"I got one that way once . . . but it didn't work as well. That's intramuscular. This is intravenous."

"Okay, Dr. Kildare. Now tell me something. Where did you get this shot?"

"Dr. Preston Alpert. He's out here now. In New York his brother takes care of me."

"And just what do these shots do for you?"

"Make you feel like you own the world."

"Send for him," he demanded.

They reached Dr. Alpert in the Polo Lounge. Within fifteen minutes he was at their bungalow. When he met Tom he was so visibly impressed that his hand shook as he attached the disposable needle to the syringe. January sat huddled on the bed in one of Tom's robes. Tom was shirtless . . . still in his white denim pants. He was tanned from the beach. In contrast Dr. Alpert looked like a spindly green grasshopper as he bent over his syringe. Tom watched the doctor carefully. January looked away as Dr. Preston plunged the needle into his arm. But if Tom felt anything, his expression never changed. He waited silently until Dr. Alpert finished. He stared at the small bandaid on his arm and reached into his pocket. "What do I owe you?"

"One hundred dollars."

"One hundred dollars!" January shouted. "Why that's crazy. Your brother only charges me twenty-five."

Dr. Alpert looked at her nastily. "That's an office visit. This is a house call. And after hours at that."

Tom slammed the money into his hand. "Look, take your money. And if I ever see you around here, I'll break every bottle you've got in that case."

Dr. Alpert was stunned. "You mean you're not pleased with the shot? Don't you feel anything?"

"I feel plenty. Too much for just a vitamin shot. That shot is loaded with some kind of speed."

Dr. Alpert started for the door. Tom went after him and grabbed him by the jacket. "Remember, I don't want you to go near her or I'll run you out of town."

Dr. Alpert pulled himself together. "Mr. Colt, if they

did a blood analysis on you right now, they'd find heavy doses of Vitamin A, E, C, and all the B's."

"And some meth as well, I'm sure. I don't doubt that you've got some vitamins in it. But it's the speed that makes the patient feel good."

Dr. Alpert tripped over the door ledge in his hurry to leave the bungalow. Tom turned to January. "How long have you been on these things?"

"I'm not really on anything, Tom. I mean . . . I've taken a few shots . . . Linda told me about it. . . ." Then she went on to explain about Keith and all the important people who used the two Dr. Alperts.

Tom took her in his arms and held her close. "Look, baby, right now I feel like I could make love to you all night. That I could start writing my next book and never stop . . . that I could dive off the highest hill at Miramar in Acapulco . . . catch the current as well as any of the professional Mexican divers. It's a great feeling. And I've had it before. I was a correspondent during World War Two. I used to take bennies and get a little of this kind of jolt. The bomber pilots who made the early morning raids ate them like gumdrops. Maybe they hadn't slept too well the night before, figuring it might be their last. But they popped those bennies in their mouth at four A.M., and an hour later, when they took off, they were soaring into that wild blue yonder positive that no bullet could hit them. Hell, half of them felt as if they didn't even need the plane. I feel the same way now. I could . . . well . . . hell . . . let's not waste the shot." And he threw her on the bed.

The following morning, the effect of the shot seemed to have worn off for Tom. But January was still in a constant state of enthusiastic energy. Tom sat her down and tried to explain the danger. "Look, I'm six foot two and weigh a hundred and ninety pounds. So my system absorbed it quickly. But you . . . you can't weigh more than a hundred pounds, and that shot is loaded with methamphetamine, I'm sure. It's not addictive like the hard stuff . . . but when it wears off, the withdrawal signs are like a bitch of a hangover."

"But can they really hurt me?"

"As a steady diet they could kill you. It races the pulse . . . makes your heart beat triple . . . Now look, if you want to get high, do it with booze. You can't drink enough to hurt you. I can—and do—but then I've lived my life. Now, no more shots . . . Promise?"

"I promise."

That night they had room service and they had barely finished dinner when he jumped up and pulled her toward the bedroom. "Tom." She laughed as she followed him. "The waiter will come in . . ."

"Let him. We'll close the bedroom door. Maybe it's the bourbon activating what's left of the shot. But whatever it is, I don't want to blow it."

They didn't hear the doorbell. They didn't even hear the bedroom door open. Then everything happened so fast that she could barely put things together. She was aware of the lights going on. Someone pulling Tom off her. Seeing a fist send a bone-crunching blow to Tom's jaw. Tom staggering and spitting blood. Then she gasped. It was Mike! . . . standing there . . . his fists clenched . . . staring at them both.

"Mike!" The word stuck in her throat.

Tom had recovered and lunged after Mike, but Mike's fist slammed into his face again. Tom struck back, but Mike crouched like a street fighter. Tom wasn't able to touch him, and Mike came after Tom with a maniacal fury. His fist smashed into Tom's face again and again. She tried to scream, but no sound came out. Tom stood up as Mike pummeled into him. He tried to lash out, but his timing was off. His face was a bloody smear. Mike's fist smashed into his jaw again . . . into his stomach . . . back to his face . . . back to the jaw—it was more violent than anything she had ever imagined. And she stood watching it in a stupor as if it wasn't quite real. It was all happening so fast. Tom flailing out . . . beginning to falter under Mike's merciless onslaught . . . Mike pulling Tom to his feet . . . his fist crashing against Tom's face again and again. The blood was pouring from Tom's mouth. His eye was cut. She saw him stand groggily against the wall and spit teeth. She rushed to her father. "Let him alone . . . stop it! STOP IT!" She screamed.

Mike let go and Tom slipped against the wall to the floor. January knelt beside him. She looked up at her father. "Do something . . . help him . . . oh God, you've knocked out all of his front teeth."

Mike walked over and pulled her to her feet. "They're caps. They've probably been knocked out before." Then suddenly for the first time he seemed to realize she was naked. His face went dark with embarrassment. He turned away. "Put your clothes on. I'll wait in the next room."

"Just like that!" she shouted. "You come in here and half kill the man I love . . . and then give orders. Why? Are you jealous?" She jumped in front of him. "Is that it? Well, I never burst into your bedroom and beat up Dee. I come to Palm Beach and smile like a good little girl."

"He's a bum!"

Tears were running down her face. "I love him. Don't you understand? I love him . . . and he loves me."

He pushed past her and looked at his watch. "Get dressed. I've got the plane waiting."

"Why did you come here?" she sobbed.

"Because when I talked to you on the phone yesterday you sounded spaced out. I was afraid you were in some drug scene. I couldn't get here fast enough. Now I wish I hadn't come. But I'm here. So let's cut out. We'll forget any of this happened. Come back to Palm Beach with me."

"No way," she said.

He looked at his watch. "I'll sit in the Polo Lounge for half an hour. If you don't come by then, I'll leave. But if you have any brains at all, you'll pack your things and tell him to call his wife to come and get him. I'll be waiting in the Polo Lounge—for exactly one half hour." He slammed the door of the bungalow.

For a moment she stared after him. Tom had made it to the bathroom. She rushed after him and got a wet towel and held it to his face. He put on a robe and with her help made it back to the bedroom.

"Tom . . . your teeth . . ."

He tried to smile and winced. "Like the man said . . . caps. I can get them fixed. It's my jaw . . . I think it's broken . . ."

"Oh, Tom!"

"Don't worry . . . it's been broken before. Your father's got a good punch."

"I'm sorry."

"I hate the bastard," he said. "But I guess I would have done the same thing if it had been my daughter."

"You're not mad?"

He shook his head. "No. He's just brought things to a head. I've always had a hunch that maybe I was just a replacement. Now I know. So you better get dressed and go to him."

"Tom . . . I love you. I told him I loved you."

"That line you pulled about his wife was the clincher, honey."

"What line?"

"Skip it." He turned away.

She got into her slacks and shirt. He looked at her and nodded. "So long."

"I'll be back," she said.

"Back?"

"Yes. I just want to see him . . . to tell him I'm staying."

"If you don't show in half an hour he'll know that."

"But I've got to tell him."

He grabbed her hand. "Listen, baby. This is it. This is the moment when you make the big choice. It's me or Daddy . . . not both. Because if you go out there, you've made your choice."

"I'm just going to tell him . . . I mean, I can't let him go off like this. I can't let him just sit and wait."

"If you walk out, there's no coming back," he said slowly.

"But Tom, I have to talk to him. Can't you understand?"

"You love me, right?" She nodded anxiously. "Okay,"

he went on. "Someone just came in here and beat the shit out of me because you loved me. Now, if you walk out on me—even for ten minutes—to make peace with that guy—then you make a bum out of me."

"But he's not just a guy . . . he's my father."

"Right now he's the guy who smashed me up . . . and you're my girl. Mike knows the rules. You walk out there for any goddam reason and it's like another clout at my jaw." He looked at the clock. "You've got twenty minutes left."

She hesitated. She thought of Mike sitting in the bar waiting. Then she looked at the bruised man on the bed. She nodded and walked slowly back to him. He held her in his arms and they both lay very still listening to the minutes tick by. . . .

When he left Bungalow Five, Mike went to the men's room and let cold water run over his hand. It was beginning to swell . . . the knuckles were split in several places. His hand felt like it was busted. He hated to think how Tom Colt's jaw must feel.

He went to the Polo Lounge and ordered a Scotch. He looked at his watch. Ten minutes had passed. She'd come. She was probably seeing to it that Tom Colt was fixed up. He hadn't meant to mangle the guy. But he had seen Tom Colt in fights before. No one had a chance against him. So he knew he had to keep hitting. All along he had expected Colt to let one fly that would demolish him. He kept expecting it—and it was that expectation that had driven him on. If he had thought about it, he might have hesitated in tangling with Colt. But the sight of him on top of his daughter . . . something had just snapped and he hadn't been able to *stop* hitting him.

He was amazed that he had come out of it with nothing more than a busted hand. But then, when a guy has just shot a load he's not exactly in fighting form. He felt sick in the stomach thinking of him with January. Her body was so slim and beautiful . . . too clean and nice for a man like Colt to handle.

He looked at his watch. Fifteen minutes. She was probably packing now. He ordered another drink. Was the captain looking at him with sympathy? No . . . it was all in his mind. They probably didn't even know she was his daughter. A guy sitting alone in the Polo Lounge always looks like he's been stood up. But he wouldn't be stood up. Any second now she'd come dashing in . . . and he would smile and not even discuss it. Hell, he had made plenty of mistakes in his time. He certainly couldn't lecture her.

Twenty minutes. Why was she cutting it this thin? Well, all that mattered was getting her back. And it was going to be different from now on. He'd take her to Cannes in May. They'd talk about that on the trip back to Palm Beach. He'd tell her about his luck, the way it was coming back.

Twenty-five minutes! Jesus, it couldn't be that she *wasn't* going to show! No . . . She'd come. She was his daughter . . . she belonged to him. But what was that crack she had made about Dee? Was she jealous of Dee? She had no reason to be . . . she knew damn well he didn't love Dee. He wasn't jealous of Tom Colt . . . he was just sick about her being with a man like him. He was too old . . . he had a wife . . . he was a drunk . . . and he had shacked up with every kind of broad around. He wasn't fit to touch his daughter.

The half hour was gone. He stared at his watch as if he couldn't quite believe it. He looked toward the door. He'd give her five more minutes. He ordered a third drink. Christ, he never drank three drinks in half an hour. His hand was throbbing, but the pain in his gut was worse. Because he knew she wasn't going to show. But he'd have the drink . . . it would give him an excuse to hang on an extra ten minutes.

He nursed it for fifteen minutes and ordered another. He was giving her an hour. Bullshit . . . he was giving himself time. He was too stunned to move. He had to think this thing out. His little January . . . turning him down for Tom Colt. He had always felt she'd walk out on the world for him. And he'd do the same for her. It had always been that way . . . it *had* been that way! But now Tom Colt had the corner suite at the Plaza. Tom Colt had Bungalow Five. Tom Colt's book was number one on the list. Tom Colt was a winner . . . and Mike Wayne was just Dee Milford Granger's husband.

Okay. She wasn't coming out. She belonged to Tom Colt for now. But when the romance phased itself out —as it had to in time—how would he go about reestablishing their old relationship? Would she ever forgive him for breaking in like that? Would she ever respect him like she did that drunken bum in there? To stay with a guy who's had his teeth knocked out . . . she had to care for him. Or feel pity. No. January wouldn't stay out of pity. She was *his* daughter, and he had never stuck with anyone out of pity. She was with Tom Colt because she respected the sonofabitch. Well, why not? He was number one. And he was probably also a great cocksman. He winced as he thought about it in relationship to his daughter. But he forced himself to face the facts. Tom Colt always charmed the broads. No doubt about it . . . he was great in that department. And January . . . well . . . she was his daughter. So she probably dug sex, too. He clenched the glass so hard it broke. Now his bad hand was cut on the inside as well. The waiter rushed to him . . . Mike brushed it off . . . it was just an accident. He wrapped his handkerchief around his hand, dropped a twenty-dollar bill on the table, and left the hotel. He had waited one hour and fifteen minutes.

He thought about it as he drove to the airport. How did he go about getting her back? No woman had ever walked out on him before. And he'd never forget the way she looked at him. As if she was seeing a stranger.

He lit a cigarette and tried to think it out. To start with, he'd have to win back her respect. He could do it. His luck had changed. So far he had won over one hundred and thirty-five thousand dollars gambling on golf, gin, and even backgammon. If he kept this up . . . He ground out his cigarette. If he kept this up he'd be nowhere! If your luck was hot you had to push it. In the old days he'd have pushed this streak and run it into a couple of million. What was he doing sitting around like a dame . . . hoarding his winnings . . . putting them into a safe deposit box in his daughter's name? What good was the money if she despised him? And if he kept up this penny ante stuff, he'd never win back her respect.

He got to the airport and walked across the field to his plane.

"Back to Palm Beach?" his pilot asked.

"No," Mike snapped. "Get clearance for Las Vegas. We're going there for a few days."

He sat in the plane as it made the turbulent flight. He remembered when he used to fly to Vegas from the Coast every weekend. One thing—being married to Dee, his markers would be good. He was going to shoot the whole works. He'd build up a big bankroll for Cannes. He was playing for big stakes again . . . perhaps the biggest in his life. He was rolling the dice for his daughter.

TWENTY-TWO

JANUARY AWOKE when she heard the rain. Oh, God
. . . not again. There was nothing worse than California in the rain. The light on the clock radio said
seven-thirteen. She closed her eyes and tried to go back
to sleep. It had been raining for three days. The monotonous clatter it made on the roof of the bungalow
was now something she accepted as part of her day—
the way she accepted the eternal clicking of Tom's typewriter. She had been in California one month and it
seemed like forever. Perhaps it was the sameness of
each day. When the sun shone . . . it seemed eternal.
And when it rained . . . the rain seemed eternal.

But with the rain, she became a captive of Bungalow
Five. Tom was still asleep. She looked at him in the
shadowy morning light. He still had a small bruise under
his left eye. His recuperative powers had amazed her.
His face had healed in less than two weeks. And his
teeth were back in three days. He explained his dentist
always kept an extra set of his caps on hand. Oddly
enough it was the broken ribs that gave him the most
pain . . . but he took it all philosophically. He had
been in too many barroom fights to let a few cracked
ribs get him down. "When your nose is broken and your
jaw is wired, then you can complain." He laughed. "And
those were fights that I won." Besides, as he put it, he

needed the rest and it gave him a chance to be on hand when his agent finalized the picture sale of his book. When the deal was set, they'd go off to New York and celebrate.

He made the deal and they celebrated. And it was her fault they were still in Bungalow Five.

Tom had been exuberant the day he had signed the contract. He had spun her around the room. "Five hundred thousand against twenty-five percent of the net profit. Do you realize what that means! They want to bring the picture in for two million. So after it grosses five million, everything is gravy. If it's a big one and goes through the roof, I could make a million."

"It will if they do the book," she said. "But I've seen so many hit books changed . . . and ruined."

"Well, let's hope they get a good writer and a hot director. But meanwhile, we'll go to Matteo's tonight and celebrate. Tomorrow I'll visit my son. And the next day we take off for New York and I'll sign the lease on the apartment."

"Tom, why don't you do the script?"

"I told you. I don't do scenarios."

"Why?"

He shrugged. "It's not prestigious."

"That's a hang-up from your early days. Plenty of novelists are writing their own screenplays. Look at Neil Simon . . . he always does his own adaptations. Besides, if I had twenty-five percent of the profits, I'd want to be damn sure that my money was protected with a good script."

He looked at her for a moment. "Know something? You've given me something to think about. I never had a share of the profits before."

And then he was on the phone with his agent and for the next few days the phone calls went back and forth. And finally, at the end of the week, they sat in the Polo Lounge with Max Chase, his agent, and toasted the deal. Tom was to get fifty thousand for the treatment. And after that was approved, he'd get another hundred and fifty thousand to write the screenplay itself.

"That'll buy the apartment in New York," he said.

"Here's to you, Max . . . the deal is great. And here's to January for making me do it."

"What apartment in New York?" Max Chase asked.

"I'm buying one. My lawyer is still checking out a few points in the deal they sent us. Mortgages and stuff. But it's practically set. The way I figure it, we can get in by June, January can furnish it, and I'll knock out the treatment. Then I guess I'll have to come back here to talk about the actual screenplay."

Max Chase smiled. "I'm way ahead of you. I managed to get a few more goodies put in the contract for you. I got Century to pick up the tab on the bungalow, plus supply you with a car while you're working on both the treatment and the screenplay. So forget about New York for the time. Besides, it's best for you to write it out here. You stay in touch with things that way. You'll be able to see who they pick for a director, the actors . . . When you're right here, you get a chance to argue about it—not read about it after the fact."

Tom turned to January with a grin. "Think you can rough it out here in Bungalow Five for a few more months?"

She nodded. "I'll tell Linda I'm quitting the magazine."

"Don't be ridiculous," he said. "She can give you some assignments to do out here. Keep you busy."

And Linda had been enthusiastic. "Sure. Get me a story on Doris Day . . . and George C. Scott . . . Dean Martin . . . and get one on Barbara Stanwyck, find out how she feels about TV, the new Hollywood as opposed to the old one . . . I hear Melina Mercouri is out there—try for her. And do something on the elegant Malibu colony where your man has a house. . . ."

But it wasn't that easy. She had tried to contact the press agents of the stars and learned that most of them were on vacation. After a few calls, she stopped trying. A strange kind of lethargy had come over her. When the stimulant from the shot had worn off she had gone through two tortuous days of headaches and nausea. But Tom had been with her and forced her to sit it out. She was all right now, but she felt oddly disoriented. As if an arm or leg had been amputated. She knew that in some way it had to do with Mike. She knew her complete disinterest in *Gloss* also related to him. She realized her job had been just a means of attracting his attention . . . seeking his approval. And now she could never win his approval. She would never forget the way he had looked at her when he walked out. And now she had nothing to live for except Tom . . . Mike had walked out on her. It was Tom who cared.

In the beginning she sat at the pool and read all the current novels. Tom was still number one. He was caught up in his writing now, and she forced herself to stay away from the bungalow until late afternoon and tried to ignore the gnawing realization that nothing was happening with them at night. Of course he had been too battered the first two weeks, and he said ribs took a long time to heal. But she felt it was his writing that was coming between them. When she came in, he would often motion her to go into the other room. He didn't want to break his rhythm by even saying hello. Occasionally he would tell her the television set was on too loud. At night they'd have room service and he'd read her the stuff he had written during the day.

Now as she lay listening to the rain, she wondered why she felt so despondent. This was the way it should be. In a way she was working with him, just by being there and listening. But something was missing. She reached out and touched his shoulder. He mumbled in his sleep and turned away. She felt the tears come to her eyes. Even in his sleep he was rejecting her. What was this ego trip she was on . . . about helping him? It was all in her mind. She wasn't helping him! She wasn't even necessary in his life! She slipped out of bed and dressed quietly.

She sat at the counter of the coffee shop and had a corn muffin and coffee. Every seat was taken. And everyone in Los Angeles seemed alert and alive at eight in the morning. Some were reading the trades. She heard snatches of conversation—distribution costs . . . foreign distribution . . . the Eady plan . . . no tennis during lunch hour because of the damn rain. She paid her

check and went upstairs to the lobby and ordered
Tom's car. The rain was still slicing down. Cars were arriving in one lane and leaving in the other. There were
cracks about the glorious California sunshine; the in-
evitable reply: "This is just heavy dew." She saw Dr.
Preston Alpert get into a car with a recording star who
had arrived from London to do a Special. Good Lord!
Was he on the shots too? Finally her car arrived and
she drove down Sunset and out to Santa Monica. Then
she sat and watched the rain pelt down on the desolate
beach.

Perhaps Tom sensed her mood, because when she returned he stopped writing and insisted they have a drink
together. He had stopped drinking while he was writing,
but now he poured himself a double, insisted she have
one also, and took her to The Bistro for dinner.

His entrance caused a rush of conversation. It
seemed he knew everyone in the restaurant. Before the
meal was over several actors and directors were sitting
at their table talking shop—exchanging stories, making
suggestions on who should play certain roles. She sat
there feeling more shut out than ever.

He was in great spirits when they got back to the
bungalow. And when they were in bed he made the
attempt . . . but nothing happened. He finally made
love to her and after she was satisfied and he thought
she was asleep he got out of bed and went into the
living room. She waited a few minutes and then peeked
inside. He was rereading the pages he had done that
day. She went back to bed. Hadn't he originally said
he'd work four hours a day and spend the rest of the
time with her? In the beginning he had often come to
the pool for a brief swim. But it was always the typewriter he rushed back to. Where had she gone wrong?
What had happened to the excitement in their relationship?

On Monday it rained again. She tried to watch the
soap operas. On Tuesday it was still raining and she
tried to read. On Wednesday she tried to write an article called "The Heavy Dew"; but it didn't work. On
Thursday, when the sun finally broke through, she

threw her arms over Tom's shoulders as he sat at the typewriter. "Come on to the pool with me . . . let's take a walk . . . let's do something."

"Why don't you take tennis lessons?" He was staring at the sheet in the typewriter.

"Tom, I play tennis real well. I don't need lessons."

"Fine. Then I'll ask Max Chase to find you some players."

"Tom, I stayed in California to be with you . . . not to play tennis."

"You are with me."

"Yes, but you aren't with me."

"I'm a writer." He kept staring at the paper in the typewriter.

"For God's sake, it's only a movie treatment. It isn't *War and Peace*."

"Writing is my work. You should understand that."

"Producing was my father's work, but he certainly took time out for someone he cared about."

"January, for God's sake, go out and amuse yourself. Buy some clothes at the shop in the hotel. Charge it to the bungalow."

"I don't want clothes. Tom, it's only eleven in the morning. I'm lonely . . . I feel lost . . . tell me what to do."

"I don't give a damn what you do just as long as you get off my back."

"I'm going back to New York," she said quietly.

He turned and his face grew hard. "Why? To crawl back to him?"

"No . . . to save what we have. I'll go back to my job. At least I'll be able to walk in New York . . . see people on the street . . . talk to a blind man with pencils and a big dog . . . go to the park and get mugged—anything. But at least I'll be off your back!"

He grabbed her in his arms. "I didn't mean it. Please, baby. I need you. I want you here. Look, you've never lived with a writer before. Our relationship is great. I've never been happier. I've never written better. If you walk out on me I'd feel I had failed you. Don't do this to me now . . . not when the end is so close. Look, this will all be over soon. And we've learned something from it. We've learned we can't live in Los Angeles when I write my next book. And that's what living together is all about—you find out what works and what doesn't. But one thing we do know that works is us. Right?"

"I don't know, Tom. I really don't. I feel . . . lost."

He turned away. "I see. It's Mike, isn't it?"

"Tom, I'd be a liar if I said I didn't think about him . . . subconsciously that is. I mean . . . well . . . I loved him . . . I still love him. I've loved him all my life. I wish that night had never happened. But I made the decision. I stayed with you . . . and I lost him."

"What makes you think you've lost him?"

"Tom, if I left for New York tomorrow . . . would I lose you?"

"Yes," he said quietly. "Because I'd know why you left."

"And don't you think Mike knows why I've stayed?"

He nodded slowly. "I guess I've been selfish. Look, let me just get this draft done. Then I'll hand it in and we'll get into a car and go to San Francisco for ten days. I have a lot of friends there. You'll like them. We'll have a ball. And I promise from this moment on, I'll only write four hours a day."

"Then I'll wait and we can go swimming at two. It's only eleven now."

"I don't feel like swimming. But you go. Maybe I'll come down later."

He didn't come down. And he spent the following day at the typewriter working straight through until eight o'clock.

On Saturday it rained again. He left in the morning to go to Malibu to see his son. He promised to be back by five. They'd go somewhere for dinner. Maybe even a movie. He called at nine. She could hear music and the sound of people laughing and talking. His voice was blurred and she knew he had been drinking. "Look,

baby, it's coming down real hard out here. I think I'd
better stay for the night. Order some room service. I'll
see you tomorrow." He clicked the phone.

She sat very still for a few seconds. He was having
a marvelous time at his wife's house. And he was in no
rush to get back to her. Why should he be? All she
had done was complain. Where had all the excitement
gone? Where was her vitality, her high spirits? She was
the girl who had once made him function like a man.
Now he never even tried anymore. Just satisfied her
when he felt she needed it. A mercy dive. Yes, that's
what Linda would call it. And now he was staying overnight at Malibu. He'd come back tomorrow. But if she
kept this up, there'd be a time when he wouldn't come
back. Suddenly everything seemed so desolate . . . so
hopeless. She couldn't lose Tom . . . she couldn't! He
was all she had. She had to make it all shining and wonderful, as it had been before.

She sat very quietly for a few minutes. Then she
picked up the phone and called Dr. Preston Alpert.

TWENTY-THREE

DAVID STOOD at the bar at "21," waiting for his father. The old man was ten minutes late. This was unusual. He glanced at the empty table being held for him at the banquette against the wall. The restaurant was filling up. Peter was checking his list as some V.I.P.'s arrived without reservations. Walter had just put up a table in the archway that divided the first and second sections. Mario was giving white carnations to three attractive women. David finished his drink and decided it would be better to wait at his table. Too many people at the door were eyeing it.

He was on his second martini when his father came in. He apologized profusely as he ordered a drink. "My God, but women can be impossible." He sighed.

David laughed. "Don't tell me you've got a romance going again?"

His father colored slightly. "David, I've always had great respect for your mother. But she— Well, she isn't what you'd call a physical person. However I've never had, as you put it, a romance going. Naturally I've had an occasional discreet foray. But never any real relationship."

"Well, who is the new impossible discreet foray?" David asked.

"Nothing like that. It's your mother who is impossible. That's why I'm late. We're going to Europe in three weeks. Our first time in six years and our passports have to be renewed. Would you believe we've been at the passport office since eleven this morning, and your mother is *still* there?"

"Was it that crowded?"

His father shrugged. "Not very. This is off-season for tourists. But she's on her third photographic session. She refuses to have an unflattering picture on her passport. Now who in the world is going to see that picture other than customs officials and some foreign hotel clerks?"

David laughed. "Well, if it matters that much to her, maybe she should have her face lifted. She'd look marvelous then."

"Good God, whatever for?"

"Her own ego. It *is* being done, you know."

"Not your mother. She goes into a panic when she has to go to the dentist. It's not for her. Besides—" He paused as a murmur went through the restaurant. Everyone was staring at the woman making an entrance.

"It's Heidi Lanz!" George Milford exclaimed. "Now speaking of face-lifts—she must have had about ten. Good Lord, the woman is close to sixty and still looks thirty."

David stared at the Viennese actress who was accepting the embraces of the owners of the restaurant and shaking hands with the captains. She was with two young men and greeted everyone as she made her way to her table. She was magnificent-looking and, unlike Karla, Heidi Lanz had *never* retired. When her luck in pictures ran out, she came to Broadway and appeared in a musical. She did a yearly Special on television and played Vegas every year.

"Don't know how she manages to keep that figure," George Milford went on. "Did you happen to see her on television last month in that clinging dress? She has the body of a twenty-year-old."

David nodded. "I saw it with Karla. She said she was positive Heidi wore a body stocking—to get that firm look."

"Well, Karla should know," George Milford said.

"Why?" David's voice bristled. "Karla's figure is sensational. But she works at it, she—"

"Calm down, son. I just meant that Karla should know about this Heidi woman's figure. They were lovers, you know."

David colored and took a long sip of his martini. "Those were just Hollywood rumors."

"Perhaps. But I recall reading stories about them in the gossip columns. In the forties there were pictures in the newspapers of the two of them dashing around in pants—that was quite daring then. Your Karla, of course, was not ducking photographers as she does today. She was just beginning to make it here, and Heidi was the big star then—"

"Karla also almost eloped with one of her leading men," David reminded him.

"True." George Milford's eyes were still on Heidi. "But let's not forget that Heidi is married and has grandchildren now. But they say she still has her little girlfriends on the side."

"Karla cares only for men," David said.

"Still going on?" George Milford asked.

David nodded. "I see her almost every night."

"January still on the Coast?"

David nodded. "Don't worry. I keep my hand in. We correspond."

"Isn't it about time you came to some decision?"

David stared at his drink and nodded. "I'm afraid it is. Especially now that Dee is back. When January returns we'll announce our engagement. Oh, don't worry. I'll make a concerted effort to get her to really care. I don't think I can stall any longer. This California trip of hers was a bonanza for me. I suppose I know the end is in sight. That's why I can't seem to get enough of Karla."

"Marriage isn't always the end of the line," his father said.

"I think it would be with Karla and me. After all, to get January to agree to marriage will mean really devoting myself to romancing her. And Karla isn't the kind of woman you can just put on ice and say, 'I'll see you every odd Thursday.' " David's sigh was heavy.

"Marriage always means sacrifice of some sort," his father said. "Come now. Let's have another drink. I've always found that brightens any horizon."

When David left his father he stopped off at the men's shop at Bonwit's and bought the Cardin sport shirt he had admired all week. Sixty dollars. But it was just right with his gray slacks. He'd wear it tonight. There was a "Movie of the Week" on television that Karla had underlined in her *TV Guide*. She was cooking steaks, and it was one of those rare occasions when she had promised he could spend the night. "It is a long movie. We will watch it in bed. Then we will make love. And since it will be so very late, I shall let you stay over."

He didn't really need it, but he shaved again when he got home. Then he sat under the sunlamp for ten minutes. It helped to hold his Palm Beach tan. He tried the new shirt with the gray slacks; then he tried it with the navy. He went back to the gray. He tied a scarf inside the collar. Then he mixed himself a martini. Karla drank only wine. And he still needed that first martini to bolster his courage with her.

He thought about it as he sipped his drink. It was insane. In a few days it would be a year that they had been together. Yet at the start of each evening with her, he still had to deal with a case of schoolboy nerves.

Damn it! He was her lover! Right now she was making salad . . . for *him*! With her own hands! For *him*! And later when he held her in his arms she would moan and cling . . . to *him*!

When would the time ever come that he could feel casual about it, take her for granted? God, if he still felt this way after a year, how would he ever be able to break it off and start really romancing January?

He couldn't! But he wouldn't think about that now. Besides, January's letter gave no hint of any imminent arrival. She had even said she might do some other stories while she was out there. He looked at his watch.

He still had half an hour. Time for one more quick drink. Straight vodka this time. He was really off the beam. Just the thought of giving up Karla had thrown him into a tailspin.

He sipped the drink slowly. The vodka felt warm. He knew he was getting slightly high. But it didn't matter. He liked to be a little high when he saw her—it made him feel more relaxed. He felt better when he finished the drink. Maybe his father was right. Perhaps marriage to January wasn't the end of the line. Maybe he could explain the entire setup to Karla, even the ten million dollars. No, she'd despise him. Then how could he explain it and ask her to wait? *No* way! He felt a heavy wave of depression. But this was ridiculous. January was three thousand miles away. She might stay away another month, maybe longer. Meanwhile he had all this time with Karla. He would not think of next month . . . or even next week. He would enjoy each day as it happened. And tonight he was going to see Karla.

The phone startled him. He jumped up and caught it on the second ring. "David, I'm so glad I caught you." Karla's low voice sounded breathless.

"I was just leaving," he said cheerfully.

"You can't come tonight."

"Why?"

"A . . . a friend has arrived unexpectedly."

"I don't understand." It was the first time he had not accepted one of her cancellations in good grace. "Karla, we have a date."

"David—" Her voice was warm and almost pleading. "I also am very sad to cancel this evening. But this is a very old friend. From Europe . . . my manager . . . he came in unexpectedly . . . And it is about business. I must be with him."

"Oh, you mean Jeremy Haskins. The man you told me about?"

"Yes, my old friend."

"Well, it certainly won't last all evening, will it? Maybe I could come by later."

"I think not. I shall be tired."

"Maybe you won't be. Let me call. Give me your phone number, Karla."

"David, I must hang up."

"Damn it, Karla! Give me your number!"

The phone clicked in his ear. For a moment he panicked. He had gone too far. She was angry. She might not call tomorrow. She might not ever call again! He tried to get hold of himself. There was no reason to feel this way. She'd call him tomorrow and they'd laugh about this. He poured himself a big slug of vodka and added a few drops of vermouth. One more drink and he'd be drunk. But why not! Why not get good and sloshed! His face was beginning to sting from the sun-lamp treatment. He looked at himself in the mirror. The shirt looked great, the sunlamp had added a reddish glow to his tan. He had never looked better. Stood up for an old man!

He finished his drink and made another. Maybe he should call Kim. It was only six-thirty. But he didn't feel like being with Kim. He was drunk and he knew it. He poured himself another drink—straight vodka now. He sat in the dark and drank it slowly and methodi-cally. He was in his new shirt and his face stung and he had no place to go. No place he wanted to go. Except to Karla's. . . .

Well, there'd be tomorrow. . . . Maybe he should take off the shirt and save it for then. But somehow he knew he'd never wear it again. It was a bad luck shirt.

He lit a cigarette and tried to sort things out. Noth-ing drastic had happened. Okay, so he had asked for her phone number, demanded it. And she had hung up on him. Big deal. But they hadn't really had a fight. To-morrow everything would be fine. After all, this Jeremy character was an old man. She had told him how he had become her agent. How he had found her in an air raid shelter. In fact it was one of the few things she had told him about her life. And Jeremy had been a middle-aged man then. He was her oldest friend. He remembered her telling him that. "Jeremy is so good, so kind . . . You two must meet one day."

He put his glass down very slowly. "You two must meet one day." Then why hadn't she brought it about tonight? Why hadn't the three of them had dinner together in her kitchen? She didn't have to cancel him out. She and this Jeremy could talk business tomorrow . . .

Unless it wasn't Jeremy who was with her. The thought made his stomach feel tight. But there was no other man in her life! She saw him almost every night. And the nights she didn't see him, it was always because she was tired. In fact she often called him and told him what television show she was watching. No. There was no other man.

Suddenly the vision of Heidi Lanz entering "21" flashed before him. Beautiful Heidi! Heidi the dyke! She had just arrived in town too!

It couldn't be! He poured himself another drink. Then he toasted himself. David Milford. Prize jock. Prize idiot! In love with a fifty-two-year-old woman with a face-lift . . . who wouldn't even give him her phone number.

Only she wasn't just a woman. She was Karla! And right now she was with Jeremy Haskins, and he was drunk and imagining crazy things . . .

Goddammit! Why did he have to see Heidi Lanz at "21" today? And why did the old man have to put that idea in his head? Sure, he had heard rumors about Karla. But then he always figured most European women had had that kind of a fling in their past just as he was sure all English men had tried it with boys. But Karla couldn't really love a woman. Not the way she reacted in his arms, the way she clung to him . . . No. She was with Jeremy now.

He felt he couldn't stay in the apartment another moment. He dashed out and walked down Park Avenue. The air cleared his head. He cut over to Lexington. And kept walking. He knew he was heading toward Karla's apartment building. Well, why not . . . why *not*! He could just walk in. The doorman would think he was expected. So would the elevator man. He'd ring her bell. If it was Jeremy and she was angry, he'd beg forgiveness, he'd—he'd tell her it was his birthday. Yes, that was a good excuse. He'd tell her he had to see her, even if it was for a moment. And then even if she said he could stay, he'd leave. Yes, that was it. Even if she was warm and felt guilty, he'd refuse to stay—just one birthday drink—and then leave. But at least when he went home, he'd be able to sleep.

When he reached her block his courage evaporated. He cut over to First Avenue and went to a bar. He had a double vodka. He felt better. There was nothing to be nervous about. He was building it all up in his own mind. She'd probably laugh, think he was charming, young and impetuous. He walked down the street. When the doorman nodded he felt reassured. He felt even better as the elevator man discussed the Yankees' winning streak as he took him up to the fifteenth floor.

He walked down the hall. He waited until the elevator door closed. Then he stood in front of her door for a moment. There was no sound inside. No television. He hesitated. It still wasn't too late. He could turn around and leave and she would never know. He started back for the elevator. But what would the elevator operator think? And the doorman? They knew she was in.

He went back to her door and quickly rang the buzzer. He could actually feel his heart pounding in his throat. He rang again. Then he heard footsteps. She opened the door cautiously—and kept the safety chain on. When she saw him the large gray eyes went dark with anger.

"What do you want?" her voice was cold.

He couldn't believe this was happening. Karla, who always flung the door open for him—Karla peering through the small chained opening, staring at him like an intruder.

"It's my birthday." His voice sounded thick. Not light and easy as he had planned.

"Go away," she said.

He wedged his foot in the door. "It's my birthday.

I just want one birthday drink with you . . . and Jeremy."

"I told you to go away!"

"I won't leave." He tried to smile, but he was frightened. The whole thing was out of hand. She was really angry. There was no gracious way out now. He had to get inside, he had to explain how much he loved her . . . How he couldn't live like this, not being able to call.

"If you don't leave, I'll have to call for help," she said.

Oh God, he had ruined everything. "Karla, forgive me. I'm sorry . . ." He backed away and in that split second she slammed the door in his face.

He stood there unable to believe it. Karla. Doing this to him! The bitch! Of course there was no Jeremy inside. She was probably with Heidi Lanz. He rang her bell again. He banged against the door. "Open the door," he shouted. "Open it and prove you have your old business manager in there. Open it and I'll leave. Just prove to me you're telling the truth!"

He waited a few seconds. He was aware someone down the hall had opened the door and peered out. He felt his face burning. The door down the hall finally closed. He rang Karla's buzzer again. "Let me in, damn you . . . let me in!" He kicked at the door. Then he took out a match and stuck it in the buzzer. "I'm going to stand here and wait," he shouted. "I'll wait if I have to wait all night. To see who comes out of that apartment." He gave the door another violent kick. He knew he had lost all control but was powerless to stop. He heard several doors opening in the hall.

Then he heard the elevator door open. And he felt two pairs of strong arms grasp him. He fought and lashed out. The doorman and the elevator man were trying to get him away from Karla's door. His old smiling friends—the doorman who had taken all the dollar tips, the elevator man who had discussed the Yankees with him. They were trying to drag him down the hall.

"Take your hands off me," he shouted. "Miss Karla just doesn't hear the bell. She's expecting me!"

"Take it easy, son," the doorman said. "She called down and asked us to come and get you. Said you were making a disturbance."

He couldn't believe it. Karla was having him thrown out! He stared at them. And then at the door. He gave it a final kick. "You bull dyke," he shouted. "You double-crossing bull dyke. I know who you've got in there, Heidi. *Heidi Lanz! Heidi.* Not Jeremy . . . *Heidi Lanz!*"

Doors opened. The other tenants on the floor stared in amazement. Tenants, who in the past had looked at him with envy because he had access to their glamorous neighbor, were watching him being dragged down the hall by the doorman and elevator man. He was kicking and yelling. He heard a rip and knew it was his new shirt. She was having him thrown out! Thrown out! This couldn't be happening. It was all a nightmare.

Then he was in the elevator, and the doorman relaxed his grip. "Now listen, son. Looks like you've had a little too much to drink tonight. Let me put you in a cab and you be on your way. Tomorrow's another day. You send her a few flowers and everything will be as good as new."

He wrenched himself away from the man's hold. He walked outside and tried to stand erect. "There won't be any tomorrow. And I'll never send flowers to that lesbian cunt again! And don't worry about getting me a cab. I don't want anything from any of you. I'll never set foot near this building again." Then he stared up at the windows on the fifteenth floor. "I hate you, you bitch . . ." he muttered. Then he staggered down the street.

Karla stood by the window and watched him until he was out of sight. Then she walked to the bathroom and tapped on the door. Her face was drawn and white. "It's all right, Dee. You can come out now. I don't think David will bother us anymore."

TWENTY-FOUR

DEE STRETCHED OUT in the foamy bathtub. WPAT was playing some old Sinatra songs. They were beautiful. The whole world was beautiful. May was such a beautiful month in New York. April had been a beautiful month too. Any month was beautiful when Karla was around. This past winter in Palm Beach had marked their longest separation. Five long months. It had been murderous. There were times when she had to summon every ounce of will power to keep from picking up the phone and pleading with Karla to come down. Maybe it had worked, because on her return she found Karla actually eager to see her.

Of course there had been that dreadful night when David had hammered at the door like a bull in heat. She would never have believed David could lose control like that. But he had been drinking. She hadn't heard too much of the racket—she had been so terrified when the commotion had begun that she had dashed into the bathroom. But it obviously finished David with Karla. He was no longer one of her "nice little" men who took her to the ballet or an art movie.

Oddly enough, David didn't seem to be suffering any loss. According to the columns, he was seeing that Dutch model occasionally, and he talked about January constantly.

He had been heartbroken when she had been unable

to come to Palm Beach over Easter. Of course it was an important assignment writing a story on a man like Tom Colt. She had been in California for some time now. She wondered if there was something going on between them. Ridiculous! Tom Colt was married and much too old-fashioned for January. Mike had been oddly unenthusiastic about the importance of January's assignment. He had insisted on flying out to see her. He had stayed almost a week and when he returned everything seemed fine. Well, she'd have to get around to changing her will. Now that David posed no threat as far as Karla was concerned there was no reason to care whether or not he married January.

When she got out of the tub, she put in a call to George Milford. He came on the phone immediately. "Dee . . . I was just leaving. How nice to hear from you."

"George, I want to change my will."

"Fine. Is it urgent?"

"No, but let's meet tomorrow afternoon."

"Well, that's why I asked if it was urgent. Margaret and I are leaving tomorrow for Paris. Her sister's daughter is getting married, and we haven't had a holiday abroad for some time. So we're doing it right . . . going by boat . . . taking a whole month off. We're sailing tomorrow."

"Oh—" Dee bit her lip thoughtfully.

"But if it's urgent, I can wait in my office now. It's five-thirty. We can draw up the changes. I don't mind staying here for a few hours tonight . . . that is, if you are free. We can go over things together and I'll make notes. Then tomorrow morning I'll have it typed up and if you can come around, say, at ten, we can have it witnessed and notarized and—"

Karla was expecting her at six-thirty. This would take too much time. "No, George, it's not that urgent. It can hold until you return. Have a nice trip, and give Margaret my best."

She hung up and began to dress. Mike was at the Friars Club. She had told him she was going to a Class

Reunion. And she insisted he stay there for dinner and play cards. "I've *got* to go. It's something I do every year. There's just twenty of us, and we sit around for hours discussing our days at Miss Briarly's. And if you get home before me, don't wait up."

The marriage was crowding her. With Karla so available, it tortured her to be with Mike. Ever since her return from Palm Beach, Karla was always exuberant whenever Dee said she was free. And lately there had been none of the old excuses. ("Oh, Dee. I've invited the Maestro over for a steak. He hasn't worked for so long and he's going to the motion picture home soon.") Karla's reasons had always been valid . . . but they had come just often enough to keep Dee off balance. Yet there hadn't been one excuse since her return. Each time she called and said, "I can get out tonight," Karla sounded joyous. "I am so glad!" . . . "I await eagerly . . ." or "I have been invited to a dinner at Boris's, but I will cancel."

Of course she could see Karla during the day if she wanted to tag along and do things Karla's way. But somehow she felt a loss of dignity in trailing along after Karla, sitting in some dreary studio and watching her do bar exercises. She had done that in the first few years when just seeing Karla—being allowed to be with her—was a privilege. Oddly enough, after all these years, she still felt a sense of giddiness each time she saw Karla. But once their relationship had become firmly established, she felt it was demeaning for her to sit around like a stupefied fan. She also wouldn't go walking in the snow and rain. She wasn't like Karla, who looked fantastic with snow on her hair or rain on her face. Dee's nose and eyes ran when it got cold. Karla could stand under a shower and come out and towel-dry her hair and look magnificent. Dee would be lost without a hairdresser to fix her hair each day.

No, the only way to see Karla and keep their relationship on an equal basis was to have Karla as a houseguest in one of her homes . . . or to see her in New York at night. No woman over forty looked glamorous in daylight. Dee had tried everything. Whatever makeup base she used looked too pink, too orange or too pasty. But at night she looked marvelous. Especially in front of a fire, or sitting with Karla and having dinner by candle-light. She had taken a firm stand against eating in the kitchen. There was no romance to it. Besides, she looked dreadful in that light. Karla always looked slightly tanned, she never needed a makeup base. Karla was Karla—there was no one like her. Even after eight years it still seemed unbelievable that Karla belonged to her. No . . . not belonged. Karla would never belong to anyone. Not even to Jeremy Haskins, who she said had been her manager and great friend. She openly ad-mitted they had made an attempt at being lovers but it hadn't worked. Dee had met Jeremy when he came to the States in 1966, and when she saw his white hair and bent shoulders, she had been so relieved she had even given a dinner party in his honor. And each year she sent him a Christmas gift.

On an impulse she took out her checkbook and wrote a check for ten thousand dollars. She had stopped trying to surprise Karla with gifts. Karla never wore jewelry. And the sable coat she had given her was used like a trench coat. She walked in the snow in it, and to the re-hearsal hall and back. Karla only really came alive when she was given money. It was a phenomenon Dee couldn't understand. After all, Karla had plenty of money. My God . . . all those years when she made those pic-tures. And she spent nothing now . . . just the main-tenance on the apartment. It was a fabulous apartment as far as the physical layout went. A decorator could turn it into a showplace. But Dee doubted if there was even five thousand dollars' worth of furniture in the apartment. Of course, it was kept immaculate. Karla thought nothing of scrubbing floors and windows her-self. And there were the paintings—a Monet, two Raoul Dufys, a Vlaminck, and the Daumier sketches. But they had all been gifts. And in answer to Dee's "Why do you need a ten-room duplex when you use only three rooms?" Karla had shrugged and said, "It was a gift

. . . and it is now worth twice the original price." She had given up trying to rationalize Karla's eccentricities. Eccentricities hell! Karla was downright penurious. Even her Christmas presents to Dee were what Karla called "gag" presents. A beer mug saying "Souvenir of New York" . . . a red flannel nightgown . . . a Polish ornament for the Christmas tree. Dee chalked it up as a wartime neurosis. All refugees were slightly peculiar.

Dee left the house at six-fifteen. She had let the chauffeur go. She took a cab that rocked and wheezed its way across town; but nothing could disturb her high spirits. It was spring and the night was beautiful and in a few minutes she was going to see Karla. Oh God, if only she could hold time still. Make tonight last forever. She played a game with the traffic lights. When the cab came to a red light, she'd count. One . . . then spell it . . . O-N-E. Two . . . T-W-O. For as many numbers as she could say and spell before the light changed . . . that's how many more months she and Karla would have together. She got to sixteen on one light . . . but by the time she got to Second Avenue, she had developed some expertise and was up to thirty-five. She frowned. That was just three more years. No, she wouldn't settle for that. They'd be together forever. Oh God, if she could only believe that. If she could really believe that Karla would never leave her . . . she'd never have married Mike. But even during their most intimate moments, Dee was aware that Karla could never be really possessed by anyone. And if Karla ever thought she was Dee's whole life, Karla might disappear . . . perhaps forever. No, Mike was her safety valve, her crutch of sanity. But Mike was also a problem . . . the devious lies she had to tell him to get her "free nights." In July, she'd insist that Karla come to Marbella. But right now it was only the beginning of May. That meant six weeks in New York to worry about. She thought she had been very clever about her enthusiasm for Cannes with Mike. There was no backgammon tournament in Monte Carlo, and she never had the slightest intention of going there in the first place. But it had to be planned carefully, and so far everything was going according to schedule. The suite at the Carlton was booked for May 14. She planned to wait until the day before and then tell him that the tournament was canceled. But she would insist that he go— the suite was reserved and he deserved two marvelous weeks with all his movie friends. She'd just rest in New York and attend to getting her wardrobe together for the summer. She had the speech all rehearsed. He had to go without her. Then she would have two fantastic weeks with Karla . . . they could be together every night!

Karla was waiting for her when she arrived. Her face was scrubbed and the heavy hair was pulled back with a barrette. She threw her arms around Dee and led her to the table near the window. It was set for dinner, and Karla pointed to the candles. "Look. I bought them today. They do not need the stick to sit in . . . they melt into themselves. Oh, it was wonderful! This marvelous little shop and the little man didn't recognize me. He liked me just for myself. And he took such pains letting me smell all the different smells. Tonight we have gardenia. Dee, do you like gardenia? I love it . . . I hope you do. . . ."

"Of course I do." In the candlelight, with the dusk just beginning to settle on the East River, Karla looked like one of her most perfect movie stills. The shadows falling across her face, the hollow under her cheekbones. Suddenly Dee realized she was staring. She reached into her bag. "Karla, I brought you a little gift."

Karla didn't even look at the check. She smiled and slipped it into her desk drawer. "Thank you, Dee. Now come, sit down. I have prepared a big salad of shrimp and lobster. And look . . . a pitcher of sangria. We shall have a feast."

And that night when they made love, Karla was joyously demonstrative. In fact her whole mood was lighter than usual. Later as they lay together she sang some Polish song she had known as a girl. Then, as if embarrassed because she had revealed some hidden facet of herself, she jumped out of bed and switched on the television set. "There's a good late movie, but I know you prefer the news. I am going to take a shower. Tell me if anything important happens to our sad little world."

Dee watched the news. She heard Karla singing in the shower. Karla was happy. And she was happy. Yet along with her own happiness there was a sense of despair. Because in a short time she would have to leave and go back to Mike. She reached over to the night table and decided to try one of Karla's strong English cigarettes. As she picked up the pack, an envelope fell to the floor. It was Karla's telephone bill. She was suddenly curious. The amount had to be minuscule. Karla rarely called anyone, and if she did, she merely stated her business or request. There was no such thing as a telephone conversation with Karla. Dee took the bill out of the envelope. Her eyebrows lifted when she glanced at the total. Four hundred and thirty-one dollars! She looked at it again. How could Karla run up a bill like that? She examined it carefully. Karla had not exceeded the maximum in local calls. But there was a long list of overseas calls to England—Bostwick 3322. Sixteen calls to that number! And all of the calls lasted longer than three minutes. There were three to another number with a Lowick exchange and two to a Belgravia exchange. But sixteen to Bostwick 3322. She wrote the numbers down on a slip of paper, shoved it into her bag, and replaced the phone bill under Karla's cigarettes. But when Karla came out of the shower and made love to her again, the entire incident went out of her thoughts. She didn't think of it again until she went home and found the slip of paper in her bag. She put it in her jewel case. Karla probably had some business in London. Maybe she was in constant touch with Jeremy. Perhaps her phone bill was high every month. People who were known to be penurious often had one crazy extravagance. Perhaps with Karla it was transatlantic phone calls.

The next day was one of those rare days, when Dee had been unable to connect with Karla. There was no point calling in the morning; Karla would be out walking. And at one, when Karla would be just getting home, Dee was trapped at a luncheon at the Plaza for Baby

Town, U.S.A., a rehabilitation home for pregnant girls who were on narcotics. Dee wasn't terribly interested in the whole thing, but it was a good way to get proper newspaper exposure. All the right people were on the committee, and this would be good for her image.

She had called Karla at five, but Karla wasn't in. Then just as she was about to try again, Ernest had arrived to do her hair. She and Mike had to go to a ghastly sit-down dinner at Princess Marina's Park Avenue apartment to honor some Senator, which meant they'd have to sit and listen to his witticisms on Washington. But the Princess gave great parties in Marbella, and if the Princess had this thing about being *au courant* about politics . . . well, she'd just have to sit through one of those nights.

The following morning she lay in bed with her breakfast tray, waiting until twelve-thirty when Karla would be home from her walk. She was also trying to think of an excuse to get away from Mike for the night. The rest of the week was filled, but tonight was free. Mike had said something about seeing two movies in one night. He actually liked sitting in those filthy theaters, and even ate popcorn. In fact he was trying to talk her into building a projection room at the Winter Palace so they could run their own movies. Movies bored Dee. She adored watching all of Karla's reruns, but today's pictures held little interest for her. She hated those dreary motorcycle pictures with young people where everyone wore blue jeans and smoked pot. She could remember when you went to a movie and looked forward to seeing the fashions. But movies were ugly and dirty now. Her own life was much more exciting and beautiful.

She glanced through the newspapers. She had made *Women's Wear* with yesterday's luncheon. Good picture —she would show it to Karla. But right now she had to think of a plan to get out of being with Mike tonight. Backgammon was no longer an excuse. He *liked* backgammon. Dear Lord, why had she ever taught him? She looked at the clock. Maybe she should tell him to go to the club and play golf, that she wanted to—she wanted to *what*? It infuriated her that she had to lie here and think of an excuse. She was Dee Milford Granger. She was supporting this man. Why couldn't she just say, "I want out tonight," as she had with all the others. Because deep down she knew she just couldn't say that to Mike. He might just say, "Okay. You can have out for good." Especially since he didn't seem as concerned about that daughter of his. He never seemed to mention her lately. Maybe that ten million she had left in trust had relaxed him. Well, when he got back, he'd learn that it wasn't an irrevocable trust. She'd change all that. Put David back as an executor. Oh, she'd let the ten million stand for January, but there would be a codicil . . . the ten million would go to January only if Mike Wayne was the husband of Dee Milford Granger. She began to smile. Of course . . . then she'd be able to walk out any night she chose. But meanwhile she had to think of something for tonight. She couldn't invent a fictitious girlfriend for backgammon anymore. He knew all of her friends. This was ridiculous! All of her life she had always done just as she pleased, and now, for the most important person in her life, she had to scheme like a criminal to get a free night.

Maybe Karla might have an idea. Not that she was ever inventive. Dee loved her insanely, but she was still a dumb Polack. It was only ten of twelve; but she tried Karla. Sometimes she got home early. She dialed, but there was no answer. Of course . . . this was Thursday. The maid wasn't in. Imagine running that place with a maid that only came in three times a week!

She picked up the *Daily News* and leafed through it. The Princess had gotten only half a column. She and Mike were mentioned. But it was the Senator who had gotten all the publicity. She tossed the paper on the floor. It fell with the centerfold open. She stared for a moment. Then she jumped out of bed and grabbed the paper. There was Karla . . . hiding her face from the camera, arriving at Heathrow Airport.

Karla was in London!

She rolled the paper into a ball and tossed it across

the room. All the while she had been lying there planning—wondering how to be with her—that bitch was in
London.

London!

She got out of bed and rushed to her jewel case and
found the piece of paper with the three numbers. Then
she went to the telephone. Noon. That meant it was
five in the afternoon in London. She placed a person-to-
person call to Anthony Pierson. The firm of Pierson
and Maitland handled all of her business in London. In
less than five minutes, they rang back and Anthony
Pierson was on. He was delighted to hear from her.
They talked about the wonderful spell of good weather
London was having, about some of her holdings . . .
Then, trying to sound casual, she said, "Tony, I know
this isn't in your line at all . . . but . . . well . . .
you see, I have to find out about three phone numbers
in London. Oh, it's not for me. It's—it's my stepdaughter. Yes, you see . . . she lives with us and I just happened to come across my phone bill and there are three
London numbers that she's been calling. And she's only
twenty-one. And naturally I worry. You know how it is
. . . some of your rock artists come over here and girls
of her age fancy themselves in love—" She laughed.
"Yes . . . that's exactly it . . . I wouldn't want her
to make a nuisance of herself or get involved with the
wrong kind of people. So if you could check out those
numbers . . . Oh, Tony, I do appreciate it." She gave
him the numbers, then she said, "How long will this
take? . . . Only an hour? Oh Tony, you are divine."

She took a bath and kept her eye riveted to the light
on the phone on the dressing table. She watched it as
she made up. And precisely at one the light came on,
and Anthony Pierson was on the line.

"I do have the information," he said. "But it baffles
me a bit, I must say. The Bostwick number belongs to
a private home near Ascot. The Lowick number belongs
to Jeremy Haskins, a retired gentleman who has a bit of
fame because he is often seen with Karla when she is
here . . . incidentally you do know her, do you not?

She's here now, staying at the Dorchester. And the Belgravia number belongs to a well-known psychiatrist. It does seem a bit confusing, because none of the numbers seem to add up to anyone a twenty-one-year-old girl would care to phone."

"Who lives in the house in Ascot?"

"A couple named Harrington. They have a daughter. I pretended I was the postal clerk and needed information on them for rezoning. I thought it was dreadfully clever of me . . . don't you think?"

"How old is the daughter?"

"I didn't ask, but the Harringtons sounded as though they were well up in their fifties or sixties."

"Tony, I have to find out more about them all. Especially the psychiatrist."

"Well, this is all a bit out of my line . . . but I do know a chap . . . a Donald Whyte . . . sort of a private investigator . . . he's quite trustworthy . . ."

"Yes . . . please . . . find out everything you can. Don't worry about Jeremy Haskins. My husband was a producer, so it's quite possible my stepdaughter would know him. But find out about the Harringtons and their daughter."

She hung up and tried to control the panic she felt. Maybe the Harringtons were old friends of Karla's . . . maybe they were people she had met through Jeremy . . . or old friends she had made when she first came to London . . .

Sixteen calls in one month!

No friend was worth sixteen calls to Karla. Unless she was in love. Maybe the girl was rich and was calling Karla sixteen times a month as well. Maybe they talked every night . . . or twice a day. That bitch probably had a double life going. Ascot was lovely countryside. The girl *had* to be rich. Maybe that was why she was always taking off so secretly.

Maybe the girl had broken up with her . . . yes, that could have been it. That would explain the sixteen calls. Karla begging to come back . . . it would also explain why Karla had suddenly been so nice and warm to her

. . . No, she couldn't picture Karla begging anyone for anything. But *sixteen calls in one month!*

When Mike came home that evening, Dee had already made her plans. She was going to learn what Karla was up to and face her with it! But she had to play it carefully with Mike.

She went to the two movies with him . . . and later when they were at Sardi's, she made her first move. She stared into space and sighed heavily.

They had ordered steak. He was almost finished with his. He looked over at her untouched plate. "Aren't you hungry?"

"No . . . I . . . Oh, Mike . . . I feel like an idiot."

"What about?" He helped himself to some of her steak.

"I made a stupid error."

"What kind of an error? It can't be the end of the world."

"Mike, the backgammon tournament is in London."

"When?"

"Oh . . . I think the fifteenth, sixteenth, and seventeenth."

"Well, no big deal! We'll get to Cannes a few days later. Are you going to eat the rest of your steak?"

She pushed the plate toward him. "Mike, I was thinking . . . Look, I'm not that wild about Cannes . . . and it is *your* town. I mean, you'll know everyone . . . and you'll want to be with your old friends . . . and there is the Casino. I'm not a real gambler, not at the tables anyway, and—"

He looked at her closely. "Stop with the build-up. What are you trying to tell me?"

"Mike . . . I'd love to go to London and—"

"I said we'll go."

"But I'll feel so guilty each day I keep you from your film festival. I have friends in London. I'd like to stay there a week. Then go to Paris and buy some clothes. And then join you in Cannes for the end."

"Fine."

"What did you say?"

"I said fine. We'll leave on the fourteenth, drop you in London, and then I'll take the plane on to Nice. I'll send it back for you and you can join me whenever you like."

"Oh, Mike . . . you're an angel."

"Look, babe, it's a two-way street. No one says you have to like a film festival. I think you'll have a great time in London."

"It won't be great," she said. "But it will be interesting."

TWENTY-FIVE

DEE SAT in Anthony Pierson's office and stared at the pictures. She was still off balance from the time change. She had arrived in London at ten the night before; but it had only been five in the afternoon, New York time. She had called Tony Pierson at home. He said he had a full report, but he hardly thought it would be relevant to her stepdaughter. She told him she'd be in his office the following morning at eleven. Then she drugged herself to sleep with three Seconals. She couldn't bear a sleepless night alone in London. There was no all-night television, and she couldn't concentrate on reading. She had checked into the Grosvenor House because Karla was staying at the Dorchester. She didn't want to run into Karla. Not yet.

She felt the beginnings of a migraine headache as she sat in Anthony Pierson's quiet conservative office, but she managed to appear calm.

She leafed through the pictures he had given her. "They're excellent," she said tonelessly.

Anthony Pierson nodded. "This chap, Donald Whyte, the one who did the—shall we say research? He covered that house with a telescopic lens for days. The poor chap actually sat in a tree. The psychiatrist is on holiday . . . left two days ago . . . so we didn't fare too well there. But the shots of Karla and the girl are quite fantastic, don't you think? Of course, I got the negatives

. . . that was part of the arrangement. Whyte is a top man and quite reliable, but what with Karla still being very much of a public figure, I think it's quite fortunate I took this precaution."

"For God's sake," Dee said testily. "It's not as if he found them in bed together!"

Anthony Pierson nodded. "Quite right. But that one picture . . . with the girl's arms around Karla's neck . . . and the other where they are kissing . . . and look here . . . walking with their arms entwined. No, they've not been caught in bed . . . but it would make for jolly good speculation in one of those scandal magazines."

Dee stared at the pictures. Her head was beginning to throb. How could she compete with anyone as young and lovely as this girl?

"She's very beautiful," Dee said slowly.

"Quite fabulous, isn't she? Whyte learned that the Harringtons are not her parents. They obviously work for her. Because the girl's name is Zinaida Jones. The house is rented; it's a lovely house. Not too large, but secluded—nice piece of land and all that. Karla has been there every day. On three occasions she stayed over-night."

Dee's hand shook as she fumbled for a cigarette. She stared at the girl. The picture was fuzzy from enlargement. She inhaled her cigarette deeply. "Have you got any aspirins, Tony? I'm afraid I've a bit of jet lag."

"Of course." He went to a chest in the bathroom. When he came out, Dee was still studying the pictures.

"It does look rather peculiar, doesn't it?" he said. "Looks like the great Karla has found herself a bit of new young love life. But then . . . there's always been that rumor about the lady, hasn't there?"

"I've heard it," Dee said. "But I know Karla. She's been to my home, and I never saw anything that would give it any credence."

"Except these pictures, I'd say," Anthony Pierson said. "Pretty damning. Why can't these people confine their amorous inclinations to the bedroom? Why would she walk around the grounds with her arms around that girl?"

"Perhaps because she didn't know Mr. Donald Whyte

was sitting up in a tree with a telescopic camera. You say it is a secluded place?"

"Has about an acre of its own ground. But my dear Mrs. Wayne, how can any of this affect your stepdaughter?"

Dee shook her head. "Well . . . perhaps . . . perhaps she knows this Zinaida."

"Oh." For a moment Anthony Pierson colored slightly. "Well . . . oh . . . I see. All the calls . . . you are thinking that perhaps your stepdaughter was, ah . . . friendly with this Zinaida Jones?"

Dee shrugged. "Why not? She went to school in Switzerland. She was raised in girls' schools." She stood up. "Do you have the exact address of the house?"

"Yes. Right here. It's about an hour's drive from town."

"Thank you. And will you take care of Mr. Whyte's services and send the entire bill to me? Send it around tomorrow to the Grosvenor. For obvious reasons, I wouldn't want this to go to New York."

She tried to think of a plan of action as she drove to the country. The chauffeur knew the way, and now they were out of London, coming into lush green scenery, approaching Ascot. . . . But then what? She couldn't just ring the bell and say to this Zinaida Jones: "Look . . . she's mine!" Perhaps if she got off outside of the house and tried to catch sight of them. The whole thing was so distasteful that she shrank back in the seat. But she was determined to go through with it. All the years of devotion she had given Karla . . . all the "gifts." Had Karla used that last ten-thousand-dollar check to dash off to be with her young new love? For the first time she knew how a man felt to be cuckolded. Cuckolded! Now how did she ever come up with an expression like that? But that's exactly how she felt. Cuckolded! It was a great word. She couldn't say she was being cheated on . . . no doubt Karla had done that off and on all the time. She had never really asked her, just as Karla never asked about her sex life with Mike. She had tried to tell Karla about it once . . . how she really just put up with Mike . . . how relieved she was when the sex part was over . . . because that meant he wouldn't bother her for at least two or three days. She thought about it now. Funny . . . in the last few months, weeks had gone by without Mike coming near her. She hadn't even noticed. The thought disturbed her. Not that she wanted him to touch her . . . but was she that unattractive? She knew there was a certain softness to her body . . . her thighs . . . her stomach. She was aware of it when she was lying close to Karla, because Karla didn't have an ounce of spare flesh. But she hadn't minded her own soft body . . . somehow it had made her feel more feminine with Karla. But why had Mike stayed away? Was it too much golf? He was always gambling lately. She wondered how much he had won.

But that wasn't her concern. Right now her concern was Karla . . . and the new girl. But maybe she wasn't a new girl. Maybe they had been together for some time. Maybe Karla was going through a "young" period. There had been David for a time . . . now this girl. . . .

The driver pulled up along a huge row of hedges. "This is the house, madam. The entrance is down the road a bit. But you said you wanted to stop here."

"Yes. I want to surprise some old friends. If the car comes in the driveway, well . . . there wouldn't be any surprise, would there?"

"No, madam."

She wondered if he believed her. The English could be so damned expressionless when they wanted to be. He probably thought she was surprising a lover. Well, she was!

The small iron gate had no lock. She opened it and walked up the driveway. It was beginning to rain. She was wearing a raincoat and she put her scarf over her head. It was a very modest driveway; but the grounds were well tended. The house was Tudor in style. There was a small English car parked out front.

Dee approached slowly. She wondered if this Zinaida owned a dog. It would be horrible if some English mastiff lunged at her throat. She could see the headline: DEE MILFORD GRANGER ATTACKED BY DOG FOR TRESPASSING. God, how would she ever explain that?

There were lights inside the house. Zinaida was probably home . . . or was she off walking the countryside with her arm around Karla's waist like in the pictures? Karla liked to walk in any kind of weather. And she could just bet that Zinaida pretended to adore it too.

She tiptoed over to the window. It was a cozy living room, nothing pretentious; and no one was there. Perhaps if she went around to the back . . . Karla always loved kitchens . . .

"Why don't you come in . . . it's very wet outside."

She gasped when she heard the voice. She turned . . . Karla was standing behind her. The rain was on her face and she was wearing a bandana and a trenchcoat.

"Karla . . . I . . ."

"Let's go inside. It is damp and cold."

Karla opened the door. Dee noticed she had a key. She wanted to run. This was the end. . . . She never should have come. Karla's face was a mask. She was obviously cold with anger and she would probably tell her that everything was over between them. Oh God, why had she done this? She had once seen a play where the mistress had done her best to have the wife find out . . . because once the wife confronted her husband with the evidence, there was nothing for him to do but admit it. And if Karla admitted it, Dee would have to walk away. Even though she would die inside . . . she'd have to walk away with pride. Because without pride . . . there could be no relationship. Yet at the same time she longed to fall on her knees and tell Karla to forget she was there . . . to forget this whole horrible incident.

Karla hung up her coat on a rack near the door. She was wearing gabardine slacks and a man's shirt. Her hair was long and straight. She looked weary but as beautiful as ever.

Dee stood very still. Karla turned and pointed to the rack. "Take off your coat. It is wet."

Dee took it off and knew that her hair was squashed down by the scarf. She probably never looked worse. And somewhere in this house—waiting for Karla—was this gorgeous young creature.

"Sit down," Karla said. "I will get some brandy." She disappeared into another room.

Dee looked around. There was a picture of Karla in a large frame. Then there was a picture of a German shepherd dog, obviously long deceased, because the girl with it was a child. Probably one of Zinaida's childhood pets. Where was she? Probably upstairs, respecting Karla's desire for privacy like everyone else, giving in to Karla's moods.

Karla returned with a bottle of brandy and poured two glasses. Dee watched with surprise the way Karla tossed down the drink in one gulp. Then she sat down. "All right, Dee. . . . I'm not going to ask how you found me. I'll save you that embarrassment."

Tears came to Dee's eyes. She got up and walked toward the charred fireplace. "I'd give ten years of my life if I could take back this afternoon."

"Do I mean that much to you?" Karla's voice was almost gentle.

Dee turned toward her, forcing back her tears. "Do you mean that much to me? Oh, God . . ." She walked across the room and went to her bag for a cigarette. She lit it and turned to Karla. "No . . . you don't mean very much. Just enough to make me sick every time you take off . . . enough to make me become a devious liar and a sneak with my husband . . . sending him off to Cannes alone while I . . . I . . . called a friend . . . and learned of your whereabouts . . . and found out about Zinaida. And I must be some kind of masochist. Instead of just putting you out of my life, I come out here . . . wanting to see her for myself . . . wanting— Oh, God knows what. Why should I torture myself like this? I know she's years younger than I . . . and very beautiful . . . and I wish to God I hadn't come . . . because if I hadn't . . . we'd still be together."

"Where did you see her?" Karla asked.

Dee opened her bag and dropped the pictures in Karla's lap.

Karla studied them. She looked at Dee in amazement. "This is the work of a paparazzi."

Dee shook her head helplessly. "No . . . it's an Eng-

lishman named Donald Whyte. Don't worry . . . I
have the negatives. Look, Karla . . . I have my car
outside . . . I'd better go." She started for the door. She
reached for her raincoat and turned to Karla. "Just tell
me one thing . . . how long has this affair been going
on?"

Karla looked down at the pictures . . . then at Dee.
Then with a sad smile she shook her head. "Yes . . .
I see . . . the pictures . . . What else do you know?"

"I know that you've been spending several nights
here."

"Ah, your man is thorough. But not thorough enough
. . . right?"

"Do you enjoy this game?" Dee snatched her coat
from the wooden rack.

"No . . . I am suffering inside more than you would
believe. But since you have come such a long way . . .
and gone to so much trouble . . . I think that before
you leave, you should meet Zinaida."

"No." Dee struggled to get into her coat. With a sudden movement, Karla sprang to the center of the room
and pushed her into a chair.

"You have snooped . . . and you now wish to walk
away. Well, a snoop deserves to see the finish. Perhaps
it will teach you some kind of lesson in the future." Karla
walked to the staircase and shouted, "Mrs. Harrington."

A small gray-haired lady peered over the balustrade.
"Tell Zinaida to tear herself away from the TV set and
come downstairs. I want her to meet a friend of mine."

Karla poured herself another glass of brandy. She
pointed to Dee's untouched glass. "Drink yours. You'll
need it."

Dee kept her eyes fastened on the stairs. Then she saw
the girl. She was more beautiful than the photographs.
She was tall, almost as tall as Karla. Her hair was blonde
and it fell to her shoulders. She looked much younger
than her pictures. Dee guessed her to be about January's
age.

Karla's smile was gentle. "Come in, Zinaida. We have
a guest. This is Mrs. Wayne."

The girl smiled at Dee. Then she turned to Karla.

"Could I have some chocolate cake? Mrs. Harrington just made it this afternoon and she said I can't have it until dinner."

"We do what Mrs. Harrington says," Karla said slowly. "Perhaps she wanted the cake to be a surprise."

"But now you know about it, so it's no surprise. So can I have it? Just one piece? Please? I'm so dreadfully sick of those oatmeal cookies she always makes."

"Go back to your telly," Karla said.

The girl sighed in disgust. Then she pointed at Dee. "Is she staying for dinner?"

"Shall we ask her?"

Zinaida smiled. "Sure, as long as you tell me the Red Shoes story before I go to bed." She ran out of the room.

For a moment Dee stared after her. Then she looked at Karla. "She's very beautiful . . . but what was all that? Some kind of a private joke? I thought she acted like a twelve-year-old."

"Actually, she's ten."

"What are you talking about?"

"Her mentality. It is that of a ten-year-old."

"And she's your great love?"

"She's my daughter."

For a moment, Dee couldn't speak. "Drink your brandy," Karla said. This time Dee swallowed it in one gulp. Then Karla poured them each another. "Take off your coat and stay for dinner. That is, if you like chocolate cake."

"Karla, when did you have this child?"

"Thirty-one years ago."

"But . . . she looks so young."

Karla shrugged. "They always look young. Perhaps because they do not have grown-up worries."

"Do you . . . want to tell me about it?"

"After dinner. But first—I suggest you dismiss your car. I will drive you back into town."

It had been an easy dinner. Dee was so relieved at the change of events that she was filled with affection for the beautiful child-woman who tore into the food and chattered incessantly throughout the meal. Mr. and Mrs. Harrington were obviously the couple who took care of

Zinaida. Dee noticed Zinaida addressed Karla as "God-mother." When dinner was finished she jumped up and said, "And now Godmother is going to tell me 'Red Shoes.'"

Dee sat spellbound as Karla half talked, half danced, and half acted out the story. She had never seen Karla give this much of herself. But her warmth toward Zinaida was fluid and easy. At nine o'clock, Mrs. Harrington appeared. "Come, Zinaida . . . Godmother has company, and it is time for a bath and bed."

"Will you come up later and hear my prayers?"

"Of course," Karla said as she kissed the girl.

Karla added more wood to the fire. She sat and stared at it morosely. "She is very lovely, isn't she?"

"She's fantastic-looking," Dee said. "I see a lot of you in the bone structure of her face . . . but her eyes are dark. Her father must have been very handsome."

"I don't know who he was."

Dee didn't answer. She sat motionless . . . afraid to break the mood. Karla spoke hesitantly. "You see, I was raped by almost a dozen Russian soldiers in one night. Any one of them could have fathered her." Then she sat down and stared into the fire. She spoke slowly . . . never moving her eyes from the flame. Her voice was low and unemotional as she told Dee about her girl-hood in Wilno . . . Sister Thérèse . . . the ballet . . . the war . . . the Russian occupation . . . and the violence and rape. She also told how it had been impossible for her to leave Wilno until after the baby was born. She talked about Gregory Sokoyen—how he had stayed with her the night she was in labor . . . how she could not cry out because of the other children sleeping in the convent . . . the nineteen hours of un-bearable pain . . . Gregory always there . . . even in the final moment when they had realized something was wrong . . . a breech birth . . . it had been Gregory who fought his own panic and reached up, straight-ened the baby, and literally pulled it out. She could still see him, standing under the awful little overhead light . . . smacking the bottom of the bloody child . . . until the first pitiful wail emerged.

Karla looked over at Dee. "In pictures, and even in hospitals, one always sees the mother being given a sweet-smelling little bundle in an immaculate blanket. But my cubicle of a bedroom looked like a slaughterhouse that night. The baby was covered with my blood . . . the long umbilical cord hung down . . . Gregory attended to everything while I went into another violent spasm of pain delivering the afterbirth."

She shuddered slightly. "I'll never forget that night . . . getting the baby cleaned first . . . then destroying bloody sheets . . . putting the baby to my breast for the first time. I had never dreamed I would have a golden little girl. Somehow, I guess I had always thought it would come out looking like a little miniature Russian soldier with a bulbous nose and whiskey on its breath. And when I held her in my arms, I knew I could never leave her."

She talked on in a quiet voice, telling of the hazardous trip with the A.K. Twenty of them, hiding in barns during the day . . . crossing rooftops and underground tunnels at night . . . carrying the baby strapped against her stomach . . . stifling the baby's cries with a few drops of vodka when the Russians were close.

"And that is how it all happened. Zinaida was about three months old . . . a beautiful normal baby girl. We were close to the Corridor . . . the Nazis were all around us now . . . and the baby began to cry. We did everything—the vodka didn't work . . . nothing worked . . . even the chocolate candy which we hoarded like gold. Her cries grew piercing. I put her to my breast . . . but I had so little milk. I couldn't quiet her. Suddenly one of the men grabbed her from my arms and placed a pillow over her face while another held my mouth so I couldn't scream. And when the Germans were gone . . . Zinaida was dead. Oh God! I'll never forget that moment . . . when we all stared at that lifeless little body. I was sobbing silently . . . And the man who had held the pillow had tears running down his face. Suddenly he grabbed her and started breathing into her mouth. We all stood so still. Twenty cold dirty people who had traveled together, slept huddled against

one another for warmth, picked lice off one another—
lived together for three long weeks with just two
thoughts. Survival and escape. And everyone had tears
in their eyes as the man worked on Zinaida. Even the
small children with their pinched faces—some were perhaps only five or six, but they knew what was happening.
And when Zinaida let out that first hint of a wail, everyone fell to their knees and thanked God. Zinaida had
been brought back to life. I suppose she was dead for
a few minutes . . . maybe five . . . maybe ten—just
long enough to lose the oxygen that damaged her brain.
But I didn't know it at the time. And when we got to Sweden she seemed just like any other baby, only far more
beautiful. I left her with a family named Oleson. They
thought she was an infant who had been abandoned at the
convent that I had 'adopted.' I was going to London and
I promised to send money for her care . . . and send for
her as soon as the war ended. You see, I was to stay at
Uncle Otto's. I could not saddle them with a child, and I
hoped to get into the ballet. Then I would be able to support her.

"You know the rest. Jeremy found me in a bomb
shelter and I went into pictures. It sounds pat and very
easy, but it was such a strange world to me, with a new
language to learn . . . I was so shy and thought everyone was laughing at my English, and I had so little confidence in my acting. Dancing was the only thing I knew.
But I was able to send Mrs. Oleson good money every
week, and she was very kind and sent me pictures of
little Zina constantly. Zinaida was about three when the
first rumblings of trouble began. Mrs. Oleson's letters
became less enthusiastic. Zinaida was a slow walker
. . . she still babbled rather than talked . . . all the
other children were ahead of her. At first I tried to tell
myself many children were slow—you know how it is.
Everyone tells you Einstein didn't talk until he was five
. . . and you push it from your mind. The child would
catch up. And then finally Mrs. Oleson sent another
letter, asking for permission to institutionalize the child.
As she put it, 'After all, it is not yours, it is an orphan.
Why should you waste any more money on it?' "

Karla began to pace the room. "Can you imagine how I felt? I insisted on having the child brought to London . . . to raise it as my own. But Jeremy was the practical one. By then I was quite well known in London, and Jeremy explained that divulging the existence of an illegitimate child—a retarded one at that—would destroy any career I might have. You must remember, this was not 1971, when that sort of thing is now accepted. This was 1946, and an actress with a bastard child would be thrown out of the business. It was Jeremy who went over and got Zinaida. He also arranged for an English birth certificate and selected the name Jones. We put Zinaida in a psychiatric hospital while the neurologists made every possible test. The reports were all the same. Brain damage. She would be teachable. . . . But what mentality she would have, one could not definitely say." Karla walked across the room and poured herself another brandy. "Well, I suppose we are fortunate in a way—she is ten years old mentally and about six emotionally."

"But a ten-year-old is capable of doing many things," Dee said.

Karla nodded. "Unfortunately, you are right. She is pregnant." Karla walked to the stairs. "And now I must go up and hear her prayers."

When she came down, Dee was standing by the stairs waiting.

"Karla . . . what are we going to do?"

"We?"

There were tears in Dee's eyes. "Yes . . . *we*. Oh, God, Karla . . . now I understand so much . . . all the times you disappeared . . . why you're so . . . so—"

"So cheap?"

"Not cheap . . . but . . ."

"Cheap," Karla said with a sad smile. "Dee, I do not have the money people think I have. I retired with a quarter of a million dollars. That is invested. I live off the interest and whatever gifts I receive." She looked at Dee with a faint smile. "Jeremy is getting old. He cannot always call me when things go wrong . . . like now. So I have come here and found a companion for

Zinaida. Actually, she is a nurse. But she will not dress as one. She will live with Zinaida and be in constant touch with me. The Harringtons are marvelous people . . . they run the house . . . and do their best . . . But they cannot be with her every second. When Miss Roberts arrives, she will be with Zina constantly. She will ride horses with Zina, play checkers, read to her . . . She will cost me three hundred dollars a week, but I will rest easier. I cannot stay and take care of her . . . the child worships me. When I stay too long she becomes attached. She . . . she tried to make love to me one night." Karla stood up and threw her hands to the ceiling. "Well, why not? Good God, she has a woman's body! It craves sex . . . it craves sex wherever it can find it. We have her on tranquilizers now. But it is best I do not stay too long. The psychiatrist we saw . . . he is arranging for a legal abortion."

"Who was the man?"

"A delivery man, we assume. Who knows? The Harringtons suddenly noticed the morning sickness, the thickening of her waist . . . and they questioned her. She was quite candid. She said a man told her if he put his number-one thing into her number-one thing it would feel good. But she didn't like it, she said it hurt. We have told her never to do that again, and she says she will not . . . But I shall feel better when Miss Roberts arrives next week."

"Karla, I want to help."

Karla smiled and took Dee's hand. "You have helped. Your checks have helped so very much."

"No . . . more than that. Look, most people with my kind of money leave it to foundations and charities. I have my foundations and trusts. But I'm also going to do some good while I'm alive. When I go back . . . I'm changing my will immediately. I'll put ten million into an irrevocable trust for you and Zinaida. I'll have it worked out so that it can go to you and Zinaida now. The interest alone will be over half a million a year. And when we get back to the States we'll start the Zinaida Foundation . . . we'll build a school in her name . . . to help people like Zinaida. We'll work on it together. And maybe later we can bring Zinaida back to the States. She and the nurse can live at a guest cottage on the grounds of the Winter Palace. I'll build a projection room so she can see movies . . . Mike wants one anyway . . . and perhaps we'll have a big benefit . . . and even teach Zinaida a little speech. Let them see how beautiful a retarded child can be. And you can come out of retirement and tell them she is an adopted godchild of yours . . . use your time and *my* time for something worthwhile. I can stop all those needless luncheons and you can stop those goddamn bar exercises. You've got some real work to fill your days now. And so have I. And Karla . . . we'll work together." She took Karla into her arms because she suddenly realized that Karla was sobbing.

And that night as they lay in bed together, Karla whispered, "I love you, Dee. I will never leave you. I will never go off again. Now I can breathe easier. You see, Zinaida has no one but me. I always worried— what if I got ill? Perhaps that is why I tried to stay so physically fit. The money I have—I could live fine. But old age or a prolonged illness could wipe it out; and then where would Zinaida be? I couldn't bear the idea of a state hospital. Also, I will die before Zinaida— the estate I would leave after taxes might not be enough to take care of her for the rest of her life. But now, because of you, for the first time I can live without fear of the future."

Dee commuted between Grosvenor House and the cottage near Ascot. She waited until Zinaida had the abortion, then she left for Cannes. Karla would stay with Zinaida for another week, and then they planned to meet back in New York.

Dee sat in her plane and wondered if anyone had ever known the kind of happiness she felt. She would even pretend to like Cannes. She would give Mike a pleasant week. She could afford to be generous. Because when she came back to New York her life was really going to begin . . .

TWENTY-SIX

MIKE THREW the third seven in a row. He was having
the same kind of hot run he had had that week in Vegas.
A large crowd had gathered behind him at the Casino
in Monte Carlo. He let the money ride and threw the
dice again. His point was eight. He covered the four,
five, nine and ten. Then he rolled again. A four came up.
He pressed the bet. "Numbers!" he shouted as he
rolled the dice. He made a nine. He pressed it . . .
then rolled two sixes, a four, three nines, a ten, and
another four before making his point. He rolled again.
Eleven! He was hot now. His next point was six. He kept
rolling, calling for numbers. He made hard eights, fours,
tens . . . he pressed as far as the limit would allow.
He made eight straight passes, and when he cashed in
his francs, he had won close to twenty-five thousand
dollars. He kept ten thousand francs in chips and
roamed around the Casino.

It had been a good night. But he felt it wasn't over.
He walked past the Chemin de Fer table and yelled
Banco. He got the bank and lost. He waited for the
next deal and yelled Banco again. He got half the bank
and won. Then he waited his turn and took the bank.
An hour later he walked away with over a hundred
thousand francs. He wandered over to the roulette
table where Dee was playing. She played a chip on number thirty-six. He reached out and surrounded it. Num-

ber thirty-five won. She stared in amazement as the
croupier pushed all the stacks of chips toward him. He
took them off the table and walked away. He went to
the cashier. All together he had won close to fifty thousand dollars. Time to quit for the night.

Time to quit. Period. He had spent a week at the
Casino without having a losing night. He had found the
picture he was looking for. A seamy story about a girl
pushing thirty who made her living entering beauty con-
tests. She never won any titles, but she was always up
there in the finals. Always in the money. Always on a
bus . . . going to another town . . . another contest.
He had seen the picture three times before he made his
decision.

It had been shot on location in Texas by two young
independent producers. They had run short on money
and borrowed three hundred thousand from a bank to
finish it. Then they came to Cannes, looking for a distribution deal. Mike got 60 percent of the picture by paying
off their bank loan and guaranteeing the advertising
costs. He ran into Cyril Bean of Century Pictures and
talked him into taking a look at the film. Before the film
was over, they shook hands. Century would get 35 percent for distribution and share in the costs of advertising. Mike Wayne was back in action again.

He planned to open it at an art house and back it
with a big advertising campaign. The girl who played
the tired beauty contestant was an Off Broadway actress,
unknown to the public. Several of the critics who saw
it in Cannes were giving it raves. He couldn't lose. Even
if it wasn't an all-time box-office winner, it would make
a hell of a splash, he'd get his money back. But more
important it would put him back in action. The girl was
a cinch for an Academy Award nomination. Everything
was set. He had the signed contract in his vault at the
hotel. He had paid off the bank, and he still had over
a half-million dollars in cash . . . and a few more
nights at the Casino. Then back to New York. . . .

And *then* he'd call January. He had rehearsed the
call in his mind, night after night. He knew exactly how
to handle it. He wouldn't even mention Tom Colt. He'd

tell her he was back in action again and ask her if she
wanted to work with him. He'd open his own office.
She could help him in the overall campaign—travel to
all the cities with him to open the picture. If she refused . . . he'd take a different attack. He'd play it
cool . . . accept her decision. Then a few days later
he'd call back, and ask a favor. He'd tell her he needed
publicity on the picture. Would she do a story for that
magazine of hers? Cover the opening . . . take some
pictures of him in his office, on the road . . . (The
story in *Gloss* was the last thing he needed. He had hired
a top publicity firm to do a tremendous job, but he
wouldn't let her know. He'd act like he *needed* her help.
She couldn't turn him down.) He was confident that
once they saw one another, spent some time together,
everything would fall into place. It would be like old
times. The old razzle-dazzle . . . the old excitement.
Because from now on he was going to generate plenty
of excitement and action. He had also done some clever
wheeling and dealing in the lobby of the Carlton Hotel
in Cannes. He had practically stolen the American distribution rights of a great Italian picture by a new director. He also had 50 percent of the American rights
of a Czech picture that wasn't going to make any money
but would win prizes at every festival. And his name
would be on it. In 1972, Mike Wayne would be right
up there again.

He was also going to leave Dee. He'd let her divorce
him. He'd thank her for giving it a try and explain it
just hadn't worked out. Of course that would mean
she'd change her will and January would blow ten million bucks. But the year with Dee had brought a lot of
things into focus. He had married Dee to get security
for January. And where was she? Shacked up with an
overaged married stud in a bungalow at the Beverly
Hills Hotel. What security did she have with Tom Colt?
She had to know his work would come first . . . and
that his wife and kid would also eventually take precedence over her. But she had gone into it knowing she had
to finish a poor third. She had taken the gamble. She
didn't want life to be giftwrapped or dropped into her

lap. And neither did he. He couldn't face another winter in Palm Beach . . . a summer at Marbella . . . the small talk at dinner parties . . . the bland empty serenity of Dee . . . No wonder she had no lines in her face—she felt nothing. She lived in a world of "small talk," backgammon, shopping . . . A life of trivia. She probably wouldn't even go into any real scene over their split-up. Oh, it might upset some of her plans for Marbella—especially the seating arrangements at her dinner parties—but she wouldn't feel any great loss. And January wouldn't really lose anything in not becoming an heiress. As soon as they got back he'd take out a healthy life insurance policy, and no matter what happened, he'd never borrow on it. He'd get his old suite back at the Plaza . . . with two bedrooms. He'd ask her to move back. No, he'd tell her the room was there—would always be there—if she wanted it.

Several times he had almost placed a call to her at the Beverly Hills Hotel. But he always caught himself in time. He saw to it that his acquisition of the picture got a big story in *Variety*. He had cut it out and mailed it to her with no comment.

They planned to leave for New York on Friday. Two days before, he made a quick trip to Switzerland and deposited half a million in cash in a numbered bank account. Then he cabled the Plaza to reserve his old suite for Saturday, May 28. He would wait until they got to the Pierre . . . then break it to Dee, and check into the Plaza.

On Thursday afternoon, Dee ran around the Rue Antibes buying perfume and little gifts for her friends. Mike ran into a producer he had never liked. He invited Mike to his suite for a game of gin. Mike hesitated. The producer was notoriously lucky. Then he nodded. Why not! This would be a final test of his luck.

He left the suite late that afternoon, thirty thousand dollars richer, and went to Cartier's and bought Dee a thin platinum cigarette case. He managed to get a rush job done on the engraving. The following day as they drove to the airport, he tossed it in her lap. The inscription said TO DEE. THE LADY WHO BROUGHT ME

BACK MY LUCK. IN GRATITUDE. MIKE. She leaned over
and kissed his cheek. Maybe he should tell her now
and get it over with . . . But then he thought better
of it. It'd be murder to be trapped in a plane for six
hours with nothing to do but rehash a "nothing" marriage. Besides, it wasn't her fault. She had bought herself
a legal escort. And now it was time for her to find another. This one was returning to the human race.

They left Cannes and boarded their plane at Nice. He
sat across the aisle from Dee. He had brought caviar
and champagne aboard. Paid for it himself. He had hesitated at first, because this was a ritual he reserved for
January. But then, this *was* for January. He was on his
way back to her and freedom.

They opened the champagne and caviar after they
were airborne. The new attendant served them. He was
a young French boy who had driven for them while
they were in Cannes. His dream was to see America.
Mike had offered him a ride, and Dee had told him there
was always room for a gardener or driver at the Winter
Palace. His name was Jean Paul Vallon, and he had
lived all of his nineteen years in Cannes. He had never
even been to Paris. His mother, and aunt, three
cousins, and his sister and brother-in-law had come to
see him off. None of them had ever been in a plane
before—and the opulence of Dee's private jet overwhelmed them.

Dee held up her glass and smiled at Mike. "To Cannes
. . . and your friends."

He held up his glass. "To Marbella . . . and your
life and friends."

She smiled and sipped her drink. Mike put his glass
to his lips . . . but couldn't bring himself to drink it.
Suddenly it seemed wrong to drink Dom Perignon with
anyone but January. He held the glass and stared out
the window. It wasn't going to be easy breaking this
to Dee. After all, she hadn't done anything . . . except
be herself. Only it just wasn't for him.

Dee opened the cigarette case and took out a cigarette.
She stared out the window at the clouds below. The in-

scription on the case was beautiful. Mike was so kind
. . . so sweet . . . he really cared about her. But she
just couldn't go on like this. She had no intention of
lying awake night after night trying to plan excuses to
be with Karla. No, after she changed the will, she would
have to tell him. And then announce that she intended
to lead her own life—and that he could do the same
—as long as he got into no scandal and was always
available when she needed him. If he accepted those
terms, then January's inheritance would be safe.

She looked over at his strong profile. She would be
castrating him. Yet there was no other way. She stared
at the cigarette case. It was the first expensive gift she
had ever received from any man. She fingered it gently.
He had spent a lot of money on it. Probably all of
his gambling winnings. Her eyes blurred. Oh God, why
was there always someone who had to get hurt? She
took a deep drag of her cigarette. Then she jabbed it
out in the small ashtray. She had given him a good year
. . . done the best she could for his daughter . . . and
the daughter would wind up being a very rich woman
if Mike played along. But her conscience still bothered
her. She looked at the case again. A man had to be in
love to write an inscription like that: THE LADY WHO
BROUGHT ME BACK MY LUCK. But there was no reason
for her to have a guilt complex like this. If a man were
in her spot, would he be as generous toward the
woman? Of course not! And he'd feel no guilt either.
Karla had left London for New York three days ago
. . . they had talked on the phone for close to an hour.
Zinaida had taken to Miss Roberts and Karla was eager
to return to New York and see Dee.

Karla's voice had been low. "Dee . . . please hurry
back."

Just thinking about it now made her feel weak with
happiness. She closed her eyes and leaned back, trying
to cement the vision of Karla in her mind. Karla belonged to her now. Really belonged to her!

The plane lurched, but Dee kept her eyes closed.
Mike's drink had spilled, and Jean Paul came rushing
over to mop it up. Mike wiped off the attaché case

he was holding. The contract for the picture was inside. Along with one hundred and fifty thousand American dollars in cash. Enough to get him started in an office and get the publicity rolling.

Jean Paul refilled Mike's glass even though he motioned that he didn't want any. He took the bottle from the boy and refilled Dee's glass. "Here's some for you too, Jean Paul. This is a big occasion . . . your first trip to America. And from now on, anytime anything special happens in your life . . . buy yourself a bottle and make this a ritual. A ritual of luck."

The boy watched carefully as Mike filled his glass. The plane lurched again, and some of the wine spilled on to his new dark trousers. Mike laughed. "That means good luck, Jean Paul." The plane lurched again and dropped fifty feet . . . then it seemed to rock. The boy's eyes went glassy with fright. Mike smiled. "Strap yourself in, kid. Looks like we're probably hitting some weather."

Mike leaned back and closed his eyes. The plane jolted . . . then leveled out. He was thinking about January when he heard an uneven sound in the jet's engine—like the revving of a motorcycle. He sat up and listened carefully. Dee looked at him questioningly. He unstrapped his seatbelt and went inside the cabin. Both pilots were working furiously at the controls. Smoke was pouring out of one of the jet's motors. The plane began to weave crazily.

"Release the motor. Drop it," Mike said hoarsely.

"I can't," the pilot shouted. "It's jammed. Wire Mayday," he told his partner. "Go back and sit down, Mr. Wayne. Looks like we'll have to go for a crash landing."

Mike returned to his seat. Dee was staring at him apprehensively. The young French boy had taken out a rosary. His face was ashen. He looked at Mike, his eyes pleading for some reassurance.

Mike managed a smile. "Everything's fine . . . we've sprung a little engine trouble. We're gonna put down and get it fixed. Just relax."

Then the pilot's voice came through. "Mr. and Mrs. Wayne, we're going for a crash landing. Will you please unstrap your seat belts. Take off your shoes and get into a kneeling position on the floor. If you are wearing glasses, take them off, and put your head in your hands."

Jean Paul began to sob. "I will never see America. We are all going to die . . ."

Dee was silent. Her face was strained and white. Oh God! This was something you read about that happened to other people. It couldn't be happening to her . . . not now . . . not when she really had something to live for . . . Oh, please not now!

Mike knelt down and held the attaché case firmly. Then he leaned over and picked up the champagne bottle that was on the floor. He put it to his mouth and took a long swallow. It was an occasion now . . . one hell of an occasion. And just before the plane exploded in mid-air, he thought of January. He would never have the chance to apologize and tell her how much he loved her. And when the explosion came, the last thing that occurred to him was the numbered bank account in Switzerland and that this certainly was one hell of a place for his luck to run out. . . .

TWENTY-SEVEN

JANUARY CLOSED HER EYES as the 747 began its descent to Kennedy Airport. She couldn't face the sight of New York knowing Mike wouldn't be at the airport to meet her. Knowing he'd never be at any airport to meet her.

Less than an hour after his plane had exploded into the Atlantic the news had flashed on television in New York, cutting into all regular programming. Fortunately, George Milford reached January at the Beverly Hills Hotel before she heard it on the air.

It had all seemed completely unreal. When she hung up, the sunlight was still streaming into the room. Tom was still banging away on the typewriter in the next room. Mike was dead . . . and the world was still going on.

She had listened quietly while George Milford told her the details. She was silent when David offered condolences on the extension phone. Should they come and get her? Should they make arrangements for the services? Should they? . . . Somewhere in the middle of one of the "Should they's" she had hung up. She had sat quietly at first, wondering why the birds were still singing . . . wondering why she was still breathing.

She didn't remember when she began to scream. She just knew she was screaming and couldn't stop . . . and Tom was holding her in his arms and pleading for an explanation. And then suddenly the phones were

436

ringing in every room and Tom finally told the operator to stop all calls, and she could tell by his face that he knew . . . and all the while the goddamn sun kept shining and the birds called out to each other and the operator paged people at the pool.

She remembered a kind man named Dr. Cutler who arrived and gave her a shot. A different kind of shot from Dr. Alpert's. This was a soft easy shot . . . it made her stop screaming. It made everything sound very quiet . . . even the sunlight grew dim . . . and she felt as if she were floating and the birds sounded as if they were far away. And then she slept.

When she awoke, she thought perhaps it had all been a dream, a crazy nightmare. But Tom wasn't at the typewriter. He was sitting beside the bed, and when she asked him if it had been a dream he turned away.

He had held her close all night. She didn't cry. She was afraid to cry because she might never stop. . . .

Keeping it locked in was almost like refusing to admit that it had really happened.

Tom had finally turned off all the phones. Linda had gotten through; she had offered to come out and bring January back. Both George and David Milford had made the same offer. But January didn't want anyone to come out for her. Tom took charge and booked her on TWA's noon flight the following day. He wired David and George her flight number and arrival time. He drove her to the airport and got permission to take her on the plane before the other passengers boarded. She sat in the front seat of the huge empty plane and suddenly panicked.

"Come back with me, Tom. I can't face it alone."

"You won't be facing it alone," he said quietly. "I'm always with you. Just remember that—hold that thought all the time. And George and David Milford will be waiting at the airport."

"Oh, Tom, I don't want it this way."

He managed a smile. "It's not what we *want* . . . but what has to be. Let's face it, honey . . . I *am* a married man. David and his father actually believe you're here doing a story on me. Not that I care what they think, but it's you I'm worrying about. After all, there will be reporters waiting at Kennedy."

"Reporters?" She looked dazed.

"Well . . . your father was a hell of a colorful guy in his time, and Dee Milford Granger was one of the richest women in the world. It is news, and the public is morbid—"

"Tom." She reached out and gripped his hands. "Please come with me."

"I want to, baby. But there's nothing I could do to help. I'd have to hide out in a hotel while you made the arrangements. Because that's all the press would need —you coming to make funeral arrangements with a married lover in tow. Besides, I'm way behind with my work. The studio is on my neck. Seems like I've been too much of a lover and not enough of a writer."

She clung to him and he assured her he'd be there . . . waiting. "You get things settled . . . and call me . . . any time . . . all the time . . . whenever you need me . . . I'll be here."

The plane was circling Kennedy waiting for ground clearance. She opened her bag and took out the *Variety* clipping and reread it again. And once again she asked herself—Why had he sent it without a note? Was it because he was still angry? But then, he wouldn't have sent it at all. It was his way of saying everything was okay. It had to mean that! Oh God . . . it had to.

The plane touched the runway. It was a smooth landing. Everyone released their seat belts . . . the Muzak came on . . . people stood up even though the stewardess kept pleading for everyone to remain seated until the plane stopped taxiing. People reached for hand luggage . . . a baby cried in the back section . . . the ramp stairway was wheeled to the plane . . . the stewardesses were standing at the open door now . . . smiling . . . saying goodbye to everyone with sincere-looking smiles . . . thanking everyone for flying TWA . . . She was walking to the door like all the other passengers. It was crazy how the world could come to an end and you still functioned and did all of the ordinary

things. Like sitting through a four-and-a-half-hour flight
. . . even picking at some food . . . and now walking
down the ramp like everyone else. She saw the photographers, but it never occurred to her that they were
waiting for her until the lights were flashing in her face.
They were crowding in on her, and then David and his
father broke through and led her into a private room at
the airport while a chauffeur took her baggage stubs.

Then there was the ride back to New York, the same
ride she had taken with Mike. The same road, the same
leftovers from the World's Fair. They were still there
. . . but Mike was gone.

". . . and that's why we think it's best . . ." George
Milford was saying.

"Best. Best what?" She looked at the two men.

David's voice was gentle. "Best for you to stay at the
Pierre. It will take some time for the estate to be pro-
bated. Eventually the Winter Palace, the place in Marbella, and the apartment at the Pierre will be sold, and
the money will go into the foundation. But until then you
are welcome to live anywhere. And you'll be comfortable at the Pierre."

"No . . . I have my own place."

"But you'll have your privacy guaranteed at the
Pierre."

"Privacy?"

"The newspapers will blow this up for days, I'm
afraid," George Milford explained. "You see, when the
news broke, the press called me to ask about Dee's
estate. And I'm afraid that I inadvertently let it slip that
you would come into ten million."

"Ten million?" She looked at them both. "Dee left me
ten million dollars? Why? I hardly knew her."

George Milford smiled. "She loved your father very
much. I'm sure she did it to please him. She told me how
much he loved you . . . and that's why you should live
at the Pierre. After all, your father wanted it that way."

"How do you know what he wanted?" she asked.
"You didn't really know him."

"January, I knew him . . . quite well, toward the
end," David said quietly. "We talked a lot at Palm

'Beach that Easter weekend when you didn't come. He told me he had hoped we would eventually get married . . . I told him how I felt about you and he said to wait, not to push it. Those were his words. He never wanted to push you into anything. He hated the idea of your living in that tacky apartment. But he said he would never let you know, just as he never told you how disappointed he was when you left the Pierre."

She felt the tears slide down her cheeks. She nodded in the darkness. "All right, David. . . . Of course I'll stay at the Pierre."

During the next four days, with the help of Librium and sleeping pills, January functioned in a mechanized manner. She had just gotten a shot from Dr. Alpert the day before the plane crash. It wore off while she was in New York, but her mental anguish outweighed any physical reaction. She almost welcomed the headaches, the tightness in her throat, the aches in her bones—this kind of pain she understood and knew would pass. The unbelievable emptiness of a world without Mike was something she could not accept.

Sadie hovered over her like a devoted nurse. She was a lost soul without Dee. She seemed to be constantly listening, as if any second she would hear one of Dee's crisp orders. Sadie had been with Dee for thirty years. She *needed* someone to "tend to," and she transferred this need to January, bringing trays of food that January barely touched, answering phones, keeping everyone away except the Milfords, standing guard like a gaunt sentry, silent . . . sad . . . waiting.

David sat beside January at the memorial service for Dee and Mike. Her face was expressionless, almost as if she were asleep with her eyes open. His father sat on the other side of her. And his mother sat next to her husband, tense, clutching her handkerchief, and looking properly distraught. The church was mobbed and the presence of all the socialites and celebrities had brought out the entire news media. The International Set was represented by bona fide royalty. Some of Dee's friends from Europe had chartered a private plane to attend. And many show business celebrities, sensing the television cameramen would be on hand, had suddenly found it necessary to pay their last respects to Mike. But it was Karla's appearance that caused the biggest sensation. The crowd of curious onlookers had almost broken through the cordon of police when she arrived.

David hadn't seen her. But he had heard the screams go up outside, fans calling out her name. He knew she was sitting in the back somewhere and he prayed he wouldn't see her. After that traumatic night he had forced all thoughts of her from his mind. He had actually used a form of self-hypnosis to exorcise her from his thoughts. He thought "hate" whenever her name came to mind. Then he would think of things the word hate conjured—Hitler, child molesting, poverty. And somewhere along the line, his mind would latch onto some other subject. He also took on new accounts and extra work. And he made sure he was never alone at night. He alternated between Kim and Valerie, a gorgeous Eurasian girl. And when word of the plane crash occurred, he dropped everything and plunged into the immediate urgency of the "care and consideration" of January.

And from now on it was going to be January all the way. His slim, pale, beautiful little heiress. The news cameras had given her a hard time when she arrived at the church. She had clung to him in bewilderment. She really was a beautiful girl, a beautiful little lost girl—a beautiful little lost girl with ten million dollars. He reached out and touched her gloved hand. She looked up, and he hoped his slight smile conveyed sympathy and reassurance.

The memorial service droned on. He knew the church was jammed. People were standing three-deep in the back. Someone had said the governor was there. Where was Karla sitting? He realized with a certain amazement that today—this minute—was the first time he had "allowed" himself to think of her. He pushed her from his mind. But it didn't work. Somehow, in the crowded church, he felt her presence. It was ridiculous. But he actually *felt* it. And now, suddenly, even the self-hypnosis didn't work. He sat helplessly and allowed his thoughts to take over his mind. Had she come alone? Or had she been accompanied by Boris or one of her trusted escorts? Or was there someone new? He had to stop this! Think of January, he told himself. Think of Dee. Think of family. He was here as "next of kin." "Next of kin," but cut out of the will. God, why did that plane have to crash! Couldn't it have crashed *after* Dee changed her will? She had wanted to change it. Why had she waited to call his father till the day before the old man was leaving for Europe? And she had also cabled from the South of France that she wanted extensive changes when she returned. Why?

Would he have been reinstated? Would January have been out? But all the speculation in the world didn't matter now. The will was airtight. And January was the new rich girl in town.

Then he heard the organ and the muffled sounds of everyone murmuring the Lord's Prayer. He bowed his head and rose automatically with the others. He held January's arm as his father and mother started out of the pew. He kept his head bowed as he led January up the aisle away from the serene twilight of the church, toward the gaping hole of daylight where the curious public and television cameras waited.

And as he passed the third row from the back, he saw her. She was wearing a black chiffon scarf around her head and was preparing to make her own dash toward an exit. But in that one moment, before she shoved on the perpetual dark glasses, their eyes had met. And then she was gone, ducking her way across an aisle, hoping to make her escape through a side entrance. He held January's arm and continued the solemn pace toward the limousine. And he managed to look properly somber as the TV cameras photographed them for the six o'clock news.

He took January back to the Pierre. And for the next three hours the drawing room housed an avalanche of celebrities, café society, and clinking glasses. Security men stood on guard as the paying of respects turned into a gala cocktail reception. He stood by January's side until she showed visible signs of fatigue. Sadie led her off into the bedroom, but the party continued. New arrivals continued to flow through the door. He watched his mother play hostess. Even the old man seemed to be having a marvelous time. There was something barbaric about the whole thing. He glanced at the shining silver frames on the piano. Most of the famous faces were represented in person in the huge drawing room at the Pierre. All but one. His eyes rested on Karla's picture. He walked over and stared at it. The eyes were distant, with a hint of loneliness, just as they had been today.

He saw Sadie come out of the bedroom. She tiptoed over and told him January was resting. She had taken a sedative. And when he was sure no one noticed, he slipped out of the apartment.

He knew where he was going. He had thought he could never go there again, that he could never face that doorman, or the elevator man. But suddenly it didn't matter. After looking into her eyes today, he knew he could face them all—an army of them. He had to see her!

Nevertheless his relief was enormous when a strange doorman stood in front of her building. Of course— he had never come around at noon. The doorman stopped him with a perfunctory, "All guests must be announced." For a moment he hesitated. If Karla sent back word that she wouldn't receive him he would have the embarrassment of facing this strange doorman.

But now all that seemed so unimportant. He gave his name and waited while the man lumbered inside to the house phone. This hulk of a stranger in the braided uniform would have the privilege of talking to her . . . and perhaps *he* might not. He lit a cigarette while he waited. It seemed forever. Maybe she hadn't come home. If the doorman said she was out, it might be the truth. But he'd never know.

The doorman walked back slowly, as if his arches pained him. David ground out his cigarette and waited.

"Apartment Fifteen A," the doorman said. "Front elevator."

For a moment David stood very still. Then he strode through the lobby quickly. This was no time to allow himself to feel any nerves. He was grateful that the elevator was waiting. And when he got off, she was standing at the door of her apartment.

"Come in," she said quietly.

He followed her inside. The sunlight turned the murky East River into shades of yellow gray. He saw a tugboat inching its way, causing miniature waves in the water as it passed. "I had no idea you had such a view," he said.

"Perhaps because you have only seen it at night," she said quietly.

"Or perhaps I never really looked," he said.

For a moment neither of them spoke. Then he said, "Karla . . . I can't live without you."

She sat down and lit one of her English cigarettes. Then, almost as an afterthought, she extended the pack to him. He shook his head. Then he sat beside her. "You don't believe me, do you?"

She nodded slowly. "I believe that you mean it . . . now."

"Karla, I'm sorry about that night," he said stiffly. Suddenly it all rushed out. "Oh, God, I must have been insane. I can't even blame it on being drunk, because I got drunk intentionally. To give me the nerve to come over, to make that scene." He looked down at his hands. "It's just that the whole scene was closing in on me. The constant worry of time, of how long we would have, when would you suddenly take off again. But today when I looked at you I got my head together and I knew what it was all about. I love you. I want to be with you . . . openly. I want to marry you—if you'll have me. Or I'll stick around as your consort if that's the way you want it. I've lived all my life worrying about inheriting Dee's money, and now it looks like I'm supposed to spend my life trying to get at January's money. And I was willing to go along that way until I saw you at church. Because until that moment I had nothing better to do. But when I saw you again—"

She put her hand to his lips. "David, it is good to see you. And I am sorry about that night."

He grabbed her hands and kissed them. "No. I'm the one who is sorry. I didn't really mean any of those things I said. I—" He knew his face was burning. "I didn't believe what I was saying about Heidi Lanz. I didn't really think she was in here."

"None of that is important," she said. "Heidi—" She smiled. "I knew her so very long ago, when I first came to America. I haven't seen her in years, except reruns of her old pictures on television."

"Of course. And I had seen her that day at '21' and she just came to my mind and—"

She put her fingers across his lips and smiled. "Please, David. None of that is important. Heidi, or—"

"You're right," he said. "Nothing is important. Except us."

She stood up and crossed the room. She smiled at him, yet there was a sadness in her eyes. "No, David, we are not all that important. I have lived a very selfish life. I have always meant to do so many things, but always felt there was so much time. Dee's death taught me differently. We never know just how much time there is. Jeremy Haskins, my old friend, is close to eighty. Every time I hear from London I hold my breath. Yet who would have thought Jeremy would outlive Dee?"

He came to her and tried to take her in his arms, but she broke his embrace. He held her by the shoulders and looked into her eyes. "Karla, that's why I'm here. For just that reason. We've talked about the age difference between us. But now it all seems so stupid. All that matters is being together, having one another."

"No, David, that is not all that matters." She turned away. Then she pointed to the couch. "Sit down. I want you to listen to me. Yes, we have had our wonderful times. But that is past. Now I will tell you about what does matter. I will tell you about a girl called Zinaida. . . ."

David crumpled his empty package of cigarettes. He stared at Karla as she stood against the mantel. Several times he had felt tears come to his eyes as she recounted her struggle to raise her child. Her quiet composure as she told him about the rape of the nuns at the convent only added to the horror of the scene. When she had finished, she said, "So you see how unimportant anything between us really is. Until now I had coasted, letting others take care of Zinaida. But now it is all different."

"Did Dee know about your child?" he asked.

Karla hesitated. Then she managed a smile. "Of course not. Why would Dee know? Actually we weren't that close. I was just one of the silver frames on her piano."

"If she knew, she might have left something in her will."

Karla shrugged. "I have enough money. But only if I change my life style. I have put this apartment up for sale. That should bring me a good sum of money. And there is a marvelous little Greek island called Patmos. Not many tourists go there. It is quiet, and I am going to buy a house there and live with Zinaida and the Harringtons."

"Bring her here," David begged. "We can all live together."

"Oh, David, you do not understand. She is very beautiful. But she is a child. She would think nothing of skipping along the streets. Or bursting into tears at Schwarz's because you would not buy her all the toys she wanted. She is a child. A thirty-one-year-old child! I am a very private person. And you know how I have to fight for whatever privacy I get. It would not be fair to Zinaida to expose her to the photographers who would chase her. Her life would become a mockery. But on Patmos . . . we can swim together, walk together, play together. No one will know me there. We will have complete privacy. Jeremy has sent a man to arrange things. I leave tomorrow to select the house."

"Karla . . . marry me! Please! You have enough money to support Zinaida. I make enough so that we can live and . . ."

She stroked his face gently. "Yes, I am sure you do. And we would have a wonderful year together."

"Years," he corrected her.

"No, David. A year at the most. Then you would see your lovely little January marry. You would think about the ten million dollars, you would think about the life style you could have had . . . No, David, it would never last. My place is with Zinaida. I must teach her so many things. Especially that I am her mother. She is so very lost. And your place is with January. I saw her today. She is also lost. She needs you very much."

"I need you," he said.

She opened her arms and for a moment he held her close. He covered her face with kisses. Then she broke away from him. "No, David . . ."

"Karla . . ." he pleaded. "If you are sending me away, then please, let me be with you for the last time . . ."

She shook her head. "It would only be harder for both of us. Goodbye, David."

"Are you sending me away again?" he asked.

She nodded. "But this time I am sending you away with love."

He walked to the door. And suddenly she rushed to him and held him close. "Oh, David. Be happy. Please. For my sake . . . be happy." And he felt the tears running down her face, but he did not turn and look back as he walked out of the door, because he knew his own eyes were filled with tears . . .

TWENTY-EIGHT

JANUARY HAD BEEN TOO SEDATED even to remember the memorial service. She knew David had been at her side. But the whole thing seemed like a newsreel without sound. Dr. Clifford, Mrs. Milford's internist, had given her some tranquilizers, and she had taken triple the amount prescribed. She knew the church had been crowded, and she recalled thinking, "Mike would have liked the idea of playing to a full house." But she felt oddly removed from the news cameras that flashed when she left the church, or the curious onlookers who called out her name.

She had been amazed at the people who crowded into the apartment at the Pierre, stunned by the fact that she was supposed to greet them as if they were invited guests. And when it had gotten too much for her, she had slipped into the bedroom and taken some more tranquilizers.

And the days that followered were just as dreamlike. Days of serious meetings and signing of documents at George Milford's office—with David always at her side. Dee had left her ten million dollars! The enormity of the amount failed to arouse any distinct emotion. Could it bring Mike back? Could it take back that evening at Bungalow Five?

Somehow the days dragged by. David took her to his parents' home for dinner each night. She managed to make some kind of conversation with Margaret Milford, who nervously tried to anticipate every wish. Through it all, she was duly grateful for David. Sometimes she felt as if she were drowning when she was surrounded by all the new strange faces and the battery of press that seemed to pop up everywhere. That was when she would cling to David . . . find relief in seeing the familiar face. And there was always Sadie . . . waiting when she returned to the Pierre. She slept in the master bedroom now, on the side of the bed that Sadie said Mike used. And Sadie would know, because she had brought Dee's coffee to her every morning.

Sadie also doled out Dr. Clifford's sleeping pills each night. Two Seconals and some warm milk. At the end of the week, January found that lacing the milk with Jack Daniel's brought instant sleep. And through it all, she called Tom constantly. She was never quite aware when she called him . . . or how many times. She called him when she woke up . . . whether it was in the morning or the middle of the night. Whenever she found herself alone, she reached for a phone and called him. He always consoled her, even though he sometimes sounded harassed or sleepy. A few times he gently accused her of being drunk.

But most of all, she liked to sleep. Because of the dream. It came every night. The shadowy vision of a beautiful man with aquamarine-colored eyes. She had dreamed of him once long ago, when she had first met Tom. It had been a disconcerting dream then, because somehow the man had reminded her of Mike. But once she and Tom became lovers, she had forgotten the dream. And when she was on Dr. Alpert's shots she never dreamed because she never really fell into a deep sleep. But the dream had come again the first night she took the Seconals and the milk with the Jack Daniel's. It had been an odd dream. She was in Mike's arms and he was telling her he was still alive . . . that it had all been a mistake . . . another plane had crashed . . . he was fine. And then suddenly he fell from her arms and she saw him slip into the ocean . . . down . . . down . . . down . . . and just as she tried to go after him, she was caught by a pair of strong arms. It was Tom . . . holding her and telling her he would never leave her. And when she clung to him and told him how much she needed him . . . she saw that it wasn't really Tom. He was like Tom . . . and he was like Mike . . . except for the eyes. The most beautiful eyes she had ever seen. And when she woke up she could still see the eyes. . . .

She asked Dr. Clifford for more sleeping pills, and he suggested that she start trying to sleep without them. "If you were a widow or an older woman, who was alone in the world, I might give sleeping pills for a longer time to help you through the loneliness. But you are a young beautiful girl with a fiancé who adores you, and you must start trying to function."

She spent a sleepless night, and then in desperation, when her head ached and her throat felt thick, she went to Dee's medicine chest for an aspirin and stumbled into the Comstock Lode. Bottle after bottle of sleeping pills. None of them had Dr. Clifford's name on the label. Evidently Dee had a "pill doctor" all her own. There were dieting pills (she recognized them because Linda occasionally used them), two bottles of yellow sleeping pills, three bottles of Seconal, a bottle of Tuinals, and several boxes of the French suppositories. She quickly took them all from the cabinet and hid them.

The dream came every night now. Sometimes it was just the eyes. They seemed to be trying to comfort her, trying to give her hope, telling her there was a wonderful world waiting for her. . . . But when she woke up there was just the loneliness of the dark room and the empty bed. Then she would call Tom . . . and talk to him until her speech grew thick and she fell back to sleep.

It was in the middle of the third week that the pills stopped working. She would fall asleep immediately . . . and wake up a few hours later. And then one night she woke up and realized she hadn't had the dream. Sleep had just been a few dark hours of nothingness. She went to the closet where she kept the pills and took another Seconal and tried a yellow one with it. She felt groggy but she couldn't sleep. She called Tom. It took several rings before he answered. He sounded groggy.

"January, for God's sake . . . it's two in the morning."

"Well, at least I didn't get you in the middle of your writing."

"No, but you woke me. Honey, I'm way behind. The studio is on my back. I've got to finish this thing."

"Tom . . . I'll be finished with everything in a few days. Then I'll be back."

There was a slight pause. Then he said. "Look, I think it's best if you wait."

"Wait for what?"

"Wait until I finish the treatment. If you come out here, you can't move in with me now . . ."

"Why not?"

"For God's sake, haven't you been reading the newspapers?"

"No."

"You've been plastered all over them. That ten million bucks turned you into an instant celebrity."

"You sound like Linda. She . . . she . . . she keeps saying . . . I'm—" She stopped. Her tongue was getting thick and she couldn't remember what she was trying to say.

"January, have you taken anything?"

"Sleeping pills."

"How many?"

"Just two."

"Well, go to sleep. Look, I'll be through with the script soon. Then we'll talk it over."

She fell asleep with the phone in her hand. And when Sadie woke her the next day at noon, she couldn't remember any of the conversation. But she had the feeling that something hadn't gone quite right.

A few days later, she invited Linda up for dinner. The room service was excellent. Sadie had chilled a bottle of Dee's best wine. But something in their old relationship was missing. Linda had let her hair grow past her shoulders, picked at her food, and was wearing a body stocking that made her look thinner than usual. "I want to be bone thin," she said. "That's my new image. How do you like my glasses?"

"They're great. But I didn't know you needed them."

"I always wore contact lenses. But I like this look better. I'm dating Benjamin James now." She waited for January's reaction. When there was none, she said, "Look, darling. He's not exactly Tom Colt. But he's won a lot of minor prizes. Actually, he's considered too literary to ever really make it. His last book of poems only sold nine hundred copies. But there's a real 'In' group that consider him to be a genius. Besides, he's very good for me right now."

"Linda, don't you ever want a permanent man?"

"Not anymore. When I saw your pictures in the papers—" She paused and looked around the room. "When I look at this layout, it only proves my point. There's only two ways to make it. With money . . . or fame. If you've got either of those things, then you can have any man you want. And when I'm famous I won't really need a permanent man."

"Why not?"

"Because when I make it, there's going to be room for only one superstar in my setup . . . me. Until then, there has to be the Benjamins who can help. But once I get there, then I'll take no more shit from any man. That's the way I want to live—not being part of a man, but being *the* Linda Riggs. And that's why I wash Benjamin's socks and cook for him—because he's bright and he's in with a lot of cerebral people. I need him for now. Until the convention. In fact I'll start working for my candidate in September. Then I'll go all out."

"For whom?"

"Muskie. Benjamin says he can't lose." Then, almost as an afterthought, Linda said, "Now, what's happening with you and Tom?"

"He's finishing his screen treatment."

"You're going back then, I take it."

"No."

"Don't tell me it's over. But then you don't really need him now."

"It's not over. And I need him more than ever," January said. "But with all the publicity I've gotten . . . well, Tom feels I'm too well known to . . . well . . . to just arrive and move in with him."

"Well, go out there and rent a big house. A mansion. Good Lord, you can do anything you want now. Hire a press agent, get yourself invited to all the 'A' parties. Give a few yourself. Now that you've got ten million dollars maybe he'll be a little more flexible about divorce."

"Divorce?"

"Look, January, let's face it. You're a born pussycat. You need a man, and what's more, deep down you want it to be all nice and legal. You've been trying to go along with this living together stuff. But I can tell, it isn't sitting right. You told me way back that he was writing this screen treatment to protect his percentage deal, to pay for the co-op. In other words, just for the money. Well, he doesn't have to worry about that now. *You* can buy the apartment for him. And if you want to really be the generous lady of all time, you can pay his wife such a big settlement that she'll hand him *and* the child over to you on a silver platter. And if he's really freaky about playing Daddy, you can offer to have your own baby with him. I mean, you're the type who wants all that, aren't you?"

"I want to be married. *Yes,* I really do. And I could give Tom a baby. I could . . . why not? Linda, you're right. I'm going to talk to him about it tonight."

Linda picked up her bag and stared at the pictures on the piano. "Did Dee really know all of these people?"

"Yes."

"See. It's just as I said. With money or fame, you can own the world."

January smiled. "I don't want the world. I just want to feel there's a reason to get up each day."

She thought about it when Linda had gone. She hadn't slept well the night before. She had waited for the dream. But it hadn't come. She had awakened feeling desolate, almost as if she had suffered some personal rejection. Lately the dreams were more real than the thoughts she had when she was awake. The beautiful stranger with the blue eyes was tender and compassionate. She could never remember whether they ever spoke . . . or touched . . . she just knew he was there when she went to sleep. Lately she had found herself lying down in the afternoon and trying to drift off. But Dr. Clifford was right. She had to face reality. Tom was real. Tom was working in Bungalow Five, working on that screen treatment just to buy their apartment. She could be furnishing it now, doing something. She'd have that reason to get up each day!

She picked up the phone and started to dial. Then she remembered the time difference. It was eleven o'clock —eight o'clock in Los Angeles. Tom would just be settling down for his evening's work. He always worked from eight until eleven. That meant three hours to wait. . . .

She tried to watch television. She switched from Johnny to Merv to Dick. To a late movie. But nothing held her attention. She undressed and took a bath. That took time. Then she stretched out on the bed. She knew she had fallen asleep, because she was aware that she was dreaming. But it wasn't "the dream." It was a nightmare. There was water and moonlight. And then she saw a plane going down. Mike's plane. It was spinning. Down . . . down . . . down . . . until it disappeared into the silvery path the moon spread on the ocean. She felt panic, as if she were falling too. And then she felt some force lift her and she was safe. Then she saw the blue eyes. He was walking to her from a distance. She tried desperately to see his face. It was in the shadows; but somehow she knew it was a beautiful face. . . .

"Do you really want to come to me?" he whispered. And before she could answer, he disappeared, and she woke up.

The dream had been too real. She looked around the bedroom, half expecting to find him standing there. Whoever he was—he was the most beautiful man in the world. And yet she had never seen his face. It was something she just sensed. But this was ridiculous. He didn't exist. He was a man she had created in her dreams. Maybe she was losing her mind. Wasn't this the way it happened? People started seeing visions, hearing sounds that weren't there. She was really frightened. Because she could still hear his voice . . . and there was a jangling noise in the darkness.

It took her a moment to realize the jangling noise was the phone. A very real sound. And she had awakened because it was ringing. In the darkness, the luminous dial of the radio clock said one fifty-five. Who would be calling her at that hour! Except . . . *Tom*!

She grabbed the phone, and when she heard his voice she wasn't at all surprised. Just elated. She needed him more than ever right now. She needed the reassurance of a real man, not a fantasy man.

"Oh, Tom, I'm so glad you called. I was going to call you . . . as soon as you finished writing for the night."

He laughed. "How come this new burst of consideration?"

She groped for her cigarettes in the darkness. "I don't understand."

"January, for the past three weeks you've called me at the rate of twenty times a day, at hours ranging from nine A.M. my time straight through till five A.M.—and now this sudden curfew."

"Oh, Tom, I'm sorry, I hadn't realized. . . . It's just that whenever I'm unhappy or lost I reach out for you. Tom, I can't stand it. I'm coming out. Tomorrow."

"Don't bother, January. All you have to do is cross the street."

"I don't understand."

"I'm at the Plaza. I just got in."

"Tom!" She sat up in bed and switched on the light. "Oh, Tom, I'll throw on some slacks and come right over."

"Baby, hold it! I'm beat. Besides, I have a nine o'clock meeting tomorrow morning at my publisher's."

"Well, when do I see you? I can't wait!"

"Lunch."

"Lunch? Oh, Tom! Who needs lunch? I want to be alone with you. I want—"

"Honey, my lawyer is meeting me at the publisher's. We'll be working out details on the contract for the next book. After that I'll need to relax and have a few drinks. So let's make it at Toots Shor's. Say . . . twelve-thirty?"

"Tom . . ." Her voice was low. "I want to see you now. I can't bear the idea that you're just across the street. Please. Let me come over."

He sighed. "Baby, do you realize you are talking to a fifty-eight-year-old man who feels the jet lag and needs his sleep?"

"Fifty-seven," she said.

"Fifty-eight. I had a birthday while you were gone."

"Oh, Tom . . . You should have told me."

He laughed. "That's hardly the thing I feel like advertising. See you tomorrow, baby. Twelve-thirty. And, January . . . For God's sake, don't bring a birthday cake . . ."

He was standing wedged in at the bar when she walked into Toots Shor's. He had already met a few old friends and was buying them drinks. He held out his arms when he saw her, and she snuggled into them as he forced a space for her at the crowded bar. He made the introductions all around, then grinned as he looked at her. "Okay, boys. I'm out of circulation from here on." He kissed her gently on the cheek. "White wine?"

"No. Whatever you're having."

"Jack Daniel's for the lady. Heavy on the soda."

"Tom, you look wonderful. All tanned and—"

"I finally finished the script. That is, the treatment. And spent the last few days at my producer's pool learning that the ending has to be changed."

"Tom! You can't change the end—"

"If I don't, they'll assign someone else who will."

"You mean you have no control?"

"None. Once I take their money for the book, the book belongs to them. And once I take their money to write a screenplay, that means I agree to write a screenplay that will please them."

"What would happen if you refused?"

"Well, for one thing, they wouldn't pay me. And then they'd put on a guy who would do exactly what they wanted." He swallowed the rest of his drink and said,

"But don't look so sad. That's par for the course. I knew what I was getting into when I signed to do it. The only thing I didn't know . . . was that it would hurt so much." Then he signaled the waiter and motioned he was ready to sit down.

She waited until they were at their table and he had ordered another drink. Then she said, "Walk away from it, Tom. Let someone else do it. It's not worth all the pain."

He shook his head. "I can't now. At least this way I'll have some control. And parts of it are great. And if I have to compromise, at least I want to be there to make sure that the compromise works."

"But you only did the screen treatment because it would pay for the apartment in New York and—"

"I did it because I have a piece of the profits. Remember? And I'm there to protect my book."

"But you also said it would pay for the apartment. And now you don't have to worry about that or . . . I mean . . . Well . . ."

He reached out and took her hand. "January, I canceled the apartment."

"What!"

"Look, I've done a lot of thinking while we've been apart. I've also gotten a lot of work done while you've been gone. And I realize I can never really write if I live with you."

"Tom . . . don't say that!"

The waiter placed the menus in front of them. Tom studied his. She wanted to scream! How could he look at food? Or think of anything when their life together was at stake?

"Try the scallops," he told her. "They're real tiny—the kind you like."

"I don't want anything."

"Two hamburgers," he told the waiter. "And bring some hot sauce. Make mine rare. How do you want yours, January?"

"I don't care."

"Make the lady's rare too."

The moment the waiter left, she turned on him. "Tom,

what do you mean? Of course you can write if I'm living with you. Maybe you can't when we're in the bungalow. But if we have a large apartment in New York, I'll never be in your way. I'll stay in the background. I won't interfere. I promise."

He sighed. "Unfortunately, you do, baby. Look. I've had a hell of a lot of love in my time. And I always thought I'd go on loving and drinking forever. But each year the work gets harder and the love seems less important. I've already faced the fact that I'm fifty-eight and I haven't written half the books I promised myself I'd write. I don't think I can allow myself the luxury of love anymore."

She was trying not to let the tears come to her eyes. But they made her voice hoarse. "Tom . . . don't you love me?"

"Oh, Jesus, January. . . . I'm so damned grateful to you. You gave me something pretty wonderful. And I'll never forget it. Look, what we had was great. But it would have ended anyhow. Maybe a few months later . . . But maybe it is best to wash it up now—"

"Tom, once you said you could never be without me. Were they just words?"

"You know damn well I meant them at the time."

"At the time?"

The busboy came by to fill their water glasses. They were both silent until he left. Then Tom reached out and took both her hands. "Now listen . . . What I said . . . I meant. At the time. And they weren't lying-on-top-of-a-dame words. I meant them. But things change . . ."

"Nothing's changed," she said tensely.

"Okay. Let's say I've changed. Let's say just the one more year changed things. Honey, at your age, you've got the world ahead, you've got time. God, that's a great word—time. And you've got it. Time for love, time for dreams, time for crazy escapades . . . And I've just been one of them."

"No!"

"Maybe I'll be an important one when you're old enough to do some looking back. Maybe the most important. But baby . . . just think—in thirty-seven years—

that's the year two thousand eight—you'll just be my age." He paused and smiled. "Seems inconceivable to you, right? And I'll lay a few more inconceivable facts before you. In two thousand eight, *if* I am still around, I'll be ninety-five!"

The waiter arrived with the hamburgers. January forced a smile as he served them. The moment he left, Tom plunged into his. January touched his arm. Her voice was low and urgent. "Tom, you said if we had a year, two years . . . whatever we could grab—it would be worth it."

He nodded. "That's exactly what I said."

"Well, let's take it. Don't cancel me out before it's run its course."

"But damn it, January, it has run its course. It can't work any longer. Don't you see? I've got to go back to that bungalow and work. Then I've got to write some more books. I've got—"

"Tom." She was swallowing hard and keeping her voice down, because she was positive the people at the banquette beside them were trying to listen. "Tom, please, I'll do anything you say—just don't end it now. I can't live without you. You're all I've got. All I care for."

He looked at her and smiled sadly. "Twenty-one, worth all that money, loaded with beauty and health—and I'm all you've got?"

"All I want." The tears were brimming in her eyes now.

He was silent for a moment. Then he nodded. "Okay. We'll try it. It's not going to be easy. But we'll try. I once promised you that I'd never leave you, that as long as you wanted us to be together, we'd make it. And I'll keep that promise."

"Oh, Tom . . ."

"Now eat your hamburger. Because you've got to get home and start packing. I've got to be back in L.A. tomorrow."

She nibbled at the meat and tried to push it around her plate. As the restaurant filled, people he knew stopped at the table to compliment him on his book, to congratulate him because it was still holding the number-one spot. Some asked about the movie, about casting . . . And through it all, she managed to smile as he made introductions. Some of the men gave Tom playful insults, asked her what she saw in an ugly old man like him. But she knew their jokes sprang from genuine admiration and affection for him.

They were finally alone as they had espresso. He spoke first. "Well, if you think you can face it, it's back to Bungalow Five."

She tucked her arm in his. "Is it still raining out there?"

"No. At least it wasn't when I left." Once again he sighed.

"You don't really want me to come," she said.

"It's not that. It's the fucking script."

"Don't do it, Tom."

"Maybe you weren't listening to me earlier when I explained . . ."

"I heard every word. I also remember you saying that you're fifty-eight, that you want to write all the books you promised yourself to write. Then why bury yourself for another six months hacking away and butchering your own work? Start doing the things you really want to do."

"There's also a little thing like seventy-five thousand bucks involved."

"Tom, I've been doing a lot of thinking while we've been apart. Look. I've got ten million dollars. I'll give your wife a million if she'll divorce you. I'll leave another million in trust for your child. That frees you from all guilts and responsibilities. We can be together, get married, have a child of our own, as many as you want . . . And you can still write."

He looked at her curiously. "This is the first time you've made noises like a millionaire."

"What do you mean?"

"Everything and everyone is on an auction block. Right? Everyone has a price. One million, two million. It doesn't matter what the poor bastard you're buying wants. As long as you pay the price, he's yours."

"Tom, that's not true! I want you to be my husband. I want us to be together all the time. I've got enough money so that you don't have to shut yourself up with that typewriter and do what the producer or director tells you to do. I want you to be able to write the way you want to write. And above all, I want us to be together. To love one another and be happy."

He shook his head sadly. "January, can't you see? It's not going to work. There isn't room for what we once had anymore. You came along when I was floundering. I needed you. God, how I needed you. And you gave a middle-aged man his last pretense at being a stud. For that, I'll always be grateful. We found something special together at the right time. You gave me warmth and a sense of pride while I was prostituting myself on the tour circuit. And in return I replaced Daddy for you. So we're even. I'll go back to my writing and you go back to the money Daddy got for you. Go back to a young girl's life. It's all out there, waiting for you."

"No! Tom, you don't really mean this. You're just depressed. I don't want any other kind of life. I just want to be with you and——"

"But my life is writing! Can't you understand that? Writing comes first. It always will."

"Fine. Okay. You can write. You can write all you want. I want you to write. I'll buy us a house in the South of France, away from everyone. You'll never have to write screen treatments. You'll never have to write anything you don't want to write. I'll be very quiet. I'll have servants to attend to everything you want. If you like writing in New York I'll buy you the biggest apartment you ever saw. I'll——"

"Cut it, January! You're talking to Tom Colt. Not Mike Wayne."

She was silent for a moment. When she spoke she stared at the table and her voice was strained. "What did you mean by that?"

"Just what it sounded like. I'm not your father. I'm not going to be kept by a rich woman."

She pushed the table away and stood up. She knew the espresso had spilled, but she never looked back as she walked out of the restaurant.

TWENTY-NINE

JANUARY SLEPT off and on for three days. Sadie diligently arrived with trays and tried to coax her to eat. Sometimes she would wave her off or mumble incoherently that she wasn't feeling well. When Sadie threatened to call Dr. Clifford, January made an attempt to eat something and explained she was just having a bad siege with the curse. This relieved Sadie, who in turn told David, "Miss January is just going through a bad time of the month."

She had reached a point where the pills no longer sent her off into a soft empty sleep. By the fourth day she lay half awake, too drowsy to read, too oversedated to sleep. She was also aware that tomorrow night she would have to go to the Milfords' for dinner with David. Because no one could have a "bad time of the month" longer than five days.

Whenever she reached for a pill, seeking the fuzzy unconsciousness it brought, she told herself that it was just for "now"—to help her get over the hurt Tom had inflicted. It wasn't that she wanted to die. It was just that she couldn't face the heavy depression that hit her the moment she realized where she was and what had happened. Mike and Tom were both gone . . . and now even "the dream" had deserted her.

She found herself reliving those last weeks with Tom. Where had she gone wrong? What had she done? She kept remembering the sincerity in his voice, the tenderness of his eyes when he had said, "I can never be without you again." How could he say that in February and tell her they were through in June? But she had to try to go on. She thought back to the days when she had fought so hard just to walk—and here she was lying in bed, trying to buy a little bit of death each day with sleeping pills. She told herself God would punish her. Then she buried her head in the pillow because it seemed to her that God had punished her enough in twenty-one years . . .

She had her health . . . and she had money. But right now, to her, they were just words. She heard the house phone ring and waited for Sadie to pick it up, but it kept on ringing. She picked up the extension just as Sadie came on. She heard Sadie state that she wasn't taking any calls. Suddenly she recognized the voice and cut in. "It's all right, Sadie. I'll take it. Hugh! Where are you?"

"I'm lying on a sand dune with my private phone plugged in to a star."

She managed a laugh. He sounded so alive . . . so good. "You nut . . . Where are you?"

"Down in your lobby. I was just passing by and I thought you might like to go out for a bite."

"No . . . I'm in bed . . . but come on up."

Hugh sat in a chair near the bed. His vitality made the room seem cramped and oppressive. "Do you want something?" she asked. "I can have Sadie get you a drink, or even a quick steak if you like. She always keeps the freezer loaded."

"No. But why don't you throw on something and we'll find a hamburger joint."

She shook her head and reached for a cigarette. "I'm not feeling great. Nothing serious. Just that time of the month."

"Bullshit."

"I mean it, Hugh."

"You never took to your bed any time during the months you went with Tom unless it was to ball him." He saw her flinch, but he went on. "I had a drink with him before he left for the Coast. He told me about the Toots Shor's episode." She studied the ash of her cigarette without answering. "It had to end, January," he said quietly. "It never could have worked out. You've got to realize that Tom's writing does come first. It always has. Personally I don't think he's capable of ever really loving any woman."

"He loved me," she said stubbornly. "He . . . he even made me split with my father."

Hugh nodded. "He told me about that. Said it was the worst move he had ever made. He regretted it as soon as he thought it all out. Because he realized from that moment on he had a commitment to you. And Tom doesn't want any commitments except to his work. He said you were the one who finally cut it. You walked out on him."

"I had no choice."

"Okay. But he feels in the clear. You gave him back his head when you walked out of that restaurant."

"But Hugh . . . Tom does love me! I know he does. He told me he could never be without me."

"I'm sure he said that. And he probably meant it at the time. I've said the same thing to women. And I've meant it too—at the time. Men always mean what they say *when* they're saying it. If women could only realize that, and not hold them to it as a lifetime contract. Look, Tom's a writer . . . and a boozer. You made him your whole life. He couldn't take it."

"Why are you telling me all this?"

"Because I care about you. I figured you might take it hard." He looked around the room. "But I didn't expect to see you laid out like a corpse. Christ, with those flowers—all we need is soft organ music."

"Tom will come back," she said stubbornly.

"It's over, January. Over. Finished! *Done*! Sure, Tom might come back if you went down on your knees and forced him back out of guilt. If you want him back that way . . . then go ahead. But if you do, then you're not the girl I thought you were. Now snap out of it. You've got everything any girl could ever want."

"I've got ten million dollars," she said. "I live in this

gorgeous place and I have a closet full of clothes." The tears spilled down her face. "But I can't go to bed with ten million dollars. I can't put my arms around this apartment."

"No. But you can start in proving that you really loved your father."

"Prove I loved him?"

"That's right." He leaned close to her. "Look, this Dee Milford Granger was a nice lady. But from what I hear, Mike Wayne always shacked up with the most beautiful girls around. He made Tom Colt look like an amateur. But suddenly he marries this rich lady and now you've inherited ten million bucks. Okay . . . you tell me. Do you think she left it to you because she loved those big brown eyes of yours?"

She shook her head. "No . . . I still don't know why she left it to me."

"Holy Jesus! You're so busy lying around feeling sorry for yourself that you haven't even bothered to think things out. Look, sweet lady. Your father *earned* that ten million for you. Maybe he worked at it for only a year, but I'll guarantee you it was the hardest money he ever earned." He stared at her as the tears ran down her face. "Now stop crying," he snapped. "It won't bring him back. Get out of that bed and go out and have some fun. If you don't, it means Mike Wayne threw away the last year of his life for nothing. And he's probably feeling worse than you, knowing you're lying around crying for a man who doesn't want you."

She reached out and hugged him. "Hugh, it's too late tonight . . . I took two sleeping pills before you came in. But how about tomorrow . . . will you take me to dinner?"

"No."

She looked at him in surprise. "I only asked you out tonight to speak my mind," he said. "I've said it all now."

"But that doesn't mean we can't be friends—"

"Friends . . . yes. I am your friend. But don't try to turn me into another substitute for your father and Tom."

She smiled and her voice was teasing. "Why? I think you're a very attractive man."

"I'm fit and in my prime. And I've met a very nice widow who is forty-one and attractive and who cooks dinner for me about three times a week, and sometimes I take her into New York to see a show, and I consider myself a lucky man."

"Why are you telling me all this?"

"Because I know you're still in deep water and you'll latch on to whatever log floats by . . . and that's all wrong. If you ever tried to be anything more than a friend to me, I just might weaken, and that would kill your old man all over again. After all, he didn't go through all this to have you wind up with an overaged ex-astronaut."

"I think he wanted me to wind up with David."

"David?"

"The flowers." She looked over at the roses.

"Do you care for him?"

"I don't know . . . I never really gave myself a chance. In the beginning I thought I did. Then, well, then I met Tom and—"

"Give yourself another chance. Give yourself a lot of chances. Whether it's David or Peter or Joe or whatever . . . go out . . . meet them all . . . the world is your oyster now. Your old man saw to that. Go out and take it so he can sleep in peace."

She began to go out with David every night. His mother had insisted that neither Dee nor her father would want her to go into any extended period of mourning. So she forced herself to sit through the blasting music at Le Club . . . smiled through the noise at Maxwell's Plum and the Unicorn . . . went to Gino's on Sunday nights . . . met new people—girls who invited her to lunch, young men who were friends of David, who pressed too close when they held her on the dance floor. Through it all she smiled, made conversation, accepted luncheon invitations. . . . And all the while she knew she was waiting only for the evening to pass so she could take two red pills and go to sleep.

One day dissolved into another. Some of the beautiful young women she met called and invited her to lunch and she forced herself to accept. She sat at "21," Orsini's, La Grenouille . . . listened to gossip about new romances . . . the latest "In" boutiques . . . the latest "In" resort. She received invitations for weekends at Southampton, a cruise of the Greek islands (three couples were going to charter a boat; David said he was positive he could get the four weeks off if she wanted to go). And then, of course, there was always Marbella —Dee's house was fully staffed, available to her at any time.

Yes, there was a bright world out there. A whole brilliant summer waiting.

It was the middle of June, and she knew she had to make some plans. Everyone told her she couldn't just sit in the hot city. No one who was civilized stayed in town. She listened and agreed and knew that David was waiting . . . patient and kind . . . holding his plans in abeyance . . . waiting for her to come to some decision . . . any decision—yet he never complained. He called her every day and saw her every night.

There were others who called every day. A Prince, a good-looking movie star, a young Italian whose family was very social, a broker who worked in a rival firm of David's.

They called . . . they sent flowers. She wrote thank-you notes for the flowers but felt the same lethargy toward them all. She read that Tom had handed in his treatment for the screenplay and had gone to Big Sur for ten days. Had he taken his wife or was there someone else?

Even Linda was going away. She had rented a house in Quogue for the month of July. She and Benjamin would spend long weekends together; Benjamin would spend the entire month . . . writing.

Everyone was going somewhere. She had read that Karla had bought a house on a Greek island called

Patmos. Yes, everyone had survived, the world was going on without Mike, without Dee and all her money. The same sun was shining. And all the people in the silver frames on Dee's piano were still smiling, still functioning and feeling. . . .

She *wanted* to feel something. She wanted to wake up one morning and feel eager to start the day. Sometimes when she opened her eyes . . . those first few seconds before full consciousness took over, she felt good. Then everything rushed back to her, and she felt the weight of depression take over. Mike was gone . . . Tom was gone . . . even the dream was gone. The man with the beautiful eyes had disappeared along with her father and Tom . . .

Hugh called several times. He gave her pep talks. Told her it was a beautiful day, that she must go out and try to be happy. It was one thing to try . . . but another to make it work.

Her closet was filled with clothes for Marbella and St. Tropez. Each day she had shopped with her new friends and made identical purchases with them. She wore a figa around her neck . . . Gucci shoes . . . Cartier gold loop earrings . . . a Louis Vuitton shoulder bag. She knew she was beginning to look and dress like Vera and Patty and Debbie because one day Vera showed her their picture in *Women's Wear*, and she had to look for her name to distinguish herself from the others.

She stretched across the bed. She had told Sadie she would rest for half an hour. But she hadn't been able to sleep. She wondered where David would want to go for dinner. She hadn't worn any of the new clothes; maybe she'd wear something special tonight.

She saw the light flash on her phone. She always forgot to turn the sound on. She picked it up just as David was telling Sadie not to bother her if she was resting. "Tell her I have to cancel tonight. There's been a minor crisis at the office. Tell her I'll call her tomorrow."

She walked into the bathroom. It was five o'clock. Might as well take a bath and have a tray. She let the water run and dropped some bubble powder into the tub. Did David really have a crisis . . . or was he just not up to another monotonous evening with her?

She stood very still. Another monotonous evening with her . . . *She* had said it! Until now it had always been another monotonous evening with David . . . but suddenly it was as if she had penetrated into his thought process. . . .

Of course she was monotonous and dull. All she did was try to get through an evening without yawning. Why should he want to spend every evening with her? Come to think of it, Patty hadn't called in two days, and Vera had said something just today about not having time for lunch anymore—she was too busy buying last-minute things for her trip. She *was* a drag. A king-sized drag . . . And soon everyone would leave her.

She walked back to the bedroom and stared down at the park. The whole world was out there. A world Mike had given her on a platter and she couldn't rouse herself to take it. What had happened to all that boundless energy she had with the magazine . . . with Linda . . . with Tom?

She stood very still. Of course! Why hadn't she thought of it before! Instead of taking sleeping pills, she needed a shot! Tom had said they were bad for her. Well, they couldn't be worse than sleeping pills and this zonked-out feeling of inertia. She looked at the clock . . . five-thirty. Dr. Alpert would still be in his office. She let the bath water go down the drain and dug into the back of the closet for a pair of blue jeans Sadie had tried to throw out. She got into them, pulled on a T-shirt, grabbed some dark glasses, a bag and dashed out.

She wouldn't chance calling Dr. Alpert and being told to come the next day. They *had* to take her now.

At first she thought she was in the wrong office. It looked like a motorcycle club convention. Boys and girls sat slouched in jeans and sleeveless T-shirts. The smell of pot hung heavy in the room. The receptionist stared at January in amazement. Then she flashed a bright smile and held out her hand. "Congratulations.

I mean . . . I'm sorry about your father, but congratulations on your fortune. I keep reading about you."

"About me?"

"Of course. You're in the columns every day. Are you really going to Marbella or is it St. Tropez? I read you were practically engaged to David Milford."

January couldn't answer. She hadn't read a newspaper since California. She knew there had been a lot in the paper about the funeral. But why were the columnists writing about her? Did having ten million dollars cause the world to suddenly be interested in where she went to lunch or where she planned to vacation?

She looked at the crowded waiting room. "I have no appointment," she said.

"Oh, I'm sure we can work you in," the receptionist said. "It's always hectic at this hour. You see we have the cast of a big Broadway show here now. They come in every night at this hour." She nodded toward the actors sitting around the waiting room. "But we'll make an opening for you. Dr. Preston is back from the Coast. So we have both our doctors here now."

"What happened to all his big clients out there?"

"Oh, he actually has no office out there. He just went because Freddie Dillson couldn't sing unless Dr. Preston was backstage."

"But last week . . . on the news on television . . . I saw Freddie being carried out to an ambulance."

The receptionist nodded sadly. "He had a complete breakdown . . . right in the middle of the show. And after Dr. Preston worked so hard—he stayed out there close to seven weeks trying to get him into shape, but Freddie's voice is shot."

"But he was so great," January said. "I played his records all the time in Switzerland."

"You should have seen him when he came here two years ago. His wife had walked out on him—he's a big gambler you know—and he was broke. Dr. Preston took him in hand, and he opened at the Waldorf and made a spectacular comeback. Then he played Vegas and fell apart. Dr. Preston went out there to try and get him in shape for the Los Angeles opening . . . and he did. But he couldn't stay with him forever. Dr. Preston isn't a nursemaid, you know."

"But if he needed the shots?"

The receptionist shrugged. "My dear, Dr. Preston has taught two of our biggest senators to give themselves I.V. shots, but Freddie just couldn't make that scene with the needle. I mean . . . after all . . . suppose one has diabetes . . . We must not be afraid of the needle."

"I'd rather have Dr. Simon if I can," January said.

"Well, he has the cast . . . but let's see what we can do. I'll tell you what . . . follow me and I'll sneak you into an inside waiting room. That's where we always put our V.I.P.'s."

She followed the receptionist down a hall just as a young man walked out of a cubicle rolling down his sleeve. He stopped when he saw her. For a moment they both stared at each other. Then he threw his arms around her.

"Hey, heiress . . . What are you doing here?"

"Keith!" She hugged him eagerly. He was thinner and his hair was longer. She suddenly was so glad to see him. "Keith, what are *you* doing here?"

"I come here every night. I'm in *Caterpillar*. You've seen it, of course."

"No . . . I've been away."

"I've read about you. Wow, have you got it made! What do you need happy shots for?"

She shrugged. "No blood, I guess."

"Well, anytime you want to see the show—" He stopped. "Say—" Then he shook his head. "Nah . . . forget it."

"Forget what?"

"There's a big party tonight. At Christina Spencer's town house. She'd flip out if you'd come . . . But I guess you're all booked up."

"No . . . I'm free."

"All evening?"

"As soon as I get my shot."

"Want to see the show?"

"I'd love it."

"Great! I'll wait. I'll put you out front, only this time I can't sit with you."

"And this time I won't run out," she said.

"There's some nudity in it," he said warningly.

"I'm a big girl now, Keith."

"Okay. Get your happy shot. I'll wait out there."

THIRTY

SHE SAT mesmerized by the frantic activity of the show.
Keith had one song, which he "talked." To her surprise
he wasn't very good. Somehow she had expected him
to be more exciting on stage. But the vitality of his own
personality never came across. There was one scene
with frontal nudity. Keith was in that along with most of
the cast. She was suddenly aware that everyone's penis
was the same size. About the size of David's. Maybe
that was standard. It looked as though most men came
off the assembly line like that. Except Tom. Poor Tom!
Wow, she could really feel sorry for him. Was it the
shot? Or was she finally able to see things in their right
perspective? She began to giggle. Imagine seeing a bunch
of penises floating around on the stage, and here she
was, philosophizing about life.

She thought of Mike. She knew he was gone . . . but
suddenly she could accept it. For the first time she could
think of Mike without feeling dead inside. Mike had
lived a full life. As he would have put it—he went out
in style. Mike had lived a bigtime life and he had enjoyed
every minute of it . . . except, perhaps, the last year.
And as Hugh had said, he had lived that year for her
. . . so she could have many many good years.

Thank God for Hugh. And thank God for Dr. Alpert.
Maybe the shots were bad for you; Tom had said they
were. But it couldn't be worse than all that Jack Daniel's

he consumed. He was fifty-eight, but even with all that bourbon, he could still write and be what Linda called a "superstar." And with that small penis of his, he could still afford the luxury of letting her walk out of his life. Suddenly it struck her as being amusing. How had she ever felt so desolate because it was over? She felt alive and eager sitting in the audience. She was snapping her fingers to the beat. She could think clearly. She was sitting in the third row watching *Caterpillar* and enjoying herself. She wasn't lying in bed at the Pierre taking sleeping pills. There *was* a world out here, a world where people were leaping about on the stage, girls baring their breasts in a frenzied rock dance . . . and it all seemed just fine.

They decided to walk to the party after the show. Christina Spencer's town house was in the East Sixties, and the night was warm and clear. January clung to Keith's arm. She wanted to skip, to run . . . She stared at the dark sky. "Oh, Keith, isn't it great to really feel good?"

He nodded. "Dr. Alpert probably gave you the full dose. He was so high himself tonight, he probably thought you were a member of the cast."

She giggled. "Is that why he didn't even talk to me? You know I felt bad that he didn't even give me a 'Welcome Home' or a 'Glad to see you.' "

Keith smiled and looked down at her. "Feel great, huh?"

"I feel like I can hear the trees grow, smell the summer coming . . . I *can* see the leaves growing. Keith, look at that tree—can't you *see* that leaf getting bigger?"

He smiled. "You bet. And it's important to see and feel all these things. There will only be this Thursday in June just once. Tomorrow will be Friday and this Thursday will never come back."

"Why did you leave Linda?" she asked suddenly.

"Linda wanted too much of me."

She nodded. No one could have all of anyone. That was why Tom had put her out of his life. She stopped and stared at the sky. This one minute, she felt on the brink of something . . . as if she could look into the future . . . understand everything . . . She turned to him. "Keith, can you get hooked on these shots?"

"No, but no matter how out of sight everything's been, it's a bad scene when it wears off. Because you drop to the bottom . . . and the colors are gone. You look up and realize there's dust on the sun and brown on the leaves and shit in the street. Well, if you want to live in a dirty tired world, you can stop taking the shots. Everyone has the right to live the way they want—the Jesus Freaks have their bag, the nature freaks have their thing . . . I'm a speed freak, and as long as it makes everything green and orange . . . fine. And one day, maybe I won't want it all to be technicolor, and on that day, maybe I'll quit. But why should I right now?"

They had stopped in front of a brownstone on a tree-lined street. There were several limousines in front. Keith led January inside. She saw a well-known rock singer standing in the hall. They pushed into the living room. It was packed solid with familiar faces. Pop artists, underground movie stars, recording artists, several young screen actresses. There were blue jeans, velvet pants suits, see-through blouses, striped jackets, and a sprinkling of Indian outfits.

And there was Christina Spencer. She floated toward them, her much photographed face a bit toothier in person. Her figure even more fantastic than the photographs showed. She had to be in her late fifties. Her face was taut from several lifts. She wore a midriff outfit of flowered silk. Her full breasts peeked above the low-cut neckline. She had the body of a twenty-year-old.

She welcomed January warmly. "I knew your father, my dear. We had a few gorgeous nights together once n Acapulco. That was right before I met dear Geoffrey."

Keith steered January away. "Personally, I think she killed Geoffrey," he whispered. "She's married three times and each husband died and left her more money. And with her luck she backs *Caterpillar* with her own money and it's a smash."

"I thought you were her lover," January said.

"Oh, I balled her. But she spreads herself around. She needs a new young lover every week to prove to herself that the doctor from Brazil who tightened everything did a good job. But she's not bad. And what the hell . . . she lets everyone do their own number. Maybe I am top boy, but tonight she thinks I'm balling you . . . and she's not mad . . ."

A girl walked over to Keith. "Baby . . . the sangria is out of sight, it's in the den upstairs."

Keith led January upstairs into a dark sitting room. Everyone was sitting on cushions. He pulled January to the floor and reached into his pocket and took out a skinny cigarette. He lit it and passed it to her. She inhaled deeply and let the smoke out in a thin stream. "Jesus, baby . . . you're smoking it like it was a Chesterfield."

"I inhaled it," she said.

"But with grass you're not supposed to let the smoke out. You got to take air in with it." He held it between his middle fingers and illustrated the technique. She tried . . . but couldn't keep the smoke down. Suddenly he said, "Hold still. I'll give you a shotgun." Then he leaned over to kiss her, only he blew the smoke into her mouth and held her nose. "Now swallow it." She gagged, but kept most of it down. He did it twice again and she began to feel giddy and light-headed. Then he lit another and this time she inhaled properly. A beautiful young girl came over carrying a pitcher of sangria. "Here's some paper cups. Want some great stuff?"

Keith nodded and took the cups she handed them. "This is Arlene, January."

"Drink the wine . . . you'll blow your mind . . . Anita is strung out in the other room."

January sipped the wine. "It's great," she said.

"Sip it slowly," Keith said. "It's laced heavy."

"What?" She put down the cup.

"Relax. There's just enough acid in it for a good trip Trust me. Look, we all have the show to do tomorrow I'm drinking it . . . Just sip it slowly."

She looked around. The sweet smell of pot was ev erywhere. Music was piped into all the rooms. Everyon was sipping the sangria. She shrugged . . . why not? Everyone here had done it before . . . and they seemed eager to do it again. The sensation had to be great. Besides, as Keith had said, there would only be this Thursday in June, once in her life!

She finished the wine. Then she handed him the empty cup. She leaned against his shoulder. She felt no great reaction . . . just totally relaxed. She had been taut from the shot, taut and high . . . overactive . . . Now everything seemed calm and tranquil. That was a funny word . . . tranquil . . . but the whole world seemed tranquil . . . she felt warm and saw the sun . . . then a rainbow of color flashed by and hung over water. She saw waves and the ocean . . . and it seemed soft and blue and she suddenly knew with a strange clarity that Mike had felt no fear when the plane went down . . . he had almost welcomed slipping into that soft blue sea . . . he would rest . . . just as she was resting her head against Keith's shoulder . . . and Mike hadn't died . . . nothing ever died . . . life existed always . . . and people were good . . . Keith's lips were warm . . . Keith was kissing her . . . he was unbuttoning her shirt and she had no bra on . . . but it didn't matter . . . everything seemed to be going in slow motion now . . . maybe it wasn't right for her to kiss Keith . . . because Linda had loved him . . . *had* . . . *had* . . . everything was so long ago and nothing was forever.

She leaned back on the cushions. Keith's lips were on her breasts. She saw a girl completely naked dancing alone . . . a boy was naked and he held another boy close to him and they danced. Arlene floated through the room and turned a switch . . . psychedelic lights floated against the walls. January rolled over and put her head in Keith's lap. He sat there gazing into space stroking her breasts. She stared up into his face, but she knew he didn't see her . . . he was listening to sounds of his own. It seemed as if she could actually see his hair getting darker . . . and everything was so still that even through the music she could hear her own heart beating, and suddenly she felt she could see the past and the future. The future without Mike. It was as if God was opening the heavens for a moment. And then she saw him . . . his blue eyes. He had come back. She stretched out her arms. He had been away so long . . . and now he had come back and she wasn't asleep. His eyes were so blue . . . maybe it was God. Did God have blue eyes . . .

She heard voices . . . they seemed so far away. One of the voices came from a young man standing near Keith. Norton . . . yes . . . he had done a big number in the show. Norton was smiling down at her . . . but she stared past him . . . where had God gone . . . Norton's eyes were brown . . . amber brown . . . golden brown.

"Man, her tits are small but beautiful . . . such tiny pink nipples . . . I dig pink nipples. Man . . . can I have them?"

And then Norton was stroking one breast and Keith had knelt down and was stroking the other. They each kissed one . . . and it was sweet and friendly and she held both their heads. Everyone loved one another . . . everything was so peaceful . . . and Christina came over . . . she had taken off the top of her dress . . . her breasts were hanging. Why were they hanging? They had been so nice and round sticking out of her dress. Christina reached down and pulled Norton's arm. "Norton, come with Arlene and me . . ." She pulled Norton to his feet. Another boy walked over. He smiled at Keith. "Hi, man. She's outta sight . . ." He knelt down and looked into January's eyes. "I'm Ricky. . . ."

She smiled and touched his legs. "You did the dance . . ." Ricky had no clothes on . . . he had worn very little in the show . . . but now he had no clothes on . . . he started moving his body . . . doing the dance from the show . . . he held out his hands . . . he wanted her to do the dance with him. She got up slowly . . . she felt she could do anything . . . even fly across the room . . . float over everyone's head.

"You can't dance with clothes on," he said.

She smiled as she dropped the jeans to the floor. Then

she stepped out of her pants. He slid his hands down her body and she smiled. She felt free . . . she moved sensuously . . . in rhythm to his movements . . . following all of Ricky's gyrations. They were a foot apart with their eyes locked together. He moved closer. Everyone began to clap in a far-away rhythm to their movements. She raised her hands over her head and joined in. Clap . . . Clap . . . Clap . . . Ricky snapped his fingers to the same beat. Keith came behind her and lifted her . . . she felt lighter than air. Someone was spreading her legs . . . Everyone was clapping . . . slowly . . . in rhythm . . . Clap . . . Clap . . . Clap . . . She was clapping . . . She saw the strong young penis coming toward her . . . Clap . . . Clap . . . Clap . . . Ricky's penis . . . Clap . . . Clap . . . Clap . . . it was a chant . . . the penis moved into her. Everyone chanted . . . Fuck . . . Fuck . . . Fuck . . . Keith was moving her body back and forth . . . a group was holding Ricky too. . . . Fuck . . . Fuck . . . Fuck. . . . Nothing wrong with it . . . The young penis entered . . . in and out . . . in and out . . . in and out . . . Clap . . . Clap . . . Clap . . . Fuck . . . Fuck . . . Fuck . . . everyone is a friend . . . Fuck . . . Fuck . . . Fuck . . . Lights going . . . Christina kissing her breasts . . . nice friendly gesture . . . poor Christina with long hanging breasts . . . across the room she saw several girls take off their clothes . . . all in a slow rhythmic movement . . . Another boy came by and kissed her breasts . . . Everyone loved everyone . . . it was nice and good . . . Clap . . . Clap . . . Clap . . . ritualistic clap . . . clap . . . clap . . . fuck . . . fuck . . . fuck . . . suck . . . suck . . . suck . . . everyone was loving her. Oh God, it was wonderful . . . She was floating . . . she had never felt anything like this before . . . Ricky's penis . . . someone's lips on her and on Ricky's penis at the same time . . . Christina at her breast . . . She felt the orgasm coming . . . she saw Keith hold something under her nose . . . Fuck . . . Fuck . . . Fuck. . . . 'Sniff hard, January . . . it's a popper." She breathed deeply . . . her head felt like it was coming off . . .

and the orgasm was lasting forever and ever. She wanted it to go on and on . . . on and on. . . . "Oh, Mike, I love you," she shouted. Then she passed out.

When she opened her eyes she was curled up on a fur rug clinging to Keith. Her blouse and jeans were on the floor beside her. She sat up. Her head felt clear and she thought about the bizarre dream. Then she looked at her body. She was naked! Ricky was sprawled across the floor . . . also naked and asleep. She stood up and slid into her jeans. It hadn't been a dream. She had been part of something insane . . . ritualistic. She carried her blouse and walked among the sleeping people. She had to find her shoes. A clock struck in the hall . . . she wandered out there . . . two girls were nude . . . locked in an embrace. They stopped when they saw her and smiled. She smiled and they came over to her and each one kissed her lightly on the cheek. She smiled at the gesture of friendship and love . . . a rush of wonderful lightness streaked before her eyes . . . she saw flashing colors . . . she felt warm all over . . . but she felt she should go home. There were sandals lying all over the place . . . she must find a pair that fit. She found her bag and slid it on her shoulder.

Keith came over to her. "Where are you going?"

She smiled as she put on her shirt. "Home . . ."

He handed her a cube of sugar. "Eat it . . . it's great." Then he shoved an envelope inside the bag she had slid on her shoulder.

She sucked the sugar cube. "What did you put in my bag?"

"A gift," he said as he began to unbutton her shirt. She felt like she was floating again . . . there was a whirring noise inside her head. But she broke away with a smile. "No . . . you belong to Linda."

As she walked back to the foyer, the two girls who were still embracing each other looked up. They each reached out and pulled her toward them. They kissed her. They opened her shirt. One slipped her lips on one of January's breasts. Both began fondling her. It wa beautiful . . . these two girls she had never seen before . . . wanting to make her happy . . . wanting to be friendly . . . she felt them unzip her jeans . . . she felt one of the soft hands touching her . . . no . . . that was wrong . . . only a penis should do that . . . or a man . . . She pulled away . . . she smiled and shook her head. The girls smiled. One buttoned her blouse. The other helped her with her zipper. Each waved and went back to making love to one another. She watched them . . . it was like a ballet . . . beautiful . . . she walked to the door.

She went outside. The summer night felt cool and clean. If possible, she felt more light-headed than before. She could see beyond time and space . . . through buildings . . . through that brownstone house she had just left, where people were making love— happy beautiful people.

It was a wonderful marvelous world, and tomorrow she'd tell Mike all about it. No, Mike was gone. Well, when she saw him again . . . because she would see him again . . . everyone existed forever . . . and he would know she loved him. Because everyone should love everyone . . . everyone should love everything . . . even a tree—a tree could love back. She stopped at a tree and threw her arms around it. "You're just a young skinny tree . . . but don't be afraid . . . because one day you'll be a big tree. And I love you!" She clung to the tree. "Such a weak little tree . . . this whole street has such young weak little trees . . . But know what, little trees? You'll all be here long after we are gone. And maybe someone else will tell you how much they love you. Don't you hope so? Tell me, tree— f that tree next to you told you it wanted to belong to ɣou forever . . . intertwine its branches with yours . . become one . . . wouldn't you like that? Wouldn't he two of you together make a real big strong happy ree?" She sighed. "But no, you've got to stand here all lone, skinny and lonely . . . and maybe some of your eaves will blow against his . . . and with the wind you oth can whisper and speak . . . and be together . . .

yet apart. Is that the way nature wants it to be? Then maybe that's the way we're supposed to be too. But oh, tree . . . it's so nice to belong to someone . . ."

She left the tree and began to walk in a zigzag pattern. She was aware of the way she walked, just as a child is aware when it is consciously trying not to step on the cracks of the pavement. She looked up at the sky. The stars were separated too. Were they lonely? Then she saw one shoot across the heavens. She shut her eyes and made a wish. Maybe right now her father was watching the same star from the ocean. Or maybe he was on one of those stars, beginning a whole new life.

"Twinkle, twinkle, little star." She laughed. That was silly, because a star wasn't little. A star was a big sun. . . . "How I wonder what you are!" She knew what a star was. She fastened her attention on one that seemed to be blinking at her. It was so bright, but she was aware that the velvet sky was starting to fade . . . morning would begin soon . . . that very special Thursday in June was over. Never to be gotten back. Only now it was a very special Friday. She got up and began to walk . . . sometimes she zigzagged . . . sometimes she skipped. The red light on Madison Avenue looked so red . . . and the green light so green. And those lights told people and cars what to do . . . when to go . . . when to stop. It was a world of stop and go lights. But who needed them? People wouldn't hurt anyone. What was everyone trying to protect her from? Why did people try to instill fear? People were taught to fear and obey. Fear strangers . . . fear cars . . . obey lights! Who needed lights! The world would be much better without stop lights. People would stop and go quite properly without those lights. Because people cared. She stood in the middle of the street and threw her head back and stared at the sky. There were no stop signals in the sky . . . and with that whole big sky . . Mike's plane had gone down . . . from that soft sky into the soft water . . . and now Mike was looking a the sky too . . . and nothing could ever hurt hin again . . . just like right now . . . nothing could hur her . . . no one would hit her . . . because at this moment she was part of infinity. Nothing bad could ever happen . . . even death wasn't the end . . . it was just part of another existence. She was sure of that now. She stared at the sky and waited for an answer . . . she heard the screech of brakes . . . a cab pulled to a stop inches in front of her. The driver got out . . . "You dumb drunken broad!"

"Don't say that." She smiled. She slipped her arms around his neck. "Don't be angry because I love you."

He pulled away and stared at her. "You coulda been killed. Oh, Christ . . . you're one of them. You're stoned out of your mind."

"I love you," she said and put her head against his cheek. "Everyone should love everyone."

He sighed. "I got two daughters your age. I work nights so they can study. One goes to teacher's college . . . the other is studying to be a nurse. And you . . . flower child . . . what the hell are you studying?"

"To love . . . to know . . . to feel. . . ."

"Get into the cab. I'll take you home."

"No . . . I want to walk . . . to float . . . to feel."

"Get in . . . no charge."

She smiled. "See, you do love me."

He dragged her by the arm and put her in the seat beside him. "I don't trust you in the back. Now . . . where's home?"

"Where the heart is."

"Look, I finished work at four, but I had an airport call. It's quarter to five in the morning. I live in the Bronx. Right now my wife is sitting, waiting with the coffee, picturing me being held up with a knife at my throat. So let's get with it. Where do you want to go?"

"To the Plaza. My daddy lives there."

He headed for the Plaza. After a few blocks she touched his arm. "No . . . not the Plaza . . . he's not there now. The man I loved was at the Plaza . . . now's he at the Beverly Hills Hotel."

"Look . . . where do you want to go?"

"The Pierre."

"What are you? Some kind of a hotel freak? C'mon . . . where shall I take you?"

She looked at his registration card. "Mr. Isadore Cohen, you are a beautiful man. Take me to the Pierre."

He started down Fifth Avenue. "And what's your name, flower child?"

"January."

"Naturally," he said.

It was beginning to rain when Isadore Cohen walked her to the entrance of the Pierre. She looked up at the heavy gray sky. "Where are the stars? Where did my beautiful night go?" she asked.

"It's turned into morning," Isadore Cohen grumbled. "An ugly wet morning. . . . Now go back to wherever you belong."

She turned and waved as he walked back to his cab. He had refused to take any money, but she had left a twenty-dollar bill on the seat. She tiptoed into her bedroom and closed the drapes. Sadie was still asleep. The whole world was asleep except dear sweet Mr. Cohen who was on his way home to the Bronx. He was a wonderful man. Everyone was wonderful if you took time out to understand them. Like Keith, now that she knew him—he was wonderful too. She undressed slowly and tossed her bag on the chair. It slipped to the floor. She leaned over and picked it up gently. "You, Mr. Bag, are a Louis Vuitton, and I happen to think you are ugly. But they say you are very 'in.' " She studied the bag. Vera had made her buy it at Saks. ("But I don't wear much brown," January had said. "A Louis Vuitton bag isn't just brown," Vera insisted. "It goes with everything.")

Well, for one hundred and thirty dollars she damn well intended to wear it with everything. Then she laughed. What was a hundred and thirty dollars if she had ten million? But the idea of ten million dollars belonging to her was impossible to grasp. Any more than she could feel that this apartment belonged to her. It was still Dee's. She wondered if Mike ever felt it belonged to

him. But the Louis Vuitton bag that cost one hundred
and thirty dollars belonged to her. That kind of money
she could understand. She sat on the edge of the bed
and stroked the bag. She put the bag on the pillow and
crawled into bed.

She wasn't sleepy. She thought about taking a sleeping pill. She reached for the bottle in the drawer of the
night table . . . then put it away. Why should she?
She felt too marvelous . . . And as Keith had said,
"There will never be this Thursday again"—only now it
was Friday and there'd never be *this* Friday again. She
lay very quietly and savored the wonderful feeling of
weightlessness that flowed through her body. She knew
she wouldn't fall asleep . . . she couldn't . . . yet she
realized she had because the dream came again. First the
eyes . . . so clear and blue. The face was vague . . .
it was always vague, but she knew it was beautiful. He
was a stranger, and yet instinctively she felt he was
someone she wanted to be with. He held out his arms
. . . and she knew she had to go to him. She felt she
was getting out of bed and going into his arms . . . yet
she knew she had to be *in* her bed dreaming the whole
scene. That was it . . . a scene . . . because she saw
herself getting out of bed . . . she watched herself follow the outstretched arms. Yet each time she reached
him it was as if she hadn't come quite close enough. He
kept waiting. She followed him into the living room . . .
to the window. But now he was outside the window! She
opened it . . . the sky was dark . . . filled with stars.
Now she knew it was all a dream because it had been
dawn just a few minutes ago when she fell asleep . . .
a gray sticky dawn . . . so that meant she was still in
bed and not standing at the window, staring out at the
stars and this mystical man. But this time, she was determined to see his face. She leaned out the windowsill.
"Do you want me?" she called out.

He held out his arms. "If I come to you, you have to
really love me," she told him. "I can't bear to fall in love
with you and have you disappear, even if you are only
a dream."

He didn't speak. But the eyes told her he would never

hurt her. And suddenly she knew that all she had to do was jump out of that window and float up into his arms. She put one leg over the sill. And then she felt someone dragging her back. Keeping her from him . . . She struggled . . . And then she woke because Sadie was pulling at her and screaming . . . pulling her inside. She looked at the street below . . . she had been half-way out of the window!

"Miss January! Oh, Miss January! Why? . . . Why!" Sadie was sobbing from fright.

She clung to Sadie for a moment. Then she managed a weak smile. "It's all right, Sadie. It was just a dream."

"A dream! You were going to jump out of that window. Thank God I was in the kitchen when I heard the window open."

January stared out the window. It was dark and there were stars. "What time is it?"

"Ten o'clock. I was just fixing myself some tea and going to watch the news. I tried to wake you at noon and you mumbled something about having been up all night. Mr. Milford called at seven and I told him you were still asleep. He was very concerned. He's been calling every hour."

"Don't worry, Sadie. I . . . I took some sleeping pills this morning. I couldn't sleep last night. I guess I just slept round the clock."

"Well . . . will you call Mr. Milford? He's very concerned."

She nodded and went to her room. "Can I bring you anything, Miss January?"

"No . . . I'm not hungry."

She picked up the phone and started to dial David. Suddenly the room went dark. Then bright lights shot through her eyes and she saw him again . . . just for a flash . . . the blue eyes . . . almost mocking her . . . as if she had been a coward. "You would have killed me!" she shouted. "Killed me! Is that what you wanted?"

Sadie came rushing in. January stared down at the phone, which was now buzzing with the phone-off-the-hook-too-long signal. "Miss January, you were screaming!"

"No. I'm . . . I . . . I shouted at the operator because I got a wrong number twice. Don't worry, Sadie . . . please. I'm going to call Mr. Milford. You go to sleep."

Then she dialed the number. Sadie hovered by and waited until she heard January say, "Hi, David!" Then she discreetly left the room.

David sounded genuinely concerned. She tried to make her voice light. But the room was growing dark again and the splashing array of colors had returned. "I went to a party," she said as she blinked hard to make the colors disappear.

"It must have been a late one," he said. "You slept all day."

She closed her eyes to block out the flashing lights. "It was late. Some . . . some friends of my father's . . . actors . . . directors . . ." The colors were gone and she was all right now. Her voice was strong again. "It was a late party . . . it didn't start until midnight. And then when I got home for some strange reason I wasn't sleepy. So I read . . . until morning. And then I took two sleeping pills . . . and . . . well . . . you know the rest."

"How are you going to be able to sleep now?"

"Easy. I'll read a dull book and take some pills. By tomorrow my time schedule will be straightened out."

"January, I don't like this sleeping pill business. I'm against all pills. I never even take an aspirin."

"Well, after tonight I won't take any again."

"It's my fault. I left you alone. And you shouldn't be alone now . . . ever. January, let's not wait out the summer. Let's do it now."

"Do what now?"

"Get married."

She was silent. He had never asked her to go to bed with him since that first time. But his whole attitude since the accident had been different. He was gentle . . . considerate . . . and always concerned.

"January, are you there?"

"Yes . . ."

"Well . . . will you marry me?"

"David . . . I—" She hesitated. But what was she hesitating about? What *was* she waiting for? Another Tom to come along to destroy her? A relationship with Keith . . . and his friends? The full impact of it was just beginning to hit her. And even the dream was dangerous. She had almost jumped out of a window. She was suddenly frightened. What was happening to her? Where was the girl she had once been . . . still was. But that girl had allowed a stranger to make love to her in the midst of a room filled with strangers. Yet it had all seemed perfectly proper at the time. She began to tremble . . . she felt unclean . . . violated.

"January, are you still on?"

"Yes, David. I'm . . . I'm just thinking . . ."

"Please, January. I love you . . . I want to take care of you."

"David—" She clung to the phone. "I do need you. Yes . . . Yes. I do!"

"Oh, January! I promise you'll never regret it. Look, we'll celebrate tomorrow night at dinner. I'll invite a few friends. Vera and Ted . . . Harriet and Paul . . . Muriel and Burt . . . Bonnie and—" He stopped. "Where shall we do it? The Lafayette? Sign of the Dove?"

"No. Let's go to Raffles. That was the scene of our first date, wasn't it?"

"January, you're sentimental! I never would have thought it."

"There's a lot of things we'll both have to find out about each other," she said. "David, do you realize . . . we really hardly know one another."

"That's not my fault," he said. "I . . . well . . . I haven't invited you back to my place or asked to stay with you because I thought you were too upset and—"

"Oh, David, that's not what I mean. Strangers can go to bed together."

"I guess I'm not very demonstrative," he said. "I mean . . . when I care for someone . . . maybe I don't know how to show it. But January . . . you don' either. Know what all my friends call you? 'Her Coolness.' Even the newspapers picked it up . . . they called you that in a column yesterday."

"Do I seem cool?"

"Detached at times," he said. "But good God, why shouldn't you? After all that's happened to you in less than a year."

"Yes, you're right. A lot has happened . . ." She suddenly remembered that first night at Raffles. It all seemed unreal. Could she really spend the rest of her life with David . . . live with him . . . sleep in the same bed with him? . . . She began to panic.

"David, I can't! It isn't fair to you."

"What's not fair to me?"

"To marry you. I . . . I'm not really in love with you."

He was silent for a moment. Then he said, "January, have you really ever loved anyone?"

"Yes."

"Besides your father?"

"Yes . . ."

He hesitated. "Is it over?"

"Yes." Her voice was very low.

"Then don't tell me about it."

"But David . . . if I know I can love someone in a certain way and I don't feel that way about you, then is it fair to you? I mean . . . oh, I don't know how to put it—"

"I understand. Because I've loved someone too. And not in the same way I love you. But no two loves are the same. If you keep searching for the same kind of love each time, then you never really love again, because each new affair merely becomes a continuation of that first love."

"How do you know that?" she asked.

"I was talking to a big shrink at a party of my mother's. Dr. Arthur Addison. My mother went to him when she began having her changes and got a little depressed. I don't believe in psychiatry—unless someone is really batty—but I have to admit he helped my mother, and since then he has become a big friend of the family. But,

January, the kind of love we're both talking about only happens to a person once. And since we've both had it . . . what we have now is something new for both of us. And we can build it into a new life and forget all the old memories."

"Do you think we can do it?"

"Of course. Only a neurotic person clings to something that's gone. And you strike me as a very level-headed girl. Now go to sleep and try to dream of me."

She hung up and thought about their conversation. David was right. She couldn't bring Mike back or regain what she once had with Tom. That part of her life was over. But how could she shut out the memories? Maybe it was easier for a man. God, if she could just shut out last night. All the feeling of love for everyone was gone. She felt nothing but loathing and disgust. For Keith, his friends . . . but most of all, herself. And then to top it all she had tried to jump out of the window. If Sadie hadn't come in time, she would be dead. Or would she? Was there something out there? Something calling to her? She looked out the window . . . at the stars . . . then she ran to her closet and found another pair of jeans. She put on a shirt, took a sweater, and grabbed her bag. It was only ten-thirty . . . she would drive to the beach and talk it all out with Hugh. Tell him everything. The happy shots . . . the party . . . the orgy scene . . . and the man with the blue eyes. She would also tell him about almost jumping out of the window.

She crept out of the apartment so as not to awaken Sadie. She knew Dee kept her cars at a garage on West Fifty-sixth Street. She walked over.

There were several garages on Fifty-sixth Street. She hit the correct one on the first try and took it as an omen of good luck. The night manager recognized her and gave her the Jaguar. She left the garage and headed downtown. She recalled Tom's driver had taken the Midtown Tunnel to the Long Island Expressway. The car handled beautifully.

There was no traffic. She'd make Westhampton by one. Perhaps she should have phoned Hugh . . . But then he might have asked her to wait until tomorrow, and she had to talk it out now. She cut off the Expressway and pulled into a garage. The attendant filled the gas tank and gave her directions for Westhampton. The gas took all of her money, and she gave the attendant her last quarter as a tip. But the tank was filled, the road was good, and soon she'd see Hugh. Somehow she felt talking it out with him would make everything come out right.

It was one-fifteen when she pulled up to the house. She rang the bell . . . it had a hollow sound . . . an empty sound. Oh, Lord . . . was this one of his nights with his widow? She got into her car. She would sit and wait. She stared out at the dunes. They seemed so far away and so high and unfriendly tonight. But that was silly . . . they were just globs of sand. Hugh often slept out there. Of course! Maybe he was out there now! She got out of the car and started for the beach.

It was hard going. Wild grass grew in crazy patches. Several times she tripped over pieces of driftwood. Sand filled her sandals, but she ploughed on. She was physically exhausted by the time she reached the dunes. She stood on the top of the highest hill and looked down the stretch of beach. No sign of life anywhere. Even the ocean seemed abnormally calm. The waves seemed to whisper a hushed apology as they lapped against the sand. Perhaps Hugh was on another dune, farther down the beach. . . .

She stood and shouted his name. There was no answer . . . just the empty sound of her voice. Not even a gull called out. Where were all the gulls at night? They were always swooping around and screeching at one another during the day. She flopped on the ground and let some of the cool sand sift through her fingers. Where *did* sea gulls go at night? She looked back toward the house. It was dark and lonely-looking. The calm night, the bright stars, and the sighs of the waves seemed much friendlier than the empty house.

She rolled her sweater into a ball and cushioned it under her head. Then she lay back and stared at the sky. It seemed to come closer and blanket her. Suddenly she felt as if *it* was the world and earth was merely the floor. What *was* up there? Other planets? Other worlds? She looked back toward the house. Maybe Hugh was spending the night at the lady's place.

She could go back to her car, and sleep there until he came back. But she wasn't sleepy and it was so peaceful on the dune. All those stars. The Wise Men had looked at these same stars the night Jesus was born. Galileo had looked at them . . . and when Columbus was looking for his new route to India he had also relied on them. How many people had made love under them? How many children had made wishes on them and prayed to the God they imagined sitting above them as she had when she was a child. God's lights. Her mother had told her that! It suddenly came to her—God's lights. Her mother! Until this second her mother had always been just a misty memory. A quiet lady always "resting." Always beautiful when she was up and about . . . great brown eyes staring adoringly at her father . . . never at her. In fact she couldn't recall ever looking into those eyes herself . . . *Yes! Once!* . . . It came to her now. The memory of snuggling in her mother's arms and seeing those great brown eyes looking tenderly at her. She had had a bad dream and cried out. The nurse came immediately. But this time her mother had come too. And it was one of the rare times that her mother rather than the nurse comforted her. And when she had shown fear of being alone in the darkness because the bad dream might return . . . her mother had held her close and told her nothing bad could happen in the night. That sometimes the light made things look bad, but the night was soft and comforting. They had sat before the window and looked at the stars together and her mother had said, "They are God's little beacon lights . . . to remind you that He is always watching you . . . always there to help you . . . to love you."

She thought about it now as she watched the stars. That was really a beautiful story to tell to a frightened little girl. What had her mother been like? Suddenly she wished she had been older and could have comforted her. Her mother loved Mike . . . but he had other girls. God, how she must have suffered. She remembered how she had felt that day Tom stayed at the beach with hi

wife. Tears came to her eyes. Her poor, poor mother.
In love with Mike . . . left alone with a little girl while
he was in California. Probably in Bungalow Five with a
girl of his own. Suddenly, lying there, it was as if she
saw herself split into two beings. She was Mike's girl in
Bungalow Five . . . and she was her young helpless
mother . . . alone too much . . . sobbing too much
. . . She called out, "Mother . . . you shouldn't have
done it. The girl with him suffered too. At least you knew
he would always come back to you. And you had me.
Why did you leave me? Didn't you love me?" Her voice
rang out in the night . . . and the stars stared back. But
suddenly they no longer seemed warm and friendly. They
looked hard and cold . . . as if they resented this in-
trusion into their privacy. They were aloof and secure
. . . so sure they would always be there. Laughing at
this little speck of humanity on the beach. And they
weren't God's beacon lights . . . they were worlds and
suns and meteorites. And now there was even space junk
floating around in that velvety darkness. She saw a
star streak across . . . then another . . . the moon
looked so low. Like a mother dominating the heavens
with the stars as her children. It was sad to know that
the moon wasn't silver and bright. That it was just a
wasteland . . . scarred . . . pitted . . . smaller than
earth . . . an ash in the sky. Man had landed on it and
revealed its mystery and taken away all of the romance.

She still felt alert and colors were still strong. The sky
was black but she saw shades of blue and purple in its
blackness.

She glanced toward Hugh's house. The moon hung
over it, its brilliant light illuminating the dark windows.
Maybe he had taken the widow to New York tonight.

She opened her bag and groped for her cigarettes. Her
hand came across an envelope. She took it out. A plain
white crumpled bulky envelope. The envelope Keith
had stuck into her bag just as she was leaving. She ripped
it open. It contained a small plastic pill bottle with two
sugar cubes. There was also a note. She flicked on her
cigarette lighter. "DEAR HEIRESS: I LOVE YOU. I CAN'T
TAKE YOU TO MARBELLA OR THE SOUTH OF FRANCE.

BUT IF YOU'LL BE MY GIRL I CAN TAKE YOU ON TRIPS
OUT OF THIS WORLD. FOR STARTERS—HERE'S TWO ON
ME. LOVE, KEITH."

She opened the bottle and held the sugar cubes in her
hand. She started to toss them away, but something
held her back. Why not take one? If she did, all of her
depression would evaporate. She'd be able to reach up
and touch the stars. She put the cubes back into the
bottle and dropped it back into her bag. No, taking acid
wasn't going to solve things. The problem would still be
there when the "trip" was over. But what was the solution? Try to conform? Try to learn to love David? Learn
backgammon? Have lunch every day? Buy clothes? *No!*
She didn't want a life that had no highs. Even the lows
were worthwhile if you knew there would be highs. And
not an acid high. A real high. Like seeing Mike stride
toward her that day in the airport at Rome, hearing Tom
say he could never be without her. . . .

But they were both gone. Tom and Mike. . . .

She took out the bottle again. What would happen if
she took *both* of them? Maybe she'd go on a trip that
would last forever. Maybe she'd never come back.

She shivered. A wind had come up from nowhere.
For some reason it chilled her. Sand began to spray
against her face. She stood up and brushed the sand from
her clothes. The wind was really blowing now. She put on
her sweater. And then as suddenly as it had come, the
wind stopped. And there was a curious silence—like
the silence she had once heard in California right before
a minor earth tremor. When the crickets had stopped
and even the leaves made no sound. She looked toward
the ocean. It was like glass, and the moon hung over it
casting a bright path over the dark water. But that was
impossible! Just a moment ago the moon had been behind her, hanging over Hugh's house. She turned and
looked back. Of course. There it was . . . A pale
friendly light over the dark strip of beach-front houses.
Then she looked back at the ocean . . . and there *it*
was! Clear and bright . . . another moon!

She was hallucinating! It was that sugar cube Keith
had given her at the party. She jumped up and turned

her back on the "new moon." She began to run, but it was like one of those dreadful nightmares where you ran but remained in one spot. It was happening to her. Her feet were moving, her breath was coming fast, but she remained on top of that dune . . . trapped between two moons.

She turned and looked back. The new moon had disappeared. The ocean was black and lonely. The stars seemed more distant than ever. She was frightened now. She started running. This time her feet moved. She stumbled and slipped in the darkness. Oh, God, acid was really dangerous. It had almost made her jump out of a window. Now it had made her see another moon. This must be what they call re-hallucinating. Or had she taken another sugar cube? Or both of them! Oh, God . . . had she? She looked back. She could see her bag on the dune where she had dropped it. She could see it because it was illuminated by moonlight. Moonlight from the *other* moon! It was back!

Maybe she *had* taken the sugar cubes. But she was positive she had put them back. Or had she? It didn't matter. She was hallucinating, seeing two moons . . . Anything could happen. It might drag her out to the ocean. If she could think she could jump out of a window and float upward, then there was no telling what would happen. Oh, God, she'd never take anything again. She'd marry David and have children. A child of her own to love. Maybe she'd never feel for David what she felt for Mike. No . . . what she felt for Tom. But at least she'd be marrying someone Mike approved of. And she would have a little boy who would look just like Mike. And a girl too. And she'd love them and be a good mother. She would! Only, please, God. Just let her make it back to that house.

Why did the house seem so far away? She was off the dune now. In a valley, climbing another. . . .

It was still there. She turned and saw it hover over the ocean. Suddenly it streaked across the sky, returned and spun around, pirouetting—as if it were doing an eerie ballet just for her. It shot into the heavens until it looked no larger than a star, until she was positive it was a star.

Then it returned to its normal size, throwing its glow into a perfect lane across the water.

She stared at it for a moment. This was no hallucination. This was real! Because when you hallucinate you don't know it. Like going out of the window. She had thought she was dreaming. But maybe *this* was a dream too. Maybe she wasn't on the beach. Maybe she was home in bed. Maybe she wasn't at the Pierre. Maybe that had all been part of a dream too. Maybe she was still with Tom, and Mike wasn't dead. Maybe the happy shots caused all this to be one long horrible nightmare. And when she woke up she'd be at Bungalow Five and Tom would be there and she would leave him and rush to meet Mike and make things up. Or maybe they hadn't had the fight, maybe the fight was part of the nightmare —then she wouldn't have to leave Tom. But maybe she had never met Tom. Maybe she was still in Switzerland, and she was getting well, and she was coming home to Mike and he hadn't met Dee, and none of this had happened . . . But then maybe there never was a Franco, and there had never been a motorcycle accident. Maybe she had never been born—because she couldn't tell just when the nightmare began.

But it hadn't all been a nightmare. Some of it had been marvelous. Going to Miss Haddon's had even been all right because there had been wonderful weekends to look forward to, the Saturdays when she'd rush into his arms. And even the Clinique hadn't been all bad because there were his visits, and most of all the expectation and the dream of getting well, especially the month before she came home, when she knew she would be with him. . . .

At least there had been that month of dreams, and sometimes dreams were better than reality. You couldn't call a month of wonderful dreams a nightmare. And the month had culminated in a moment of fantastic reality that afternoon when she found him at the airport waiting. She didn't know about Dee then. So for a few hours he belonged to her, as he had in Rome until Melba came on the scene. There had been happy moments once. Just as her mother had probably been happy—once—and then had to face it, accept the fact that everything was gone, a special kind of happiness comes only once . . .

"No!" she cried out. "Once is not enough! Oh, Mother, how did you ever live through it as long as you did!"

She stood very still. She had shouted at the ghostly light. And all the while she stood rooted in one spot. She stared at it as it hung over the ocean. It looked exactly like the other moon. Only this one didn't have any dark areas.

And then a new thought struck her. Maybe there was a logical explanation for all this. Maybe this was one of those UFO's that occasionally crop up in the news. Well, if it was, she certainly couldn't be the only person in Westhampton who was seeing it. She looked toward all the dark houses. Wasn't anyone in town awake? Wherever Hugh was, couldn't he see it? All those nights he spent on the dunes, nothing like this had ever happened to him. She had to come along *one* night . . . And look at the mess she was in!

She stood there bathed in that strange light, alone on the beach. Somehow she felt that if she stood very still it wouldn't see her. But that was ridiculous. Whatever it was, it couldn't possibly see her—it was thousands of miles away.

Maybe she should try to remember everything. How large it was, how many miles away it seemed, what direction it was traveling. Maybe she should report it. Oh, sure—that's all she'd need!

But it was there, hanging in front of her. She began to shout. "WAKE UP, SOMEONE! DOESN'T ANYONE IN WESTHAMPTON KNOW YOU'VE SUDDENLY GOT TWO MOONS!"

There was nothing but silence. There was no use in running, because she felt locked in that one spot. She dropped to the sand. It felt cool and soft. She felt the glow of the new moon upon her. It almost felt like sunlight—warm, comforting. And then she saw him walking toward her. He was coming from the shoreline. And when he walked directly into the path of the moonlight his face was in shadow. But she wasn't the least surprised that he had those startling blue eyes she had seen so many times before.

And as she watched him approach, she felt no fear. She suddenly remembered a verse from a poem by John Burroughs called "Waiting." Long ago she had memorized it in Switzerland and . . .

> Serene, I fold my hands and wait,
> Nor care for wind, nor tide, nor sea;
> I rave no more 'gainst time or fate,
> For lo! my own shall come to me.

And now for the first time, she felt all the waiting was over. He came closer and suddenly she couldn't breathe. It was Mike!

But it wasn't Mike. His smile was like Mike's, he looked like Mike . . . yet he wasn't Mike. He stood before her and held out his arms. She scrambled to her feet and went to him. He held her close. "I'm glad to see you, January."

"Mike," she whispered.

He stroked her hair. "I'm not Mike."

"But you look like Mike."

"Only because you want me to."

She clung to him. "Look. This is my hallucination. So it's going to go my way. Whoever you are—I've wanted you all my life. Maybe I always knew you would come. Maybe I loved Mike because he looked like you. Maybe I love you because you look like him. Maybe you both are one. It doesn't matter . . ."

She dropped to the sand, and he took her in his arms. When their lips met it was everything she knew it would be. And when he took her, she knew it had been the moment she had waited for all her life. His caress was gentle yet firm. She reached out for him and held him close . . . closer . . . until they were united like the sand that joins the wave that draws it back into the sea.

"Please don't ever leave me," she whispered.

And he held her close and promised he would never let her go again.

JUNE 29, 1972

NEW YORK (AP)

TODAY MARKS ONE YEAR SINCE THE
DISAPPEARANCE OF JANUARY WAYNE,
HEIRESS TO THE GRANGER MILLIONS.
HER FIANCE, DAVID MILFORD, WAS
UNAVAILABLE FOR COMMENT, AS HE IS
VACATIONING SOMEWHERE ON THE GREEK
ISLAND OF PATMOS. BUT FRIENDS STATE THAT
HE STILL CLINGS TO THE HOPE THAT SHE IS
ALIVE. DR. GERSON CLIFFORD, MISS WAYNE'S
PERSONAL PHYSICIAN, SAID MISS WAYNE HAD
BEEN IN A DEEP DEPRESSION OVER THE DEATH
OF HER FATHER AND STEPMOTHER. IT IS DR.
CLIFFORD'S THEORY THAT MISS WAYNE MAY
HAVE WALKED INTO THE OCEAN AND DROWNED,
SINCE HER CAR WAS FOUND PARKED NEAR
A BEACH ENTRANCE THE MORNING AFTER
HER DISAPPEARANCE.
LATER THAT SAME MORNING, TWO YOUNG
BOYS, EDWARD STEVENS, 9, AND TOMMY KAROL,
8, FOUND A HANDBAG ON THE BEACH WHICH
WAS IDENTIFIED AS BELONGING TO MISS
WAYNE. THERE WAS NOTHING IN THE BAG
EXCEPT AN EMPTY WALLET WITH CREDIT
CARDS AND A PLASTIC BOTTLE CONTAINING
TWO SUGAR CUBES . . .

ABOUT THE AUTHOR

JACQUELINE SUSANN was born in Philadelphia. Her mother was a school teacher and her father was Robert Susann, the famous portrait painter. At the age of sixteen, Miss Susann announced that she wanted to be an actress. Before she had a chance to reconsider, her parents bought her a one-way ticket to New York.

She acted in several Broadway shows and appeared frequently on television. In 1963, her first book, *EVERY NIGHT, JOSEPHINE!*, was published and became an immediate success. It was followed by *VALLEY OF THE DOLLS, THE LOVE MACHINE* and *ONCE IS NOT ENOUGH*, each a worldwide and world-famous bestseller.

Miss Susann is married to television and motion-picture producer Irving Mansfield. She divides her time between New York City and California.

VALLEY OF THE DOLLS by JACQUELINE SUSANN
Valley of the Dolls is about the world where sex is a success weapon, where love is the smiling mask of hate, where slipping youth and fading beauty are ever-present spectres. It is a world where the magic tickets to peace or oblivion are 'dolls'—the insider's word for pills—pep pills, sleeping pills, red pills, blue pills . . . and pills to chase the truth away.

Valley of the Dolls is the story of three of the most exciting women you'll ever meet; women who were too tough or too talented not to reach the top . . . and unable to enjoy it once they were there!

Valley of the Dolls is the all-time bestseller you can't afford to miss!

552 07807 7 — 60p

THE LOVE MACHINE by JACQUELINE SUSANN
THE LOVE MACHINE
is the story of Robin Stone—a brilliant, ruthless man—and of three women who love him. It is a story set against the background of show business and big-time television—the world Robin Stone has set out to conquer—a world of uninhibited orgies in London, of 'gay' parties in Hollywood, of sordid deals in which love and sex are coldly bartered.

In this hidden world, seeking to satisfy longings he can not admit to himself, Robin Stone is driven from those who love him and whose love he cannot accept to a series of harrowing experiences and—ultimately—to the agonised discovery of the truth about himself and his past . . .

552 08523 5 — 40p

PORTNOY'S COMPLAINT by Philip Roth
PORTNOY'S COMPLAINT—a disorder in which strongly felt ethical and altruistic impulses are perpetually warring with extreme longings, often of a perverse nature. Alexander Portnoy is 33 years old, a bachelor, the Assistant Commissioner for the City of New York Commission on Human Opportunity, and a Jew. . . .

The book is written in the manner of a confession to his psychiatrist, and Portnoy says: "This is my life, and I'm living it in the middle of a Jewish joke. I am the son in the Jewish joke—ONLY IT AIN'T NO JOKE!"

"A deliciously funny book, absurd and exuberant, wild and uproarious." *New York Times*

0552 085979 — 40p

GOODBYE COLUMBUS by Philip Roth
"The first time I saw Brenda she asked me to hold her glasses."

From this innocuous beginning, Neil—a college boy—and Brenda, the pampered daughter of a wealthy manufacturer, spent a long summer celebrating their new-found love. They spent the hot days teasing and tantalising each other, and the hot nights making love.

Included with this story, which won its author, Philip Roth, the coveted National Book Award, are five of his short stories: THE CONVERSION OF THE JEWS, DEFENDER OF THE FAITH, EPSTEIN, YOU CAN'T TELL A MAN BY THE SONG HE SINGS, and ELI THE FANATIC.

GOODBYE COLUMBUS was also made into a highly successful film, starring Richard Benjamin and Ali MacGraw.

0552 095702 — 40p

THE FIRES OF SPRING by JAMES A. MICHENER
Tells the story of David Harper . . . from his childhood
in a poorhouse, his first love for a young prostitute, the
gangster and great musician who befriended him, the true
love he found in Greenwich Village, to his final emergence
as a novelist who understood himself and thus all men.

0 552 08404 2 — 50p

TALES OF THE SOUTH PACIFIC
   by JAMES A. MICHENER
Tells of the adventures of a young wartime naval officer,
whose duties take him up and down the South Pacific and
on to the coral specks called islands . . . islands full of
tropical love and violence.

0 552 08501 4 — 45p

A SELECTED LIST OF FINE FICTION
FOR YOUR READING PLEASURE

☐	09018 2	**A SOLDIER ERECT**	*Brian W. Aldiss*	35p
☐	08651 7	**THE HAND-REARED BOY**	*Brian W. Aldiss*	35p
☐	08786 6	**COFFEE, TEA OR ME?**	*Trudy Baker & Rachel Jones*	40p
☐	09410 2	**THE COFFEE, TEA OR ME GIRLS LAY IT ON THE LINE**		
			Trudy Baker & Rachel Jones	35p
☐	07765 8	**GIOVANNI'S ROOM**	*James Baldwin*	30p
☐	09396 3	**THE WILD BOYS**	*William Burroughs*	35p
☐	09574 5	**THE SOFT MACHINE**	*William Burroughs*	50p
☐	09573 7	**THE NAKED LUNCH**	*William Burroughs*	65p
☐	09089 1	**THE HORSES OF WINTER**	*A. A. Davies*	45p
☐	09174 X	**A CHEMICAL ROMANCE**	*Jenny Fabian*	35p
☐	09589 3	**SUCH GOOD FRIENDS**	*Lois Gould*	65p
☐	08985 0	**THE WELL OF LONELINESS**	*Radcliffe Hall*	50p
☐	09086 7	**BLUE DREAMS**	*William Hanley*	40p
☐	09051 4	**THE ANALYST**	*Alec Hilton*	35p
☐	07904 9	**THE CONSULTANT**	*Alex Hilton*	35p
☐	09046 8	**STRANGERS WHEN WE MEET**	*Evan Hunter*	35p
☐	09047 6	**MOTHERS AND DAUGHTERS**	*Evan Hunter*	50p
☐	08818 8	**THE BAWDY WIND**	*Nan Maynard*	25p
☐	08597 9	**PORTNOY'S COMPLAINT**	*Philip Roth*	40p
☐	09570 2	**GOODBYE, COLUMBUS**	*Philip Roth*	40p
☐	09571 0	**LETTING GO**	*Philip Roth*	75p
☐	08372 0	**LAST EXIT TO BROOKLYN**	*Herbert Seloy Jr.*	65p
☐	08523 5	**THE LOVE MACHINE**	*Jacqueline Susann*	60p
☐	07807 7	**VALLEY OF THE DOLLS**	*Jacqueline Susann*	50p
☐	08433 6	**EVERY NIGHT, JOSEPHINE**	*Jacqueline Susann*	30p
☐	09460 9	**THE WORD**	*Irving Wallace*	75p
☐	08483 2	**THE LOVERS**	*Kathleen Winsor*	35p

All these books are available at your bookshop or newsagent: or can be ordered direct from the publisher. Just tick the titles you want and fill in the form below.

CORGI BOOKS. Cash Sales Department, P.O. Box 11, Falmouth, Cornwall.

Please send cheque or postal order. No currency, and allow 10p per book to cover the cost of postage and packing (plus 5p each for additional copies).

NAME (Block letters) ....

ADDRESS ....

....

While every effort is made to keep prices low, it is sometimes necessary to increase prices at short notice. CORGI Books reserve the right to show new retail prices covers which may differ from those previously advertised in the text or elsewhere